A Game For Assassins

A Game For Assassins

The Redaction Chronicles Book I

James Quinn

'You have to learn the rules of the game.
And then you have to play better than anyone else.'
Albert Einstein

Contents

Book One:
Enter the Assassins

Chapter One

*Dominican Republic – 30*th *May 1961*

The harsh daylight sun was finally receding, giving way to a more comfortable and cooler evening. Despite this, the bugs and gnats from the nearby swamp still swarmed about, hoping to gather in the last vestiges of the day's heat and occasionally picking at the six prone bodies lying in the roadside ditch.

The killers had been in place for the past three hours, waiting, sweating, and ignoring the bugs and the heat. They numbered eight in total; six Dominicans and two Europeans. The Europeans and four of the indigenous team were waiting in the ditch for the target; the remaining two were parked a few hundred meters up the road in cars, acting as spotters. It was also their job to act as ramming vehicles, to trap the forthcoming limousines of 'El Benefactor' in the center of the kill zone.

The 'Catalan' glanced over at his partner the 'Georgian'. They were both dressed in civilian clothes, short-sleeved shirts, hard-wearing slacks and work boots. The field radio crackled into life. The two Europeans glanced at each other one more time and their eyes met. They knew this was it. No false alarms, no backing down, no mistakes. The killing would start soon.

"La luz Es brillante, la luz Es brilliante," the spotter shrieked into the radio. "The Light is Bright." It was the code for the imminent passing of El Benefactor's motorcade.

The killers had been funded and encouraged by the Americans from the Embassy, and the arrival of these two European specialists had spurred them on from what had once been the kernel of an idea, into something that was about to become very real.

The Agency had quickly tired of El Benefactor's growing unpopularity, and fearing that he would not put up much of a fight to fend off a Communist takeover, they'd decided it would be beneficial to remove him from power. Their opinion was 'If we can't own him – nobody can', and it wasn't long before the Agency had called in its most versatile freelance operators – the two Europeans – to plan out and organize the largely untutored and inexperienced freedom fighters into a small but effective assassination team.

Now the code was registering into the group of killers. Men tensed, weapons were checked, safety catches were flicked off, and rifle butts were jammed into shoulder positions. They spotted the dust cloud first, kicked up from the arid country road as the two-car convoy sped along. The intelligence they had received told them that the road, a quiet back route, was the most likely to be taken when El Benefactor visited his favorite mistress in San Cristobel. It was the perfect ambush spot.

The dust cloud grew nearer and the growl of the heavier engines got louder. And then it happened, not hurried or at a frantic pace, but slowly. The mid-speed amble of the two-car motor convoy of gleaming Lincolns'; the roar of the gunned engine in the ambush truck as it gained speed to block the motorcade; the growl of the truck when it turned in a perfectly formed 'U' into the center of the road, causing El Benefactor's vehicles to brake hurriedly. And then the noise of the multiple automatic weapons as they spat out death, which was aimed, very accurately, at the prone motorcade.

For a few brief moments, nothing more, the noise was deafening. The men of the killing team were all keen to get into the fight and put as much ammunition as possible into the President's vehicles. Each wants to be able to tell the tale to his grandchildren. Each one wants to be the man who killed that brute Trujillo.

The first volley was impressive and completely incapacitated the cars. Then, as several of the President's security men struggled to regain the initiative, and even contemplated fighting back, the freedom fighters were on the move, firing, closing down their enemy, changing magazines so that they can continue with the salvo.

Leading from the front was the Catalan's partner, the stubby, hard-looking Georgian who shouts to them to "Atacar hacia adelente", before emptying his own weapon into an unfortunate bodyguard who had decided to run. It seems there can be no survivors... or witnesses. Then the noise falters and stops, the smoke starts to dissipate, and the removal of a seemingly unbeatable dictator is almost at an end. It is so quick – and so easy after all.

The Catalan got up from his prone position and motioned for the Georgian to attend to the President's backup vehicle, where the few remaining bodyguards were being unceremoniously dragged from the car and beaten. They wouldn't last much longer. He sauntered over to the mortally wounded lead vehicle. His face was a mask of sweat and tension, from the serious business of killing. The sides and windows of the car had been shattered by multiple bullet holes and smeared with blood from the interior. Already the smell of death was making its existence known.

"They fought back bravely, commander," said Rafael, the youngest member of the team. The Catalan nodded and peered inside the vehicle. It was a charnel house. The driver and bodyguard had been pulverized. A series of single shots rang out from nearby.

The Catalan straightened up and looked around to find the Georgian and his team executing the remaining bodyguards. "Where is Trujillo?"

"He ran for the tree line, Ramon shot him in the legs. He's guarding him and waiting for you."

"El Benefactor is still alive, though?"

"Si senor."

"And for us, no casualties?"

"No senor. They never knew what hit them."

The Catalan made his way over to the tree line and there, with the little freedom fighter guarding him, lay the man who had held a small nation in his vice-like grip for more than thirty years. Blood was oozing from his legs, which lay at an unnatural angle, his suit covered in mud and dust, but the face... the face still held contempt and arrogance. *But not for much longer,* thought the Catalan.

"El Presidente. Do you know who I am?"

The rotund, white-haired man glared back. "You are a pig of a 'freedom fighter' and mother-fucker who sucks on the cocks of traitors!"

The Catalan smiled and shook his head. "No senor, I am not from your pretty island. I am from far from here... but I have a message, a message from the Norte Americanos." *The shock on Trujillo's face was clear,* thinks the Catalan. *He has been outwitted by the Americans.*

"Your time here is over," murmured the Catalan, and in one fluid movement he drew a large caliber revolver, a Smith & Wesson, and fired a single shot through the eye of the dictator. An old man dead in a ditch. "Ramon, you and the boys take the body away and hide it. And here..." he handed over the revolver to the only other witness to the execution. "If anybody asks, *you* shot Trujillo. Okay?

Ramon took the pistol and stared down at it, feeling its weight and the grease running across his fingers. It was a good weapon. "Si senor. We can hide the body at one of the safe-houses until it is time to display it to the world."

The Catalan nodded in approval. "Good, then organize yourselves and go! Get out of here as quickly as you can."

"What about you Commander, you and La Bala?"

La Bala was the nickname the boys had given to the Georgian. It was a term of affection. La Bala, 'the bullet', because the small Georgian did indeed resemble a bullet. Small, stubby, hard, balding...

"We will be leaving by a separate route. You will not see either of us again, our job here is over. Go well."

The Catalan and the Georgian would have to move fast. They had a separate vehicle parked several minutes away along an arterial route, which would take them to the safe-house they had been using for the past few weeks. A clean up and fresh change of clothes would be in order, before they offered an after-action report to their in-country CIA case officer, Tanner, at a meeting in the bar of the Hotel Rafael in Cijaud Trujillo.

By the time the news of 'El Benefactor's' disappearance had started to filter through, the men would be on a fast seaplane to Miami and their CIA contact would be reporting back to Langley that Agents QJ/WIN and WI/ROGUE, the Catalan and the Georgian respectively, had completed the terms of their current assignment and were on their way stateside for a final debrief by the Chief of the Executive Action department.

* * *

Beirut, Lebanon – August 1962

The small, stocky man stood on the corner of the busy thoroughfare. He checked his wristwatch nonchalantly. Supposedly for the time, in reality to see if he was being observed. He gave a quick glance either way to his periphery. Nothing.

He wore a lightweight, cream colored suit that he'd had made on a whistle-stop visit to Hong Kong years ago, and a pale blue, open necked shirt. The Middle Eastern sun had filtered through his cropped, white blond hair leaving his scalp burned. He wore a pair of dark wraparound sunglasses to reduce the glare. He was early-thirties, trim, in shape, and alert. His cryptonym was 'Gorilla'. It was a name which fitted him like a glove, not because of his size or bulk, but because of his rolling gait when he walked, the furrowed glower behind the sunglasses, and the hint of a hirsute nature peeking out from beneath his well-tailored suit.

He was on the move again, pushing his way through the pedestrian walkways, past the crowded restaurants and coffee bars. Exotic looking women with liquid hips were shopping in the designer stores, businessmen were conducting meetings over a plate of *meze*, and friends were chatting over cups of Cafe Blanc, the herbal tea made from hot water, orange blossom and honey. *It was easy to see,* thought Gorilla, *why Beirut was described as the Paris of the Orient.*

He moved at a steady pace along Hamra Street, being careful not to catch anyone's eyes directly, or bump into the mass of bodies packed onto the pavements. If he had 'bumped' anyone it would have been greeted with a respectful "*Pardon en moi.*" Today, he was using French as it fitted in better with his cover and would disguise his identity for later.

It was then that he saw his 'Squire'. A fat man with a standard moustache and swarthy complexion, he was sitting in an old Buick. His cover was that of a *Servee* driver, the name for the local taxi service. Both the car and the driver had definitely seen better days. A Squire was a local, low-level intelligence asset who provided equipment or services to visiting field agents. Forged documents, money, safe-houses, weapons and transport all fell within a Squire's remit, and very much like their counterparts from the Middle Ages, they were expected to be on call at short notice.

A quick glance, then Gorilla strode across and smoothly entered the rear passenger side of the vehicle. If he thought that it was hot out on the street, it was nothing compared to the stifling mugginess that he faced inside the car. On its plus side, the vehicle had limited visibility, partly due to the dust-laden windows that had never been cleaned, thus allowing the meeting inside the vehicle to be as discreet as it was ever going to be.

The Squire remained stock still, and he continued to stare out of the window at the passers-by. Hamra Street was busy at this time of the day, and it made it harder to spot local surveillance teams, so he spoke out of the corner of his mouth and flicked an occasional glance in his rear view mirror.

"Sallam Allaikum," said the driver.

"Allaikum Sallam," replied Gorilla. With the formalities complete, they settled down to business.

"You know where you are going?"

Gorilla nodded. He'd read the reports and knew the route from studying a local map.

The target had a small office located in a quiet corner of Rue Jeanne D'Arc and Gorilla had telephoned that very morning to arrange a 'business meeting' with the target, using the ruse that he was a French investor looking to hire the target's services through his Import/Export business. Gorilla had hinted that he had an illegal cargo to move and hoped that he had pricked both the target's curiosity and greed. At least this way, the target would be alone and exactly where Gorilla wanted him.

"The package?"

"Under my seat. It's the best I could do at short notice, but I think it will suffice."

Gorilla reached under the driver's seat and withdrew a small satchel. Inside, covered by a square of muslin, lay his work tool for the day – a Beretta M1951, complete with a bulbous noise suppressor. Old but reliable – not his preferred weapon – but given the limited resources available, it was certainly acceptable.

He quickly tested the spring in the magazine, checked the action of the weapon, attached the sound suppressor, smacked home the magazine and let the slide roll forward. A quick chamber check, to ensure the bullet was seated properly and then he flicked the safety on.

His only other piece of equipment was a bouquet of carnations. To the casual observer, he would look like a man on the way to meet his lover or mistress, but the bouquet would hide the silenced Beretta in a sleeve nestling against the flowers. Gorilla concealed the weapon inside the bouquet and cradled it in the crook of his left arm.

The target was a Lebanese-born contract agent by the name of Abu Qassam, who had been playing both ends against the middle in French

North Africa, operating for the British but betraying their operations to the FLN, the French National Liberation army.

Things had come to a head when it was discovered that he had personally taken part in the torture and murder of a key British intelligence asset in the region. Realizing that he'd gone the length of the rope, he'd fled to his native Beirut where, mistakenly, he had assumed he could hide and would, years later, be safe.

The British could forgive him his betrayal, to a degree. But the murder of one of their own – never! They had set about planning retribution. A tracking team was assembled; favors were called in throughout the intelligence community, sources were cajoled and leaned upon... until they had his new name. Then they had an address. Then they had a time and date. And it was at that point that the small man in the lightweight summer suit, Gorilla, was summoned.

His unit's expertise was dealing with enemy agents, traitors, extremists – and this was his fledgling operation for them. A 'hit' they said, a quick in, quick out. Do this right and there'll be a step up the ladder, maybe even permanent secondment. In truth, Gorilla knew very little about the background of the case, the bare minimum, and to be frank – that was way too much anyway. For this kind of operation, the only information he required was a time, a location, and a description; anything more was showing off on behalf of the case officer running the show, in his opinion. His only priority was to get the job done and get out with a clean pair of heels.

"I will wait here," said the Squire. "I can give you at most five minutes, after that you will be on your own."

Gorilla nodded. "Five minutes is more than enough time; I'm not planning on having a chat with him. Keep the engine running."

A quick scan of movement on the street and he exited the car, nonchalantly clutching his lethal gift.

He had killed men before during his time in the military, some in situations not dissimilar to this one, but never in such a coldly targeted, ruthless way. He knew he was more than capable of the task the colonel had given him; why else would he have been chosen? Gorilla had a special collection of skills that made him useful for jobs like this. He knew it, the colonel knew it and the hierarchy at Broadway knew it.

He glided along the street, scanning from behind the dark glasses for people taking an interest in him, but again nothing. He moved like a spectre. That was one of Gorilla's talents, the almost intuitive skill to become unnoticeable. One of his instructors had once commented you could lose him in a crowd of two people.

Moving into an empty side street, he saw the target location up ahead: a small doorway with a brass plaque outside stamped with 'Import/Export', accessed by a twelve step flight of stairs. He climbed the darkened hallway, counting the steps slowly in his head as he moved forward. He settled the carnations more comfortably in his right hand and walked up the last few steps to the heavy wooden door with a glass viewing window that was the office of Al Saud Import/Export Company. He turned the handle of the door with his left hand, entered and closed the door gently behind him.

He instantly assessed the layout of the room and its contents – the shadows of the curtained room, the ornate cabinets and pictures adorning the wall, the languid figure reclining back in an office chair behind the desk. The man was smoking French Gauloises and a small glass of Arak lay half empty before him on the desk. No other people present. Good.

The assessment took a fraction of a second.

Then Gorilla was moving forward, seeking to dominate the room. It took three strides to reach the desk. The man began to stand, extending a hand in greeting, smiling. "Monsieur Canon, how…" he started to say, but Gorilla had reached the front of the desk and quickly, but not hurriedly, raised the bouquet with both hands to chest height. The motion was deceptively casual.

Confusion passed over the target's face. Why was this client pushing a bouquet of flowers at his face? Was it some kind of strange French custom? As the target reached his full height, he perhaps realized, belatedly, what was happening. Gorilla touched the delicate petals to the man's forehead, gently brushing his skin, and pulled the trigger hidden within the lethal bouquet twice in rapid succession. PHUT, PHUT!

The sound was barely noticeable, nothing louder than a vigorous cough, certainly nothing to attract anyone's attention from outside. With the first shot, the man stared at Gorilla as though he had been smacked in the forehead with a cricket bat. His head rocked backwards, and through his own momentum, started to crane forward again just in time for the second shot to hit him, inches away from the first bullet. This time, however, the bullet didn't rock the target any further, instead his legs simply gave way and he dropped like a marionette whose strings have been swiftly sliced through. He fell in a crumpled heap behind the desk, work papers and invoices scattered all over him. What had been white was now red.

Gorilla made his way around the desk and fired two more shots from the now ragged-looking bouquet into the target's head. Just to make sure – but he knew from experience that they were not necessary. The whole operation had taken no more than fifteen seconds. *A bit slow,* thought Gorilla, who hated shoddy shooting, especially in himself. No fancy stuff, no long speeches, just BANG and the target is dropped.

After the extreme act of violence there was silence, the only ambient sound being the tat-tat-tat of an old air fan in the corner of the room.

Gorilla's heart started beating at a rapid pace as a surge of adrenaline hit him. He took two slow, deep breaths, closed his eyes and started moving. He quickly returned to the office door, turned the door sign to read 'Reunion en cours', pulled down the blind and locked the door. He discarded the flowers on the desk and set about searching the rest of the office, striding swiftly from room to room. He moved silently, with the suppressed Beretta leading the way like a lethal tribune. Less than a minute later he was satisfied that he was alone.

Job done, he thought. Now all he had to do was leave without bumping into the bloody cleaning woman, or whatever random happening was liable to throw itself into the mix on these types of operations. But his concerns proved unfounded.

He disassembled the Beretta, breaking it down into its component parts – suppressor, magazine, and slide. Picking up the spent casings from the shots he'd fired, he placed them all into his inside jacket pockets before leaving the office. His presence raised not even a glance as he exited the office and made his way onto Hamra Street, heading back to the Squire's taxi. Moments later, Gorilla opened the rear passenger door and dropped down into the seat.

"Okay. Off we go. But take it easy, no gunning the engine or high speed," he said to the driver.

The Squire nodded and began to move the car out into the busy traffic. "Was everything okay my friend? Any problems?"

Gorilla placed the pieces of the Beretta into the satchel before tucking it back under the Squire's seat. "Everything was fine. The less you know about it the better."

"I understand. You will tell your organization that I performed well. That I was of use?"

Gorilla nodded. This Squire had performed exactly as he'd requested. Good driver, adequate weapon choice, no flapping. "Of course. My people will no doubt reward you well. You were very good."

"Inshallah. Thank you, and where to now, my friend?"

"The airport. I have a flight to catch."

By the time the body of the target had been discovered, Gorilla would be winging his way to Paris before travelling home to London. A circuitous route for sure, but it would at least keep the trail he left down to a minimum.

He settled back and watched the sun cast the Corniche and the mountains in the distance in a yellow haze. Glancing down, he noticed a single speck of blood on the lapel of his jacket. It was a testament, and in fact the only proof, of his first Redaction.

* * *

Warsaw, Poland – October 1962

12

The long watch of Tomasz Bajek began on a bright Saturday afternoon and had started some three hours earlier when he had taken over the surveillance shift.

The operation, bizarrely enough, was in Warsaw Zoo, which to Bajek seemed a strange place for a group of fully grown men to be trying to blend in unnoticed on a warm weekend. But he supposed that foreign agents did not have the luxury of working only on weekdays.

The zoo had been rebuilt in 1949 following the bombings of the Second World War, and was now one of the main attractions of the new Poland. He had already completed three rounds of his sector of the zoo and was now sitting down, rocking the pram that he'd been pushing for the past few hours. To the casual observer, he no doubt looked like a devoted new father who had been ushered out of the house by his frantic wife on the weekend, to spend some time with his progeny. The zoo was a relatively inexpensive day out.

However, all was not as it seemed. Bajek was not a new father, and the pram held nothing more than a toy doll, wrapped up in multiple layers of blankets and bonnets on the off-chance that an overzealous member of the public should desire to see the baby. All that was visible were two bright blue eyes peeking out. He could think of nothing worse than wandering around a zoo for hours on end. He had never visited the zoo before, he hated bloody zoos, and after this job was finished he would never want to visit it again.

In reality, Tomasz Bajek was a young, junior officer in Poland's internal security service. He had been working in the counterespionage department for the past four years, helping to catch spies and traitors.

Normally he was tied to a desk, but today, due to a shortage of staff, he had been seconded to one of the roving surveillance teams. A break from the drab head office was always a pleasure.

He was the sixth operative in an eight-man team, which ranked him somewhere above a headquarters cleaner, but below the filing clerks. Each of the team had their own designated areas inside the zoo's grounds. Two surveillance vehicles were also part of the operation - one was disguised as a refuse collection truck, circling the perimeter, whilst the other was that workhorse of security services; a repair wagon, complete with a suitably slothful workman who'd taken many hours to do not very much at all.

Bajek had the area covering the park and wild boar enclosure. Pleasant enough, but not when you're waiting nervously to capture a western spy.

The job had been passed to them by the Russians. Unusually, a senior KGB officer by the name of Major Krivitsky was in command of the operation. Squat, vulgar, disdainful of the Polish intelligence officers under his command, Krivitsky had set out his stall in a blunt manner at the morning briefing.

He stood at the head of the team, his large knuckles resting on the desk, chin jutting forward, soulless black eyes fixed on them, daring them to challenge his authority. He had then proceeded to lay out his experience. Fought in the Great Patriotic War, lifelong communist, an NKVD officer before they had changed their name to its current anagram; agent-runner, spy-catcher, hard bastard and the one person you don't want to cross. And all spoken in the absolutely lousiest Polish Bajek had ever heard. The man's voice was guttural, and at times almost incomprehensible, but it was clear enough to get his briefing across.

A network of Polish spies had been rolled up and now the Russians wanted the chance to get their hands on a live, western case officer. But no ordinary western agent, not someone who worked through the Embassy, someone who had the safety net of diplomatic immunity.

No, this was a non-official cover operative sent in on the 'black' to retrieve incriminating material. "The deal is this. You can have the Polish agents, we want the westerner," glowered Krivitsky. "A show trial," said Krivitsky, "to embarrass the Americans, the British, whoever the fuck it was. Then a prolonged interrogation, some Gulag time and then we sell him back to the West for one of our agents in a few years' time."

So who was this agent? What did he look like?

"We don't know, so don't ask. Tall, maybe, young, sure. That's all we got, and we won't be getting any more where that came from," murmured Krivitsky, who seemed loathe to give out any more information than he absolutely needed to. The rumor Bajek had heard was that the Polish spy Krivitsky interrogated hadn't had a strong enough constitution, and had decided to play the game no more. Permanently.

"We got a trap set for him," Krivitsky had announced. "A time and a place. We set the 'all clear' signal. Chalk mark on a lamppost on Marszałkowska Street. Means come and empty the post-box. Dead letter drop. He thinks he's getting the keys to the Kremlin, but we are going to be there rolling him up. So remember… you work for me. You do as I say. You don't, I make sure that you are sweeping the shit from the sewers for the rest of your life."

The dead letter box was in fact a loose brick, third row down, sixth brick across in a wall that surrounded the Herpetarium. It was located behind a small bush that provided, briefly, cover from any surveillance. The repair wagon which housed a member of the surveillance team had a discreet long lens camera pointing at the entrance to the pathway.

The plan was to observe the target entering the tiny pathway between the wall and the shrubbery, alert the rest of the team, and they would then move in to make a hard arrest on the foreign agent and detain him once he'd exited.

Over the past few hours they'd seen a few possible candidates for the soon-to-be-captured spy, but none of them fit the profile of a foreign intelligence agent. An elderly couple walking arm in arm, a mother on a visit with her two playful children, the usual retinue of courting couples. The most likely candidate had been a tall man of middle years, western business suit, but who had quickly been identified as a party official.

One of the team had 'worked' him months ago after a suspected security leak from his Ministry, and the most contentious thing about him was his love affair with a junior secretary from the admin section. The team quickly ruled him out and minutes later, he was seen walking towards the park, hand in hand with a young flaxen-haired girl who was definitely not his wife.

Bajek glanced at his watch, it was 4.45p.m., the light was starting to fade and the zoo would be closed within the hour. Maybe they were in for a no-show, or maybe the spy had picked up on the surveillance and decided to abort the emptying of the letter box, which meant that he might be stuck walking around the zoo again tomorrow. Damn.

He heaved his heavy frame off the seat and decided on another series of ambles around his route, pushing the pram, and feigning interest in the limited selection of animals the zoo had to offer. He completed one circuit, returned for a second, and it was at the commencement of his third, and what he hoped would be final rotation around the zoo, when he heard the sound of the whistle.

The whistles had been issued to all members of the team and were the equivalent of an early warning system. Not especially cutting edge, but effective nonetheless. "You see him – you blow the whistle. Got it?" Krivitsky had warned at the briefing session.

Bajek turned his head in the direction of the peal. At first he saw nothing – just the zoo in its familiar state, visitors examining the animal enclosures. Normality. Then he saw a movement. A man of similar age to him, dark haired and skinny compared to Bajek's bulk, dressed in a workman's overalls and jacket, running at full pelt from the direction of the dead letter box, and seemingly, heading towards the main pathway which led to one of the exit points.

Closely behind the runner, although with no chance of ever catching his quarry, was Stefan, the oldest member of the surveillance team, sporting a bloodied nose. Poor old Stefan had one hand pressed to his nose, trying in vain to stem the flow of blood, and the other swinging, in an effort to propel him forward faster. It appeared the spy hadn't wanted to be taken and had fought back.

Then all the whistles seemed to be blowing at once, alerting the rest of the team to move in, and it was then that Bajek seized his chance. He wasn't a natural runner, nor was he particularly fit despite his youth, but he did have one vital advantage. He was standing at a 45-degree angle to where the spy would be in a matter of moments. If he could cut across the grass he would be able to intersect the runner's route, blindside him and bring the man down with a body charge. Bajek's bulk would be no match for the thinner man; he would simply knock him off his feet.

The pram which had been his surveillance partner for the past few hours was flung, discarded, toy baby and all, and he was off! Pumping his arms, thrusting his legs along to propel him forward, he caught sight of the man from the corner of his eye. It was a race for survival. Bajek for his chances of promotion and escape from his prison-like desk; the spy, he was sure, for his life and liberty. Ten seconds to go, he was sure he could make it…

Five seconds to collision. Bajek, the hero of the service, the man who brought down a ruthless western spy… blood is pumping in his ears… the only sound he can hear is the noise of his heart thundering…

He can see the man clearly; young, certainly, but with a tough, handsome face… three seconds, almost…

But then something strange happened. The man seemed to trip, stumble, but then regained his balance. Bajek nearly has a hand on the spy's jacket collar when he finally hears the report.

At first, Bajek becomes aware of the Russian shouting, in fact, screaming would be a more accurate description. Then the crash of numerous rounds being fired, the 'whizz' of bullets passing by him, the screech of the caged animals as they react with fear. Then the spy seems to stagger – at least to Bajek – but still the gunfire continues. *Who the hell had a gun on the team?* Bajek thinks. *I thought we all had whistles.*

The final few bullets seemed to explode into the running spy. One to the shoulder, and the final one – the most serious – took him in the rear of the skull, providing him, momentarily, with a pretty red halo before he crashed unceremoniously to the ground. The world seemed to stop, a breath held in anticipation of more to come. But no more do come. The bullets have done their work. The spy was splayed out face down, his arms and legs twisted at odd angles so that he resembled a child's rag doll, tossed aside in a fit of pique.

Bajek knelt down to examine the wounded man. There was a mass of blood and grey matter, caked all over the concrete path.

The left side of his head had been blown away, a fatal wound, but to the man's credit, he was still clinging to the last remnants of life. His body twitched every few seconds, his eyes rolling wildly and his jaw worked as though he was trying to speak.

Bajek moved closer, so that his ear was almost touching the man's lips. At first there was nothing, then with a massive effort a word came out in a hoarse whisper... to be repeated again and again and again. Each time, the strain on the dying man took its toll, but still he expelled the same word until finally he had nothing left to give. His eyes rolled back into his head and he slipped away. Bajek closed the man's eyes and raised himself to one knee.

The rest of the team stood stock still, like mourners at a funeral, which in a way they were, Bajek supposed, providing a cordon to keep the public onlookers away. And there at the back of them all stood that bastard bloody Russian, the so-called professional, the big man from the KGB, who had fired the fatal shots.

The Russian stood now like a child chastised, hands at his side, pistol still in his right hand, a guilty look, a look of shame in his expression. His eyes cast around the Polish team and he dismissed the shooting with a shrug. It was then that Bajek, the junior officer, who was only a rung up from the office cleaner, snapped and lunged at the man. No deception, no thought or planning, just a straight charge and jump to reach the Russian's throat.

"I almost had him... you... you... *butcher!*"

Both men went down in a tangle, the pistol dropping to the floor as Bajek started beating at the KGB man with fists, elbows and feet. Bajek found himself being pulled back hurriedly and restrained. He was pulled one way while Jan, the team leader, picked up the Russian, dusted him down, and began to apologize, moving him in the opposite direction.

"I'm sorry about that, Major. You have my word, he will be punished, he is a junior officer with little experience of how operations in the field work. He is young. The shooting? Accidents happen. No, of course you didn't intend to kill him. A tragic accident. The man should not have run. Please, let's get you back to base; my team can sort this out, so that we can prepare our reports together."

Bajek was aware of the Russian storming back toward the vehicles that would spirit him away from the scene. The rest of the team were re-grouping, calling in the 'meat-wagon' to take the body away, dispersing those members of the public who were brave enough, or stupid enough, to continue showing an interest.

Bajek slumped down against the wall of the Black Bear enclosure. Jan, the team leader, came to stand over him, hands on his hips. "Do you know how much trouble you're in? You'll be lucky if you don't get kicked out of the service for this."

"That stupid Russian panicked. He blew the whole operation," growled Bajek, his anger still prevalent, but slowly receding with the increasing realization of what he'd just done.

"So what? It's his head on the line, or at least it was, until you waded in with your fists. Now you've embarrassed the service and made an enemy of a Major in the KGB. Well done."

"I thought the KGB were supposed to be the professionals and we're just the poor country cousins? If that's their best, God help them," Bajek complained.

Jan shook his head, appearing resigned to what he had to do. "We *are* the poor cousins. Let's be realistic, we can't operate without the Russians' help. They own us. The deal was, we got the local agents of this network and the Russians get the Western case officer running them. I'll have to escort you back to base, Tomasz. The Director will want to read you the riot act, before he decides which dark hole he's going to drop you down."

Bajek staggered to his feet. Jan gently gripped his arm and started to lead him away. "What did he say anyway?" he questioned.

"Huh?" Bajek flicked a look back over his shoulder to where the body of the western spy lay. One of the team had draped a coat over the body, trying to conceal it until the meat wagon arrived. The zoo animals had started to react, perhaps due to the odor of the dead man's blood that wafted upon the air, invigorating their primal senses. Bajek paused for a moment, deep in thought.

"Well," Jan pressed. "What did he say? Are you deaf? It might be important."

"He said nothing, nothing at all, he was probably just trying to breathe."

It was only later, when he sat at his desk, sweating while the senior officers of the Service decided his fate that Bajek allowed himself to recall what the man had whispered again and again. He'd repeated one word, in English, in his last dying moments. At the time Bajek wasn't sure what the man was trying to say. So once back at headquarters, he had picked up the well-thumbed office copy of the English/Polish dictionary and rifled through its pages until he had found a match for the word the man kept repeating.

In Polish the word was 'Tata'. In English the man, in his dying breaths, had repeated and repeated and repeated; "Dad... Dad... Dad..."

Book Two:
The Rules of the Game

Chapter One

The recruitment of the first European killer, who would later go on to be the operational field controller on the ground, took place on a freezing cold evening in Luxembourg in a small and privately run villa called the 'St. Hubert' in the pretty town of Clervaux. It was a fairy-like house situated in a fairytale hamlet.

The 'Man from Luxembourg' as the Catalan-born killer was collo-quially known within the international mercenary milieu, was greeted at the door of the small villa by Max Dobos, the American's Hungarian factotum, contact man and cut-out. The Hungarian was also there to ensure that the Catalan and the American were not disturbed and that their meeting would remain 'Sub Rosa'.

"He's waiting. Been in town since lunchtime. I have to search you, it's routine," said Dobos.

A frisk, and a pat down – good, but not up to the Catalan's standards by any means. Then a disrobing of his winter coat and a quick-paced climb up a winding staircase to a first floor landing, and a closed, heavy wooden door. A rap on the door and a muffled "Enter" sounded from within.

The door opened up into a sparsely dressed room with an oak ta-ble, several comfortable-looking couches, and at its center, two up-holstered leather reading chairs facing each other. The large windows were curtained to prevent any outside surveillance, but the Catalan knew that the view of the valley outside would have been breathtaking.

"Allow me to introduce Herr Knight," said Max Dobos to the Catalan, overseeing the formal shaking of hands. They were using English, the common language that bonded them all, and with the introductions complete the American was keen to take charge.

"Max, if you would be so good as to leave us and make sure that we aren't disturbed. Thank you."

The Hungarian middle man gave a curt nod, and exited swiftly. A click of the door and the distant sound of him scampering down the flight of stairs ensured they were alone. With the chaperone gone from the proceedings, the American and the Catalan appraised each other as only men of a certain confidence and experience can do; with professional respect and a little wariness.

The American was known only as 'Mr. Knight', no first name given, and as with all aspects of his tradecraft he had performed perfectly and planned everything down to the last detail. He was medium everything. Medium height, middle aged, salt and pepper hair, middle-ranking business suit. He exuded ordinariness, except for the eyes. The eyes had a hard coldness to them that could, on occasion, change from an icy glare to a fiery rage. They were the eyes of a zealot.

To the American, the Catalan was tall and patrician, with slicked, jet black hair that had horns of grey streaking the temples. He was well dressed and well presented. Yet the American wasn't fooled for a moment. This European was dangerous and an experienced killer of men. His reputation preceded him.

"Shall we perhaps sit and make ourselves more comfortable?" suggested the American, keen to control the pace of the meeting, as agent runners are always apt to do with possible future agents.

And so they sat, face to face across a living room, hands resting comfortably on their respective laps, with only the American's briefcase between them.

Elsewhere in the villa, and unbeknownst to either the Killer or the Spy, a tape machine slowly began to turn, covertly recording every word...

* * *

"You did some exceptional work for us in the past. I've studied your file. Very capable, very professional, especially that operation in the Dominican Republic, taking down Trujillo."

The Catalan merely smiled a self-deprecating smile and shrugged. "I was glad to have been of service. Your organization was very generous... while it lasted." The Catalan's voice was thick and deep.

"I know, I know, believe me. The people in charge of operations back then had their backs to the wall, especially following the assassination of President Kennedy. A lot of senators and public bodies decided they wanted to clip the Agency's wings. We had to step back and cut contact with anyone who was involved in what they would class as even mildly contentious activities. We're sorry about that. Let's move on."

The Catalan nodded his sympathy. "Such is the way of our trade and we are all at the mercy of those higher than us. But obviously things have changed, otherwise you wouldn't have travelled all the way from Langley to make contact with me."

Mr. Knight leaned forward, bringing his guest closer into the fold. "Even politicians are pragmatists in this day and age. We are fighting a Cold War, whether we like it or not, and in order to conduct operations against the Soviets, we need soldiers. Capable men such as you, men not afraid to get their hands dirty. Not 'Wild Cards' – far from it, but professional operators who know how to run an operation."

"You are very kind."

"No, I am not kind, far from it. But I am honest and I like to tell it straight. The cull after the murder of the President was a blip, nothing more. Now we have serious work to do and I would like to have you working with us. How do you feel about that?"

24

The Catalan inhaled and pondered the raindrops drying on his leather shoes. "I have other business interests these days that take up much of my time. If I were to work with your people again, I would need a strong incentive."

In truth, he was keen to work with the Americans again. Since his enforced retirement as a contract agent, he had confined himself to his legitimate business enterprise, the running of an art and antiques store here in the center of Luxembourg. After operating around the world, he'd decided he needed a refuge; somewhere small, discreet, quiet and cultured. Luxembourg, for him, had fitted the bill perfectly. Despite his lifestyle as a small businessman, he had also been a part of several not-so-legitimate enterprises, namely the funding of several small-scale heroin smuggling operations across the Mediterranean, which, while making him a tidy profit, had failed to provide him with the adrenaline rush of his previous work for the Americans.

Mr. Knight locked eyes with him, his stare direct. "My friend, if you sign up for this operation, I can assure you that the resources available and the remuneration will exceed anything that we offered you before; on that you have my word. There's a new broom heading the Agency and he wants to sweep away the crap that the Soviets have been hitting us with, while we've been distracted by being raked over the coals. At this juncture, I am merely enquiring to see if you would be interested in principle. If that is the case, then we will move on with the details of the project, if not, well… then we shake hands, you go your way, I go mine, and you never contact or work for the Agency again."

The Catalan held the American's gaze for a brief moment, weighing up his options. To commit or to refuse; both held advantages and disadvantages, and when all things were considered, it really didn't come down to the money, welcome as it was. It was more the desire to be an active part of the great game that he had been a part of for most of his adult life.

So, the decision was clear, to carry on being a small-time smuggler on the fringes of the European underworld, or to take on the challenge and be a major player in the Cold War? It was always useful to have powerful allies such as the Americans, especially if his less-than-legal enterprises and investments turned sour. He smiled a sad smile of resignation and acquiescence. Really, there was never any doubt.

"Mr. Knight, please, tell me more about this operation. It intrigues me. How can I be of service?"

* * *

The American poured them both a shot glass of schnapps, a taste for which he'd acquired during his time in Germany after the war. It was a nice opportunity to halt the 'pitch to the Catalan. *Leave him dangling, keep him off balance and lets me set the pace,* thought Mr. Knight.

But the hiatus in the conversation had to be timed correctly. Too keen with the details and the Catalan may be scared off, too much of a pause and he wouldn't take it seriously. Mr. Knight knew from experience of handling agents in the past that the trick was never to go directly to the matter at hand. Instead the wisdom was to start out wide and gradually bring it in to a narrow focus, hence the offer of the schnapps and his next preamble.

"Following the death of Kennedy, the Soviet intelligence apparatus and their satellite services began to test the boundaries of what they could get away with in operations against any number of Western intelligence services. They'd already had success penetrating French, British and German intelligence, but the CIA was proving a tougher nut to crack. So they decided to take advantage of our inability to conduct covert action operations and chose to up the stakes, by eliminating several of our agents and operatives in Europe and Asia. When the politicians closed down our Executive Action capability, they also threw out its operations chief. Without him, his assets and his planning skills we were left effectively unarmed. A bit like a gun without the bullets."

The Catalan nodded his understanding. He'd met the Chief Operations Officer of the CIA's covert action capability several times, mostly in Italy. An overweight drunk who had gone to seed a little bit, but still a man of great experience and an excellent covert operator, none the less. Both men raised a silent toast to the absent CIA man and downed their schnapps.

Mr. Knight continued sipping at his drink. "Damn... that's good. Anyway, the Agency put up with this for as long as it could stand it, then it started to fight back. Oh, not against the Russians, hell, that would have been the easy part. No against the damned politicians, oversight committees, and shit heels that know as much about running covert ops as they do about astrophysics! Our argument to them was clear. Some very high up people in the Agency formed a quorum and approached several sympathetic congressmen, some of whom had helped us out during the war and knew where we were coming from. Good men, lovers of freedom and democracy."

Mr. Knight poured himself another shot of schnapps and downed it. "Look, we know we got a bit carried away recruiting and running all kinds of assets in some very unsavory parts of the world. Our people said to them, 'We fucked up. But if you guys want to win this Cold War of ours for all the freedom loving people of the world, then for the love of God take the gloves off so that we can at least hit back from time to time!'"

"Very commendable," said the Catalan, eager to get to the nub of this American's proposal. "So, what is the contract? Which dictator are we to neutralize this time?" The Catalan noticed a frown pass across Mr. Knight's face. *Maybe I have misunderstood the proposal,* he thought. Then, just as quickly, the cloud passed and the American regained his composure.

"No, not a dictator. Not this time. Not some African butcher, or some Latin American hard man. The Agency has very wisely decided that we are not in the dictator-removal business anymore. We've had our fingers burned too many times," explained Mr. Knight.

There was a frown this time from the Killer. "Then I am confused. In our previous contracts, we were always directed toward such targets, that was our specialty?"

"Oh, I can assure you, your skills will not be wasted, otherwise why else would we have chosen to re-activate you? No, not a high profile target such as a head of state, but important enough to this operation to warrant your attention. Seven people… excuse me seven 'targets'… to be eliminated within a given time frame. They are scattered across Europe, have minimal or no protection and are totally unaware that they are being targeted," Mr. Knight explained calmly.

"Soviets?"

"Of course. Soviet agents to be more precise, but it amounts to the same thing. I'm afraid you will be off the KGB's Christmas card list for the foreseeable future."

The Catalan nodded. He was not unduly worried; he knew how to cover his tracks. "And the fee?"

"Double the usual monthly retainer from your previous employment with us, with a $25,000 bonus upon satisfactory completion of the contract, plus the usual expenses and resources available."

The normally poker-faced killer raised an eyebrow at that. A payoff of $25,000 would set him up for the rest of his life and would easily see him into retirement. The Americans must want these agents removed very badly indeed.

"We already have much of the plumbing in place, but we can go over that in more detail at our next meeting," the American continued.

Plumbing, the Catalan knew, was the Agency's euphemism for pre-operational planning. Before any job was given the green light, the case officer in charge had to provide the necessary resources to actually make the operation viable.

"However, because of the deniable nature of this contract you will need to source certain things for yourself. We want everything done at arm's length, to keep the facade of plausible deniability in place. Passports, vehicles, specialist equipment and so forth. Is that a problem?"

"No, not at all. I have a good man that I use in Antwerp for false documentation. He is very professional, very discreet. However, I will need assistance to help me execute this contract. Suitable personnel. Qualified people."

Mr. Knight leaned down and lifted a manila folder from his brief-case, opened it and made a small notation with his pen. "Yes of course. We would in no way expect you to carry this out on your own. We were rather hoping that you would take it upon yourself to perhaps approach and recruit your former partner on our behalf. Is that acceptable?"

"Certainly. He is a fine operator, and one of the few men I would trust to work with," said the Catalan smoothly.

"I understand he can be a little reckless at times. A little wild?"

The Catalan thought back to his time working with the Georgian. The little man *was* both reckless and ruthless at times, but remarkably, he had always been able to rein him in and control him. "He does have that reputation, but not with me. If you wish me to take this contract, and I'm guessing that you have gone to a lot of trouble to arrange this meeting, then I want the Georgian as my back-up man. This is not negotiable."

The American seemed satisfied with the answer. He clicked his pen to retract the ballpoint, returned it to his pocket and sat once more staring directly at his guest. They had reached a point of no return and, from this moment on, the operation would either go forward or be stillborn.

"So who are these targets? Until I have an understanding of precisely who and what they are, I cannot give you an accurate assessment of success feasibility," said the Catalan.

Mr. Knight pulled another manila folder from his briefcase, and with a quick flick through the pages with his fingers, he handed a single, typewritten sheet of paper to the Catalan. The words 'TOP SECRET' were emblazoned in red diagonally across the page. He evidently had his own copy as he immediately turned his attention to the folder resting across his lap and began to speak. "I think for brevity's sake, for the moment we should refer to them by their professional titles," said Mr. Knight.

The Catalan nodded his agreement and returned his gaze to the briefing document, while Mr. Knight cleared his throat and assumed the mantle of a teacher conducting a lecture.

"So we have the *Soldier*, an army colonel currently assigned as his country's liaison officer to NATO headquarters in Paris. There is the *Diplomat*, who is operating out of an embassy in Hamburg; he is part of a diplomatic policy think-tank for creating strategies to counter Soviet expansion. The man is also a closet homosexual."

Mr. Knight ran his finger down the page until he reached the next targets on the list. "The *Engineer* is a senior scientist currently believed to be seconded to a project designing a new missile delivery system. The man was a leading light in the Nazi war machine during the war, a protégé of Werner Von Braun, no less. Then we have the *Financier* who is a senior banking official with a noted Swiss banking house in Żurich. He has direct access to various government funds and is an expert in re-routing and hiding KGB monies in the West.

"The *Politician* is Special Advisor to the current UN Secretary-General and a former member of the Italian parliament. She is very influential, with many friends across Europe and the USA, apparently also has the ear of the current Chief of Staff in Washington. Finally, we have the *Quartermaster*; a respected businessman who runs a secret sideline, procuring illegal arms for Soviet-backed operations across Africa."

The Catalan sat quiet for a moment. It was an impressive list, no doubt, but there were several nagging doubts running through his mind, not the least of which he decided to voice. "Would it not be better to try to turn these agents? I know from my own experiences during the war that the perceived wisdom is to use agents to catch more agents. Killing them merely leaves you with a dead end."

Mr. Knight sighed. He'd expected this reply at some point and his carefully constructed response had been prepared in advance. "That is the usual way of doing things, certainly, and as a professional I agree with what you're saying. But this operation is just one part of a bigger project. The reasons don't concern you, only the conditions."

The Catalan frowned. "There are only six names on this list; you said there were seven targets."

Mr. Knight cleared his throat and placed his hands carefully on his knees, almost as if he didn't trust them to remain still. When he spoke, his words were clipped. "The seventh target is, we believe, the KGB controller who runs these agents personally. At the moment, we only have limited information about him. That will change over the coming months. We know that he's currently active in Europe somewhere. As soon as we find him, we will pass you the information."

Both men stared openly at each other for a moment, weighing up their options. It was the American who finally spoke. "So we have now reached a line in the sand. I think I need a clear answer." There was a deliberate pause before he spoke again. "Are you able to handle this operation?"

Chapter Two

Was he able to handle the murder of seven people, seven people who made up a Russian intelligence network?

Oh, he was more than capable. In his time he had caused – either directly or indirectly – the deaths of more than a dozen people, for just as some people are born to be academics, surgeons or musicians of the highest order, so the Catalan was a natural in the art of murder. He had, after all, spent half his life engaged in the dangerous world of espionage, criminality and professional terrorism.

Juan Raul Marquez –aka the Catalan; the man from Luxembourg; the Killer – had been born forty-five years earlier in the Catalonian region of Northern Spain. His affluent family background had been a melting pot of Catalan extremism, and while the political firebrand of his youth had long since left him, what had remained was the wisdom and experience of the born survivor. The life blood of intrigue coursed through his veins, and like all natural survivors who have walked through the constantly shifting sands of the secret world, he played the game superbly.

As a young man he had travelled extensively around Europe, affiliating himself with all manner of revolutionary and counter-revolutionary groups. He was like many of his generation, outwardly wealthy, cultured but still struggling with his fortunate place in the world. He had so much, while many had so little.

So he raged; raged against the elitist European royalty, the corrupt governments, the puppet politicians, the lies of communism, and it was this anger and this searching that led him into contact with his first underground political cell.

In truth, it had been his infatuation – perhaps even love – for the cell's leader, a charismatic and handsome Swiss doctor named Michel who was eager to stem the rise of communism, which had led him to being one of the bomb throwers in an attempted assassination of a visiting communist party leader to Geneva. Unfortunately for the fledgling terrorists, both bombs had failed to ignite and Marquez and his cohort were quickly arrested by the authorities.

Prison, even a Swiss one, had brutalized him. The beatings, the rapes, the hard labor were bad enough; but six months into a ten year sentence he had learned through the underground network the harsh reality of the secret world. His beloved Michel had been an *Agent Provocateur* for the Swiss authorities. It had been a trap designed to roll up a cell which had been getting too well known.

People take to prison in many ways, some acquiesce, some blend in, and some fight back. For Marquez, it was the latter. Following months of abuse and the final cut of betrayal, he'd proven to be a difficult prisoner for the guards to handle. The beatings increased and solitary confinement seemed to be his way of life. Fortunately, for both himself and the guards, he was handed an early release from prison, thanks to the intervention of influential, and very rich, friends from his social circle who were able to hand a hefty bribe to the Swiss authorities. That, and the promise that he would never return to Geneva again, seemed to be a fair deal.

The experience had left him with a clear understanding of several things. Namely, that he would no longer be fooled into believing the lie of political ideology. They were fools the lot of them, ready to commit to a baseless system and yet so easily brought down by human fallibility. How weak.

He decided that in the future, he would be responsible for his own planning. He spent most of his twenties hiring himself out as a smuggler and thief and eventually moved to Paris.

He moved in wealthy circles, had tempestuous affairs with several men, and cultivated friendships with those in power. He was fast becoming a power player.

With the outbreak of war, Marquez fell firmly on the side of the Petain government and had many patrons inside the Vichy regime. He soon came to the attention of the *Abwher*, German military intelligence, and earned his credentials in the early part of the war by spying on his French hosts. He was caught *in flagrante* by the French authorities, spying on a munitions factory, and given a prison sentence for his trouble.

Fortune was once more on his side however, and he was released by the intervention of his friends in the Vichy regime, not least being Pierre Laval, the new head of government. Once he had regained his liberty, he went straight back to the spying game, this time in Bordeaux working as an intelligence agent for the *Sicherheitendienst, also known as the* SD – the Nazi intelligence organization. Capture, murder and torture were his stock in trade and he used them to excess.

By 1943, and sensing that victory was turning in the Allies' direction, Marquez offered his services as a double agent to a British intelligence network operating in Paris. He also had a lucrative sideline, smuggling expensive works of art and diamonds stolen from wealthy Jewish families to Lisbon. He used this 'route' to pass sensitive information he had gleaned from his inside position in the Nazi intelligence service in France, to the British SIS and American OSS stations in neutral Portugal.

In the intelligence war, however, there are no old and bold spies and it was only a matter of time before a rare mistake was made by Marquez. He lasted a year before he came under suspicion by the Gestapo; he was hauled into the interrogation center at the Avenue Foch and questioned for days. Through good luck and a cast-iron cover story, he was able to soothe the German's concerns, at least initially. He was released and placed under surveillance by the Gestapo, who waited to see if he would make contact with anyone from the Allied spy networks.

Marquez, with his trademark cunning, knew when he had been compromised and did nothing except sit in his Paris apartment drinking expensive wine and entertaining several young men. After a month's worth of surveillance, the Germans, being no fools, decided that he was too much of a risk and chose to exile him from France. The knock on the door one December morning by two heavily armed Gestapo agents who were under orders to 'escort' him to southern Luxembourg confirmed that his espionage career was over. Marquez, if asked, would simply state that it was part of the great game; the risk, the thrill, and the elegant blood rush of danger that made him become embroiled in such intrigues. He traded the lives of men and women as a stockbroker might play the market, with ruthlessness and cold calculation. He never looked back, only forward.

By 1945, the Germans were on the run and the Americans were rounding up all manner of former German agents, spies and operatives. Marquez was hauled out of Luxembourg and placed before a British Colonel with responsibilities for intelligence work. The stern Colonel assured Marquez that his valuable work as a double agent would certainly go in his favor, if he could "just give us a few more details about his former compatriots."

Marquez spent the remainder of the year giving as much evidence as he could about German and Vichy intelligence operations to investigators and prosecutors at the Nuremburg trials. With the war over and his freedom assured, he moved back to a civilian life in Luxembourg. He opened a small art dealership and antiques business, and to the casual observer, lived a quiet and unremarkable life. It provided him with excellent cover for his much more lucrative secret life consisting of international smuggling operations, both in precious minerals and narcotics, as well as working as a freelance agent for the French, Belgian and West German Intelligence Services.

And so a decade after the end of the war, Juan Raul Marquez had once again returned to his chosen trade of smuggling, espionage and murder. It was a trade in which he excelled, and a trade which sooner rather than later would bring him to the almost omnipotent attention of the CIA.

Chapter Three

Marquez stood at the window and gently peeled back the curtain, so only the smallest aperture was made allowing him to view the frozen scene outside. He scanned the street for any sign of a threat, but saw only the empty streets below him. He turned to the American. "Who would be my contact?"

"You would work directly with me. No contact, either overt or covert, with the American Embassy or the local CIA stations where you are operating. You work at arm's length, independently, with no chaperoning. You try knocking on Agency doors, they'll tell you to take a hike and that they don't know what you're talking about. I will give you a series of telephone numbers and you will be required to check in regularly, to give and receive up-to-date intelligence. After each successful hit, I will release a designated amount to a personal bank account of your choice. You don't complete the contracts; you don't get paid. Questions?" said Mr. Knight.

"I would need several weeks of planning, to organize my team and work out how we would complete the operation."

"Of course," Mr. Knight agreed.

"Monies are to be paid directly into my private account at the Banque International de Luxembourg. I will distribute the funds as and when I require them."

"Absolutely."

"I will look over your intelligence and planning so far. If it can't be done, I will say so. I will not waste our time. If that is the case I would require $5000 as a severance payout. My time is precious, you understand."

"Agreed."

Marquez gave the scenery outside one final look before turning to the American. "Then if all that is acceptable, I would say you have a contractor."

* * *

"Max. Our guest is leaving, please fetch his coat." The call went out to the factotum, down the stairs in the lower level of the building. A distant "Yes, Herr Knight," was the reply.

With the successful reactivation of Marquez, Mr. Knight, ever the practical intelligence officer, had a more pressing problem, namely the tying up of loose ends. Conversely, it was also a fine way to test the Catalan killer's loyalty to the operation and to see if his skills had diminished in any way over the years since he had last been employed by the Agency.

"Herr Marquez," he whispered as the man stood to smooth down the creases in his tailored suit. "I suggest that we meet one week from today in Vienna. There I will hand you all the biographical details of the targets, funds and a list of resources available to you. I would also like to go over your plan at the same time." The American reached into his inside jacket pocket and removed an envelope. "Here is a ticket to Vienna, some expenses and an itinerary."

Marquez pocketed them; he would read through them later. "What about my cryptonym?" he asked.

"Well, I think if you are agreeable, we will stick with your original Agency codenames; QJ/WIN and WI/ROGUE. Is that satisfactory?"

Marquez nodded his approval. He knew that the CIA used cryptonyms that began with a two-digit prefix called a digraph. This digraph usually denoted the locale where the agent had first been recruited. In his own case QJ stood for Luxembourg, the place of his initial recruitment. His partner's digraph of WI represented the Congo, the place of his first operation and the country that had brought them together.

The latter part of the cryptonym was usually something random, or that fitted together to make a complete word. However, in the case of WIN and ROGUE, there was always a sneaking suspicion on Marquez's part that some anonymous CIA officer had judged their personalities well: one a ruthless winner, the other a risk taking criminal. He smiled. It felt like he was back where he belonged, safely inside the protection of a CIA sponsored operation. This contract, possibly his greatest challenge, he was sure would also be his greatest masterpiece.

* * *

The following week was a whirlwind of activity for Marquez. He temporarily closed down his little antiques business in Luxembourg, citing the need to visit an elderly relative in Spain and warning his customers he may not be back for weeks, possibly even a month or two.

He also made discreet contact with several members of the European underworld, with whom he had worked in the past. Each was a specialist in their chosen field. They were expensive, but well worth the price that their expertise brought. Finally, he locked himself away in his beautifully furnished apartment above his little shop and set to work. By the second day, he had the workings of a plan and a strategy of how he would complete this most challenging of contracts.

His plan was simple. Take out the easier targets first, without arousing the suspicions of the KGB. Accidents were always good as they weren't as obvious as a bullet to the head. They bought the assassin time to escape and didn't alert any investigators to the fact that foul play had been used.

Experience also told him that the higher profile the target was, the less likely the use of 'accidents' was, of being an option. Their security was invariably higher and therefore they had a level of protection that made it much harder for the erstwhile assassin to get intimately close to the target. Close quarters work may be an option in this case, but he doubted it. Besides, he would know more once he had a chance to read through the American's intelligence assessments on the targets.

The devil is in the details, he told himself. He sat back in his chair, stretched, then reached across to the telephone sitting on his desk. He heard the click of the operator picking up and asked her to connect him to the private number of a bar in Portugal, which belonged to his former partner.

* * *

The meeting of the two European killers took place at a small cafe located on the Stallburgrasse 2 in the old town area of Vienna, exactly eight days after Marquez and the American had first met. It was discreet, off the beaten track, away from its flashier rivals and a perfect place for two old friends and business partners to reacquaint themselves.

It was commented on by the SIS intelligence analysts who later reviewed the case, that this momentous meeting was a pivotal point in the operation; as much hinged on the successful recruitment of the Georgian killer. It had been a good length of time since the two men had last worked together and much could have changed in the little killer's attitudes. He had, after all, found a new country, a woman and a lifestyle.

The SIS analysts also felt that if he had turned down the offer of a lucrative contract, it would have signaled his imminent death sentence. Contract killers, especially top level ones, despise being turned down by former partners as they are invariably seen as security risks or even worse; there are fears they may try to undercut the original contractor. Hell hath no fury like a deceived assassin, it would seem.

However, on this occasion the analysts and naysayers needn't have worried. The killer had reverted to type and just as a leopard is said to never change his spots, so it was for the small Georgian – he would never turn down a lucrative contract sponsored by his old partner.

David Gioradze, the Georgian, arrived at the cafe at the appointed time. He was dressed in a thick, fur-lined coat, gloves and a hat to keep the cold at bay. He had spent the past few years enjoying the warmer climate of Portugal where he had made his erstwhile home, running a small bar and enjoying the many pleasures of that country, not least, the wine and the women. Having to travel to Vienna during the winter months did not exactly fill him with pleasure.

He made his way through the tables to the counter, ordered a *Kleiner Schwarzer*, the Austrian name for a small black coffee without milk, and pointed the waitress to the corner table in the shadows, where the unmistakable figure of his former partner reposed. He took in the man's long aquiline face, his perfectly groomed hair, his cultured manner, his fashionable, yet conservative clothes made by the finest tailors in Italy. This seemingly cultured and urbane businessman was one of the best contract killers in Europe. Inwardly, he sneered. In truth, he disliked the man, hated his aloofness, his penchant for young men, his sometimes effete manner. They were not friends, never would be, and the fact that they came from different social classes only widened the gap. But on occasion, the two men would come together to form a symbiotic relationship. The iron hand in the velvet glove was how they had once been described; Marquez the planner, Gioradze the hammer.

"It's been a long time since Leopoldville," said Gioradze, shaking the other man's hand.

They had first met in 1960, when both had been working, separately at first, for the CIA in Africa. To the CIA officers who ran them, and to the headquarters staff at Langley, these two Cold War mercenaries were better known by their registered codenames, the ones that would be used in confidential communiqués. Gioradze was known, perhaps in reference to his penchant for taking risks and daring nature, as WI/ROGUE, while Marquez, in reference to his single mindedness and commitment to finishing a job successfully, was known as QJ/WIN.

Marquez smiled back at his partner. *He still has that ice cold smile,* thought Gioradze, *the smile that invites you into its embrace, just as he plunges a dagger into your back.*

"Indeed," said Marquez. "Not to mention Mexico, Brazil and Bolivia. Come, my friend, sit down. We can talk about the old times, once we have discussed our bright and prosperous future."

Chapter Four

Leopoldville, Republic of the Congo – November 1960

The CIA agent QJ/WIN had arrived in Leopoldville operating under the name of Lucien LeClerc. His cover was that of a French business-man from Marseilles, who was looking to import agricultural machin-ery from Europe in order to assist the Congolese economy. His travel papers were valid for the next three months and in that time, he was expected to travel across the region, visiting businessmen, govern-ment ministers and local political leaders. In truth, he had no intention whatsoever of doing any of this. His real mission was much more in-teresting.

He had first been recruited in the late 1950's, following a success-ful career as a smuggler. Two large Americans had visited him at his apartment one evening with an interesting proposition. "Thanks for agreeing to meet with us. I'm Frank and this is Tony," said the larger and meatier-faced of the two. "I'm the guy fighting the Commies; Tony here is fighting the drug war. We have a proposal for you."

It had started from there. Because of his underworld contacts across Europe, especially with the Corsican and Sicilian drug gangs, he had been an excellent agent to infiltrate himself into a network involving Chinese Communist heroin that was being given freely with the clear understanding that it must be flooded into the United States. As an *Agent Provocateur*, Marquez had been exceptional. He had bought his way into the deal using American funds and had arranged for collection points and private transport en route. Of course it had all been a ruse and on a given date, the shipments had been intercepted by the US Coast Guard, but more importantly several of the main arterial routes into the USA had been compromised, with several others being placed under surveillance.

Following the counter-narcotics operation, he had been approached six months later and met with an overweight, almost obese CIA man in Rome. The man looked like a disheveled drunk, but he had a confidence and swagger about him that hinted at hidden resources and tenacity. "Call me Bill," the CIA man had said as they dined on seafood at the Restaurant Villa Venezia, a small, family run place a stone's throw from the Vatican.

"I liked what you did for us against those Chinese commies, nice work. I'd also like to thank you for some of the potential agents you've talent spotted for us. I'm in charge of a new outfit. We deal with Executive Action, which is a bullshit euphemism for getting our hands dirty in covert operations. I think you're the type of guy that we'd like to have working with us."

Marquez had been put on the payroll, a nice monthly retainer and all he had to do was establish enough cover to be classed as deniable to the overt world. The Congo operation was his first mission and although he was listed as an Executive Action department agent, he would in truth be seconded to the CIA's Africa Division for the duration of the project.

The ride from the airport into Leopoldville had brought back old memories of his time in Africa, not here in the Congo, where he was unknown, but in other regions of the Dark Continent; Chad, Nigeria, Algeria, Dakar. The smell, the noise, the heat; all gave Africa its own unique pulse. The drive through the streets did nothing to dispel any of these sensations and also confirmed what he had already been told by the CIA; the Congo was sliding slowly into a whirlwind of chaos and feudal fighting with the military on the streets and militias in the back rooms.

Marquez had booked himself into the Intercontinental Hotel, a large, high-rise slab of concrete in the center of the city. It was the hotel of choice for businessmen, journalists and visiting VIP's. He left his suitcase in the room and immediately ordered a taxi from the hotel reception. His first port of call was to be his briefing with the CIA station chief, Deakin. The venue was a one-bedroom apartment in Binza, a suburb of Leopoldville and one of the many safe-houses the Agency kept for covert meetings. The knock on the door and code phrase gained him entrance to the inner sanctum of the safe-house.

"You clean? No surveillance on you, they're pretty easy to spot. They trail around together like a bunch of virgins at a frat party." *Deakin was the archetypical CIA case officer* thought Marquez, *young, sleek and a smooth operator.* They made themselves comfortable with Deakin playing the host and pouring the drinks; coffee, black and strong.

"So, Langley wants me to give you the edited version of events here and then brief you on your mission while you're in country." Deakin lit a Camel cigarette and relaxed back into his chair, readying himself to deliver the intelligence briefing.

"What we have here in the RC is a four-act play with the main power players – Kalonji, Lumumba, Tshombe and Mobutu – all ready to slit each other's throats to gain the high seat. Mobutu rules here in Leopoldville, Kalonji has South Kasai, Tshombe has control of the mining franchise in Katanga and is backed by the Belgians and their mercenaries, and finally, there is Lumumba and his clique who have set up an enclave in Stanleyville. We have tribal, financial and political factions, all armed and all willing to take the country to the brink of chaos in order to get what they want. You with me so far?"

"Of course," said Marquez. "Although it sounds like most African 'democracies' these days."

"It is, you're absolutely right, but it's our job to ensure that as few countries as possible don't topple to the commies and the word from high command in Washington is that the Republic of the Congo is to be saved at all costs, even if that means rescuing it from itself. Since the summer, Washington has been in a tailspin about how to go about securing this country. The main threat for the USA and the West comes from Lumumba. He seems to have communist backing and the theory is that if he continues to hold high office, it will pave the way for a Communist takeover. The Agency cannot allow that to happen."

"Which is where I come in," prompted Marquez.

"That's right. We want you to see if it's possible to penetrate Lumumba's entourage. We've tried to deal with him over the past few months; negotiation, bribes, political concessions, but it seems he's either very much his own man or is in the back pocket of Moscow. We have our sights on the Chief of the Army, Mobutu. Washington thinks he is a man we can work with. Lumumba needs to be removed, to give Mobutu a clear run."

"So, the rapier rather than the Claymore for this operation?" asked Marquez.

"Yes, a subtle approach is always preferable. We want you to get under his skin, gain his trust and then we can see about removing him."

"And this is sanctioned by Washington?" Marquez didn't want to be left out in the cold if the operation went sour.

"The best I can tell you is that this operation is officially unofficial. Don't worry about it yet; just get close to the target first."

Marquez noted Deakin's pause and his non-committal reply. Was the CIA man not giving him the whole picture, perhaps retaining some operational piece of information? Spies! Who knew how their little minds worked? "Alright, where do I start?"

"There is a man who works for Lumumba, name of Patrick Kivwa, a political fixer and lawyer here in Leopoldville; he transcends the Congolese players and the Europeans. He handles the money and arranges meetings. We have heard that they are in need of financial support, after all counter-coups don't come cheap. They certainly wouldn't entertain an approach from an American businessman looking to bring wealth into the country. We rather screwed up our pitch there."

"But a French citizen looking to trade with a new government… yes, I see. Very good, I like it," said Marquez.

"Exactly," said Deakin. "Langley says we can have up $100,000 to get them interested and get an asset inside. So that's your start point."

"And once either I or a sub-agent can gain access to Lumumba, then what?"

"Kill him. No fucking about. Langley and Washington may dress it up with all kinds of euphemisms, but the short version is we want him dead."

"Silenced pistol. Explosion, what?" asked Marquez, eager to work out *how* he would be able to do it.

"Again, something subtler is in order. We have at our disposal a chemical agent that we would like you, or your nominee, to administer. The toxin is designed to be administered to Lumumba orally through food, perhaps at a dinner party."

Ah, thought Marquez, *poison.* The oldest of the assassin tricks.

* * *

Marquez had to wait three days before he could hold his initial meeting with Lumumba's man. Deakin had given him a contact number and told him to call at a certain time of day. The man who answered the phone spoke in a high pitched, excitable whine. Marquez introduced himself by his cover name of LeClerc and gave an outline of his proposal.

"Mmm, come to my office later today. We can talk in more detail face-to-face," said Kivwa.

Kivwa's office was on the second floor of a commercial block in the business district. The office looked out onto a street filled with cafes and taxi cabs; the canopy of the building was shielding them from the worst of the sun. The man himself was a giant, whose physical dimensions were only just being held in check by a tailored, three-piece suit. He was greying and weary.

"So, you French want to take over our country, is that it? You have more colonial aspirations, Monsieur LeClerc. Agricultural machinery! Do you expect me to believe that?"

47

Marquez held up his hands in mock surrender. In order to gain access to this man's principal, he felt it best to be honest with the Congolese lawyer, or as honest as his cover story would allow him to be. "It is true, I did use that story in order to gain some credibility and to get you to meet with me. I also represent interests in European banking who are keen to assist with the mining and development of minerals included; copper, gold and diamonds. I have been authorized to make a proposal to your principal."

Kivwa laughed. "But you are already too late my friend, Tshombe and his Belgian dogs already have that market under control."

Marquez nodded in understanding. "My people in Europe believe that Patrice Lumumba would be a much better option for everyone concerned. We believe that he is a man who could unite the country and bring back stability."

Kivwa moved the papers on his desk to one side and leaned forward to make his point. "My friend, Lumumba is for all purposes, a hunted man. He cannot move freely without risk to himself. He is currently under house arrest. Where would he go and how would he get there?"

"I have the authority from my patrons to offer him protection in Europe as a guest; we can guarantee it." Marquez watched Kivwa closely. The man was unsure how to react. Perhaps his pitch had come in too sharply, too sudden?

"Umm… I do not know about this. I will need to consult directly with Lumumba. Where can I contact you?"

Marquez gave him the name of his hotel and the direct number to his room.

"I will contact you when I have spoken to Lumumba, but I have to tell you honestly that I think you are wasting your time," said Kivwa.

* * *

Marquez had no choice but to return to his hotel and wait. He checked his watch, discovering it was sundown. *Time for a drink*, he thought. He turned around and headed straight for the bar, a group of journalists checking in at reception. They looked like modern-day versions of colonial adventurers, coming to take the Dark Continent by storm, except this time, instead of rifles they were armed only with cameras and tripods.

The bar was quiet and wouldn't start to fill up for another half an hour. He pulled up one of the stools and leaned forward against the bar. The barman made his way over, a glass already in his hand. "Mon Dieu, I need a drink, a large one, a Ricard. It's been a hell of a day," said Marquez.

"Make that two," a voice said from behind him.

Marquez turned and looked down to find a small bullet of a man, beaming a huge smile in his direction. He looked him over with a closer eye. There was something not quite right about the man's appearance; it was like trying to decipher an optical illusion.

The man was dressed in a summer business suit, the type that seemed to be so fashionable these days, and he had a thin narrow nose and suntanned features. Marquez would have described him as ordinary and peasant-like. But there were two things which set him apart, that didn't quite fit. First was the hair. It was obviously a toupee, an excellent one certainly, you could hardly see the join, but still a hairpiece – of that there was no doubt. Secondly was the scar that ran the length of his cheek. No accident, a scar like that, in that location it could only have come from being cut with a knife. A duel or a fight, perhaps? Marquez wondered who had won the encounter; the unknown knifer or this tough-looking European.

"You are new in town," said Scarface.

"A few days ago. I'm Lucien LeClerc."

"Franz Donner," said the man, holding out his hand.

"German?"

"Austrian, but it amounts to the same thing these days to most people. What are you doing here in Leopoldville? Business or pleasure?"

Marquez laughed. "I wouldn't have thought there was much pleasure to be had in the Congo's current state. Business. The company

I work for is trying to cut a deal with the Government. We sell farm equipment."

The little Austrian laughed. "Whoa, there's no money in that around here my friend. Jules, two more drinks here, we're both dry as the scrubland." The last was directed to the bartender, who swiftly brought them two beers. The Austrian settled himself into the chair next to his new friend. "Now, the big money in this part of the world is in arms and ammunition. If you can supply those, you can make a killing in a place like this. No pun intended."

"Is that what you do here? Gunrunning?"

Donner shook his head and smiled. "Not at all, I'm new here myself. I've only been here a few weeks. I run a small shop in town, selling cameras and photographic equipment. I get a lot of business from journalists."

Marquez nodded, more out of politeness than appreciation of the man's business acumen. On the whole it seemed a strange place to open up a new business for a European, but in his time he had met all kinds of strange people, with even stranger ideas. They chatted for another hour, each giving a somewhat sparse account of themselves. They were both of a certain type; adventurers, players of a great game, eager to make a difference, but both motivated by money. Mercenaries. Well dressed and cultured certainly, but mercenaries all the same, if only of the commercial type.

"What do you make of all the Russians here?" asked Donner.

Marquez sipped his drink and shrugged. "To be honest, I haven't seen many of them, certainly haven't spoken to them. Why? Have you had problems with them?"

Donner sneered. "The Russians are always a problem, no matter where in the world you go. They were welcomed here by that fool, Lumumba. I think that he will live to regret it… or maybe he won't."

Marquez cocked his head curiously. *Maybe this conversation with the Austrian might prove useful,* he thought. He decided to press the topic further, after all, who knew where it might lead. "Why? Do you know something that the rest of us don't? Lumumba is certainly unpopular in certain quarters, but my reading of it is that if he could rally enough support from his people he could regain power."

Donner shrugged, "Possibly, but if that happened, he would open the gates of the city and the USSR would simply walk right into Africa. Think about it. No more free trade, a semi-communist state, no room for European investors. All Soviet owned."

Marquez nodded. "But what can we do Franz, we are after all, only small businessmen. We don't have the means to pressure the Soviet Union, unfortunately."

"Maybe not directly. But if you are interested in helping the people here, there are things that can be done to at least halt its takeover in its tracks. Practical things, things that happen on the ground. Things that would benefit European businessmen like you and me."

Then it occurred to Marquez that this tough-looking little man actually imagined that he was trying to recruit him! If it hadn't been so amusing, he might have taken offence. Marquez looked at the Austrian with new eyes.

"I could use a man like you. I see it in your eyes, Lucien – beneath that veneer you are a man unafraid of action. I am in touch with people who are disgusted at the way these communists are treating Africa and its peoples, by putting up their puppets in the seat of power."

Marquez drained the last of his drink. "There will always be people who revel in power, *mon ami*, it has always been that way."

"Of course, of course, but these friends of mine have taken it upon themselves to act, to stop the rot that is ruining the Congo."

"Who are they?" Marquez asked curiously.

Donner considered this man carefully. Could he trust him? He was a European after all and his brief was to organize and run an assassination unit, ready to act at a moment's notice to bring down whichever of the players the Americans saw fit to eliminate as a contender to power over the Congo. "Not here. Too many ears here and none of them trustworthy. What about a nightcap at the *Numero Dix* nightclub? Do you know it?"

Marquez shook his head.

"It is run by a Corsican tough guy; it would be a good place for us to talk more, no disturbances and most of the clientele are discreet, plus the girls are very accommodating."

They took a taxi and arrived at the *Numero Dix*, a large, expensively furnished bar, five minutes' drive away from the Intercontinental. It was dark inside, with glass and chrome in abundance, giving it a sinister edge. Marquez was aware of exotically-dressed waitresses flirting with several patrons. They found a booth, ordered drinks and only then did the Austrian begin to speak.

"I'm sorry about all the cloak and dagger, but there are certain places in this city where you feel secure and some that you don't, especially when discussing matters of life and death."

"No problem. And are we? Discussing life and death, I mean?"

The Austrian huddled in close, their conversation, murmured, would be lost in the noise and bustle of the nightclub. "Not initially, but things can change fast. I'm putting together a team, a team of useful individuals who can be ready to act at a moment's notice. A team willing to do whatever's necessary, even getting their hands dirty. Does that bother you?"

Marquez shook his head; he knew what the man meant, but thought it best to play down his emotions. "Not so far. Although I'm not sure in what way I can help. I have no experience of combat," he lied.

"Not everything has to be about combat. There are other ways that you could help the team I have; passing messages, moving equipment, watching an address, perhaps even giving us a piece of information that you have come across. Obviously we wouldn't expect you to do it for free. Three hundred American dollars a month to start with, more if special jobs come up."

Donner didn't say what 'special jobs' involved, but Marquez guessed it was the type of job involving sub-machine guns and a human target. He pulled out a huge roll of Belgian Francs, tore a half a dozen from the pile and pushed them over to Marquez. "Don't decide now; think it over, there's no hurry. We'll call this a payment for taking up your valuable time. Questions?"

Marquez had several but thought it better to stick to the obvious one first, if nothing else, to see how professional this spy was. He decided to approach it in a half humorous, half curious way. "These, 'friends' of yours – who are they? Not locals, I assume. Is this for a foreign government? Are you a spy, Franz?"

The little Austrian gave a cursory look around the nightclub to make sure they hadn't been overheard. When he returned Marquez's gaze, he was smiling. "Come, my friend, I can neither confirm nor deny your conclusions."

"But Franz, at least give me an inkling *who* would be paying my wages. If I'm to risk my life, I've a right to have a rough idea who I'm risking it for."

Donner nodded in sympathy and Marquez could see that he was working out how much to tell his potential 'sub-agent'.

"Okay, what I can tell you is that I represent a modern nation that has seen the error of its ways since the Second World War. They are a country reborn, despite their recent difficulties and they feel that helping a nation in trouble, such as this one, will bring them back into the fold and gain the trust of their former enemies. I think that gives you enough clues as to who our supporters are."

Marquez was impressed with the pitch; he even bought part of it. Donner was giving all the clues to point towards West Germany, but experience had told him that the Germans had enough to worry about, rather than concerning themselves with a flyspeck in Africa. No, things didn't add up and would need further investigating. "I will need time, as you say. Don't worry Franz, I will be discreet, but I need to think on this proposition."

The Austrian looked at him, full of false bonhomie. "Of course, my friend, of course. We are men of the world and I wouldn't expect anything less than for you to be cautious. But I sense hidden depths in you, Luc. There is more to you than meets the eye."

* * *

Marquez arrived back at his hotel an hour later. He had walked, enjoying the cool night air and besides, it had given him time to clear his head and correlate his thoughts. He wasn't drunk, far from it despite the amount of cheap alcohol he'd imbibed. But he needed to place the information from the night's encounter in some semblance of order.

There was always a sense of unreality about being on a mission. It didn't matter who it was for – the underworld, the Nazi's, French, Belgians or Americans – there was always that strange, out of body experience, as if the rules didn't apply when you were part of the secret world. He had felt it before and he would no doubt feel it again until he stopped with this strange business he had chosen as his own.

He stood in the darkness of his hotel room and stared out at the nighttime cityscape which greeted him. Large pockets of darkness, interspersed with small jewels of light, but further out in the distance the overpowering blackness of Africa.

Marquez focused his attention on a small area west of the city. Somewhere out there, a man was settling down for the evening, perhaps reading or writing some notes for his next speech or press release. The man was his target. He would find this target and he, Marquez, would ultimately be the cause of the man's demise.

Chapter Five

"I think someone was trying to recruit me the other day," said Marquez.

Deakin had picked him up outside the Botanical Gardens, on the thoroughfare fifteen minutes' walk away from the Intercontinental. It was busy enough that no one would have noticed the foreigner slip quickly into the passenger seat of the anonymous black sedan the American was driving. "Really. Who?"

"He says he's an Austrian, name of Franz Donner. He says he's trying to set up a camera shop business here in Leopoldville, which has to be the worst cover I've ever heard."

Deakin laughed, he had heard worse in his time, certainly, but had to agree that a photographic business in chaos-driven Congo was a bit like trying to sell inflatable rafts in a desert. It was pointless. The Congolese had bigger things to be concerned about than cameras. "So what makes you think he's a spy?"

"He talked about the new resistance against the communists in the Congo. He claims that he's part of a group of Europeans who are ready to take up arms against the communist leaders here. I assume he's talking about Lumumba. He says he has a team at his disposal, ready to do some killing."

"A hit-team! He's trying to recruit you to be part of a hit-team?" laughed Deakin. "Oh, the irony."

But Marquez could see Deakin's mind ticking over, weighing up the information and seeing if it could benefit him. They were heading out toward the fringes of the city, so Deakin turned the car around and started to drive back to its interior.

Like most intelligence officers, he felt comfortable in the hustle and bustle of a city. You were less exposed and more vulnerable to being spotted by a canny surveillance team.

"So tell me about him," said the CIA man.

Marquez thought carefully for a moment. "He looks like an operative, despite his attempts to disguise it. He's small, tough talking, looks as if he could handle himself in a fight. He says he's from Austria but his accent is all over the place. It might fool the locals here, but he's no Austrian, there's a touch of a French accent hidden away in there somewhere, it flits from one dialect to the other as if he doesn't have control of his own voice. He hinted that he was working for the Germans. Who knows, it might even be true."

"Where did you meet?"

"The bar of my hotel, surprisingly enough! We got chatting, had a few drinks and then decided to go for a drink at *The Numero Dix*. It was then that he pitched his assassination team idea. If you want my opinion, based on my own experience, I would say he looks like a mercenary who was given an intelligence operation."

"Okay, leave it with me, I'll check him out see if his name rings any alarm bells back at Langley. Keep him on the dangle, okay? Encourage him, see what you can find out, but don't commit yourself to anything," suggested Deakin, steering the car back onto the main road.

"Understood," said Marquez.

They passed an open-backed military truck, carrying a dozen soldiers with all their weapons on show. Both men tensed until it had passed them. Deakin kept an eye on the truck in the rear view mirror until it disappeared from view. "That's Mobutu's boys, flexing their muscles. Now, to other business. The target. How's that going?"

"So far, excellent. The go-between is arranging a meeting, where and when is still to be decided. It's a case of sitting and waiting it out."

"But they seemed keen? They bought the story you fed them?"

"They appeared to. I would guess that they're trying their best to check out my bona fides."

Deakin laughed. "Good luck with that one. They'll hit a wall. No, I think curiosity and the fact that they can feel the proverbial noose tightening around their necks will bring them around. Now, to one other piece of business."

Marquez perked up. The waiting game over the past few days was beginning to take its toll on him. Spying, he knew was a game of patience, but sometimes he just yearned for the thrill of action.

"I have a couple of gifts for you, or more accurately for our friend the target. An asset from Langley brought them in directly to the Embassy today. Do you understand?"

Marquez nodded. This 'asset' was evidently someone from the CIA's Technical Services Division, bringing in the chemical agent that was to be used against Lumumba.

"Good," said Deakin. "Open the glove compartment."

Marquez opened it and found a tube of ordinary-looking toothpaste. The brand name was 'Gleamer', a generic title from a fictitious company. There was also a loaded Colt. 45 semi-automatic.

"The pistol's for you, keep it with you at all times more for personal protection than anything else. You can't be too careful around these parts. The toothpaste is for our friend. Looks normal right? Well, it isn't so don't you go touching it, or be tempted to brush your teeth with it," said Deakin.

Marquez slipped the tube back into its cardboard container and placed it in his inside jacket pocket.

"It's odourless and untraceable to most toxicology tests," said Deakin. "At least, anything that the people in this part of the world would be able to find. A pea-sized amount is enough to kill him."

"How does it work?"

"It attacks the respiratory system, then the heart; the target will be dead within twelve hours, so I've been led to believe. You had any ideas about how to administer it to the target?"

Marquez shook his head. "Not yet, it's too early to say. I'll know more once I've had my first meeting. Possibly as a gift parcel from my supposed principals in Europe. Failing that, I'll have to see if anyone in Lumumba's entourage is susceptible to a bribe and introduce it that way."

Deakin liked that plan. If the poisoned toothpaste was going to be the method of assassination, they were the most likely scenarios to ensure its success. "Good," he said. "After that, all our problems will be over."

* * *

The phone call to his hotel room came early the next morning. It was Patrick Kivwa, Lumumba's go-between and legal advisor. His voice sounded tinny and under stress. "The meeting is on, later today. A driver will pick you up in front of your hotel at midday. Bring your passport with you, so that the guards will let you through. You have one hour to talk. After that, the driver will take you back to the hotel."

Promptly at 11.55am, Marquez stood and waited in the baking sun to take the journey to finally meet his target. The car was a 1960 Lincoln Limousine and the driver was a young, smartly dressed man who gave his name as Samuel.

Since being deposed in September, Lumumba had been under house arrest at his former official residence on the outskirts of Leopoldville. The Prime Minister's residence was an ornate colonial affair set in well-manicured grounds. The United Nations protection team manned a permanent guard and brooded over this unwelcome task. Guarding a target for political assassination was not a task they welcomed.

The car arrived at the residence twenty minutes later and Marquez was greeted at the entrance by Kivwa before being whisked through the reception area, up the main stairs and into the private office of Patrice Lumumba. Lumumba, dressed casually in a dark shirt and light cotton pants, came forward to meet him. Marquez thought he looked like a Sunday school teacher, rather than a politician engaged in an African coup-counter-coup conspiracy.

"Monsieur LeClerc, I am Patrice Lumumba, please sit so that we can be comfortable while we speak." Marquez took in the man's face; bespectacled, somber, honorable. There was a lot to like about this man, Marquez sensed.

"I understand that you are a representative of certain outside interests. At least, that is what Patrick has told me, is that not correct? How can I help?" said Lumumba.

Marquez settled himself. This was probably going to be the highest risk pitch of his career. He knew there was going to be no middle ground; either Lumumba would believe every word and welcome him with open arms, or he would be cast out and the operation, at least from his end, would be over. He cleared his throat and looked the man square in the eyes.

"Prime Minister, I will be open with you and will not waste either your time or mine. I am but a messenger for a group of individuals who are sympathetic to your country's situation. We hope that you will give us an opportunity to help you."

Lumumba inclined his head; "Monsieur, I am a reasonable man and will gladly listen to all voices of reason. But please tell me, who are these people you represent. Is it the French, the British, or please God, not the Americans again!"

Marquez shook his head. "No, not the Americans," he lied. "We are subtler than that. Although I understand that you have had unhappy dealings with the USA."

Lumumba cast his hands in the air, in a motion of exasperation. "Oh, the Americans are fools. They think of me as 'Moscow's man', but that is far from the case. Yes, I have accepted assistance from the Russians – why not? But I am not their puppet. I am my own man; I make my own allegiances. The Russians serve a purpose for now, but this country will never be a communist state. Not if I have my way."

"And the Russians, do they know this?"

"The Russians can believe what they want. They assume that I am just as corrupt as my rivals here. But I am in no way like them. Kalonji is ineffective as a leader, he will do whatever he thinks people want. That is not leadership, it is weakness. How can he hope to rule the RC when he can't even rule himself? Tshombe has been bought by the Belgians and their mercenaries. He is venal. As for Mobutu; the Americans believe that they can control him, which makes them even more foolish than I first thought. The General is a dictator in waiting."

"So what could you offer your people?" prompted Marquez, genuinely curious to know what made this man tick.

For the first time Lumumba seemed angry, affronted by his visitor's remark. "I have only the need to serve my people, to carry them through this crisis and give them a country they can be proud of. I have no wish to be anyone's puppet, but even I recognize that in this war of words between the west and the east, small countries like mine can be seen as mere pawns on a chess board."

"I may have a third option, one that removes the Russians from the equation," suggested Marquez. Lumumba watched him carefully as if deciding whether to listen, or have him thrown out of the building.

"We can get you to Stanleyville; there you can gather in -country support before a quick flight out of the country, a meeting with my principals, and then return to your base to remove your opponents."

"And you are doing this out of the goodness of your heart, you and your leaders?"

"No, Prime Minister we are not. I know we are not; you know we are not. My people are businessmen. We have spotted a commercial opportunity to help, nothing more."

"Ha, oh, so easy for you," mocked Lumumba. Then his face set in stone as his mind turned to the serious business of money and what it could achieve. "And of the Congo's natural resources, what of them? Raped and pillaged, no doubt."

Marquez shook his head. *Give him what he wants, tell him what he wants to hear and then reel him in.* "No. Businessmen and corporations are there for a profit certainly, but we are not governments and politicians who want to control and decimate. We would want the vast majority of the Congo's resources to be used to benefit the peoples of this nation; the money that my investors would make would be marginal by comparison. We are not the Belgian's after all; we are pragmatists and humanists."

"But where is the profit for them in that!"

"Monsieur, even a small percentage of profits can be worth billions to the right people. We can supply engineers, surveyors; public relations people, a whole range of assistants who can make the Congo a stable proposition with Patrice Lumumba guiding his people. Imagine returning Katanga and South Kasai back into the fold of the Republic."

"It sounds almost too good to be true," said Lumumba.

"It could happen. I can get you to Stanleyville within twenty-four hours. By the end of the week, you can be in a safe European country, meeting with the consortium that I represent; serious men, practicable men, men who want to assist you in your struggle. By the end of the month, we can turn the tide of this crisis in your favor and we can start to re-build the Congo."

Lumumba's eyes glazed over, almost as if he was in the depths of a dream. Then he turned his gaze to Marquez. "You are very persuasive, LeClerc. I will think on your proposal, Monsieur. Kivwa will be in touch. Thank you for your time."

* * *

Marquez spent the next few days waiting, sweating and drinking. It was the way the game was played. You weren't paid for the final action; you were paid for waiting around for your contact to get in touch.

It was more tiring than actually killing the target. He just hoped he'd done enough and that his story, while not believed totally, was at least plausible enough to keep the target interested.

He stayed close to his hotel in case an emergency message came through from Lumumba's people. He ventured to the bar and ate in the restaurant, but didn't come into contact with the little Austrian spy. At this point in the proceedings, Marquez imagined that this was a good sign. The last thing he needed this deep into an operation like this was a rival spy, poking his nose around.

* * *

They came for him as he was approaching the Intercontinental. He had been to visit an acquaintance who he had been trying to recruit; a Yugoslav Air-Force pilot who was here teaching the Congolese military how to fly. The meeting had seemed to go well, the pilot had appeared interested in helping and had gladly taken the 'expenses' which had been offered to him. Yes, Donner was sure he would make a good agent for his little 'unit'.

An old, rusty, green-colored camper van pulled up when he was within twenty feet of the door to the foyer. The first he knew of it, was when his arms were pinned from either side by an enormous set of hands; two left, two right. They lifted him off his feet; he barely had time to shout before someone else had grabbed both his legs and he found himself being carried like a rolled up carpet.

Donner did what he always did in physical situations like this; he fought back. If he'd had a weapon he would have drawn it, used it and to hell with the consequences. But he didn't and the punch to the stomach took the wind right out of him, but it was the elbow to his temple that not only stunned him, but finished the fight.

Through a haze he heard the roller doors of the camper van slide open and he was thrown deep into the darkness of the van's interior. Then bodies, three, four, five large and strong, piled in and began to handcuff his wrists and ankles.

The doors slid shut and the engine was gunned. He felt the weight of his abductors holding him down until they were satisfied he was secured.

The whole snatch had taken less than a minute, and the *faux* Austrian Franz Donner had, to all intents and purposes, disappeared off the face of the earth.

* * *

The knock at his hotel door came just after he'd returned from his evening meal in the hotel's restaurant. It was Deakin and he looked like a man who had only hours to live. "I've got some news, not much of it good," he said.

They sat perched on the end of the bed. Marquez poured them both a Cognac and Deakin took a slug and beckoned for a refill. "Okay, I'll speak fast. Time is of the essence here."

Marquez wondered if things had taken a dramatic turn, possibly even a dangerous turn, and that was why the American was so furious.

"The Austrian that you said tried to recruit you does work for an intelligence service – he works for *our* intelligence service. There's a turf war going on in Langley, between Africa Division and Executive Action and we're caught in the center of it all. Those assholes manning a desk in Langley didn't see fit to let me into the knowledge that I had another operative working on my patch, I mean fuck, I'm only the goddamned Chief of Station in this cesspit, what do I know?" ranted Deakin.

So that's what has angered him, thought Marquez; *the fact that his bosses have kept him out of the loop.* It was understandable given the circumstances.

Deakin drained his glass and put it rim down, gambler style, on the bedside table. "He's here on a similar mission to yours. Lumumba is his target, same as yours. He's a former French mercenary by the name of David Gioradze. He's wanted for attempted murder, bank robbery and gunrunning. His Agency name is ROGUE."

"So what's changed?"

"Things have taken a turn and our 'other' agent here Mr. ROGUE, has only gone and gotten himself lifted by the security police. Word is that they don't know who he is, or what he's up to. At least not yet anyway, but knowing the methods that they use here, it won't take long for him to spill."

"Why did they lift him? What tipped them off?"

"Apparently, my source in the security service says that ROGUE was snitched on by a Yugoslav Air Force pilot who he had attempted to recruit for some kind of intelligence work. Probably something to do with this assassination team he was trying to put together. The guy's a yo-yo and without doubt the worst spy I've ever had the misfortune to come across."

Marquez thought back to the man's crass attempt to recruit him. No wonder he'd come to the attention of the police.

"It's been told to me in no uncertain terms by the geniuses in Langley that I have to arrange to get him out of jail. I may need your help with this," said Deakin.

Marquez nodded. "Of course, if I can."

"We also want to bring the Lumumba thing forward. Forget about the chemical agent, we're trying a different tack. Do you think you could persuade him to leave his compound?"

Marquez frowned. He didn't like it. This operation was fast spiraling down into chaos and he was being asked to do things over and above his original orders. Control of the mission was being lost, fast. He breathed out softly to calm himself. "It is certainly possible. In fact, we have already discussed it at our initial meeting. It will depend on whether he thinks I'm serious or not. Put it this way, luring him out of his residence is a much more viable option than using that ridiculous poisoned toothpaste you gave me."

Deakin let out a howl of laughter, slapping his knees as if he'd just heard the best joke of his life. "Well now, on that one I grant you, it was a little comedy of errors. Okay, what can we do to make Lumumba bite? What is the one thing that he wants?"

"That's easy. To be taken seriously, to have an influence on the world's stage."

"And how do we do that?"

"Simple. Give him a signal that an influential politician outside of Africa is keen to meet with him. Someone who is accepted by both sides of the conflict," suggested Marquez.

"Perfect, that sounds like the final bit of bait to get him to leave the safety of his compound. A personal letter should do it, signed by the man in question. I have a very good forger on staff who should be able to rig something up."

"And then?"

"And then he's fair game. Shot while trying to escape in the time honored tradition of escaped prisoners the world over. You lure him out, isolate him and then hand him over to Mobutu's men. Job done."

Marquez thought it over. It could work, but he still had the thorny issue of the 'other' CIA agent, languishing somewhere in a prison cell. Despite his misgivings about – what was his name? Gioradze, that was it. As a spy, Marquez actually liked and admired the gutsy little fighter. "Okay," he said, "but I have some suggestions first, conditions, to be more precise."

"Alright, shoot," said Deakin, who found the idea of an agent telling his case officer how to run an operation almost comical.

Marquez spoke for five minutes without interruption and laid out a plan that would ensure that their erstwhile colleague, the other agent known as ROGUE was freed and the Lumumba situation was brought to a swift conclusion, and all for a fraction of their operating budget.

"It's good, I like it," said Deakin. "It covers all our bases, gets our man out and finishes the target off. Plus, we also get to send a little warning signal to the security police, let them know who the boss is here."

* * *

That same night, in a different part of Leopoldville, former Prime Minister Patrice Lumumba was taking an evening stroll in the gardens of the official residence.

He enjoyed these nocturnal moments of solitude, listening to the night's insects and animals vocalizing their existence. It gave him time to ponder, calmly and meditatively, on the situation he had found himself in. He looked over at the United Nations troops who were on permanent watch outside the property. *Were they protectors or prison guards,* he sometimes wondered.

One thing he was sure of was that the status quo couldn't continue indefinitely. Somewhere along the line, and sooner rather than later, he would have to decide his own fate and make a stand. *A stand for right or wrong,* he thought, *even if it means risking my own life.* He turned and called back into the residence, shouting the name of his personal assistant. The middle aged aide came running, his hands smoothing out his shirt as if he was on a parade ground. "Oui, Monsieur le Premier Ministre."

"Cyrille, could you telephone Monsieur Kivwa for me and pass him a message. Tell him to contact the Frenchman. I would like to accept his proposal and meet with his principals."

Cyrille accepted the message without comment, turned and made his way back inside to complete his errand. Lumumba turned back to the UN guards; they were still there in place, pacing, watching. If this 'escape' plan was to work, he would need to circumvent the soldiers outside the residence. Not only the UN, but also Mobutu's secret police who, he was sure, had the place under surveillance.

Was he sure this was the right thing to do? Perhaps he could make a deal with the others to go into exile and live a happy life with his family?

But Lumumba knew better. That was not the way that rivalries were settled in the Congo. There was no middle ground of exile, only victory or death at the hands of a sword. He just hoped the Frenchman was everything he claimed to be. *What choice do I have,* he thought, *except to put my life in his hands?*

Chapter Six

The call connected to the Security Police headquarters. A series of clicks as the operators switched the plug from one port to the other, a crackle and then a voiced rumbled, "Hello?"

"This is Deakin, from the American Embassy, can I speak with Major Koroma please?"

"Hello, Mr. Deakin, I am Major Pierre Koroma, how can I help you today?"

"Major I am told that you are the man I should speak to. You can make things happen. I am speaking here on a matter of urgency and discretion. You know which organization I work for, I assume?"

"Of course, Mr. Deakin, we have great respect for your organization," said Koroma smoothly.

Yeah, plus you like our money too much, thought Deakin. "Major, it appears that you have something of ours. One of our people who was, I assume, mistakenly arrested. Your security people obviously didn't know who he was. We would like him back, please."

Deakin heard Koroma let out a long sigh. "Mr. Deakin this is a very disturbing state of affairs and something that General Mobutu would take very seriously, despite our cordial relations with the American Embassy. We are not keen on foreign agents operating on our soil."

"Nevertheless, Major, he belongs to us and we would like him returned."

"Mmm, that is difficult. I am a soldier, Mr. Deakin, I work directly for the General, but those security police animals, whilst being under his control are a law unto themselves. I am not sure how much influence I would be able to have over them," said Koroma.

Deakin sensed they were about to reach an impasse. He knew the play; every spy, gambler and hard-headed businessman did. They were angling for a deal; it was just a case of what deal they wanted. "Major, can I just cut to the chase. I'm a very busy man, but I think I've found a solution that could benefit everybody."

"Really?"

Got you, thought Deakin. He had pricked Major Koroma's interest, now it was time to reel him in. "I can offer you five thousand US dollars for the safe release of our man." Deakin heard the laugh. In truth, he was expecting it.

"Mr. Deakin, five thousand would not even cover the costs incurred by the security police officials involved, it is—"

"Excuse me, Major, but I had not finished. Thank you. As I was saying, five thousand for the release of the prisoner, plus we are in a position to hand over to you your biggest political rival. I think you know who I mean."

The silence was palpable. Deakin drummed his fingers on his desk. Come on, come on...

"I know who you mean. But Mr. Deakin, Lumumba is under house arrest. He is already in our custody, of a sort," said Koroma.

"Major, we have information that suggests he is planning to flee the Prime Minister's residence, make his way to Stanleyville and raise a counter-force."

There was a moment's silence on the line as Koroma weighed up whether the American was yanking his chain. "So, at last, the snake shows his true colors... treason it is, then."

"Indeed. However, we have an agent on the ground who can deliver Lumumba directly to you during his 'escape.' "

"I see, and when is this to happen?" asked Koroma.

"Within the next twenty-four hours. We will take care of all the arrangements. I will telephone you directly with a time and a location for the rendezvous. You, in return, will contact the security unit that has our man in custody and inform them of our deal."

Koroma pondered this, desperately trying to figure out the angles. Was this American playing him for a fool, or would he get the chance to be part of the capture of a traitor? "And then?" asked Koroma.

"One of our operatives here will hand over Lumumba, directly to you personally. You will give him the location of our imprisoned agent; he will pay the guards directly and retrieve our man."

It sounded plausible, thought Koroma. "And we can trust you on this?"

Deakin laughed. "You'll have to. Just wait for my phone call." He hung up. *Leave them dangling,* he thought to himself, *always leave them dangling.*

* * *

On the first day of December, the assassin sat comfortably in the rear of the Lincoln limousine and watched from the window as the streets of Leopoldville passed by.

The man was grey-haired, with a beard to match, and wore a thick pair of spectacles that covered most of his upper face. His suit was tailored and expensive. He had in his pocket a passport that identified him as one Jose Silva, a Portuguese diplomat who was assigned as a liaison official with the United Nations. The other item in his pocket was a signed personal letter to Prime Minister Patrice Lumumba from UN Secretary-General Dag Hammerskjold, stating that he wished his friend well and that he was offering his utmost support, both political and moral, in these difficult times.

Of course the wig, beard and glasses were nothing more than stage make-up supplied by the CIA station officers. The passport and letter were also forged, once again provided by the paper experts of the Agency. Marquez knew that the work which had consumed the last month of his life would be finished within a matter of hours. He had played the game out to its natural conclusion, and barring a few detours along the way, it had pretty much gone according to plan.

They were minutes away now from the Prime Minister's residence and he patted himself down, making sure that everything was in place. He could see the UN soldiers manning the gates and he reached inside his jacket for his passport.

A soldier stepped forward and motioned for the driver to wind down the window. Marquez leaned forward and offered his papers for inspection; the soldier crouched down and peered in, his eyes slowly adjusting to the gloom of the interior. His eyes flicked from the passport to the man sitting in the rear of the car then back to the papers again. He handed the papers back, saluted and waved the car through the main gates. The car drove up to the main entrance and Marquez stepped out to be greeted by Kivwa. They shook hands like old friends.

"Welcome, Senor Silva," said Kivwa, playing out the charade for the guards to clearly hear. "Come in and have some refreshments, Samuel, go and park the car around the side."

The two men disappeared inside while the chauffeur reversed the Lincoln and steered it around to the servant's entrance where the car could not be seen. No sooner had the car stopped than Samuel had gotten out and opened the rear passenger door. A figure quickly moved in a crouch from the servants' door to the back seat of the Lincoln, a fleeting glance, no more, and then the door of the car was slammed shut and the figure covered itself with the thick blanket which had been provided. The heat was stifling underneath it, but he knew he only had to endure fifteen minutes or less until his escort was due to exit from the front entrance.

Fifteen minutes later, the Portuguese diplomat shook hands with Patrick Kivwa on the steps of the residence. Underneath his breath Kivwa whispered, "Good luck, just get him out of the damned country and to safety."

Marquez looked the man in the eye and nodded. Almost there... almost there...

The Lincoln pulled up and Marquez got in. The subterfuge had worked and the limousine ambled calmly past the UN guards manning the compound. "Just keep driving at a steady speed until we are out of sight," Marquez ordered Samuel. He saw the young man nod his understanding in the rear view mirror.

"Thank you Lucien, your assistance and bravery will not be forgotten in the new democracy," said Lumumba. The man sighed and relaxed back into the seat, confident he had outwitted his enemies.

"Get some rest Mr. Prime Minister, we have only a short drive to the escape plane," reassured Marquez, as he began to remove the glasses, wig and false beard glued to his face.

The drive continued out of the city for a further half an hour with bright streets giving way to dark roads. *The time was nearly right,* thought Marquez, *only a few more moments to the rendezvous.* He was aware of Lumumba speaking to him again. The time for the charade to end was nigh.

"What will you do once I am in Paris, Lucien, will you perhaps visit or be a part of..."

In one swift movement Marquez had grabbed Lumumba's head and was forcing it down to the floor with one hand while with the other he pulled out the Colt.45, pressing it to the man's temple. "Down, down...down on the floor! Try to fight and I will shoot! Get DOWN! Quiet!"

Lumumba was no fool and knew better than to argue with an armed man. He slumped into a sullen silence.

"Keep driving for another half a mile, you'll come to a fork in the road. That's the rendezvous; the collection party will be waiting for us," Marquez ordered Samuel. The driver, to his credit, kept calm and guided the car along the dirt track for another few minutes. Then slowly from out of the darkness the silhouette of several military jeeps and wagons began to appear. They flashed their lights in recognition and the driver of the limousine beeped his horn to complete the code.

The limousine slowly pulled to a halt, the driver aware of the soldiers with their fingers on the triggers of their weapons. A man stepped forward, large, in command, his outline cast against the glare of the truck's headlights.

"I am Major Pierre Koroma." His voice was a deep basso and rumbled. He stood composed and confident; one hand wavering near the pistol he wore on his hip. He was military, through and through.

The door of the limousine opened and Marquez dragged out the terrified Lumumba, the gun still pressed against his temple, and forced him onto his knees between the two groups.

"Hello, Patrice," said the man and then waved a hand for unseen shadows to take the deposed Prime Minister away. Marquez stepped back as the guards grabbed the fallen man. He didn't even look at the doomed prisoner. For Marquez, the target was now a thing of the past, a burden he had put aside.

"I have been asked to pass on our thanks on behalf of General Mobutu," said Koroma.

"Thank you."

"The General says that he is in your debt for this service. He says if there is anything he can do for you in the future, he will consider it an honor to help."

The noise of a scuffle broke out from the rear of the trucks. Marquez assumed that the ANC soldiers were having fun with the deposed politician, fun involving punches, kicks and rifle butts no doubt. Marquez turned back to Koroma. "I will remember the General's kind words. It is always useful to have a patron as wise and powerful as the General. I thank him."

Koroma nodded. It was good that this foreign spy should show proper respect to the General. "That is good. I also have the other piece of information that you wanted, about the kidnapping of your 'friend'. "

"Yes?"

"He is being held in a warehouse out near Panza. It is a private place which belongs to the security police. He has been there for days. If you go there now, they will be told you are expected so that you can collect him." Koroma handed Marquez a slip of paper with the address.

"Thank you, Major."

"Our friends in the Security Police will also be expecting the agreed sum for the release of your friend."

"That is understood Major. I have the funds, five thousand dollars."

"Excellent," said Koroma happily. "Then our business is complete."

The man stalked back to his jeep, issuing orders as he went. The engines of the convoy rumbled into life and within seconds the trucks and jeeps were a distant light down the dirt road.

Marquez stood for a moment, breathed, and took in the coolness and tranquility of the night. *The first job of the night complete,* he thought, *now for the rest of his chores.* He walked around to the driver's window and motioned for him to open the window. "Samuel, are you alright?"

The driver nodded, but Marquez could see his hands were shaking. He gripped the steering wheel fiercely, trying to halt the tremors. Marquez opened the door and eased him out, leaning the traumatized man against the side of the vehicle. "Relax, it is over now. You have earned your money. You would be better if you forgot everything that you saw here tonight. Come, let me give you a cigarette. Let me get my pack from the back seat."

The shot, when it came, shattered the night air; the sounds of the wilderness taking flight and the echoing report of the.45 caliber bullet. The sound of the body hitting the dirt at full force was negligible. Marquez stood and looked down at the body for a moment. The bullet had exploded right in the driver's eye, taking away a section of his head. Marquez moved quickly, grabbing the dead man's heels, dragging him out into the scrubland and concealing the body behind a small clump of bushes. It might take weeks before the corpse was discovered and once the wildlife and desert dogs had their fill of the flesh, identification might take even longer.

* * *

David Gioradze, the spy who had been operating under the pseudonym of the Austrian Franz Donner, had been sitting handcuffed to the uneven iron chair for the past five hours.

The rusty metal of the handcuffs had worn away the skin around his wrists and the thick black hood that covered his entire head was saturated with sweat. The sweat wasn't from the temperature, but from the sheer physical effort of keeping his body under control.

He was naked, freezing cold and bruised along the full length of his torso. He prayed they would kill him soon. His only escape from the torture, discomfort, and pain was the refuge of his own mind.

Hide David, his mama would have said. *Hide and you'll be fine.* He had learned that trick well as a child when his father would come home after a meeting with the émigré group he was a part of in Paris. His father, a man with a short fuse of a temper, had taken badly to being an exile in a country which he despised. The émigrés would meet once a week in a small bar in Montmartre and the talk and the wine would flow, so that by the end of their 'political meeting' they would be fired up with patriotism, revenge, hare-brained schemes, and cheap vodka.

By the time his father had made it home, his temper had been at boiling point and the likely target for his temper and frustration was his wife. "Hide David, papa will be home soon," was the usual routine, and always followed by the reminder to, "Whatever you do stay in your room, don't look and cover your ears. Papa is tired, that's all it is, emotional and tired."

The family had 'escaped' from the ravages of the Georgian/Armenian war in 1918, when David had been no more than a year old. With distant relatives in France, Paris seemed the logical place for the family of Pytor Gioradze to seek sanctuary. The intention had been to return to Tbilisi at the end of hostilities, but no sooner had one skirmish finished than three years later the Red Army had stormed its way into Georgia. Pyotr Gioradze, a committed anti-communist, saw the writing on the wall and decided that to return to his homeland would mean repression or even death for him and his family.

They had lived an uneventful life as exiles. His father drank himself to death and his mother lived a humble life in a two-bedroomed apartment until she finally succumbed to cancer. For David, he simply became self-sufficient and made his own way in the world working as a laborer, or in a host of other manual jobs. He didn't worry too much – he was young and without any commitments. He could do as he pleased.

During the Second World War, he'd seen Paris being stormed by the fearful Wehrmacht, and like many young men of his time he had decided that the best way to free his adopted country was to aid the Maquis resistance fighters any way that he could. Gioradze had only been allowed on the fringes of the French resistance; running messages, moving sabotage material, surveillance of German officers, but it had given him a taste for adventure. Compared to some, he'd had a good war until 1944 when he had been captured at a Maquis safehouse during a Gestapo raid.

He had been operating as a courier for a local sabotage network, unfortunately by 1944 the Germans were taking no prisoners, the tide of the war was going against them and mass executions were the norm. He had been held in the local secret police cells, awaiting execution and it was only when Paris fell that he was finally released by the Americans.

After the war, he'd run with a gang of organized criminals; safe blowing and bank robberies mostly. The last job he'd been on had ended up with him being caught and doing five years in La Santé prison.

After five years of hard stir, he'd been released and came right back out to work with his old gang. Then a fight outside a bar one night had turned sour and Gioradze had ended up killing a member of a rival gang who was trying to muscle into their patch. A knife was pulled; Gioradze was slashed across the face. In return, Gioradze simply pulled out his .38 and shot the man dead in the street. His fellow gang members got him out of Paris that very night. He headed south, determined not to go back to prison again under any circumstances.

He made his way down to Sidi-bel-abbes in Algeria and signed up for the French Foreign Legion for five years.

He made it to Corporal and had fought his way across Asia and North Africa; jungles, swamps and deserts were his battlegrounds. He liked the action, adventure and the spirit of the men he worked with. He had faced death, looked it in the eye and had retaliated at times with almost reckless abandon. At the end of his five year 'stint' Gioradze returned to Europe, looking to start a life away from the Legion and to make some serious money. He bumped into an old Legion friend in Belgium and heard that the Americans were hiring mercenaries for an operation in South-East Asia.

Rather naively, he approached the US Embassy in Belgium in the hope of gaining a meeting with the local Military Attaché. The man on the desk simply nodded, asked him a series of questions, took his contact details, and politely told him that he would pass the information on to the relevant department. David Gioradze returned to the apartment that he was renting and went about his business. He heard no more from the Embassy. He was not unduly worried about money, he still had his savings from his time in the Legion, and if he did run short of cash, well, there was always a bank or jewelers that he could turn his attention to. He was happy to while away the days in Belgium drinking and whoring, at least for a while.

A month later he received a letter inviting him to attend an employment interview in Germany. The letter suggested some possible work that suited his experience and skills. The name on the letterhead said 'Farthing & Co – Munich' and enclosed was a time and date and a request to 'keep all travel receipts for reimbursement purposes'.

A week later he arrived in Munich for his job interview. He sat in a sparsely furnished office while a patrician-like German interviewed him for over an hour. "We understand that you're good with languages – French, German... Russian," the man had said. "And that you're experienced in military matters."

"Is this about the job in Asia?" asked Gioradze.

"No, we know nothing about that. We have something more important to concern ourselves with. You're the kind of man we're looking for. How do you find the idea of working in Europe? It would mean a quick stopover in another country first, just to check you out and give you a bit of training. Nothing too intense and certainly nothing you haven't done before I would imagine. We work in the acquisition of information."

And that had been it, the start of his career as a contract agent for the CIA. His initial mission had been as one of two agents who were to 'trail their coats' in Berlin in the hope that the KGB would pick them up, offer them some money in exchange for a trade in information. Except of course that the information, codes, actually, would be fake, but would give the Americans a chance to peek inside the Russian's code-breaking capabilities.

The weeks' worth of training at a CIA safe-house in Maryland included the use of tradecraft, cover and secret writing. It was intense, but not difficult. The mission was a 'go'. He would be in West Berlin within twenty-four hours, he was ready and primed.

Then the bombshell landed. The job was cancelled with just twelve hours to spare. He never knew why or what had gone wrong, only that the project had been 'dismantled' and that he was now spiked. His handler came to visit him. "We're thinking of resettling you; give you some money so that you can start again. The Europe operation's a busted flush; how do you fancy Mexico? Maybe we can use you again in the future for something. Think about it."

He did, and decided that Mexico would do just fine. Maybe he could get a job working armed security for some of the big *Fincas* owned by the growing drug gangs. It was something to think on, certainly.

A week later as he was packing, two smart-suited Agency officers paid him a visit. They were from the CIA's Africa Division and they had yet another job offer for him. "David we have something else for you, something has come up in Africa. It's a little operation that we're keen to get involved in. It would be dangerous, I won't lie to you, but it's more your kind of thing," suggested the senior of the two.

He had snapped at the offer, anything was better than sitting around the CIA safe-house in Maryland staring at the ceiling, and Mexico, well, Mexico would always be there at some point in the future.

This time he had been flown by USAF cargo plane to an ancient fort in Malta, where the Agency kept a discreet paramilitary training base for its covert operators. Two weeks' worth of demolitions, small arms and surveillance training made him feel alive and he relished the thought of becoming an 'action agent'.

Halfway through the training his case officer came to him for a final preparation. "You'll need some cosmetic work, toupee, new identification, and a new cover. You've operated in Africa with the Legion, we don't want you running into old contacts and being caught out. Don't worry about that we'll take care of it."

He had flown to West Berlin and from there direct to Leopoldville. His mission was to prepare a plausible cover for himself – someone mentioned a small retail business – organize a base of operations and begin to recruit suitable personnel for a covert intelligence network and a covert action team. Armed with a bit of money, some basic information and a lot of guts, he had thrown himself into his new role of a covert operator.

But now as he sat among the feces, blood and vomit that had spewed from his body, and with all things being equal, he wished that he had never opened that letter in Belgium and had told the CIA officers to go and royally fuck themselves.

* * *

It was the soft scuffing of feet on the concrete floor outside his cell that awoke him from his dream.

He twisted his head around inside the hood, craning his neck, trying to gauge whether it was food time or beating time. Maybe it was a trick, another mock execution, or maybe this time it was going to be the real thing.

The clank of the bolt on his cell door being retracted made him involuntarily tense his muscles, bracing himself for whatever degradation they had in mind for him this time, except that this time there was no violence, no shouting, no cold water, no rubber hoses, only silence and the occasional whisper and slow careful movements of persons'unknown. He felt the handcuffs being unlocked before he was unceremoniously lifted to his feet and told to stand. They dressed him quickly and with no grace; pants up, shirt unbuttoned, no shoes, because his shoes had been stolen over a week ago. He was clothed, but barely.

Strong hands grabbed him from either side, fingers digging into his biceps and then he was propelled forward moving left, left, left, up some steps, right, and all the while his bare feet bearing the brunt of the stone floor. It was the air that hit him first; coolness after the stifling confines of the cell. *It's an execution,* he thought; *firing squad in the courtyard. Best to take it outside; don't want to foul the cell with more blood and brains.*

A creak of un-oiled metal came from what he later learned was a car door being opened and he was pushed into a seat. The heat returned again. His heart was pounding now, his breath coming in rasps. Through the hood he was unsure, but he thought he could hear a muffled conversation taking place outside the car. It went on for several minutes; perhaps French, perhaps English. Again he was unsure. He heard another door open, felt the weight of another body entering the vehicle on the driver's side. An engine was gunned and the vehicle fled at speed.

The drive went on for, he guessed, the next ten minutes or so. *Say nothing, just wait until an opportunity presents itself. And then what?* he reasoned. *I'm beat up, exhausted, can barely walk! What good could I do?*

He felt the speed of the vehicle drop until it casually slowed to a halt. The sound of tires crunching on the rubble road told him they were out in the countryside. He felt the hood being removed slowly from his head and experienced that wonderful moment of pleasure when cool, fresh air enveloped his bruised and cut face. Slowly he opened his eyes, partially at first, aware that any bright light would hurt the one good eye which wasn't completely shut from the beatings.

He opened it to its full aperture and saw darkness. He was in the front seat of a car, what make he didn't know, and next to him in the driver's seat was the dark shadow of a man. They were definitely out in the countryside – that much he could see; no buildings, darkness, isolation. "I'm going to turn on the courtesy light. You might want to shield your eyes for the moment," said the dark shadow man.

The voice was speaking in English, but was also strangely familiar. The light clicked and bathed the interior of the car in a yellow tinge. Almost immediately, insects began trying in vain to penetrate the windows.

"How are you, my friend?"

David Gioradze turned his head towards the man, squinting his one good eye against the light, but at the same time eager to see the face of his savior. The man was dressed impeccably, as usual, in a summer suit and silk tie, and even in this extreme heat he looked relaxed and in control. The only addendum to his normal attire was a Colt .45 tucked at an angle into his waistband. "Luc... Luc, is that you? How..."

"Relax you're safe now, those animals have done their worst to you. They can do no more."

His mind whirled with surprise, confusion, mistrust and panic. Was his cover still intact? Had he told them anything of importance? He didn't think so. Those animals had been more interested in information about local forces, rather than freebooting foreigners interfering in Congolese politics. He was quite happy to give up the local agents he had managed to recruit, anything or anyone as long as he wasn't 'blown'.

He risked another look at the man he knew as Lucien. Who was he? How was an agricultural salesman from Marseilles able to spring him from a secret police torture cell? He gathered his thoughts, took a breath and started again. "Why did you come and get me, *how* did you get me?" he muttered through cut and bruised lips.

The man known as Lucien LeClerc switched off the interior light, started the engine and began to drive.

He pressed the accelerator down to the floor, keen to reach his destination as soon as possible he tore up the road leading away from Panza. Gioradze lay back in his seat and watched in a daze as they drove further and further into the darkness. Occasionally he would close his eyes, only to jerk them open moments later to escape from the horrors of the torture cell; punching, kicking, burning and beating. It was when the knives and machetes came out that he had really screamed in terror.

"Take it easy, just breathe. I'll tell you what I can on the way."

"On the way to where?" said Gioradze, the mistrust in his voice evident.

"Don't worry, I didn't rescue you from one torture cell to take you to another. There's a makeshift airstrip not far from here. A private plane is waiting for us."

"Thank, thank you." He felt a wave of relief wash over him; he might even get to see the end of the day without being murdered. "How did you get me out?"

Marquez nodded. "It wasn't that difficult. The hardest part was finding out where you had been taken. I knew that you'd been lifted after leaving the hotel. After that, well, a serious bribe into the right pockets helped smooth your release. They said that you would be returned unharmed. Obviously they lied. How was it?"

"I don't want to talk about it… it was rough… the bastards."

"Seems reasonable, I don't blame you. If it helps, I left them a little present inside the briefcase containing the ransom money." A smile touched the corners of Marquez's mouth.

Gioradze looked at him quizzically. His friend Lucien looked back at him with a cold smile, a callous smile. "The case is lined with plastique. On a timer, the moment they spring open the lock well, let's just say that they'd better spend that money soon. I'm just sorry that we couldn't see the explosion. It's the very least I could do; we do, after all, have something in common."

A confused look crossed the little man's face. Lucien leaned in closer and whispered; "We have the same employer, David."

There was a pause as Gioradze began to work out exactly what the man meant. "What…the Americans…but how?"

Marquez shrugged as if it was a matter of no concern. "Different departments employ us certainly, but it amounts to the same. We both do the Agency's dirty work. Your Agency codename is ROGUE. In truth you are David Gioradze, former soldier, mercenary and bank robber, according to the local CIA man at the Embassy who briefed me. Is that correct?"

Gioradze leaned back in the seat and nodded.

"Well then, allow me to introduce myself, my true self should I say. I am Juan Raul Marquez, Agency cryptonym, WIN."

"Two CIA operators in the same place, but the odds of us meeting must be huge!"

"Really, do you think so? The CIA is nothing if not prolific and does tend to scatter its money and its agents profusely. I was sent here on one mission, you were sent here to do a different one, but we are both of the same ilk. It isn't *that* surprising that we would come into contact eventually, Europeans in a strange land do tend to gravitate towards each other."

Gioradze let the implication of the night's events sink in.

"Besides, I recognized you for what you are straight away; a spy, like me. Your rather embarrassing attempt to 'recruit' me only confirmed it," teased Marquez.

Gioradze began to cough and wheeze, the sucking of the air into his lungs was no longer to help him breathe, it was to give out great bellows of laughter. "Oh… that… is so… good! Of all the people to try to recruit and it turns out to be a fellow agent… well, that's my contract with the Yankees over and done with."

"Um, not quite. If I have learned one thing about working with the Americans, it's that they don't throw away good resources at the drop of a hat," said Marquez.

"What do you mean?"

"It seems, or so I have been informed by my case officer, that they have further use for both of us. The situation has altered while you have been locked away. The Congo is no longer on their radar; it seems that the Congo crisis has been resolved. Lumumba has been captured; hence your assassination operation is now void."

"Captured or killed?"

"For the moment, let's say captured, but from what I hear he won't see the next forty-eight hours out. Firing squad, I hear. The Americans will have their man Mobutu in place, the Russians have been kicked out of the country and normality for the CIA has been restored."

"So where does that leave us?"

"In quite a fortuitous position actually. Despite your rather inept agent recruitment methods and your exasperating skills at organizing a covert attack team, I have been singing your praises to the CIA."

"Why?"

"Because you are, I believe someone that I could work with, so long as we understand the chain of command," replied Marquez.

Gioradze knew what that meant. He knew how the chain of command worked. "In other words, you're in charge," he said.

"Let's just say I'll be the first among equals," purred Marquez.

Gioradze thought for a moment. "Okay, I can live with that. Besides, I owe you for getting me out of that hell hole. What's the plan?"

Marquez nodded, satisfied that his plan had worked out as he expected it would. "Good. The Agency has decided that we are to be partnered up. They have big plans for us and the word from the man in Washington is that they have plenty of work for us to do."

"Such as?"

"The details are a little sketchy at the moment, but broadly speaking, the CIA want us to do what we do best, covert action, assassination, sabotage and kidnappings. The benefit for them is that they will have two experienced covert agents running their operations for them."

"I could see how that would be attractive to them," said Gioradze.

"Our first job starts as soon as we get back to Florida. There is a little problem in the Dominican Republic that the CIA wants us to take care of as soon as possible. Interested?"

"Okay, fine, but first I need a cognac. Better make it a double." Gioradze turned away and looked out the car window at the dark night sky.

In the distance a faint light hinted at landing lights where a small plane might land, for example. Could he trust this man, let alone work with him? He was an enigma certainly, but Gioradze took seriously the risks that this killer had taken to save him from certain death. It was a life debt and one that he would honor.

In that respect he knew he would be Marquez's man for life – or at least until he was killed, or Marquez found someone better to work with. But that was alright, Gioradze had survived on far worse odds than that in the past.

Chapter Seven

Vienna – December 1964

Now, four years after their first meeting, the two killers and former partners sat once again face-to-face over coffee and pastries in Viennese cafe society.

Since their time in the Congo, they had worked in Africa, Latin America and had latterly been part of the operations against Castro's Cuba. All had been deniable and all had been successful. However, following the assassination of President Kennedy last year, the two men had been 'retired' as contract agents for the CIA. It was hardly surprising given that, with their own President having been the victim of a political assassination, senior CIA officers would want all links to their own assassination operations and operatives removed and hidden from sight. In fairness, the Agency had paid them well and commended them before cutting them both loose.

"How have you been, Juan, busy? You look well," said Gioradze shaking the other man's hand.

They had last met nearly a year ago on a private contract which Marquez had found for them: the kidnapping of a Turkish drug importer who had double crossed one of the major players in the Middle East heroin distribution network. They had lifted the man in Marrakech, torturing him for several days before the man finally relented and told them that the rest of the money had been spent. Marquez had shot him in the head and then burned the body. Job done.

Marquez nodded. "I did some work for the Corsicans a few months back. Nothing terribly difficult, a small job really. Besides, I have my investments and business back home to keep me busy. And you David, all goes well with you?"

Gioradze smiled and leaned back in his chair. "I too have become a legitimate businessman," he said proudly. "Nothing in your league, but the bar turns a profit, the weather is pleasant and I have a woman to keep me warm at night."

"It sounds... glorious," said Marquez, sipping his coffee and trying his best to sound impressed.

Gioradze nodded, not believing the man's kind words for a moment. Marquez was cut from a different cloth and Gioradze knew that the thought of domestic bliss, especially one with a woman, would have filled the Catalan with revulsion. "It is. I love it. But that's not why you dragged me away from it, all the way to the freezing, pissing rain in Vienna. Something's happened, I can see it in your eyes, Is it a problem? Is someone after us?"

Marquez shook his head. "No, nothing like that, not at all. In fact, it is exactly the opposite. How would you like to get back into the game?"

That statement captured the Georgian's attention immediately and the Catalan spent the next thirty minutes outlining the broad details of their new 'contract'." Marquez had spent the previous day with Mr. Knight giving his American controller the broad outline of how he would conduct the contract. What he would need, what his time frame would be and in which order the contract would be completed.

Never the *full* details of course – never – for no contract man alive ever tells his case officer everything. It is partly borne of a long mistrust of officers safely back home and tied to a desk, but also because Marquez wanted to keep a certain level of control over the running of the operation.

The two killers spent the next hour discussing in detail – as only men of a certain profession can do in their chosen trade – the logistics, tactics and pitfalls of such a unique contract. By the end of the hour Gioradze had made some suggestions which Marquez had decided to incorporate into the planning phase. He knew it had been the right thing to do to bring the little Georgian on board; the man was a natural soldier and spotted an easier way to carry out several of the killings.

"I think we need to talk in more detail back at my hotel," said Marquez.

Gioradze nodded, began to push his cup aside and started to remove his gloves from his coat pocket. Marquez, however, remained locked in his seat. "You will need to close up shop back home for the next few months David," he said.

"I'll get Maria to take over running the bar. It's no problem."

"Good. Hmm… but here in Vienna we have a problem."

Gioradze cocked his head quizzically and returned to his seat. "We do?"

Marquez nodded. "The American wants us to take care of a small administrative issue, to tie up a few loose ends."

"Tell me more."

"There is a man who has been helping the American, running errands, translating, that sort of thing. He knows what the American looks like and he knows what I look like."

Gioradze smiled. "Ah, I see my friend. I'm glad to see that you haven't lost your cautious streak."

Marquez shrugged. "I'm just being prudent. Why risk the success of this operation or indeed our liberty on the say so of a man of no importance? It protects the Americans and it protects us."

"And you, of course, want me to take care of it," said Gioradze, his mind clicking back into his old ways.

"It shows that you are committed to this contract, a sign of good faith. Besides the target has never seen you, so it will be like shooting a rat in a barrel."

"A fitting analogy. Okay, when and where?"

"Tonight. Here take this photograph of him that I got from the American," said Marquez. He slipped a small piece of paper across the table to the Georgian, who quickly glanced at it and placed it inside his glove for future reference. "He is expecting to meet me in front of the Parliament Building at nine o'clock for what he believes is a final payment for his services. When I don't show up, he'll know to go home and wait for a phone call from me as a backup. He will simply think I've been delayed and will wait for a re-schedule time. Follow him."

"So follow him, finish him." It was a statement, not a question from the Georgian.

Marquez moved his eyes searchingly over his partner, looking for a clue to his next question. "You are armed?"

"Of course, always," replied the Georgian.

"Okay. Good. I don't want to know the details, just deal with him." "And then?"

"Then meet me at my hotel so we can go over the next stage of the plan. The Hotel Imperial, room number 229. I'll be waiting. If you don't arrive by 11.30, I'll assume that you've been captured or killed. In that eventuality I'll be out of Vienna within the hour."

The Georgian stood and made ready to leave, pulling his gloves tighter. "Don't worry, I won't fail. I'll be back as quickly as I can."

Marquez nodded and watched the little mercenary make his way to the door of the Cafe, and for a brief moment he felt a pang of pity for the man who would be the target of the Georgian killer tonight. A brief pang only, before the moment passed.

* * *

Max Dobos, wearing a black cap, polo neck and knee length leather coat, stood freezing in the dark, beneath the statue of Pallas Athene, the Greek goddess of wisdom, strategy, war and peace, in front of the Parliament Building on the Ringstrasse.

The time was 8.55pm by his old and tattered wristwatch and he had five minutes to wait before he met Marquez for his final payment for the 'American job'. It would, he hoped, be a brief meeting as the less time he spent in the Catalan killer's company, the better. This would be the third time he would have met Marquez in person.

The first was when he had been recruited by the American, Mr. Knight, and he had made a personal visit to the little antiques store that was the 'front' for the assassin's more lucrative business. He had not liked the man from the moment he had set eyes on him. Cold and aloof, he turned Max Dobos's blood to ice.

The next time had been when he was in charge of security during Marquez and Mr. Knight's meeting in Clervaux. He had liked him even less then; again the eyes looked at you as though they were figuring out the most effective way to kill you.

But tonight was to be the last. A brush past meeting with minimal conversation and after that he would never work with them again. If his little plan worked out well this would be his last job in the intelligence marketplace for a very long time. *If* his plan worked out. But in the meantime, he waited.

Waiting! Waiting was the bane of intelligence work, he decided. You made an arrangement, you went, you waited. Your guest didn't show, so you went for the fall back location. Then sometimes they didn't make that meeting and you had to start the whole thing all over again. He glanced at his watch again. 8.58pm.

The other rule of the waiting game was that you didn't give them a few minutes after the allotted time. That was bad security and could turn out to be lethal, as so many had found out to their cost. But not Max Dobos. When the time was up it was up. So you gave them, up to and including the minute that had been agreed upon, then you simply walked away ready for the next rendezvous.

He had been working as a peddler of intelligence information since the end of the war, when as a displaced person he had been allowed to settle in Austria, and thus far he had made a successful career moving information around from one spy service to the other. And while it was true that he was something of a whore in who he worked for, he had always had a close affinity with the British station in Vienna.

The Americans were good payers, certainly, the Germans were thorough and demanded respect, even the Russians provided him with the odd chores, but it was the British that he had chosen to make his first among equals. They had picked him up after the war and employed him, first as a translator and had pulled the necessary strings to enable him to live a relatively unmolested life in Vienna. Over time they had used him more and more, latterly as an informant and taught him the ropes of working at the coal face of the intelligence game.

He slowly paced up and down in front of the statue, impatience irritating him and the cold seeping into his lame leg that was travelling carelessly behind him. The leg! That and his eye were remnants of the war when he had been beaten mercilessly by a sadistic SS officer in an interrogation cell who, wrongly, assumed that he had some long forgotten piece of information.

He had worked first for the fascist government of Hungary as a communications technician, but as a Jew, he had no doubt that the Germans would soon implement the same treatment to Hungarians as they were doing to the rest of Europe. He was right and in 1944 he found himself in the hellhole that was Auschwitz.

The beating had left him blind in his right eye and lame in his left leg; an awkward combination in anyone's book. When he looked in the mirror these days he saw an old, old man and though his age was actually fifty, most mornings he looked nearer to seventy. *A harsh life can take its toll most certainly*, he thought.

But he was a survivor. He had survived the fascist politics of early Second World War Hungary, the hunting down and subsequent incarceration of the death camps of Auschwitz and the new war between the Soviet and western forces. He stayed below the radar, he was invisible and he thrived.

He gave another look at the watch. 9.01pm.

That's it, he decided. Head back home and wait for the call for the backup rendezvous. Despite his misgivings regarding the Catalan, he hoped that nothing had happened to him. If Marquez was caught, captured or even killed, then the last of the money was gone forever.

So he walked, determined to get home quickly and put as much space between himself and the Parliament Building rendezvous.

In truth, he was sick and tired of peddling intelligence to the great and good of Vienna's covert marketplace, sick of his menial job working at the university as a repairman, and tired of Vienna. What had once seemed like a vast stage for him to work on was now in his eyes, a crowded Babel that he had long since become weary of. He dreamed of an apartment in Paris, warm nights, a simple life with no looking over your shoulder or wondering where the next double cross was coming from. He had gone the length of the rope with this phase of his life and he knew that he needed to reinvent himself or risk becoming an outdated player. So Paris sounded just the right spot to while away his days.

The kernel of an idea for his retirement had come when he had been approached by the American, Mr. Knight. He knew the moment that the CIA man had offered him a well-funded stipend that whatever it was he was planning; it was going to be big. This was more than double his usual fee and experience told him that with a well-funded purse came an operation of great importance – and risk, of course, as risk was an elemental part of the trade.

Information is power, he knew, and the only questions to be asked were what the meeting was about and who was this intelligence useful to? But without solid evidence, the head spies would throw him out. A little fishing trip was needed, nothing too technical, simple electronics really, a little eavesdropping perhaps. After all, he had responsibility for the security at the meeting in Luxembourg, so it wouldn't be too difficult to rig up some self-made surveillance equipment. Not for Max Dobos, oh dear me no.

The device he had decided on was a Stuzzi Portable Reel to Reel Tape Recorder which was made in Vienna. It was commercially available, relatively cheap to buy, and being the size of a small toaster, fitted snugly in his overnight case. He had bought it directly from a contact who provided discreet surveillance equipment to private investigators. The Stuzzi also came with an adapted eight-foot-long string-like microphone wire, which Dobos hoped would be adequate to fit into the safe-house.

He had travelled to Luxembourg several days before to make all the arrangements, such as the approach to the Catalan killer, securing the 'safe-house' in Clervaux and to rig up his elementary recording device.

When the Catalan and the American had gone into their meeting, he had quickly rushed down to the basement, uncovered the recorder from behind the mattress and pressed the PLAY/RECORD button. The tape whirred slowly and Dobos listened intently through the head-phones. What he heard only confirmed his suspicions about the American operation. This was no mere information gathering exercise. This was a list of agents being targeted for 'termination' and outside of the Catalan and his American case officer, only he knew about it. And that made it very valuable information, very valuable indeed to the right recipient.

With the American having flown out the next morning, Max Dobos made preparations to retrieve the tape from the hidden recorder. He was in no hurry; the house in Clervaux had its rent paid up until the end of the week and, sooner rather than later, he would have to remove all traces of the meeting which had taken place a few nights earlier. He spent the next day cleaning and removing any material that had been left. His final job was to uninstall the Stuzzi recorder and place it back in its little carry case.

Once back in his rented apartment, he had listened intently again to the recording. The quality of the tape was reasonable with the excep-tion of one or two sentences being muffled due to the two men moving around the room and out of the microphone range.

What he heard was a gold mine of intelligence. Agents, operational planning and state sponsored executions. He knew that on the open market, this information would be highly valuable. But who to trade this information to, that was the crux of the matter. Reason would say that his first approach should be to the Russians. After all it was a Soviet network that was being targeted for termination. The KGB would welcome the intelligence with open arms.

But Dobos didn't think so. He knew the Russians to be poor payers, except for their star agents, and besides, Dobos hated the Russians for what they had done to his home country following the war and the Hungarian revolution in '56. No, he needed a different buyer.

He mused about it for the rest of the night, weighing up the pros and cons of each of the contacts that he had in the numerous secret services, before finally settling on the British service. He had done numerous jobs for the British spies over the years and they had always been fair and paid him well. He trusted them, as much as anyone could trust a spy, and he was sure that with the right approach, they would be able to accommodate him. After a number of tense telephone conversations with the local SIS station, he had been ordered, against his better judgement, to leave the only copy of the material at one of his old dead letter drops that SIS used to pass secret information and orders to their local informants.

He had visited the dead drop site in the Karmelitermarkt, the one his SIS contact had told him was codenamed ABEL. It had been a while since he had personally had to use it and he just hoped that it was still active. That very morning, he had lodged the small packet containing the tape recording between the brick wall and the base of the billboard. His next task, the one he was least looking forward to, was the brush past meeting with the Catalan killer from Luxembourg.

All of this he was reflecting on when he noticed the clack of footsteps somewhere in the distance behind him. Don't look around, was the age-old tenet of the counter-surveillance game. He was now passing the edge of the municipal buildings, which he knew would stretch out onto the side streets. The following footsteps kept a steady pace with his. He turned down a side walkway, with no one about. *Keep moving, Max*, he told himself. Had his plan been discovered? Had he been followed to the dead letter drop? And who was it – the Russians, the Americans – not the British, surely.

He started to move faster. If he could make it past the open ground, he would be back onto the main streets and from there it was only a matter of a few minutes until he could reach the safety of his own address. He moved faster; strong leg, weak leg, strong leg, weak leg, the same as he had learned in the camps to keep away from the beatings of the guards and...

Something occurred to him. He could no longer hear footsteps behind him. His pace slowed and after a few more tentative steps he risked turning around. He expected to see men in trench coats, ready to pounce on him, but instead he was treated to the cold darkness of the pathway he had just walked. His breathing had grown shallow; he calmed himself before moving on. He only needed to reach the end of the walkway past the wall, and he would be back onto a well-lit main road with good lighting, people and cars.

Nearly there, he thought. *Don't lose your head now.*

He calmed himself again. It was just his imagination, the deal with the British and his aborted meeting with the killer Marquez had spooked him, that was all. Strong leg, weak leg, strong leg, weak leg... just keep thinking of retirement in Paris or London or Madrid...

As he passed the end of the wall, he saw a flash of silver, felt a dull thump to the underside of his chin and then a searing pain, pain he had never felt before – ever – and never would again. His hands reached, instinctively upwards and he staggered forward, feeling the warm flow of arterial blood coursing between his fingers...

Dobos managed to twist his body around. Had he run into a fence, a spike, what? Instead, he saw a small, angry man in dark clothes, his hat discarded and flung on the floor, obviously dislodged during the initial strike. The man was approaching him fast. The man lashed out with his foot, Dobos felt his knees buckle and he fell forward onto all fours. With his hands now supporting him the blood from his throat gushed freely out onto the cobbles.

I'm dying, he thought, his mind in turmoil. *This is how it ends, on a dark backstreet on a freezing cold night, with no one to care or to miss me or to bury me.*

Then he felt his body being wrenched up violently to a kneeling position. Putting his arms up to protect himself, he was aware of the man with the blade slashing at him, trying to cut through the barrier of his forearms. The searing pain shot up through him and then he was spun around and felt the THUMP, THUMP, THUMP and the searing pain once more as the blade was pumped forcefully into his kidneys. He knew then –had seen enough of death and violence in the camps – to know that his end was imminent.

Finally, his head was wrenched backwards, exposing his throat to the stars in the manner of a sacrifice, and then for the final time and from the corner of his eye, he saw the dull red colored glint of the steel blade as it made its way towards his throat.

He was just another casualty of the intelligence war.

* * *

Gioradze had been in place for a good twenty minutes before the limper had arrived, had seen the man arrive, wait, study his watch, and as the time drew nearer to the brush past meeting that he was supposed to be having with Marquez, seen the man's evident impatience as he was stood up.

The Georgian was at an adjacent angle to the front of the Parliament Building, across the road and concealed behind the trees that lined the boulevard. He was perfectly hidden in the night and despite the chill, was comfortable. There had only been one or two people passing by, several cars, but nothing out of the ordinary. No hostile surveillance of the proposed meeting of any counterintelligence officials or security police ready to spring a trap. Whenever a pedestrian came too near his hiding spot, he simply melted back into the shadows.

He glanced over at the limper. That was how he thought of his target. The limper. He observed as the man glanced at his watch more frequently before deciding to cut his losses and abort the meeting. Gioradze gave it sixty seconds before moving out of his position and onto the darkened streets.

He knew the ambush site that he wanted. He had earmarked it earlier; it was underneath a bridge that ran across a small stretch of open ground, further up the main road. As far as killing grounds go, it was perfect. Quiet, isolated, and with few lights, so that dealing with the body of the dead man would be that much easier, allowing him to manipulate and make any last minute corrections to the corpse. He just hoped the limper went the expected way. If not, he would have to improvise. Either way, the man wouldn't make it back to his apartment tonight.

He saw the limper cross over the main road further up and knew that he was taking the expected route. Now Gioradze's priority was to get ahead of him and hide at the ambush site. He estimated he had a little less than two minutes to sprint, to reach the ambush point before the limper arrived there. For a man of Gioradze's stamina and energy it was no problem.

He ran quickly, sticking to the grassy verge lest his shoes make a noise in the still of night and alert the limper. The grass expanded out to make a small hill, rising up at a gradient, and from his elevated position Gioradze was in the perfect position to look down at his target scampering along below him. Within seconds the hill began to decline and Gioradze could see the wall that was to be his hiding place. He squared his back against it, took a deep breath and unbuttoned his heavy jacket to give his arms more freedom of movement for when the attack began. *No one ever expects an attack from the front,* he thought. The limper would be so busy worrying if someone was still behind him that he wouldn't even consider someone is in front of him.

His weapon of choice, in fact the minimal amount of protection he carried when he was not on a job, was always a knife. On this occasion it was his favorite German Paratrooper gravity knife which he had won in a poker game on a drunken night during his time in the Legion.

He had felt the weight of the weapon in his hand; it felt good, solid, and dependable. He gave a brief peek around the corner to confirm his target was near. He was no more than twenty feet away, shuffling along, dragging his lame leg. The Georgian sharply flicked the handle of the knife downwards and heard a satisfying 'click' as the inertia of the blade sprang forward, his thumb moved the lock into place and at last the full ten inches of knife was steady, resting in his hand. He cocked his body, his knife arm primed, ready to swing. He could hear the shambling movements of the man, edging closer and closer until... He could not have timed it better. He swung his arm around 180 degrees, saw the silver trail as it gleamed in the streetlight's glare, sensed rather than felt the knife's impact so sharp was the blade, and watched as the man went down in a gurgling agony. Then he pounced on his victim.

Of the violence, later he would admit, that he could remember very little of it. But then that was always the way for him. He was only aware of fast movement – kicks, grabs, stabbing and slashing the man – before sitting the man up, cutting out his throat and then pushing him away as the arterial spurt let loose.

With the limper gurgling out his last breath, Gioradze did a cursory search of the body, more out of habit than of expecting to find anything: some identity cards, some money, and a set of keys to the man's apartment, nothing of any use. He dragged the body off the main path a few feet away and folded it over until it was completely concealed. With any luck, it wouldn't be found until at least daylight the next day, by which time, of course, he expected to be out of Vienna and on his way home.

He checked his watch. 9.25pm. He had a little under two hours to report back to Marquez at his hotel. No problem. He would walk the rest of the way with a spring in his step, glad to be back working at the only job he had ever excelled at.

* * *

The next day, the early morning flight from Vienna's International Airport took off as usual. Among its many passengers was a tall, somber man of Mediterranean appearance and a smaller, bulkier man who huddled himself deeper into his hat and coat to keep the unappetizing cold at bay.

They were perhaps businessmen who had been visiting Vienna on a commercial trip and were now returning to their respective countries.

They did not sit together; each had a separate seat at either end of the aircraft. They never made eye contact and they were never seen to speak. If any of the other passengers had been asked, they could honestly say that the two men seemed completely unaware of the other's existence.

The flight's destination was Brussels International Airport. Once the plane landed, both men would go their separate ways. One would travel back to his home in Luxembourg and the other would later take the connecting flight that would edge him nearer to his adopted home of the Iberian Peninsula.

Meanwhile, back in Vienna, it would be another three hours before the butchered body of what was initially assumed to be a vagrant was found hidden in some bushes on the parkland.

Chapter Eight

Ten hours later, two men stood in the cold, grey mortuary staring down at the recently deceased body of Max Dobos. One was a criminal investigation officer with the Austrian police; the other was a senior British diplomat from Her Majesty's Embassy.

"Whoever did it to him knew exactly what they were doing," said the Austrian police officer.

Cecil Rowlands nodded his aging, shaggy head in agreement. Even to someone as untutored in forensics as he was, he could see the range of defensive wounds on the forearms of the corpse. Not to mention the butchering of the poor wretched devil's throat. Nasty.

Vienna was a village, a big village certainly, but a village nonetheless, and everybody knew someone who knew someone. As the SIS Head of Station in Vienna, it was good old Cecil's business to know the people in the know. People like Inspector Krupp, who took a monthly stipend from him.

Rowlands had been on a long weekend break, his first in many months; Thursday through to Sunday. The call to his private line when it came on the Saturday evening had ripped him away from what he hoped was going to be a quiet weekend of fishing, drinks and one of Joyce's pre-Christmas dinner parties. Joyce, his wife, did so love putting a party together. The evening phone call had put paid to that little luxury and he knew the moment he had heard Inspector Johan

Krupp's voice that his weekend was going to be ruined. Joyce would be furious with him for days over this.

He had arrived at the hospital and been whisked down to the mortuary by a police sergeant, only to find Johan Krupp, doyen of the Viennese police waiting for him. Krupp was tall and grey with a bad suit and a habit of flicking ash from his cigarillos onto the floor whenever he had things on his mind. A thing he did now, despite being in the confines of the mortuary.

"So Inspector, what made you think that this man is connected to us?" asked Rowlands.

Krupp stared down at the floor. Catching his meal ticket out was something that didn't sit well with him. "I found one of your Embassy telephone numbers hidden in his sock. Didn't know what it was at first, it was only when I ran it through the reverse telephone directory files that it was flagged as the British Embassy. I thought I'd better let you know before the security police got wind of it."

Rowlands smiled. "It's much appreciated Johan, and don't worry, there'll be something extra in the pot this month for you and your good lady. You did the right thing."

"Thank you Herr Rowlands."

Rowlands frowned. "In his sock, I wonder why he had it hidden there."

"Well, there were signs that his body had been searched before the killer fled. Obviously he either didn't think to search the feet, or else he was disturbed."

The body of Maximilian Dobos lay naked underneath a thin cotton shroud and over sheet that reached up to his tortured neck. Rowlands could see the beginnings of the 'Y' shaped pathology scar that ran from his left ear, down the torso to the abdomen.

The body had been found by a cleaner on her way to work in one of the municipal buildings. The elderly woman had noticed a shoe lying along the path that led to the adjacent alley. A quick glance around and she discovered track marks in the muddy verge, where the victim had been dragged before being concealed under an old carpet. Thirty minutes later the police were on the scene in the form of Inspector Krupp and his team of detectives. It was now a murder scene and Krupp and his men had control from here on in.

The deceased had been taken in a sealed body bag to the Vienna General Hospital and the unknown man's details had been recorded and then he had been placed in a locked fridge until the resident pathologist was ready to conduct his investigation. An hour later the post-mortem began with Krupp attending. It wasn't the first that he had been forced to sit through, wouldn't be his last either, but nevertheless it wasn't an experience that he looked forward to at any time.

The corpse had been weighed, measured and photographed. Next came the washing process, before what Krupp called, the 'butchery' started. He made himself scarce and decided to take a look at the man's clothes and possessions. It was starkly uninteresting. Normal clothes, virtually empty wallet, identity card, cheap watch. The items of a single man and nothing more. A dead end. He started again, this time more thoroughly moving through each item of personal belongings until on his second pass which turned the gloves inside out and then the socks, he found something. There it was. It was nothing more than a small piece of paper with a series of smudged numbers written on it. Krupp stared down at it for what seemed an age. It could be everything or nothing, he decided. But there was something familiar about the number, something that connected with him.

He excused himself, said he would return, then made his way back to Police Headquarters to check something. Just a hunch, but hunches in his experience had a way of turning into definitive clues. A quick flick through several contact files and confidential reverse telephone directories confirmed his suspicion.

He sat back in his office chair, lit one of his cigarillos and made the phone call to the home address of the Right Honorable Cecil Rowlands of the British Embassy in Vienna, the British resident spy and Krupp's confidant, friend, and paymaster.

* * *

"So, how long had he been dead before he was found?"

Inspector Krupp flicked through the pathology report that he had attached to his clipboard. "The pathologist suggests between six to twelve hours. So he died sometime around eleven o clock last night. It could be a few hours either way, but last night definitely."

"And the weapon?"

"A very sharp straight edged knife. No sign of that, most probably dumped in the river. Whoever did it certainly wanted to finish him. The wounds on the arms were put there to make it look like a robbery gone wrong. It buys the killer time to escape. He obviously thinks that we're all idiots on this force and will waste our time pulling in all the known robbers."

"Is there *any* suggestion that this was a black market thing? Chaps falling out about sugar or tobacco or what have you?" asked Rowlands, determined to rule out as many possibilities as he could before his thoughts turned to espionage.

Krupp shook his head. "Max Dobos wasn't known to us, but it's certainly possible. Maybe he crossed someone he shouldn't, but it must have been big for them to send this kind of message. Our underworld usually just resorts to beatings. Did you know him?"

The question caught old Rowlands off guard, but being a professional he did what he always did on such occasions; he dug deep into his trouser pocket, rummaged around, fished out an old handkerchief and began to clean his spectacles. Yes, for old, dependable Cecil Rowlands it was a tactic that had bought him time on many occasions.

He peered in close to examine the chasm that had once been the dead man's throat; he squinted, and then stood back up to his full height. "No. I didn't know him," he murmured, and then quickly moved the analysis onwards. "So; we know the cuts to the arm were committed post-mortem. What's the order of play regarding the rest of the wounds?"

Krupp shrugged and glanced at the report. "The first wound, we believe, was a stab to the throat, which caught him on the left side. That's probably the one that would have killed him; it's certainly the most lethal. Then multiple stab wounds to the kidneys and surrounding internal organs from the rear. The butchering of the throat, that was done as a supplementary strike, and in my professional opinion, was totally unnecessary. It was just the killer showing off."

"And making sure the job was done in case he didn't get a second chance," said Rowlands.

Krupp nodded, silently admitting to himself that could have been the case.

"Anything at his home? The poor fellow must have had something to his name."

"Nothing of any use to us, he seemed to live a frugal life. A shabby apartment, a cooker, a radio, a bed, a phone. No money, no frivolity it seems. We'll keep digging, but..." Krupp's words tapered off, and he shrugged his shoulders, resigned to the fact that this would probably be a dead-end case.

Rowlands was sure the Inspector would keep digging. He was a good man, a good detective, but sometimes, certain cases have a habit of coming up against a brick wall when leads fizzle out. That was something that the police and the spies had in common. "What will happen to him now Johan?"

Krupp winced, as if these matters were of no concern to him. "There will be a simple burial courtesy of the state probably by the end of the week. If anything else comes up, I'll let you know."

Rowlands thanked him and made his way out of the mortuary. From behind him, he heard the hushed tones of Inspector Krupp. "And you can, of course, rely on my discretion Herr Rowlands. We guardians of decency must stick together through thick and thin in these perilous times."

* * *

Cecil Rowlands called home. He didn't like to think of Joyce hanging around, waiting for him to turn up, especially after all the effort she had made with the dinner party he had to miss out on. "No darling,

I'm still at the hospital and will probably have to go to the office from here. You go on to bed, get some rest and poor you, having to deal with the Radleys' and Herr Marks all on your own. You're a trooper, I'll make it up to you I promise," he cooed down the phone.

With his domestic problem – if not totally resolved – at least contained, he made his way down to his car and drove the ten-minute journey at that time of night to the Embassy.

The British Embassy was an ornate fifty room villa located on Reisnerstrasse and had once been the summer residence of Prince Metternich. Rowlands waved his way past the guard on the gate, said hello to the night duty officer manning the front desk and climbed the stairs to his private sanctum at the rear of the building on the second floor. These offices were only accessible, via a multi-deadlocked steel door, to the officers of SIS.

His first port of call was the file registry room. He worked quickly and expertly, removing several buff folders before taking them to his office. He sat at his desk, placed the folders and files in front of him and opened up the confidential agents list for the Vienna station. He flicked through a few pages until he came to the 'D's'.

His finger moved down the page until he came to the entry for 'Dobos, Maximillian' and read through the brief biographical details of the agent and his contact tradecraft.

Name: Dobos, Maximillian
Agent: CH41/V
Details: Born 1914. Hungarian, confidence trickster and low-level source. Used mainly in Soviet deception operations and for routine surveillance/security operations with Vienna Station. Outsourced to other friendly intelligence agencies when required.

What followed was the man's last known address and what method was used for him to communicate directly with the station. Then Rowlands noticed a small tick in the 'communiqué' chart. It was dated the previous day. So Dobos had in some way attempted to communicate with the station over the past day or so. Rowlands closed the ledger and made his way to the station's communications section in the next room. He unlocked the secure door with his personal key, went straight to the main desk and looked through the pending file of communiqués.

It took him five minutes to find what he was looking for. Three separate transcripts. All phone calls to the station on the direct agent phone number were automatically recorded and then transcribed. It seemed that agent CH41/V had called the direct agent line three times in a twenty-four-hour period. *Interesting*, thought Rowlands. The man obviously had something important to offer, judging by the frequency of the communications.

He pulled the three separate transcripts out of the ledger and worked his way through them methodically. Each began with the usual administrative jargon – agent identity code, officer identity code, time and date – which was all part of the minutiae of running an overseas SIS station. Rowlands ignored them; he knew them by heart anyway. It was the text that he craved in the hope that it would yield a clue to the man's intentions and perhaps reveal why he had been murdered so violently.

The first communication had been received less than 48 hours ago and to Rowlands' experienced eye Dobos had been bullish and overconfident in his first contact. *It was as if he had a good hand in poker and couldn't wait to tell the rest of the table about it,* thought Rowlands.

AGENT: *This is [deleted]. I have valuable information, valuable material which may interest your service. I would prefer to speak to Colonel Ellerington. Only Ellerington will I deal with.*

STATION: *No names, please on an open line.*
AGENT: *I understand, but this information is relevant and timely. It will have great benefit for the British.*
STATION: *That may be the case, but if what you say is true, we would need to assess it to verify its worth and authenticity. We would suggest that you leave it at one of our collection points as usual.*
AGENT: *No, you do not understand. This information is very sensitive. I would be foolish to let it out of my control. I demand a face to face meeting.*
STATION: *I'm sorry, but as I'm sure you know that is not how this works. Leave the information with us so that we can look it over. If it is useful we can negotiate a price.*
AGENT: *I have a specific price for the material. It is non-negotiable and I will only deal with Colonel—*
STATION: *I said no names. You know the protocol. No names. No face to face meeting unless the material is useful to us and to do that you have to pass it to us first. Also, WE set the price.*
AGENT: *Damn you! I will offer this to the French or Germans if I have . . .*
STATION: *That is your choice. Those are our terms. This call is terminated.*
ENDEX.

Rowlands smiled at the conversation. Colonel Ellerington was his working name, the name he used when contacting local agents for off the cuff meetings. The station officer, actually his deputy John Green, had done a good job of unsettling Max Dobos and keeping him dangling. They all came in cocksure of themselves, ready to believe that they have the latest top secret, no, *above* top-secret, information ready to trade. He'd seen it a million times before and in most cases, it was worthless scraps that the informants had gleaned from drunken conversations in a bar somewhere.

Rowlands preached to his officers that the role of the professional intelligence officer was to downplay what the agent thought was priceless information, not only to bring the price down, after all no one wants to pay top prices no matter how good the intelligence is, but also to give the officer time to accurately assess and analyze the material. Is it real or is it a fake? *There you bugger, that will take the sting out of your tale,* thought Rowlands.

He flicked through to the following communication transcript. It was the same day, but two hours later. Dobos was going for his second bite of the cherry. Either the Germans or the French had told him that they weren't interested or he was determined to get a deal exclusively from SIS. Either way, he had put himself at a serious negotiating disadvantage which Rowlands knew his deputy would have taken ruthless advantage of.

STATION: *Yes. Number please.*
AGENT: *CH41. I would like to talk to someone else.*
STATION: *You can talk to me. What do you want CH41?*
AGENT: *I. . . I called earlier. We spoke. I understand the need for protocol. Of course I do. But you must look at it from my position. I have something of great value. I would be foolish to just hand it over.*
STATION: *How were the French and the Germans? Did they welcome you with open arms?*

AGENT: *I. . . I. . . I have not yet approached them. I have worked well with the British before and wanted to offer you the chance first. If you hadn't been so obtuse then. . .*

STATION: *Goodbye CH41, I'm terminating the—*

AGENT: *No, no, please wait. Can we not reach an understanding?*

STATION: *CH41, a face to face meeting is impossible. We are all very busy. Imagine if we had to have a meeting every time someone had some chicken feed to sell.*

AGENT: *It is NOT chicken feed. You will see this when you examine it!*

STATION: *As I was saying. . . we would never get any work done. The deal is this. Leave the material at my Cousin ABEL's house. You remember ABEL?*

AGENT: *Of course. . .*

STATION: *Good. We will collect it, look it over and see what we think of it. If it's good, or as good as you say it is, we can negotiate a price. If it's not for us, then we hand it back to you.*

AGENT: *But it will be too late, then you will have already seen it.*

STATION: *You know the way the game works CH41. That's the risk you take. Besides, we have worked with you in the past. Have we ever let you down? You simply have to trust us.*

AGENT: *(pause) I will think it over.*

STATION: *Good idea CH41. Good day to you, sir.*
ENDEX

Green had handled it well, thought Rowlands. He had given the agent a tentative option whilst also being fair and professional. Anything less and it turns into the tail wagging the dog with the agents trying to run rings around their case officers.

Rowlands rubbed his eyes, God, he was tired. Only one more to go he thought as he flicked through to the final transcript. The final message was short, terse, as if Dobos was at the end of his tether. The message read:

STATION: *Hello. Number please.*
AGENT: CH41. *Today the postman delivered to ABEL. Repeat ABEL. I will await confirmation of value and payment. I am placing my trust in your service's good character. I hope the agreed terms and conditions are met. Goodbye.*
STATION: *Thank you CH41 we will be in touch.*
ENDEX.

He rubbed the tiredness from his eyes and ruminated about the previous few days' events. Dobos had approached the Vienna station with possible high end intelligence. He had agreed to terms and conditions for a trade of the material and had lodged it in the dead letter box codenamed ABEL.

Rowlands checked the duty reports for the station operations over the past week. He found the correct file entitled 'Agent Management' and flipped through the section dealing with deliveries to and from the three main dead letter box sites for low level informants like the CH4's which were KANE, ABEL and ENOCH.

According to the file the only one to have been serviced by the station officers over the last few days had been ENOCH, which meant that the team hadn't gotten around to emptying ABEL. *I'll have their balls for that,* he thought. He scribbled his initials next to the ABEL heading, meaning that he would take sole responsibility for collecting whatever Dobos had left for the SIS station there. *But not tonight,* he thought. *I need to get home and get some bloody sleep.* He checked his watch. It was 2.30am. Just in time to make his way home, trying not to disturb Joyce, grab a few hours of shut eye before he had to go and empty an agents' dead letter box on what was effectively enemy territory.

He sighed and rose from his chair, felt the muscles in his aching back click, picked up his set of keys to lock the station office and headed for his car. His weekend break was ruined, and in those tired few minutes in the middle of the night he was sick to the back teeth, in fact had had a bellyful, of Vienna, being a spy and getting himself involved in murder mysteries where the victim had had his throat ripped out like a stag that had been gralloched.

* * *

The very next morning, looking refreshed and wearing his best suit and overcoat, Her Majesty's diplomatic servant the Right Honorable Cecil Rowlands strolled casually along Krummbaumgasse, his destination was the old Karmelitermarkt.

He did his best to fight his way through the busy Christmastime shoppers and keep the rain from his spectacles, which was not an easy task for someone of Rowlands' size and grace. He was more your strongman than your athlete, his wife would say.

If anyone had taken the time to ask this distinguished member of the diplomatic community where he was off to on that fine morning, he would simply have said that he was on a small errand of a personal nature before he began his day's toils in the British Embassy. If pressed further, he would have confided to his acquaintance that he was on a mission to get back in his wife's good books. A small, but modestly expensive pre-Christmas gift, to apologize for ruining their weekend together when he had been called back to the 'office' to deal with a temporary problem. Some truffles from the specialist truffle seller in the market, he would say. Joyce did so love to cook and it was a rare treat that he was able to afford luxury items.

Of course it was a good story – not true – but a good tale nonetheless.

"Cover, ladies and gentlemen, is important," he would drum into his field agents. "Always have a good reason for doing anything nefarious. You want to meet an agent at the opera; then I recommend that you at least know your Wagner's from your Verdi's, because you can bet your yearly wage that you'll bump into someone who will chatter about it for days and be a fully accredited aficionado. I'm not saying you have to be an expert, but you at least need to be able to hold a conversation without making anyone suspicious… at least until you get the opportunity to bugger off double quick!"

Why the Karmelitermarkt? Well the most obvious reason was that there was an excellent truffle stall on the far side of the market. The ruse also gave him the opportunity to visit the ABEL dead letter box which was located nearby on the fringes of the market. Its exact location was behind a billboard at ground level. He just hoped that Max Dobos had secured it properly behind the loose wooden panel that held the timber frame together.

He strolled casually, moving through the throng, nodding to his fellow shoppers in greeting or in thanks. He perused the various meat, cheese and coffee stalls. There was nothing hurried about his manner and aside from his duties at the Embassy he looked like a man content to while away the rest of the day exploring the commerce of Vienna.

Rowlands did two rotations of the ABEL site, passing by it to confirm that there was no overt surveillance, then around the block and back for one more pass. A third pass would have been suspicious, shopkeepers and market traders do have a tendency to remember a face that they have seen before. The third and final time would be the emptying of ABEL.

Was the vegetable seller looking at him a bit too closely? That road sweeper – he'd been there an awfully long time, since his second pass in fact? Or what about that couple at the cafe who were drinking their coffee, had they been observing him all along as he passed by the ABEL drop? Were they Russian informants or were they KGB agents running a hostile surveillance operation on a suspected SIS drop site?

In truth, there was no way of knowing and Rowlands knew that when it came down to the wire all the field agent on the ground could do was pray, hope for the best, and take a massive leap of faith that he wasn't about to be caught or compromised.

The dead drop was within a few feet. He did an awkward duck-shuffle and looked down in mock annoyance at his shoes. He had purposefully loosened his shoe laces this morning when he had set off knowing that they would work themselves free in time. A few more steps and he was finally at the billboard. Not stopping he began to bend in one fluid motion and then the seasoned intelligence officer reached down casually to tie his lace, and when he was sure that there were no observers his fingers explored around the gap between the brick wall and the billboard. It was only a space of roughly four inches, but it was big enough to conceal a decent-sized package.

Nothing! Damn!

He pressed his fingers in further, groping into the crevasse, a bit more, and then... there it was. Roughly the size of a pack of playing cards wrapped in sturdy brown paper and sealed with heavy duty tape and glue. A quick glance around the street revealed no one, and then the package was swiftly placed in his inside coat pocket. A quick tying of the laces and he was up, off and on his way. He spent the next thirty minutes running counter-surveillance maneuvers, just to be sure. Rowlands was an old pro who had done his fair share of shaking off a tail in his long and murky past.

* * *

An hour later Rowlands arrived back at the SIS station. He threw his overcoat into his office and gave strict instructions to his secretary, a Welsh harridan by the name of Eleanor, that he wasn't to be disturbed for the rest of the day.

He sat in the security room and unpacked the package from the dead drop. "Now then Herr Dobos, let's see what all this fuss is about." Rowlands carefully opened the package, removing the tape with small neat cuts with his penknife. Inside was a single sheet of paper, handwritten in English, and a small pool of audio tape.

The note read:

> "Recording taken November 1964. Luxembourg. Freelance job. Can give more details once you have listened to the tape. Tape assures my bona fides."

He placed it to one side and went to fetch the audio tape player, a big brute of a machine that came complete with headset, from the station equipment cupboard. He locked his office door and set about rigging up the tape in the machine. When it was all connected and tested he took a single piece of paper and a pencil, pressed the PLAY button, closed his eyes and began to listen. His pencil would make a short scribble every now and then, picking out a word or a phrase that interested him.

Thirty minutes later the tape had finished. Rowlands removed the headphones and stared down at the notes on the paper. Dobos had either edited the tape not to include too much detail, perhaps hedging his bets for a better deal later, or the people speaking on the tape were security conscious, thus suggesting that they were indeed professionals. He scribbled out things that he judged unimportant, donned the headset once again and listened to it for a second time.

"Bloody hell," he said to himself when he'd finished. If the information was accurate and judging by Dobos previous work for them it always had been, then he had inadvertently stepped into the fringes of an American-backed operation. Not just any old operation either, from the sounds of it –a bloody assassination plot.

He now doubted that the Max Dobos murder had been a robbery gone wrong or a gangland affair, as there was just too much coincidence in the timing. Day One: Dobos offers information relating to a series of contract killings. Day Two: Dobos is murdered, violently, and his body searched. There was more to this than he'd expected, and false modesty aside, it was becoming unwieldy and needed to be looked at by people higher up the chain of command.

So, with the winter sun glaring through his office window, he pulled out the station codebook and started very carefully to compose what was to be in the fullness of time, an explosive communiqué to Broadway.

Book Three:
Counter-Attack

Chapter One

London, January 1965

"*You would work directly to me. No contact, either overt or covert, with the Embassy or the local CIA stations where you are operating. You work at arm's length, independently, with no chaperoning.*

You try knocking on their doors, they'll tell you to take a hike and that they don't know what you're talking about. I will give you a series of telephone numbers; you check in regularly to give and receive up to date intelligence. After each successful 'hit', I will release a designated amount to a personal bank account of your choice. You don't complete the contracts; you don't get paid. Questions?"

The tape player clicked off with a deep thunk. It had come, mid conversation, toward the end of the spool.

"So is it fortune or fraud?" asked C.

The faces – all men he knew and trusted, stared back – all non-committal. They saw the deceptively youthful looking face of C, reclining in his chair, debonair with spectacles perched precariously on the end of his nose as he read through his files. He looked like a gentleman official from one of the better banking institutions: amiable, kindly, forgiving – all of which he could be if the occasion warranted.

But the four men knew this to be a facade. C was as tough as an old iron-spike when he had to be. The Chief of the Secret Intelligence Service, or C as he was known to his officers, knew what they were

thinking; they needed more concrete information before they were
willing to give their opinions. He didn't blame them. But that did nothing to confront the problem they were facing, and he needed answers
pretty damn soon.

The five men, the hierarchy of the Secret Service, were sitting
around the old mahogany conference table in the 'War Room', which
was situated on the top floor of 54 Broadway Buildings. The room
was dark and brooding and was in sync with their collective mood.
Stacked all around the rooms and corridors were boxes and security-
sealed filing cabinets, all in place ready for the organizations big move
over the coming weeks.

Broadway was a huge monolith of a building; slab grey, austere and
parked away in a quiet backstreet in Westminster. It had, for over
thirty years, been the headquarters of the British Secret Service. Its
maze-like corridors and annexes had, over the years, baffled even the
most intrepid of spies and visitors alike. It had survived wars, conflicts,
skirmishes and political intrigue, but with the onset of the Cold War,
even its most ferocious protectors had recognized that Broadway's day
had come to an end. Plans were afoot to make a move across the river
to a more modern building in Lambeth, with internal rumblings that
the powers that be were intent on keeping the spies away from the
corridors of power and moving them further away into the shadows.

The five men had been here for the best part of the morning, thrash-
ing out the contents of the scratchy audio recording that the technicians had done their best to clean up. It was audible, but muffled, and
the boffins had decided that it was prudent to supply a transcript of
the recording lest anything be misunderstood or misinterpreted. The
empty teapot, cups, saucers and overflowing ashtrays had been pushed
to one side, ignored, and the men had their noses firmly pushed into
the transcripts hoping to find a clue that could give them a definitive
answer.

C sat at the head of the table, as his seniority allowed. To his immediate left sat his Vice-Chief, Barton, a bullish man who had cut his
espionage teeth working for the sabotage service during the war. To

his immediate right sat the Director of Soviet Operations, Harper, a career intelligence officer who had been at the helm of Soviet Operations for as long as anybody could remember. Both men had different styles of operating within SIS, something that caused much internal friction.

Bringing up the lower echelons of the table was the 'Constellation' network controller and its senior case officer, Bernard Porter, a former Oxford Don who had been recruited from academia. The final officer present was the Head of the Redaction Unit, Colonel Stephen Masterman.

It had been several weeks since the audio tape had been recovered from the dead letter drop by the Head of Station/Vienna. The tape had been listened to, and then listened to again, phone calls had been made and then it had hastily been posted into the diplomatic bag marked "URGENT – C – EYES ONLY" and then headed for London.

When it had arrived at Broadway it had dropped on them not with a bang, as would be associated with red hot intelligence, but instead with a whimper. No one seemed to know what to make of it. Was it genuine and if so, said the old intelligence hands, what does it have to do with us?

There was the argument that the information should be shared with Broadway's sister service, MI5, the Security Service. After all, the mention of Soviet agents who had been recruited for Western organizations could provide vital clues to the spy hunters. This was quickly pooh-poohed by the older hands at Broadway, who preferred to keep it to themselves until they knew exactly *what* they were dealing with.

Finally, at the weekly department heads meeting, someone had mentioned to the Director of Soviet Operations about a report that had come in from Vienna. It was nothing out of the ordinary, just another possible piece of the intelligence jigsaw. That was until someone mentioned the phrase 'a military liaison officer in NATO is alleged to be working for the Russians'.

Then the explosion of activity had happened. The Soviet Operations desk had quickly swung into action demanding an in-depth report and investigation into the recording and its background. It had caused panic, concern and not a little consternation. The follow-up reports of the murder of the informant Max Dobos had sent the top floor of Broadway into a flurry of action. Hence the high level meeting that was now taking place.

"So… thoughts?" prompted the Chief, determined to kick-start the analysis. The group had been batting forth ideas about the overall meaning of the information contained in the recording, now he needed them to look at the fine detail.

"Well, from the unconventional way we received it, it's bound to be a fake," said Barton, bullish as ever.

"And yet, Head of Station Vienna mentions in his report that he had used this man, Max Dobos, on and off for years," countered Harper. "Low level stuff certainly, but always reliable."

"He's an intelligence hawker; he sells bits and bobs of information all over. To us, the Americans, the Germans, even the French, God help him," said Barton.

"Just because he sells intelligence to a variety of services, doesn't equate that he's a liar. He evidently thought it was important enough to pass it on to us," countered Harper.

"Bit thin isn't it… hardly cast iron evidence," replied Barton gruffly.

"Well, that and the fact that he was found recently with his throat slit suggests that he was involved with something that was nefarious, even in our trade. Was he out of his depth? Is someone tying up loose ends?" said Harper in his most courteous tone.

The two men – Harper and Barton – came to the end of their sparring match. They both sat there, each weighing up the other, planning their next move in an ever continuing turf war that had become legendary within headquarters.

"The tape is obviously incomplete. Almost as if we've come in half way through a conversation. Therefore, we have to assume that this Dobos character either didn't start recording the conversation soon enough and he ran out of tape before the meeting finished," said C.

"Or he was disturbed and had to stop the recording," said Barton.

"Possibly. The fact that he was killed in Vienna rather than in Luxembourg where we are led to believe that this meeting took place, seems to suggest that he simply ran out of tape rather than being caught in flagrante. If he had been caught red handed, it is assumed that he would have been murdered on the spot," replied C.

The committee all nodded their agreement at the Chief's assessment. In their shoes, they would have done the same thing. Why leave a witness to your crimes?

"So are we to assume that the people in this recording are completely unaware that they have been the victims of surveillance? To them, they are in the clear, haven't been compromised and the killing of this informant in Vienna has been standard procedure for them?" mused the Chief.

"Agreed. They think the integrity of their operation is intact. That gives us the tactical advantage… for the moment at least," said Harper.

"And we're definitely sure it's the Americans, are we?" asked Barton.

"On the face of it that certainly seems to be the case. An American player, numerous mentioning of the Agency, a former CIA asset by all accounts being re-recruited, the targeting of Russian agents. Has the Americans Cold War policy perhaps gotten a bit out of hand?" replied Harper.

A smile spread across C's face. He didn't think the Americans knew the meaning of 'out of hand'. They always seemed able to raise the bar to the next level of recklessness. "And have the technicians been able to identify anything useful from the voices on the tape?"

Harper shrugged. "Not much, Sir. The American voice is West Coast, late 50's, educated. 'Mr. Knight' is almost certainly a working name and aside from that, we haven't been able to positively identify him from the conversation."

"And the other voice, what of him?" asked C.

"Again, not much. European certainly, possibly from Spain or France, but the accent has been eroded over the years. Hint of German in there somewhere, so possibly travelled around a lot. Younger, somewhere in his 40's. I've checked through our agents files in the registry and it's no one that we've used before. Apart from that, it's a dead end."

There was a nod from C as he considered his options. "Mmm… So what to do," he said.

"Well, excuse me for stating what is glaringly obvious, but can't we just pull these agents out and temporarily isolate them until the threat has passed?" said Barton.

"Or at least put a security team with them?" suggested Harper.

"I'm afraid that won't be possible or indeed feasible." This time the voice was the jowly rumble of Porter.

"Please tell us why, Bernie? Give us reasons why we can't, perhaps some background to your operation might make it clearer to us mere mortals outside your games," said C.

And it was then that Bernard Russell Porter, a tubby little man of indeterminate age, gave the collective minds of British Intelligence the harsh truth about running a covert network of double agents at the sharp end of the Cold War.

* * *

Porter leaned in to them, almost trying to project his argument even more by the crowding of his body. He looked the exact opposite of the debonair agent-runner who existed in the current spate of spy movies or indeed the adventure novels of fiction.

He was neither youthful nor attractive to women. He was mid-fifties, bumbling, with a mop of dark curly hair flecked with grey and settled above a frayed, three-piece pinstripe suit. His speech came in a staccato machine gun fire that people sometimes found hard to decipher.

"The Constellation Network started as a small mission to disrupt Russian operations in Europe. Nothing fancy, nothing too technical, just a simple smoke and mirrors operation. Things that we do all the time to make the Russians look one way while we do devilish things the other. This was post-Philby."

The name 'Philby' still sent chills around the corridors of SIS and Porter hurried on with his briefing, lest the name should stir up evil ghosts from the past.

"We had been decimated by his betrayals and we had to start from scratch, rebuilding networks, operations and planning. Constellation was a part of that, small at first as I say, but it quickly grew. Its overall aim was to spread disinformation into the Russians' backyard."

Porter cleared his throat and continued. "Our head agent is *CIRIUS*. British Army Major stationed in Germany after the war and later when the wall went up. He has a lot of experience in Berlin. We worked it so that he got himself involved in a sex-trap and therefore, at least in the eyes of the Russians and East Germans, had compromised himself. We also added in his frustrations with post-war British colonial policy, lack of promotion, a shortage of cash and we had a nice little 'dangle' for the Russians to bite at, which is exactly what they did. The Major himself is a very brave man, a true patriot and is the longest serving agent in Constellation."

All eyes looked over the transcript once again as if to confirm that the man that Porter spoke of was the same person mentioned in the report. Porter continued with his briefing, his pace slowing, so as to ensure that each man understood the gravity of the situation they were dealing with.

"With our head agent in place, our aim then was to slowly integrate more operatives into the KGB's line of sight and set about building a network. Want the run down on who the rest of them are, within reason of course?"

Murmurs of agreement rose from around the table and a confirming nod came from the Chief to carry on. Porter counted each of the agents off on his fingers, holding onto each respective one like a man holding onto a rope in a sea storm.

"So," continued Porter, "we have *ORION*, a Dutch citizen who has risen to be a senior executive with the AGIG Bank in Zurich. He passes the information to Moscow about IMF funding and advises the KGB on the moving of monies for its agents and operations in the West."

"*CIRIUS* we know, and then we have *LYRA*. If *CIRIUS* is our longest serving agent, then *LYRA* is our star agent. *LYRA* is a former Italian Member of Parliament and currently Special Advisor to the UN. British mother, Italian father: she was married to an American businessman who had close ties to the current US Administration. He died several years ago. Moscow believes that she is the KGB's eyes and ears inside both the UN and the White House. Her importance to the network can't be overstated."

"Next we have *SCORPIUS*. I know, that codename sounds very dramatic doesn't it, but it belies his commitment to destroying the KGB and the Communist regime. He's a former Nazi engineer, a protégé of Van Braun no less, who currently works at the Weapons Research facility in Hampshire, where he is part of a team heading the next phase of submarine delivered nuclear missiles. He passes his KGB control 'doctored' technical information about missile guidance and propulsion systems."

"Finally, we have *PYXIS*, a junior officer at the Government Code and Communications Headquarters outstation in Cyprus. He's of the post-war intake. He had family at Bletchley during the war. The Russians seem to trust him as the KGB is more and more interested in not only new technical code developments, but also who is listening to whom in the Middle East. Plus, there is the whole stable of sub-agents, couriers, safe-houses, de-briefing teams and of course the agent handling team. Not to mention the policy making and disinformation unit that provides the intelligence that we feed to the KGB. All in all, that's a pretty big operation to risk."

Porter leaned back in his seat, spent after delivering the revue of his agents. But it was only a brief pause. He shrugged and continued with the outline of his operation.

"From the KGB's point of view, the agents of Constellation were perfect, high access, low maintenance. The only thing that concerned them was that not one of them was a thoroughbred, Russian born communist; they were all Western turncoats, and were therefore, by default, classed as completely untrustworthy and totally unreliable. But that's the Russian psyche for you; they see conspiracy and intrigue everywhere. They could have Stalin himself providing the intelligence and they'd still think he was a traitor. It's who they are."

There were several discreet rumblings of laughter from around the table. All the men recognized the truth in Porter's statement. He pulled a wry grin at his own wit before carrying on.

"But – and it took a long, long time – the Russians began to see the merits of using these agents. They proved themselves again and again and again. Oh, not in the big things, but in the small details of intelligence. A piece of gossip that turned out to be factual, a sub-agent who allowed himself to be recruited, a shred of information that confirmed a piece of intelligence. The usual things. It was an operation within an operation. First to get the network recruited and then to establish their bona fides. And eventually the Russians started to have a little faith, and then a bit more trust, until eventually someone in Moscow was having a nice little career promotion on the back of Constellation's intelligence product. And that was when we knew that they had bought into us hook, line and sinker."

Porter could see Sir Richard, C, nodding in silent agreement. He knew that Sir 'Dickie' had been on the front-line of the espionage war during the second round of unpleasantness, running German agents first in Europe before 1940 and later running them back as doubles, and he knew the pitfalls from first-hand experience.

"Constellation has been able, over the past few years, to influence Soviet policy on political decision making, strategic armed forces, missile strength and a wide variety of technical capabilities. At times we've made it appear as if the West is weak and at other times as though we are strong. Our aim is to keep the Russians off balance and thus far, we have been quite successful." Porter sighed and looked at his hands; sadness had descended over him and C had recognized it immediately as the melancholy of the agent-runner. "They're my boys and gals, you see. I've borne them, carried them, bullied them and fretted over them in some of their darkest days."

Another pause for breath, then Porter once again hammered out his theory on what *not* to do, to save his beloved network. "Now to our options, as I see it, in my role as their controller. Simply removing those agents from danger, oh, were that it was at all possible. That would be the easy option, certainly, but I fear that even the slightest hint of something out of the ordinary would cause ripples throughout Russian Intelligence. The KGB is nothing if not suspicious of everything, even its own agents. We move them, and remember that's a whole network, questions will be asked by the Russians. Why are you all going to ground? What is this, a group holiday?"

There was no laughter this time. They were into serious territory and they all knew it.

Porter became more earnest, his voice taking on more authority. "If we alert them, again it will cause them to act out of character. Something they've spent many a year building up, to gain the trust of Russian Intelligence. A scared and frightened agent begins to do silly things, takes risks, and acts like a bloody nightmare. What we need to do is keep them operationally unconscious for as long as we can about this assassination team. Apart from anything else, one of Constellation's agents, *LYRA*, before she was widowed, was married to a very influential American citizen with close personal links to the hierarchy in the White House...the current President's Chief of Staff no less. Links she still retains to this day!"

Masterman, who so far had shown very little interest in the whole briefing did, however raise an eyebrow at that. *This portly, slovenly man must be one hell of an agent-runner to have such a prize of an agent,* he thought to himself.

"She's a very clever lady who believes that cooperation between Europe and America is essential for dismantling the Communist regime. If we declared the details of Constellation's work to the CIA, it would mean bringing forth details of American citizens working indirectly for us," said Porter.

125

"And knowing the CIA, they'd want to take over the whole shooting match," said Harper, who knew from bitter experience how the Agency had a reputation for running roughshod over someone else's show.

"Not to mention the considerable embarrassment that it would cause, not only between services, but also on a political level. We spy on our friends as well as our enemies. It would bring the whole house of cards down," said Barton.

"What about agent *PYXIS*? Why doesn't he make their list?" asked C.

Porter nodded as if he had been expecting the question. "*PYXIS* is our new boy, Chief, and has only been active for a little over a year. Wherever the original intelligence came from, it appears to have been *before* he was recruited."

"I see," said C. "Well, that's good luck for him – shame it can't be said for the rest of the network. Poor buggers."

"But that's not the most surprising thing about this recording. Far from it," said Porter.

"Well, what is Bernie? Come on man, speak up," said Barton.

"Well, Sir, it's the fact that only four of the targets mentioned are a part of Constellation. The remaining names don't have anything to do with us. They appear to be legitimate Soviet agents!"

"Good Lord!"

"Yes, the Diplomat and the Quartermaster. We seem to have run into a genuine Soviet intelligence operation," said Porter, amused at the irony of it all.

"And what do we make of the seventh target, this so far unnamed Russian Intelligence officer?" said C. "Surely if we go around bumping off each other's spies, it will cause no end of chaos between services."

Barton took out his pipe and lit it. He waved the match like a man with recently numb fingers and then ceremoniously tossed it into a nearby ashtray. "That is harder to manage I agree; after all there isn't much of a description of the man. More importantly, why do they want him dead? Agents, well alright, I can see how that may be expedient, we do the same ourselves from time to time," he said flicking a brief glance down to Masterman's end of the table. "But it's a little extreme to start eliminating a fellow professional, even if he is a bloody Russian."

The men around the table all knew the unwritten rule of the intelligence business: no sanctioned killing of other service's officers, no matter how tempting it might be on occasion. They were professionals and after all such a lunatic action was only one step away from all out warfare. The Cold War was already at fever pitch and it wouldn't take much to tip the balance.

C turned to Porter. "Anyone you know, Bernie?"

Porter considered this. "Well, Sir, the Russian intelligence officer that runs several of the Constellation agents, sort of my opposite number if you like, has a reputation for being ruthless. Perhaps the Americans have tired of having to play against him. Of course it could be a dozen other KGB officers of equal experience, but without further information it's only guesswork about which one it could be I'm afraid."

C nodded. He knew that agents could, over the course of their careers have several different case officers; it was normal routine in the spy world. "Maybe you could have a dig about with your agents Bernie, see if there is anyone that fits the bill from their Russian contacts. At least if we can identify him we can make a more informed decision about whether to feed him to the dogs."

* * *

They stopped for another tea break, a stretch of their legs and backs and a quick trip to the toilet for several of the older members.

When they resumed it was C who moved the meeting on to the next phase. "So Bernie, we were talking about Constellation and how it is necessary to protect it. Perhaps you could share some more information about the time constraints that we have placed upon ourselves in carrying this out. I know that some of us are up to speed in this operation of yours, but it would rather help if you could lay out what you are hoping to achieve in the endgame."

Porter, refreshed and cleansed, once again leaned forward across the table and spoke with a quiet authority. "Gentlemen, Constellation is only one facet of this operation. It is in fact running in tandem with a much larger and more complex strategic intelligence operation. If Constellation is the means, then Operation SHREDDER is the end result."

Porter turned his gaze to Harper, the Director of Soviet Operations. "Perhaps you might like to take over from here, sir. SHREDDER is after all, under your direct control."

Harper nodded. The senior intelligence officer checked through his notes, made a small annotation, and began. "Thank you Porter. Over the past few years the Russians have been carrying out more and more aggressive operations and ramping up the tensions of the Cold War to unparalleled levels. Assassinations, rolling up of networks, plus the recent crisis in Cuba seem to have caught the West on the hop, which, let's face it, is an unenviable position for any intelligence service to be in."

The men around the table mused on the thought of recent Soviet operations, both military and espionage, and how many Western intelligence services had taken a beating on more than one occasion.

"Well," continued Harper, "after being in such a low position it was decided that an operation should be mounted, a long term operation. Its aim was to frighten the Soviet Union into a stalemate. I think that the phrase that was used at the time was that if you can't fight, then you should wear a big hat."

"Oh, I say, I rather like that," said C, a sly grin spreading across his face.

"Indeed, Chief. As you all know the thought of going to war; dare I say it, a nuclear war with Russia is something of a pipe dream by the hawks in the military. Nobody wants that. It would be the end of all days."

"It's why we do what we do, to stop the madness happening," said Barton.

"Agreed and Constellation has played a huge part in containing the excesses of the KGB and its subordinates," replied Porter.

"So what is the endgame that is so important Harper? What has Constellation been working for all these years?" queried C.

Harper ran a hand over his smooth mane of hair, dislodging several strands before he hurriedly brushed them neatly back into place. "It's a bluff, pure and simple. A big bluff that says we are the scary ones so do not dare to challenge us. There is to be a meeting later this year, in the autumn actually; exactly when is just guesswork at the moment. What we do know however is that in attendance will be several senior KGB officers, senior officials from the Russian military and numerous members of the Politburo. The purpose of the meeting is for the KGB to present, in a sort of symposium I suppose, the latest evidence of Western powers arming to the hilt to stand against the Soviet Union arms proliferation."

"What will this evidence show?" tested Barton.

"It will lay out in minute detail that we in the West have developed a range of inter-continental ballistic missiles and armaments that are far in advance of anything that the Russians have or are likely to have for the next decade. The evidence that is provided is expected to give the Russians pause, wrong foot them and make them reconsider any aggressive actions."

"And this false evidence comes from your Constellation network, Porter?" asked Barton.

"Yes. Each of the Constellation agents has, over many years, provided a piece to a jigsaw that is leading to this final operation. On their own, these pieces of intelligence are meaningless, but put together – like a jigsaw – they make up a beautiful picture of a fully armed, technologically advanced and determined Western nuclear policy," replied Porter.

"So the survival of Constellation, both literally and figuratively is essential for the success of Operation SHREDDER. Is that a fair summation?" said C.

"Absolutely. The ramifications of SHREDDER failing, being exposed or not believed, would set back our military and strategic advantage over the Russians by years. Something that I'm not sure we could recover from. Therefore, the survival and safety of Constellation is paramount, especially agents LYRA and SCORPIUS," answered Porter.

"Why those two agents in particular, Bernie?" asked C.

"Because they will provide the final clues to the Russians, Sir. SCORPIUS will provide the technical evidence and LYRA the evidence of a more aggressive Western policy in that area. They are our two best agents within Constellation; they are trusted by the Russians and have proved themselves to the KGB again and again. If they confirm what the Russians have been told, then we will have a classic closed loop; namely intelligence supplied and authenticated by several members of the same network," said Harper.

It was a huge gamble; they all knew that, risking a long term intelligence operation on a very spurious deception plan. But then that was what SIS was there for: to take on the jobs that were harder than most.

"And if it is a success, what is the outcome you're hoping for?" queried Barton.

"Best outcome for SHREDDER is that we scare the living daylights out of the Russians and give them pause about their future actions. Second best outcome is that at the very least we set the KGB off against its military counterparts," said Harper.

"Explain?" queried C.

"Well, the Soviet military machine, like most military organizations, always wants to have the best hardware and the latest weapons. If we can offer them proof that the weapon systems at our disposal outshine anything that they have by a country mile, then their military can't hope to compete with what they believe we have in the West. They will revert to type and try to dismiss the KGB's intelligence as rubbish."

"A case of if we don't have it, no one can have it. Their Russian generals will spend so much time bickering with the KGB that they'll cause an internal war. Excellent work," commented Barton, rubbing his hands beneath the table with glee.

"So it would seem that we are playing for some very high stakes. I must say I do rather like the subtlety and complexity of it all. I suspect it's the type of operation that we all dreamed we'd have the chance to run when we were toddlers in spy school," considered C.

Chapter Two

"So, the agents, what do we do next?" asked Barton.

"There's only one thing you can do!" The voice when it came caused them to startle. Seated at the far end of the table was Masterman, who so far, hadn't been a contributor to the discussion. His voice was deep and filled with a military style authority. It was a voice that resolved disputes.

The four intelligence bureaucrats turned to their colleague, but it was only the Chief who spoke. "Go on Stephen, you have a suggestion."

Masterman looked at them. "Thank you, Sir Richard. It seems to me that obviously we can't go cap-in-hand to the Americans and make it known that we have stumbled, albeit inadvertently, onto one of their operations. It would compromise our successful double agent network. Correct?"

"Absolutely," said Barton.

"We can't pull them out of the game because that would send a warning signal to Russian counter-intelligence, I mean all those agents mysteriously disappearing at the same time. The same for putting a security cordon around them at close quarters. It's too invasive, too easy for the Russians to spot even the most discreet of bodyguards and far too risky. Besides, these extra agents could be a blessing in disguise."

"In what way?" asked the Chief.

"Because it would make it easier for a good tracker to pick up the scent. These killers have to come out of hiding at some point, who knows, maybe we'll get lucky and they'll make a mistake whilst they are planning to hit one of the genuine KGB agents."

"Ah... and if the killers target the legitimate agents..." said Harper.

Masterman nodded. "Exactly, no matter how distasteful it is I'm sure we'd rather have proper iron-toothed Russian agents being eliminated than our own network. We alert them or give them security of any kind, the chances are they're blown. We move them – they are definitely blown, which leaves us with only one feasible outcome."

"Which is?" enquired Harper.

"We keep them in place and tell them nothing," said Masterman.

It was Harper this time who expressed shock, while Porter sat with his hands clasped tightly together, his brow furrowed in concentration in case he misunderstood what was being proposed.

"You can't mean it. Leave them to this pack of wolf killers?," replied Barton.

"Yes, I'm afraid I do, especially if you want the network to remain intact and the deception operation to continue. If our counter-terror operation is successful, maybe we can get in there and turn these legitimate Russian agents, or at least have them rolled up and arrested," said Masterman.

Once again Barton was at his bullish best. "Well, you're the Head of Redaction, Masterman, this is your bailiwick... what do you have in mind?"

Masterman knew exactly what he wanted. "A small team to track, identify, and eliminate these mercenaries. We hit them before they hit our agents. Hopefully," he suggested.

"You're talking about a counter-terrorist operation, to eliminate these killers? Lure them in and kill them. Bit risky for our agents, isn't it?" said Harper.

"The agents are the bait, yes. And we prefer the term 'Redaction' for what we do," replied Masterman.

"Hmm... I bet you do," said Harper. Everyone knew that Redaction had a reputation for the heavy work and for carrying out the rough stuff. It wasn't known as the 'Thug Squad' for nothing. "Do you have someone in mind?"

Masterman nodded. "I do actually. He's a good man, very capable, very experienced. He'd fit the bill for this operation."

The Chief looked around the table. "What do you think?"

There were nods of agreement. In reality it was the only option. Choice was a luxury they didn't have.

"If you think your man can do it," challenged Barton.

"Oh, he can do it alright. He'll cut out these contractors like a surgeon removing a cancer. He'll leave you with a network still intact and operational, and the Americans won't even know we've been players in this game."

"You, of course, understand the protocols, Masterman," said Barton brusquely.

Masterman nodded. He understood them alright, had been made aware of them numerous times over the past four years as Head of the Redaction Unit. If it blows up in your face, you're on your own. If your people are lost, they better damn well shut up or put a bullet through their own heads. There would be nothing written down, no verbal command authorization; nothing that could be traced back to the Chief, and aside from the five men in this room there would no other witnesses.

Everything would stop at and come from Barton, the Vice-Chief, who in real terms would be the cut out between 'operational tasks' and the Chief's executive level. For the sake of proprietary, the mission would be run under the cover of a 'training exercise'. It was to be plausible yet deniable, as their American Cousins would, ironically, phrase it.

"So do I have the green light?" asked Masterman, looking around the room and making eye contact with each man.

And with an imperceptible nod from the Chief, really nothing more than a slight inclination of his head in the general direction of the far side of the table, Operation: MACE, as it was to become known within the history of the Secret Service, was born.

Chapter Three

WI/ROGUE and QJ/WIN began the contract as reactivated agents for the CIA by both heading for Germany. They had decided that, unless circumstances altered along the way, they would complete the killings in geographical order, hopping from one country to the next working down the body of Europe picking off targets on their list.

They had a timetable and itinerary for each of the hits. From this they knew that they would be able to plan out surveillance of the targets and what type of weaponry would be needed. Both men knew that the biggest risk was traversing the various borders of the many countries that they would have to operate in. It was going to be difficult certainly, but not impossible.

Following their initial meeting in Vienna, they had reconvened to a safe-house that Marquez had rented for them in Auvers sur Oise, a quiet village thirty kilometers from the center of Paris. The small chalet just outside the main town was overlooked by acres of woodland and came complete with a barn adjacent to the main building. It was quiet, isolated, off the beaten track and was perfect for hiding out and planning the rest of their operations. It was to be one of their main bases over the next few months. Once inside, they had spread out their target list in front of them across an old oak dining table and stared at the scale of the operation.

"What about weapons," asked Gioradze. "I could have a word with some people in Belgium, but it would need to be a big order for them to be interested." The bullet headed killer knew that in order to accomplish the terms of the contract they would need a wide range of equipment, weapons that would be far beyond the range of small time gangland arms dealers whose limit would be an untraceable revolver or a few hand grenades.

Marquez shook his head. "No, we keep our regular weapons sources out of the loop. You know these mercenary arms dealers; they're leaky when it comes to who's buying what and where. We could never trust that they wouldn't simply tip off someone in Russian intelligence and double cross us. Besides, we have an alternative option thanks to our American friends, although it will mean a short trip for you."

"Where?" asked Gioradze.

"Up in north east Italy, near the Gorizia gap," replied Marquez.

The CIA had a hand in a secret project known as 'Gladio. Gladio's aim was to fund and run a stay-behind network in the event that the Soviets planned a full out invasion of Europe. The network spread across Eastern Europe and had access to a wide range of equipment, resources, personnel and weapons hidden in a number of concealed caches. Most of the weapons caches were deep in the forests of Italy, Switzerland and Belgium and were far away from prying eyes. Mr. Knight, their CIA contact, had given them the coordinates of several weapons caches that they could access. The two assassins studied the map and the coordinates and routes that would be needed.

"We'll need silenced pistols, explosives, grenades, rifles, submachine guns. Take a bit of everything, that way we're covered for most eventualities," said Marquez, drawing a circle around the three weapons dumps that they intended to 'dip' into.

"The big problem is getting them stored away and across the borders," said Gioradze.

"It's something I've considered. Did you notice the barn out back?"

Gioradze nodded. He had seen the old building as they had driven up the road to the rented property.

"Inside is a VW camper van. It has specially fitted compartments that I had an old smuggling contact of mine in Paris rig up. It has three metal containers on the under carriage, two behind the seating and two over the wheel arches. Not large compartments, but big enough to stash a few rifles, pistols, explosives and grenades in," said Marquez.

The two men went out to the barn and Marquez gave the smaller man a tour of the secret fittings, allowing him to judge for himself the feasibility of the plan. After inspecting it Gioradze nodded. "Okay, it seems good. What about a decent route? The less entanglement I have with police or border guards the better."

"If you set off tomorrow and drive down past Lyon and cross the border into northern Italy. It should take you about ten hours hard driving," said Marquez.

"Wouldn't it be quicker to cut through Switzerland and then drop down into northern Italy?" asked Gioradze.

Marquez shook his head. "No, the last thing we need is to be alerting the Swiss authorities. The Swiss are more thorough than the Italians. A flash of a passport, a quick wave and the Italian guards will just wave you through, whereas the Swiss if they smell something's wrong, will strip the van down to bare metal."

Gioradze nodded, accepting Marquez's wisdom. "Okay, then what?"

"You lay up for the day. Sleep in the van and then visit the three weapons sites. All are in woodland, so at least you won't have anyone looking over your shoulder."

"And if someone does see me?"

Marquez laughed. "I think you know the answer to that. You can't be captured or identified. Kill them."

"Even if they are part of the CIA's operation down there?"

"The message I have from Mr. Knight is that this mission supersedes everything else. So just don't get spotted."

"And then?"

Marquez shrugged and folded up the map before handing it to Gioradze. "You do the same in reverse. Take your time. Think of it as a slow getaway. You have five days to get there, get the weapons and get back here safely."

The next morning Gioradze had set off in his little camper van and travelling on a Swiss passport in the name of Blattner, began the long and dangerous journey south. Marquez had stood at the door of the chalet, gave a quick wave and then returned to his desk inside to make sure he had covered every part of the planning.

They had enough real time intelligence in the files that the American had given them. They knew where the targets lived and their day to day routines, and only that morning he had made arrangements for travel and accommodation that they were going to use while they were in Hamburg, Lichtenstein and Zurich; the locations of the first three hits.

What he didn't know *precisely* at this moment, and wouldn't until Gioradze had returned with his 'booty', was *how* they were going to carry out the respective killings on the targets.

* * *

Four days later the little Georgian returned. The camper van struggling to climb the hill that led to the barn at the rear of the property. Marquez immediately dropped what he was doing and rushed outside to open the archaic wooden doors so as to allow the van to drive straight in.

The Georgian climbed out of the driver's side and shook his partner's hand. Marquez thought he looked like a man worn away from travelling across Europe in an old camper van that was stocked with illegal arms.

"Any problems?" asked Marquez.

Gioradze shook his head. "No, just a lot of driving, a lot of cold nights, and a lot of praying every time I passed a police car."

"And the border crossings?"

"Smooth as silk, couldn't have been friendlier," replied Gioradze. "Want to see what we've got?"

The two men set about removing the seals from the hidden compartments in the van with spanners and screwdrivers and carefully extracted the items inside. Thirty minutes later the stash of weapons and munitions was laid out in front of them on the floor of the old barn. To Gioradze it was a treasure trove. "Where do we store them," he asked Marquez.

The Catalan waved a hand over to the far corner of the barn. "There is a hidden cellar in that corner, concealed underneath the old bales and hay; I think it was once used as a wine cellar. We'll put the equipment in there."

He looked down at the arms. Gioradze had picked well, as he knew he would. Pistols with silencers, grenades, a silenced rifle of some kind, plastic explosives, detonators, sub-machine guns, even a bazooka with three grenades. "And you're sure no one spotted you at the Gladio caches?"

"Don't worry, Juan. They were all in the middle of nowhere. I went when it was dark and started digging until I hit a fiberglass box, the size of a wardrobe. They were huge. I took what I needed and covered it all up again."

Marquez placed a hand on his partner's shoulder. "An excellent job, David."

The Georgian's chest swelled with pride. "Which ones do we take first?" he said, nodding at the equipment.

Marquez pondered for a few seconds and then seemed to make up his mind. "We'll start with a big bang; the bazooka. You take it to Lichtenstein, visit the arms dealer and take care of him. I'll deal with the diplomat in Hamburg."

The next day they travelled by car, but would, before they reached the border, break off and go their separate ways. One would travel to the cold north of Germany by train, whilst the other would head south by road.

Chapter Four

The Diplomat had his disguise on and was resplendent in his finery.

Disguise was perhaps the wrong word, maybe a bit too over-the-top: costume was probably more correct – but either way, the clothes he wore this fine evening were a mile away from what he would normally wear during his working life.

He was a man of secrets. Some secrets related to his job working for the British Foreign Service, some related to the 'secret work for peace' that he conducted for the Russians, and some related to his private life. Tonight's assignation was most definitely a part of his private life.

Julian Cowan, the Diplomat, walked along the Reeperbahn and as he walked, he considered that of all the places in the world, this was where he belonged. He was glad he'd been posted to Hamburg. Berlin held a much stricter legal punishment than the more forgiving Hamburg when it came to indulging his particular sexual tastes, and while it was still legally classed as a crime, there was always a member of the vice squad who would turn a blind eye or take a bribe, to leave the 'golden boys' in peace.

Tonight he wore his favorite killer outfit of purple suede and black leather, which was the polar opposite of his usual, stuffy three-piece-suit, regulation brogues and neutrally styled hair. He wore his killer outfit, because he hoped, no, prayed, that the eye candy he'd met last night would return for a repeat performance. So far, it had only consisted of drinking and a little flirtatious conversation as they watched the boys dancing. But who knew, tonight maybe, they would take it a tad further. He certainly hoped so; it would do him good to experience a release. It had been a stressful week.

First, the current spate of meetings at the Embassy and a quick stopover in Bonn, to take part in the current Anglo-German think tank on the future of a unified Germany; then back to Hamburg to meet with his Russian 'friend' to pass over the latest gossip and intelligence he had acquired. But for now that was all to be forgotten – the Embassy, the espionage, the Cold War. Tonight was to be about indulging himself in his pleasures.

Die Blaue Lagune was situated at the far end of the Reeperbahn, a downstairs bar that was one of the most secret and exotic locations in Hamburg for the discerning gentleman requiring erotic assignations and dalliances. The clientele was predominantly male and affluent, with the only exceptions being the few regular lesbian couples who frequented it.

Cowan approached the black steel door, rapped his knuckles on the wooden knocker and was scrutinized from behind a small Judas peephole. He straightened his leather overcoat and heard the bolts and locks being withdrawn inside. The door quickly creaked open, revealing a faint red glow and emitting the smell of sweat, cigarettes and beer.

The bar and the dance floor were busy; couples drinking in corners, holding hands or kissing, while the single boys and girls gyrated to the local beat music on the dance floor. Cowan moved through the crowd to the bar, nodding to several people he vaguely knew.

Now where was he? Cowan scanned the room one more time, but nothing. Then from out of the toilets he saw the object of his affections; the tall, dark haired man, with a long drooping moustache and wearing all-black clothing. The man walked across to an empty seat at the bar and picked up his drink.

"I thought you wouldn't show again, Esteban," said Cowan, placing a playful hand on his shoulder. He settled on the bar stool next to Esteban and waved the other hand toward the barman.

Marquez turned to him and smiled warmly. "I never miss out on a good thing, my darling."

* * *

Two hours and many drinks later they were back in Cowan's apartment.

They had chatted over some wine, Cowan flirting outrageously, while his older beau acted cool and aloof, not wanting to rush the night's inevitable events. Flirting had led to petting and petting had led to the bedroom where Cowan now felt his newly acquired lovers' hands, slick with oil, move up the back of his legs strong and hard, then playfully across his buttocks, quickly and firmly pressing with his thumbs along his spine until they reached the nape of his neck. They massaged carefully; once, twice, three times...he could feel himself growing hard.

More importantly, he could feel Estaban dropping his weight down onto his back, could feel his arousal as the length of his shaft playfully toyed with the crease of Cowan's buttocks. He pushed his head down into the pillow, a smile of pleasure spreading across his face. "Take me, take me," Cowan heard himself whisper, his voice hoarse with longing, as his new lover entered him gently.

* * *

Thirty minutes later, Marquez was washing his hands in the bathroom sink. Amazing how that oil got everywhere and lingered. In that respect it was very much like blood.

It had been twenty minutes since he had garroted the Englishman, the spy.

The whole operation had gone smoothly. An easy pick up of the target at the club and an unobserved exit from the bar. No witnesses had seen them leave and no one had seen them enter Cowan's apartment.

He had waited until the man was in a relaxed state following their love making and then, when the Englishman was at his most vulnerable, Marquez had quickly removed the homemade garrote which he'd secreted underneath the mattress. Marquez far outweighed the slimmer man and he dropped his knees down onto Cowan's upper arms, pinning him face downwards to the bed. Cowan yelped, more out of surprise than pain. *Perhaps he thought I was going to fuck him again,* thought Marquez.

The rest was the simple mechanics of murder. The garrote, a piece of thin piano wire connected by two dowel handles, was slipped expertly under the prone man's chin, pulled back and then twisted so that Marquez's forearms crossed. Then he pulled and pulled…

It was in that moment when Cowan began to realize that this was no sex-game, this was something else entirely, and began to panic. His body, trying to fight gravity, began to jerk and buck. But Marquez was an experienced murderer and had accounted for his victim's reaction. He shifted his weight to his left side and thrust his right knee into the small of the man's back, pressing him further down into the bed.

Marquez imagined that he looked like a rider trying to control a wild horse, the garrote his reigns as he stretched back, making the wire as taut as possible. He could see Cowan's face turning a bright red as his brain searched for oxygen, a croaking sound came from somewhere deep within his throat… and still Marquez pulled on the wire, pulled so hard that the sweat poured from his body due to the sheer physicality of the act.

He had no idea how long it had been since he slipped the garrote around the man's neck, it seemed like hours, but still he pulled and still he held the weight of the body down. He gave a final surge of effort and was rewarded with an arterial fountain of blood leaping free from the side of Cowan's neck.

The wire had cut so deeply it had severed the man's main artery, and the blood pumping onto the bed covered the once white sheets in a layer of crimson. Marquez felt the man beneath him lose strength and his body slumped forward like a balloon which has had the air slowly released from it. He worked the garrote now with a sawing motion, moving it from side to side, feeling the wire cutting through tissue and sinew until it eventually reached Cowan's spine.

He let go of the blood-soaked garrote's toggles, his hands aching from the exertion, and let them fall onto Cowan's naked back. Then he reached forward, grabbed Cowan's hair tightly with both hands and ripped the head backwards.

The head swiveled as if it was attached to Cowan's body with a one-sided hinge, turning to stare accusingly at Marquez. He looked down at the body on the bed, resembling so much butchered meat, and wrinkled his nose in disgust. Now that the killing was over, he could allow himself to feel. Not at the time, though, during the midst of a kill he was too focused and motivated on doing what was necessary.

Garroting was a first for him. Knives, guns, poisons and explosions – he had used all of them, many times in the past, but thus far, he'd never used the Italian rope. He reflected on the fact that the method of execution for this wretch of an Englishman was intimately plausible in the context of his death. What could be more personal, than murdering someone you had just had sex with using your own hands? It was quite fitting, in Marquez's opinion.

He lifted himself off the body, made his way to the bathroom and stared at himself in the shaving mirror for a long time. The mental battle raged in his head until he was finally satisfied that he'd justified his actions to his own conscience. *A job, nothing more... this man meant nothing to you. You fucked him and then killed him. That is all.*

He carefully removed the false moustache he'd worn for the last few nights during his surveillance of the Englishman. The disguise was no longer necessary. Then he found Cowan's shaving brush in the bathroom and dipped it into a pool of its owner's blood. On the wall over the bed, he daubed the word *'hure'* – whore. When the body was eventually discovered, it would be assumed that the man had been the victim of a psychopathic lover or queer-basher who had taken his anger too far. By which time, Marquez would be back on a plane and making his way to Zurich.

The first 'hit' of the contract was complete.

* * *

Vaclav Kader sat in the back of his chauffeur-driven Mercedes, working on the paperwork needed by the start of business that morning, and reflected on how blessed his life was.

He signed his name on several documents and scanned a cursory eye over several more, before placing them neatly by his side on the upholstered leather seat. Outside, the gentle flurries of snow increased giving the streets of Vaduz, Liechtenstein a dusting of white.

"Dieter, turn the heating up, please. I feel as if someone just walked over my grave," he said to the driver. Dieter, his chauffeur/bodyguard, smiled in the mirror and set about adjusting the Mercedes' heating system. Dieter was a good man. Reliable, dependable, trustworthy, and a good man to have on your side in a fight, or to take care of any unpleasant business.

They had both been in the same displaced persons camp after the war, and had come up the hard way. Black market goods and a little smuggling had made Vaclav, the wheeler dealer, and Dieter, the young enforcer, successful. But that was an age ago. Now Vaclav Kader was the CEO of one of the most successful companies in Liechtenstein.

Not that Vaclav Kader hadn't had a little help to build his post-war shipping and transportation empire; oh no, far from it. A member of the Czechoslovakian Communist Party all his life, he had been picked up by the Russians, recruited as an agent and had been 'played back' into the displaced person camps in Austria in the immediate post-war era. His mission was to infiltrate himself into western society, gain a foothold and see where it led. In truth, he was one of dozens of small time agents that the Russians would routinely 'ship' over the border, in order to worm their way into the West.

After months in the camps, where he'd gained a reputation as both a trader and fixer, he had been released with legitimate identity cards and a bright new future. The hopeful spy had then set about building his new life.

A year later he had, through the funding of a covert Russian intelligence investment, established himself in the city of Liechtenstein where he set about building Schon International Shipping Ltd into the global company it was today. But that was many years ago, and the excitement of running his legitimate business empire was far overshadowed by the thrill and danger of running his far more lucrative and illegal business, that of international arms dealer.

He had never fired a weapon in his life, had certainly never killed a man, but Vaclav Kader could reel off verbatim the pros and cons of various types of explosives, small arms, artillery and heavy-mechanized hardware. He had warehouses in Belgium, North Africa and Bolivia. He had a fleet of aircraft and ships that could be called upon to transport his secret cargoes all over the world. He had dined with warlords and revolutionaries, terrorists and presidents. He was known and respected. His work for the KGB these days was his crowning glory and the role that truly satisfied him. It was the business he had been born to run and he took pride in the title of 'Merchant of Death', which had been bestowed upon him.

He would regularly travel all over the world, ostensibly on Schon shipping business, but in reality to buy, broker, and transport all manner of small arms and munitions to KGB-backed end-users. Africa, South America, Cuba, and the Middle East had all fallen within his fiefdom over the past decade or more. He enjoyed the good life; expensive suits, the finest wines and first class travel, which for a committed Communist as wealthy as he, was a difficult juggling trick to manage with his own conscience. It was all the more remarkable, because the police and security services of the West had no real proof he was involved in any of this illegal trade.

The Mercedes turned the corner into the main street which housed the offices of Schon International Shipping Ltd. The pavements were already starting to fill with people scurrying to work, trying in vain to avoid the increasing snow fall.

His wife, a red headed beauty from Bremen, ran Schon for him these days. She was an excellent CEO and ran the company like a well-oiled machine, leaving him free to dedicate himself to his less public operations for the Russians. He knew that she had already been at work for an hour, in preparation for an important client meeting today. She was his rock and he loved her simply and completely.

"I'll pull up right outside, the snow's getting quite heavy," murmured Dieter as the car began to slow down. As they approached the ornate entrance to his business headquarters Vaclav Kader was aware of the main double doors to Schon swinging open and his wife striding out to greet him, a radiant smile spreading across her stunning features.

Yes, he decided as he heaved himself out of his luxury car, greeting his beautiful wife outside of his global business headquarters – he really was blessed with a good life.

* * *

David Gioradze sat concealed in his perch and cradled the 'Eagle' in his hands.

The perch was a grey tarpaulin hide that he'd constructed the previous night, made from old hessian sacking. Not enough to provide cover and concealment up close, but from a distance, he would blend into the flat roof of the apartment building.

He had chosen his spot well; it was far enough away to keep from the prying eyes of the locals, but within the effective range of his killing ground. When the time was right, he would simply pop up out of the hide, center on his target and melt back into the landscape before anyone could figure out where the explosion had come from.

The 'Eagle' was the nickname he'd given to the Rocket-Propelled Grenade launcher that was his weapon of choice for this type of long range killing. The RPG-7 was a 40mm warhead that would send a kinetic shockwave through anything it hit. Its main military function was to destroy heavy artillery and vehicles. He knew that against a normal car, its effect would be devastating.

Back in his Legion days, Gioradze had attended a course as part of his basic training, on the tactical battlefield use of rocket propelled weaponry. His instructor had been – before his fresh start with the Legion – a former SS commando who had used the Panzerfaust to great effect on the Eastern front against Soviet tanks. "My boy," the scarred German veteran had said, "they are the greatest weapons in the world if used correctly and aimed at the right target. They are like the eagle, swooping down, bringing death to the small lamb."

He knew his target did most of his legitimate business from his company offices located on Stadtle Street, the main thoroughfare in Vaduz. International shipping, so the intelligence files said, which in Gioradze's opinion was a useful business to have when you're buying and selling arms and munitions to the dictators of Africa and Central America. He thought it strange that a committed Communist agent who supplied military hardware to KGB-backed end-users was also in love with money for its own ends. Strange. Who knew, maybe it was the thrill of putting the deals together that was the rush, rather than venal thoughts.

Gioradze had driven the 700 kilometers overnight from France, easily passing over the border in his little camper van with the RPG-7 carefully hidden in the concealed tubing which had been expertly welded to the undercarriage of the vehicle. He had arrived as dawn was breaking over the small town of Vaduz.

His first job had been to scout out the target location, a non-descript, three story office block that was the headquarters of Schon International. Then he'd driven the campervan around the circular one-way street and stored it at the rear of the building which was to be his 'perch' for the next few hours.

Scaling the outside of the buildings had been child's play. It had merely been a case of climbing up one outside metal drain pipe, the RPG broken down into two sections and carried in a fishing bag, and then he'd clambered up onto the roof of a small outhouse. From there, it was like climbing up slowly ascending building blocks, until he reached the second story roof of the restaurant he'd chosen to be his sniper position. With the hide made, there was nothing left to do but shiver against the icy cold and keep the warhead from freezing by snuggling it against his prone body.

He checked his watch regularly. He knew his target would be arriving for work that morning at 8.45am to the minute. Again, the trusted intelligence reports had provided this information. Every morning during the working week, the arms dealer arrived precisely fifteen minutes before the rest of his staff. He would arrive in a grey Mercedes, driven by his chauffeur-bodyguard.

At 8.30am, just as the town of Vaduz was coming to life, Gioradze carefully assembled the two pieces of the RPG and locked the warhead into its firing tube. A small *clunk* and he was satisfied it was secured in place. All he had left to do now was fire. He knew what would happen when he pulled the trigger of the RPG-2. The trigger would send an electrical impulse signal to the rocket motor, which in turn would initiate the propellant, causing the grenade to leave the launcher. The grenade would then 'sprout' seven metallic fins, giving it stability in flight. Basically, Gioradze thought of it as a modern version of an archer's arrow.

He pushed back the sacking from above his head and peered up at the grey sky; a light covering of snow had turned the rooftop white. He craned his neck and chanced a look down onto Stadtle Street. It was just a normal suburban street, a few cars dotted here and there, and many people on their way to work, battling against the increasing snowfall. A check of his watch told him it was now 8.43am. *Keep it together, keep it together,* came the mantra in his head. He locked his gaze on the front of the building; he didn't want to miss the target.

Less than thirty seconds later, the target made his way along the main stretch of the road. *Closer, closer, keep coming,* he told the Mercedes, willing the car along its normal route, begging that today wasn't the day that the target deviated from his normal course of action. The Mercedes, a dark grey, powerful machine, cruised up to the entrance of Schon International. With no other cars parked in the vicinity, the driver brought it right to the door, eager to get as close as possible so that his employer wouldn't be exposed to the elements.

Gioradze heard the engine stop and watched as a large, heavyset man in a business suit climbed out of the driver's seat. *The protection,* laughed Gioradze to himself. But not today *Mon ami.* The bodyguard adjusted his jacket and spryly moved around to the pavement side to open the door for his employer. On the rooftop, Gioradze smoothly folded back the sacking which had been a makeshift blanket and stood, lofting the RPG to his shoulder and clicking the cocking button. He carefully peered through the metal sights, aligning the forward sight with the roof of the Mercedes.

Two things happened simultaneously. A woman, tall and red headed, emerged from the entrance to Schon, just as the target – the arms dealer – exited the car. Gioradze just had time to see the fit-looking arms dealer turn to inspect the street, before the woman appeared in the sights. A smile of recognition spread across the arms dealers' face when the woman came forward to embrace him. Old friends, perhaps? A lover? A wife? It didn't matter. Her death would merely be incidental.

The trigger, pull the trigger! Gioradze's head screamed. *Now, do it now!* He braced himself, the launcher tight against his shoulder when he pulled the trigger. There was a deafening *whoosh* against his right ear and then the grey morning was illuminated momentarily with a brilliant flash. He watched as the eagle of death flew toward its target.

The grenade took approximately two seconds to reach the car. It hit the vehicle directly, killing the target, the woman and the bodyguard instantly. They were simply vaporized; with the exception of a clothed limb here and there. The Mercedes seemed to be picked up by an invisible hand and then slammed back down onto the road with such force, the doors and wheels seemed to burst outwards from the main bulk of the vehicle. Then there was fire, and a lot of screaming.

Like a child watching a fireworks display, Gioradze let his eyes linger on the violent spectacle that lay below him in the street. It was a myriad of fire, smoke, charred metal, and screams. Then something else flashed into his mind, a remark from the old German who'd taught the boys how to use the 'Eagle' in the Legion.

"And when you've done the killing, don't hang around to admire the roaring fire you've created; you turn and run unless you want some sharp-eyed sniper to target your firing position."

Gioradze dropped the launcher tube and walked briskly to the rear of the roof. He hurried down, down, down through the buildings until moments later, he reached street level. There was no worry about anyone targeting this building just yet, there would be too much panic on the street and he suspected with the chaos surrounding him, it would be a while before the police arrived. He estimated he had a good ten-minutes of getaway time, which was more than enough, given that his vehicle was literally parked around the corner. From there, he would take the main arterial route out of Vaduz.

He walked out onto the Stadtle, keeping his gaze lowered. He was aware of people behind him, around him, to the side of him. People were running towards the chaos, whilst he walked in the opposite direction. He glanced back, aware of the smoke in the distance, before increasing his pace. A young girl, perhaps a waitress on her way to work a morning breakfast shift, briefly locked eyes with him. He pulled his cap further down, partly to conceal the top half of his face and partly to protect himself from the snow.

Moments later he was back in the campervan. He checked around for witnesses, seeing none, he gently removed the false beard which had been glued in place, and then took of the hat, the wig and the spectacles. They would be dumped on the roadside, as soon as he left Vaduz. He turned the key in the ignition and started the engine and the nondescript little campervan gently ambled out onto the road, heading away from the flames.

'Hit' number two had been completed.

* * *

James Quinn

Over 2000 miles away Mr. Knight, the American, received a letter from Europe. Because of the distance involved, it had taken a little over two weeks to arrive. He sat and breakfasted on coffee and pancakes while he watched the young girls swimming in the hotel's pool below and then he picked up the letter, which had been delivered to his hotel suite. European postmarks. He slit open the envelope and caught the two pieces of paper which fell out. Both were clippings from German newspapers.

One covered the assassination of a respected Liechtenstein resident and businessman, in the quiet town of Vaduz.

The report stated that Vaclav Kader, the Chairman of Schon International Shipping had been assassinated in a targeted attack. His wife and driver had also been killed. The assassins had escaped. It was assumed because of his alleged (and so far unproven) connections to the illegal arms trade that he had been killed by a rival who was trying to muscle in on this deadly and lucrative business. Police were continuing their enquiries.

The other newspaper cutting covered the death of a junior British diplomat, Julian Cowan, who had been found murdered in Hamburg. The British Embassy was vehemently denying claims that Mr. Cowan had been the victim in a homosexual sex game murder. Both articles had barely caused a ripple, relegated to pages nine and ten in the newspapers.

Mr. Knight smiled to himself, feeling very satisfied. He picked up his lighter and set both pieces of paper on fire, dropping them onto his empty plate. Seconds later, there was nothing left but ash. He thought for a few more moments and then made his way to the bedside telephone and placed a call to his bank in Switzerland. He gave the order for the first block of funds to be transferred over to his 'contractor's' bank account in Luxembourg.

Chapter Five

With Operation MACE now officially sanctioned by the hierarchy at Broadway, the resources of SIS swung into action. Masterman put in an urgent request to the Registry. *Find me the link,* he told them. Find me the name, the clue or what have you, but get it to me by yesterday!

The intelligence analysts began the long search through the archaic files of the service. What they were looking for even they weren't sure, but Masterman was an experienced hunter of men and knew that even the most careful of killers, especially those who were paid to do it for a living, always left a clue or a residue of information somewhere. It was almost impossible not to.

He gave the archivists a list of what they knew. Professional killers, European, definitely in the Dominican Republic in 1961, CIA linked definitely. Dominican Republic in 1961 equaled the assassination of President Trujillo, something the CIA was rumored to be heavily involved in. The clerks turned their attention directly to the SIS Caribbean Desk for that year.

At first there was nothing and Masterman and his unit had to settle for the silence of the telephone and the moribund action of the telex. Masterman – never one to relax – had ignored the silence and set about working out an operational plan. The intelligence would turn up, he knew sooner or later and when it did, he wanted to have a strategy in place so that he could act. Look further; look deeper, he urged them before going back to his desk in Pimlico and his planning.

And then like a radio signal breaking through static, the information slowly started to filter through... an old report from the SIS station in the Dominican Republic... a fragment, nothing more... report from a junior officer... bar room gossip, nothing more... two men and a known CIA operative... it could be nothing... really.

But to Masterman it was the break he needed. An eye witness; what's more, an eye witness who was assigned to the SIS Station. He sat at his desk in Pimlico, lifted the phone, and made a direct call through to 'Personnel' at Broadway.

"Hello Colin, it's Masterman over at Pimlico. I wondered if you could do me a little favor."

* * *

The girl rolled off of Jack Grant, body glistening with sweat from the exertions of the past hour, turned onto her front and stretched a hand over to the bedside table, reaching for her cigarettes.

Her breath was still shallow, panting, and her face was flushed with the aftermath of their lovemaking. He lazily stroked the small of her naked back, tracing his finger along the curvature of her spine. He took in the thick black hair which cascaded over her shoulders, her coffee colored skin and long, full figure. "So who's next?" he asked.

The girl laughed as she reached for her watch. It was 9.35 in the morning. "Why, you want me to hang around? Isn't an hour long enough for you... or is it that you're jealous, Jack," she teased.

He raised an eyebrow at that. Jealous? Never! Well, almost never. He had seen the girl – Coco, that was her working name – he had seen Coco four times over recent months. He always used the same discreet 'Escort Service' from Soho which provided high-class girls for discerning gentlemen. Her accent fluctuated between Jamaican, or possibly Cuban, and East End Cockney, giving it an unusually pleasant lilt.

His employment protocols dictated that she should be checked out by the snoopers at the Security Service and that, if nothing else, their assignations should be at a separate location from his home address.

But screw that, thought Grant, *he liked his home comforts.* He found her good company; and they had a similar style of love-making – active and intense! She didn't ask too much of him or he of her, and yet he always had this moment of sadness when she was due to leave. Was it guilt, or just the craving for another human being to be with?

"We all have to do things we don't like from time to time," he said.

"Even you?" she asked.

"Even me."

"What does an accountant have to do that they don't really want to?"

"Tax forms, love, tax forms. They're a bloody nightmare," he said, the beginnings of a smile on his lips.

"Hardly the same thing, Jack. Besides, why aren't you at work on a Tuesday morning, it's a bit early to be hiring me."

"It's never too early for you, Coco."

A light giggle followed as she rushed to put on her underwear and find her dress. He knew her day job was working at a coffee bar somewhere, the escort work was just a sideline, but she wouldn't tell him where and if he was being honest with himself it would cause more problems if he did know. Better to keep their relationship purely carnal.

She ran her fingers through her hair, straightening out any kinks. "Well, whatever you decide to do, have a lovely day doing it. I've got to go. Will you call soon?"

"No..." he groaned. She laughed at that, knowing full well that he would, the next time he wanted a roll between the sheets. She knew she was that good.

He heard the door slam as she scuttled off to work and he lay there enjoying the sanctuary of an empty bed, stretching, staring at the ceiling and rubbing a hand over the fresh growth of stubble on his chin. Christ, he was bored already; time to get up and move. Day off or not, he hated lying in any later than he had to.

Grant had been on enforced leave for the past month and it was starting to grate on him. Enforced leave was sometimes necessary for

agents, who had a tendency to become fatigued on operations and
after the length of his last job in Asia, which had run on for several
months, he'd been told to take some time off. *Do normal things; take a
holiday, fishing, perhaps, a bit of mountain climbing. I hear the lakes are
nice this time of year – anything, but forget about the office and being
operational for a month or two.*

But that was not Jack Grant. Not by a long mile.

So he drank, screwed attractive and available women and occasionally took himself to the Flamingo Club in Soho. In truth, he was no
lover of jazz, but the company in the club itself – hookers, gangsters,
pimps and hop heads – he felt an affinity with. They lived a secret
life and asked nothing of their fellow party goers, which suited Grant
just fine.

But for him, copious amounts of alcohol and sex equaled one thing;
that he was getting bored and he had too much free time on his hands.
It was purgatory and he needed to get back to work and quickly, if only
for the sake of his liver. He'd spent too many mornings throwing up,
after the haze of the previous night's session, and he knew that if the
office found out he'd be flogged and put on the static list, destined to
push paperwork for time immemorial.

His ability with a firearm and his skills as a tracker of men were his
greatest assets and vital to his role in the service, but even the Secret
Service had limits as to how much leeway they would offer to one of
their best men. So, he hid his excesses from the Service while he was
on leave, as best he could. He knew the only one he couldn't hide it
from, was himself. He hated himself for his laziness.

The loud peal of the telephone on his bedside table roused him from
his gloom. He grabbed the receiver and barked. *"Yes!"* Coco's leaving
had gotten to him, despite his protestations. He heard the click of the
security line being activated and he knew instantly. It was Masterman.

"It's me and I think you mean, hello *sir!*"

"Sorry, I was… in the middle of something," he muttered.

"Well, get your clothes on, I've got a little errand for you, something
to stop you from being bored."

"Too late. I've been bored for the past fortnight."

"Yes, well, we've a new recruit being seconded to our unit and I'd like you to give them the once over, meet them, greet them and then give me your assessment of how it went."

"Okay, anything to get out of the flat. When and where?"

"Around twelve-thirty. The American Bar at the Savoy, no less," replied Masterman smoothly.

That caught Grant by surprise. "Very nice. Not normally in my league, that place, I normally get the transport cafe and the ex-squaddie who thinks he can cut it with the big boys."

"What can I say? It's your lucky day and besides, the Mirabelle would be just too flashy. Just keep the bill down and don't go wild with the wine list, or it's coming out of your pay packet. Get receipts for everything," said Masterman.

"Okay, fair enough. So who is it who gets the five-star treatment?"

"Oh, just someone we think has value for an upcoming operation. Give them the hairy eyeball, Jack, don't let them have an easy ride, try to trip them up and see if you can unnerve them. We don't want any wilting daisies in our mob."

"Recognition code?" asked Grant, his mind instantly switching back into operational mode.

"The usual one we use for the greenhorns," said Masterman. "They've been told to spot the most likely-looking spy in the place and make contact."

Was that a hint of devilment in Masterman's tone, thought Grant. "Okay. And then?"

"And then send them on their merry way and report directly to me later today. The usual place, the usual time."

"I'll get onto it now," said Grant, already reaching for the bundle of clothes laying by the foot of his bed.

"Oh, and Jack…"

"Yes, sir."

"Make sure you have a decent shower to get that young lady's perfume off you; I understand that Chanel No. 5 does tend to linger."

"Sir ?"

"Yes, Jack."

"You are a bastar—" A click sounded as the phone went dead in Grant's hand.

* * *

Jack Grant, over the years of his career in espionage, had met all manner of agents, traitors and targets in numerous diverse locations. Some he had been trying to recruit. Some had been nothing more than disposable informants and some had been targets who he knew would not survive the meeting. Back alleys, souks, cafe's, cars and even once on a Baltic fishing trawler.

But he was sure – no, he was certain – that none of them, past or present, would ever match the sheer grandeur of his current 'rendezvous' location where he was to meet the as-yet unidentified field agent, namely that of the exclusive Savoy Hotel in London.

Whoever the prospective addition to the Redaction Unit was, they must certainly be special to carry this type of weight, he reasoned. Perhaps a professor or an academic who was accustomed to such elegant surroundings, rather than the working men's pubs that most of the Redaction operatives were used to.

Maybe it was even one of the new breed of Special Forces troopers who Masterman was keen to get his hands on. They were from his old wartime regiment after all, and despite Grant's initial skepticism that they were merely army grunts and therefore not used to operating in an undercover role, he had trained with several of them at their base in Wales and found them to be tough, efficient operators. He had even made a few quid off them in wagers when he'd been talked into running through a CQB pistol shooting session in their killing house. It had been like taking sweets off a nipper.

He just hoped it wasn't some limp-wristed fop, fresh out of academia or it would be a quick interview.

He was absently pondering all this as he strolled leisurely along the Strand on that chilly morning, when he noticed the woman heading directly for him. It was going to be a race to see who could make it to the ornate entrance of the Savoy first.

She was attractive and fashionably dressed in a stylish winter coat of sunburnt orange, one that accentuated her slim figure. Wearing dark sunglasses to keep out the harsh winter sun, a demure headscarf covered long auburn hair, and all the while, she held her head firmly jutted downwards against the cold. The winter disguise meant that her age was both undetermined and mysterious.

As they both headed for the doors, it was almost inevitable that they were going to collide – they were on a direct course, and it was only when the woman stumbled that Grant reached out to stop her falling flat on her face. He was greeted with an *"Oh excusez-moi, monsieur, je Suis tellement désolé,"* as he lifted her upright, feeling the delicate weight of her against him. He began to smile in her direction, trying to make eye contact, but she was already gone, her head once more stuck in her phrase book and heading into the hotel itself and up the staircase straight ahead. He watched her go. It was a literal brief, but beautiful, encounter.

He shook off his daydreaming. The weeks of nothingness had dulled his senses, but he was operational now and he negotiated the revolving doors to the Savoy, nodding to the Commissioner as he did so. He sauntered through the foyer, past the elegant reception and headed up the stairs on his left towards the American Bar. If, the Savoy staff that day had been asked later to describe the visitor who had passed them just after noon, the majority of them would have struggled to even remember him. He had that kind of skill – he could disappear like a ghost.

The more alert members of the hotel's staff might have, between them, remembered a small, stocky man… maybe. Short white blond hair that hinted at his northern European ancestry. A good quality, single breasted suit in a somber grey and a conservatively discreet tie to match… possibly. Of the man's features, any answers would have been even vaguer. Few would remember the whole man. He was, to all intents and purposes, a social ghost.

The American Bar was famous throughout the world as being one of the most exclusive watering holes for the discerning traveler. He was greeted by the Maître d', a small-boned man in black tie and white waiter's jacket, and shown to a table at the far end of the room, seated by the rear corner window with his back to a main wall. He liked that, partly because of his training – it was easier to spot a threat and fight if need be – but more importantly, because he liked to watch the passersby hurrying through the streets of London. He wondered if there was something of the voyeur about him; an observer rather than being the observed.

The bar itself was elegantly furnished with bottle after bottle of world-renowned brand names and the light from the high chandeliers reflected onto the glass and chrome giving it an ethereal feel. The Bar Manager, Joe Gilmore, stood in perfect command of his fiefdom; in the corner, the piano player was musically discreet, keeping the volume to a minimum so as not to disrupt the conversations of the handful of guests who were dotted about the booths and tables.

He noticed that one of the waitresses was complaining, in whispered tones, that her boyfriend wanted to take her to the 'flicks' to see one of those awful spy-movies which had become so popular. "I mean really, does he think I'm interested in seeing a supposedly secret agent shooting people, and cavorting with young girls half his age on a beach somewhere? Really…"

Noticing the new customer, she detached herself from her complaining and hurried across to him. He ordered a whisky, an eighteen-year-old Speyside with water on the side. When it arrived, he took a sip, enjoying its warmth and sat back to immerse himself in his surroundings and to ponder on the nature of his life, his trade and how, even in his most delusional moments, he would never class himself as your typical looking Intelligence Officer. He was certainly nothing like the 'secret agents' from the current spate of popular fiction that he loathed.

He had, over the past few years since joining the Service, fast gained a reputation for getting difficult jobs done. Too 'rough-edged' and without the proper pedigree from the correct universities or military regiments for the mainstream of intelligence work, it didn't take long for his recruiters to move him sideways, into a unit that would appreciate his unique talents and temperament. He was a ball hammer to the rest of the Service's subtler ice picks.

And why Gorilla? Where did *that* title come from?

Some thought the title came from the disdain career intelligence officials had for people they thought of as working at the 'coalface'. A laborer, a knuckle dragger, a rock crusher, an ape to do the heavy lifting. Someone to come in and do the manual, dirty work, the jobs they deemed beneath themselves, but which was far more suited to some 'oik' from the army.

The choosing of his cryptonym – Gorilla – had in fact been a testament to his maverick attitude and disdain for the snobbery of the rest of the elite of his Service. One of the 'perks' of being assigned to the Redaction Unit was that officers were allowed to choose their own cryptonyms. It was a small, but important, concession for what was seen as the elite among the intelligence service.

One thing he'd noticed early on was that there were a lot of standard choices for codenames amongst his colleagues over the years. Lots of Greek Gods and mythological heroes – Apollo's, Achilles, Centurion and the like – which was all very bombastic and reeked a little of overcompensating in his opinion. Grant was determined not to fall into that trap.

He wanted a cryptonym that was unique to him and unobtrusive in the general scheme of things. Of course, in the great bureaucracy that was a secret government service he was given a rather bland code number – 2308 – which would forever be used on official communiqués. However, things had taken a fateful turn when some wag in Personnel had discovered that Grant's nickname during his time in the army had been 'Gorilla' and had scrawled it onto the buff folder that held his life story.

It had been a great joke and had caused much merriment among the rank and file. When he'd showed them what he could do, his reputation within 'Redaction' had grown quickly, and the sniggers and jibes had stopped and the name had, unofficially, stuck.

The Redaction Unit, or 'Redaction' as it was more commonly known, was housed safely away from SIS head office on Broadway, instead preferring the relative anonymity of Pimlico. It was based on the second floor of a rather drab office block on the Belgrave Road, with creaking floors, draughty windows, an intermittently working heating system and operated under the cover of a firm of business accountants, more specifically 'Simcock, Jones and Halifax – Business Accountants', a company which allegedly specialized in providing tax advice and services to a range of wealthy and private overseas clients.

In reality, the unit comprised six officers who had been selected for the types of assignments that Redaction specialized in, namely the rough trade of the intelligence war. They received daily cables from Masterman, the Redaction Unit Chief at Broadway, and operations were conducted at 'arm's length' from the more regular intelligence officers. The cover of having to visit overseas clients for the accountancy firm proved useful for explaining away the comings and goings of the staff on trips abroad.

And the man behind the title? Who was he? Who was Gorilla?

He was alone – that was for certain – but not a lonely man. He had precious little family left, and while his origins had been some of the humblest, he was a man who appreciated and enjoyed the culture, lifestyle, and experiences that a post-war nation had to offer. As an operative, he had been forged in the early days of the Cold War fighting hard in very hard places, and on operations he carried himself with a level of confidence which hinted that he was able to draw on hidden resources at a moment's notice.

His accent wavered somewhere between a rough South London twang and a Celtic burr, almost as if he had spent too much time in the company of men who had been born at opposing ends of the country. To match his voice, he had the look of someone who was naturally physically fit and hard-boned despite his short frame; a dock worker or a mechanic who was used to hard labor. He had an easy going manner with his contemporaries and looked senior officers straight in the eye when he had something to say, though whether this was to inform or challenge them depended on the moment at hand. And when he let his anger get the better of him, which could happen from time to time, his voice and the fiery glint in his eyes gave clues to the streets where he'd been raised.

Despite his acerbic manner and gruffness, he had little time for what he saw as the humorless and privately-educated elite batch of officers who ran the service. He owned little and wanted, at the moment, for nothing more. His modest apartment in Maida Vale, a constantly temperamental Ford Zephyr, and the occasional foray into the retinue of drinking clubs and bars that he knew of in Soho were all that he desired.

He took another sip of his whisky and was shaken from his day-dreaming by a delicate hand placed on his shoulder. Whoever it was must have already been in the bar to his right and blindsided him. Crafty! From his left came the soft voice of his field agent contact. "Darling, sorry I'm late, the traffic was a nightmare."

* * *

She was not a field agent to his eyes, at least not initially, but instead a flawless, doe-eyed beauty that he'd already bumped into only moments before at the hotel entrance. Coincidence? Certainly not – in this game, coincidence was something that only happened to normal people.

Tall, slim, with elfin-like features and dressed elegantly for her surroundings in a simple, above the knee dress of green, as was the current fashion, and complemented with a string of delicate pearls at her throat. The mystery of her age was now resolved and Grant guessed that she would be late twenties. A modern and confident woman of the 1960's and he knew the instant he set eyes on her that she was out of his league; even a blind man could recognize that, for God's sake. He was having the problem that he infrequently came across with very beautiful women – the feeling that he couldn't meet her gaze, lest he was dazzled by her.

Pull yourself together man, he berated himself. *You're a trained intelligence officer, you've bedded dozens of women and killed almost as many men; so why are you going weak at the knees just because a good looking young woman, a colleague in fact, has turned up for a predetermined meeting at—* She was saying something to him! What had he missed! Oh damn! "Er…sorry?"

She smiled, evidently amused at the confused series of emotions passing over his face. "I said, darling, that the weather is particularly cruel today. Very harsh… wouldn't you agree?"

The recognition phrase! "That's right," he said, regaining his composure. "The weather report says that today the Thames may…"

She smiled, a sweet smile. "…freeze?"

"That's right, freeze. I'm Jack, nice to meet you." No handshakes or any kind of formalities were used, lest the unwary fellow drinkers spotted a flaw in their cover.

"Nicole, Nicole Quayle, my pleasure Jack… or can I call you Gor—"

"Jack will do just fine. Drink?"

She had settled herself into the comfortable high-backed chair which engulfed her frame. She had been about to use his cryptonym. Where had she gotten that from? Masterman probably, he had a penchant for throwing mischief into an agent-to-agent contact meeting.

"Please, and seeing as we are in such fine surroundings and I don't suppose I'll be able to afford to visit again anytime soon, a glass of Tattinger would be lovely," she said.

Grant called over the waitress and ordered. As protocol demanded, they waited until the waitress returned and delivered the champagne before resuming their conversation. "Tattinger. Good choice."

She frowned. "Is it? I honestly know nothing about champagne; it was mentioned in a movie I saw recently and I thought it sounded about right for our surroundings. Cheers."

Probably the same kind of movie that the waitress's boyfriend was keen on watching, thought Grant. They raised their glasses to each other then took a sip, and with a flick of the eyes over their respective drinks, each gauged the other.

"I'm surprised you made it in here, without having another trip."

"Sorry about that. I spotted you from the very basic description they gave me and I needed to get a closer look to make sure it was you. It seemed the most unobtrusive way to do it," she said.

"You were good, very good indeed. So I understand you may well be joining our section."

"So I've been led to understand, although I assumed it was more of a temporary secondment," she said.

Grant frowned. "Most of the Redaction personnel are temporary. We don't tend to have a long shelf life. Bullets, bombs, and beatings do tend to ruin a good career. Does that discourage you?"

She shook her head, dislodging a fleck of dark hair. "Not so far, Jack, although it does sound a little bit intriguing."

"Good. Well, as I don't really know anything about you, how about you tell me a little about yourself? How did you come to be involved with the Service?"

She sipped at the champagne, took a breath and steadied herself. "Partly, I wanted to be of use to my country. I'm good with languages, observant and wanted a challenge..."

A young woman joining the spies – it was certainly that, thought Grant.

"...but mainly because of my parents I suppose."

"In what way?" he asked.

She put down her glass and delicately placed her hands across her lap. "Dad was an engineer who had been posted to Paris by his employers. When war broke out, he and Mum quickly returned home and joined up. Because of their French background, they were quickly recruited into the sabotage organization which had been set up, mainly to run an intelligence network. On his first parachute jump into France, Dad had a bad landing and seriously damaged his leg. It still isn't right, even now, all these years later. My mum took control of the network and helped nurse him until he was fit enough to take control of operations again."

"Where are they now, your parents?"

"Dad lives in Bath, he retired many years ago. I was born in 1937; during the war I was farmed out to my grandparents in Surrey whilst my parents were operating in France. In 1942, Mama had only been back in the country a matter of weeks after a brief return to London when she was captured by the Germans. Dad, not being one to take this lying down, mounted a rescue attempt. He and a *Maquis* team mounted a full-scale assault on the local Gestapo station. They killed an awful lot of Germans, but it was too late. Mama was already dead. We never knew for sure, but we assume she died during interrogation. So you see, I never really knew her. At best I have a few memories of her, some photos, but mainly only stories about her from Dad."

"I'm sorry," Grant mumbled. He was never adept at shallow emotions. He either felt it, or he didn't, without any middle ground.

She smiled a wonderful smile. "Don't be. I have a wonderful life, a great father, which, I'm sure, is not a very fashionable thing to say these days, and I have a fantastic job that I enjoy."

"Is that why you came to be working in intelligence, because of your father?"

"As I say, only partly. I entered the Service in a minor clerical role at Broadway, and was lucky enough to get promoted to an overseas posting. It was still clerical, just in a more exotic range of locations than rainy old London. Although I'll not deny that Dad put a good word for me with his former comrades."

"Like it, do you? All this cloak and dagger stuff?"

She smiled. "It has its moments. To be fair, I haven't had that much to do in the mystery department – oh, the odd dropping off of a package or drawing a line with a piece of chalk on a pavement, but certainly nothing in your league. It's been mainly filing, typing and taking the odd message when the Head of Station is out of the office."

In fact, this meeting was the most interesting thing she'd been asked to do for months. True, this was work and London, and while the Savoy could in no way be compared to the Souks of the Middle East or a meeting in the shadow of the Kremlin, it was still thrilling enough for a junior staffer like Nicole to treat it with reverence and respect. Besides, after her last posting, the relative normality of 1960's London was a positive step in the right direction.

"Any ideas why you're being attached to our unit?" he asked.

"My section chief made me aware of it yesterday. He said I was to report here at this time with a code phrase and was to meet an officer of Redaction and it would be taken from there – I assumed, to see if I was suitable."

"Did anybody give you any idea what it was about?"

She shook her head again. "Not really, it was hinted that it had some-thing to do with my posting to the Caribbean several years ago, but no real detail."

Okay, time to earn a crust, thought Grant. "Redaction. Do you know what we do in the unit?"

She shook her head, "Only canteen gossip, I'm afraid; whispers, rumors, something terribly secret, obviously, which is why you're farmed out to an office in Pimlico. Whatever it is, it seems to be on the dangerous side. That's what the rumor mill says."

He took a sip of the Speyside and leaned forward. "We operate inde-pendently from the mainstream of SIS operations, although we always have full access to their resources, which annoys the hell out of them, I'm glad to say. We redact, we edit, we delete, and we cut."

"Redact what? Delete what?" she asked, looking confused.

"Whatever is required of us. Rogue agents, traitors, and extremists all fall within our remit. We take the fight back to the enemy and hit him when he's not expecting it. Then we melt back into the under-ground and disappear. That's what Redaction is."

"It doesn't seem very British. A bit below the belt, not cricket or playing by the rules," she said.

Grant pulled a grin. "That's what makes the Redaction Unit so effective. The majority of other intelligence services have no idea that SIS has this capability or that the unit actually exists. They think that good old fashioned MI-6 is all monocle-wearing gentlemen spies who work to the rules of fair play and honor."

Of course, she thought, when he presented it like that, it made perfect sense. Who would suspect the good old Brits of running a secret team that handled the rough stuff? The Americans, certainly, the French well you only had to look at the papers to see the things they were doing in Algeria, but the British. Never!

Grant's face grew serious and his manner stiff. "Can I ask you a question?"

"Of course."

"If it was a choice between you and the enemy, could you kill in cold blood?"

She paused; the directness of the question momentarily throwing her. Could she do that extreme act? She wondered what her father would say to this man and if he'd ever had to shoot a man down in cold blood during the War. Unsure of herself, she decided to err on the side of caution and answer honestly. "The truth is Jack; I have no idea. Could I do it – certainly. But would I? I guess until it happens, no one knows for sure. I'm sorry, that's not the expected answer, but I think it's best to tell the truth."

He raised an eyebrow. The answer seemed to make his mind up for him. "Do you always tell the truth?" he said.

"Only about the important things," she answered. "Do you have any idea what they want me for?"

"No. I haven't been briefed on that, at least not yet, but can I be honest with *you* and give you some friendly advice?"

She nodded and waited for him to speak.

"You're not cut out for Redaction, either physically or mentally."

She looked at him wide eyed, mouth agog.

"I'm sorry if that sounds harsh Nicole. You're a nice person and chances are you lack the cunning that one of our operators needs to infiltrate an enemy's rank and kill him. I think it's better this way; I might have just saved your life."

It was then that it happened. She fleetingly transformed from a beautiful woman into a snarling Medusa as she hit him with a steely-eyed stare that pierced into his skull. Their eyes locked and then it was gone, but the cold stare remained, albeit more subdued. She seemed to have decided on her plan of attack. He drained his glass and made a motion for the bill.

"So that's it?" she said.

He nodded. "I'm going to inform my boss that you should remain in your present position and that in my opinion, you don't have enough field experience for our unit."

The waitress arrived with a silver saucer containing a discreetly folded bill. He opened it, raised an eyebrow at the amount and then she saw him reach inside his jacket pocket, noted the confused look, and watched him as his hand transferred to the other side pocket, then trouser pockets, before he began the whole process again, patting himself down. Nicole thought that it really was quite amusing to watch, made even more so because the waitress was now raising her eyebrows at her customer's evident discomfort before she discreetly made herself scarce. Enough was enough, time to put him out of his misery. *Here goes,* she thought. "Do you like Maida Vale? Not too quiet for you?"

Now he was checking under the table, his face growing red. "Huh?"

"And the Grant name. Does that give a clue to some Scottish Heritage? Do I detect a slight Celtic twang hidden beneath your South London accent? It's buried, but it's definitely there."

"How do you know my—"

"What about the girl in the picture? She's very pretty, who is she? Wife, girlfriend, sister? It seems to have been taken in Germany. That's the Brandenburg Gate in the background isn't it?"

He glared at Nicole. She was holding up a bruised and battered black wallet between her thumb and forefinger. *His* black wallet! She removed several notes before tossing it onto the table dismissively.

"Waitress," she called.

The girl reappeared, "Yes, ma'am."

Nicole handed her the notes on the silver saucer. "Keep the change, thank you."

Grant, fuming, gathered up his wallet and checked through the contents. Satisfied, he placed it back in his inside pocket. He sat back in his chair and considered the young woman in front of him. "It was when you fell wasn't it? When I caught you at the front of the hotel?"

"Of course it was. It's something I've always been very good at; nimble fingers you see. I was a natural on the burglary course for new intakes. But then again I'd had a good teacher – I'm not my father's daughter for nothing," said Nicole coolly.

Her eyes remained locked on his face. Was there a begrudging sense of respect behind the man's glower? She leaned forward to make her point, and when another lock of hair fell forward across her face she brusquely brushed it away. "You see, I knew you'd take one look at me and dismiss me straight away. Pretty face, but only useful for answering the phone or for filling a senior officer's bed on a cold Friday night. Well, I can put your mind at rest – that's not me. Never has been and never will be. And if you want cunning and streetwise, I'm pretty sure I could run deceptive rings around you any day of the week."

"Because you think you're a field agent?"

"No, because I'm a woman." She thought she may have gone too far, made too much of a point and dented his pride. So she was surprised and not a little pleased when he beamed a wonderful glowing smile at her. *He should smile more often,* she thought. *He has such a good smile.*

"Well, Miss Nicole. I think we should maybe have another drink and begin again. What do you think? I'll start; my good friends call me Gorilla."

* * *

They spoke for another thirty minutes until the conversation had come to a natural conclusion. In truth the little stunt she had pulled had told him far more about her than a whole series of interviews ever could. Grant busied himself swirling his whisky in his glass, Nicole pretended to find the fellow drinkers in the bar interesting. Luckily, none of them had seemed to notice the tension. Either that or they were all too polite to say anything.

"So what about you," she asked, determined to break the hiatus. "What makes you suitable for the Redaction Unit?"

He thought about it for a moment before he answered. "I have a certain set of skills that are always useful to the top people in this business and unfortunately or not, there's always someone willing to use it."

"And the work name 'Gorilla' where did that come from?" she asked innocently enough.

He took a sip of his Speyside. "That was from years ago. A nickname that stuck."

Nicole looked confused by his irritatingly obtuse answers. Damn him, he could be so frustrating. He smiled, sensing her impatience with him. "Sorry, Miss Nicole, I don't do war stories. You'll have to look elsewhere."

* * *

An hour later, Jack Grant was making his way to his meeting with Masterman. It was their usual meeting place in any type of weather – rain, snow, sleet or baking sun – it mattered not.

Restaurants and pubs were out due to either the noise, or the risk of being overheard by third parties, and there was no chance that Grant or any of the remaining team from his unit would be allowed within a mile of head office. In the Redaction Unit, everything was kept at arm's length, deniable, out of sight and out of mind until they were needed.

It was on the south side of Westminster Bridge, at the base of the steps that led onto Albert Embankment where Grant would meet with his boss. Big Ben glared down at them, stoically, from across the river.

Stephen Masterman, retired Colonel of Special Forces and now
Head of the Redaction Unit for the British Secret Service, stood with
his hands pushed deep into his trench coat. It had been several weeks
since Grant had seen him last. He was tall, broad, blond and uncom-
promising, but was not without humor and affection for those he commanded. As an officer, it was easy to see why men would follow him
into battle and help him storm the gates of hell if he so commanded.
Jack Grant had been his shadow in some very dangerous situations on
more than one occasion.

"Well, you certainly caught a tan in Vientiane. Got some color in
your cheeks, at least," said Masterman.

"You're joking, aren't you? I spent the first few weeks peeling off
burnt skin! I looked like a bloody lobster."

Masterman laughed. "Well, regardless of your ruddy complexion, I
have been asked to pass on to you, congratulations and give you a pat
on the back for a job well done. The Chief was very impressed."

"Was he impressed enough for a pay-rise?" chanced Grant.

A wry grin from the taller man. "Unfortunately not, but I do have
something else for you, something of great importance. A job has come
up."

"Okay. Sounds good," said Grant, eager to hear more.

"Let's walk." They walked at Masterman's pace, with Grant, as
usual, keeping up regardless of his size. The rain had come in from
the West replacing the frosty start to the day and both men ducked
their heads so as to keep the worst of it from their faces. Their conversation only halted when 'civilians', as Masterman insisted on calling
the general public, came too near. "How're your language skills these
days?" enquired Masterman.

"Fine, a little rusty, but nothing a quick brush up wouldn't fix."

"Some French, bit of Spanish; that's right isn't it. German? Used it
much recently?"

A pause from Grant, then, "No. Not recently. Probably the last time
was Berlin."

The word hung like a shroud over the duo. Berlin was their mutual scab, one they liked to pick at in each other's company. It hurt, but they couldn't resist the urge to keep inflicting pain upon each other with its memory. "Ah," said Masterman. "Berlin... So what did you think of the girl?"

"What girl?"

Masterman snuck a hostile glance at his smaller companion. "Which one do you think? Your contact at the Savoy; did it go according to plan?"

Grant shrugged. "She seemed to know what she was talking about. Let's put it this way, she didn't make any fatal blunders. She kept it discreet which is always a good sign."

"But you liked her?"

"Are you trying to set me up on a date or something? She looks like she's still at school," growled Grant.

The big man stopped dead in his tracks, turned and barred Grant's way so that he couldn't continue with his march along the Embankment. The Palace of Westminster was framed in the background of Masterman's bulk. "Surely that's the point of people in our trade Jack; I mean you're a case in point, aren't you. A wolf in sheep's clothing. Don't let that shy office worker act fool you, she's a tough nut. Has to be to even get a foot in the door in our grimy little organization... and I heard that she's not too shabby at lifting a wallet, either."

"Very funny. So what's the operation, and why the need to bring regular officers in?"

They were on the move again, at a quicker pace this time. Masterman, as was his way, would often start out wide in his descriptions before coming into the fine detail at the end. "It's something a bit unusual. We have information that the CIA has put together an operation to eliminate a Soviet intelligence network spread across Europe. When I say eliminate, I mean eliminate in the most lethal sense, not just arresting them and giving them a smack on the wrist."

"So the Yanks want blood. What's that to us? Let them get on with it."

"Ah, well, these things do have a tendency to get rather complicated very fast, especially when the CIA get their dander up and start clomping around in hobnail boots. It seems the Americans want to give the Russians a taste of their own medicine."

Grant smiled. "And how do you know about that, sir?"

The steely eyed glare from Masterman flashed again, and then softened. He and Grant went back a long way; they'd shared too many bad times to try to pull the wool over each other's eyes. If in doubt, keep it vague. "Oh, you know the usual, gossip at the monthly Intelligence liaison meetings – the powwows we call them – but with some signals intercepts and the like for a bit of flavor."

Grant wasn't fooled for a moment. The CIA wasn't in the habit of giving away a little gem of intelligence like that, even to one of their closest allies. That could only have come from a human source. Their pace had steadied again and Grant was sure they were getting close to the nub. "Okay, so I'll ask again, what's that to us? The Americans want to start blotting out Soviet agents, of whatever description; doesn't that benefit us in the long run?"

They had turned onto Lambeth Bridge, their pace increasing, and they pushed against the cross winds that were blasting off the Thames.

Masterman turned his head sideways and shouted down at the little man against the noise of the gale. "Well, that's the problem Jack. Things aren't always what they seem. They're not the Russians' agents – never have been in truth. They're *our* agents, double agents in point of fact. They cast out a net, see what the Soviets and their ilk are interested in; we provide them with sanitized intelligence and use them to pass it on, spread disinformation and get them to perform sleight of hand tricks to keep the Russians guessing."

"And how did the Yankees get the names of these doubles? What is there; a leak on our side?"

Masterman shrugged. "Who knows? The Agency has been playing its cards close to its chest over recent months and has been cutting our service out of the loop. I don't think they've forgiven us for Philby yet. What we do know for sure, is that this time the Agency is going for assassination rather than incarceration. They're not using Agency staffers, but apparently contract agents who they've used before. Mercenaries. They're sending a message, pure and simple, straight into the heart of the KGB."

"So we can't be seen to upset the Americans by telling them to bugger off," said Grant.

Masterman nodded. "Exactly. We have to bite our tongue. The harsh reality is that we're the ones with the intelligence begging bowls at the moment, and the Americans are the ones running the officers' mess. We need them more than they need us at the moment."

"So we have to toe the line, is that what you're saying?"

"Sometimes we have to disrupt the games of our allies in order to save them from themselves," declared Masterman.

"What, by sabotaging their operations?"

"Precisely. It's a game; they lie to us, and we fool them. That's the way it works. As long as we come out of it with the better portion of the deal, we're quite happy to carry on with the deception," said Masterman, who had spent his career frustrating both friend and foe.

Grant was determined not to let his boss off the hook that easily. "And we can't move these agents; put a security screen around them? Protect them in some way?"

Masterman shook his head. "The word from the top is a resounding 'No'. The Americans and their contractors would smell a rat straight away, as would the Russians, and the word from the Chief is that this double agent network is in no way to be compromised any more than it already has been. The best defense at the moment is total ignorance. That way, they will carry on as if everything is normal. Besides the removal of a few mercenaries is very, very minor compared to the integrity of a long established intelligence network."

"Which is where I come in?" asked Grant.

Masterman nodded as they moved over the base of the bridge and headed towards Westminster Abbey. "We want the problem of these American contractors to be quietly removed, with little or no fuss. By that time, the Americans will have lost all enthusiasm for revenge and will simply put it down to experience... that's the hope anyway."

"How conscious is this double agent network that they're being targeted?" said Grant.

"Not at all. Even more worrying is that I fear we may already have to play catch up rather quickly. There have been reports that two individuals who fit the profiles of the suspected KGB agents on the list were killed last week. One was blown up by a rocket propelled grenade, and the other was garroted."

"So whoever these contractors are, they're already at work."

"It would seem so, and what we don't want is for the rest of the network to follow."

"Um... difficult start point," Grant mused.

"All is not lost; we do have several aces up our sleeve which can help you in your quest. We have a couple of rumblings of this hit-team's previous work history for the Americans, just rumors, but even rumors generally have a lot of truth in them, which may assist."

"What kind of rumors?"

Masterman waved a hand, as if the details at this juncture didn't matter. "Oh, stuff in the Caribbean, one or two things in Africa, as well as the possibility of a couple of freelance jobs for some criminal organizations on the continent. As for this particular operation, they think it's an easy contract, soft targets, easy pickings, minimal risk. That will be their downfall, as they won't be expecting you to sneak up behind them and clip their wings!"

"What's the other ace?" asked Grant.

"Ah yes, well, we think we may have a visual I.D. on them."

Grant turned and looked at Masterman. "Really? What, photographs?"

"Unfortunately, no. We have a spotter, one of our people who was stationed in the Caribbean and saw our two possible suspects meeting with the Americans in the Dominican Republic shortly after Trujillo caught a couple of bullets to his head. They fit the rather limited picture we have of them: one tall and swarthy, the other short and stocky with a bad toupee and a scar."

"That's it? Not much. Frankly, it describes half the mercenaries in Africa," said Grant.

Masterman smiled a smile which said, 'Well then, you're going to have to make the best of a bad job, old boy'.

"Okay. I'll need to question your spotter. When can I meet him?"

Masterman stopped and looked up at the spire of the Abbey. "Him, Jack ? Who said anything about it being a him? Besides, you've already met *her*."

"What…"

Masterman, when he looked down at the other man, was smiling. "That young lady who you met today. She was our officer in the Caribbean and what's more, it's been decided that she'll be going with you on this operation to confirm identification."

* * *

They had decided to walk along and were sat on a bench watching the boats sail upriver. Masterman had opened up his umbrella and was humming a little Mozart tune softly.

"You can't be serious, Colonel. She'd be a liability; I mean, has she even been on operations, let alone something like this?" said Grant, his voice deepening with anger.

"Calm down, Jack," said Masterman playfully.

"I am calm!"

"Your volume level says different. Besides, you only ever call me 'Colonel' when you're angry," Masterman teased.

Grant let out a sigh and continued to stare at his rain spattered shoes. He wished he'd stayed in bed after all.

"Look, she won't be there pulling the trigger with you. We're not stupid. But she has seen these two Europeans, something that not many people have, it seems, and we need a confirmed ID before we can sanction the killing. Apart from anything else, she can be your eyes and ears in places where you can't go. Good for basic surveillance duties, carrying out reconnaissance, passing messages... even a bit of burglary. Think about it," said Masterman.

Grant conceded that in the predominantly male world of Cold War espionage, a female passes relatively unnoticed: unless she's serving drinks or you want to sleep with her.

"As every part of this operation is to be kept at arm's length away from our stations in Europe, she'll be your cut-out back to us. Besides, I can think of worse ways to earn a living; travelling around Europe with a pretty girl in tow to keep you company," laughed Masterman.

He knew better than to argue against Masterman. When you're out on the operation certainly, really, there's not much they can do about it then. But at the early planning stage he had learned that it was best to have the top floor set the rules. "So what's the next step?" he asked.

"There's an intelligence briefing pack waiting for you back at the Pimlico office. It has everything you need to know about what we have so far. I suggest you get yourself over there double quick and start getting acquainted with the state of play before tomorrow."

"Why, what's tomorrow?"

"There is a meeting scheduled after lunch where you get to meet the Constellation Network controller and the rest of your team. So it's back to work for you," said Masterman.

The rain was getting heavier, the sky darker and Grant sensed that the briefing was coming to an end. Masterman stood up and they made their way at a brisk pace, pausing to look over at the Thames as it flowed like grey steel before them. "As you'll be the Operational Field Controller on this one, I want a blueprint and a shopping list from you as soon as possible. I need your eyes on this one, Jack, your keen mind."

In Redaction parlance a 'blueprint' was an operational execution plan and a 'shopping list' was the nefarious tools he would need to carry out the killings.

The two men separated without another word, and Masterman began the long walk back to Broadway. He enjoyed the walk around Westminster, through the seat of the British political classes, it helped clear his mind, but today he couldn't help but wonder if the mission he had given to one of his best men was one that he would ever be able to return from.

Chapter Six

The morning had not started well for Willem De Veen. He had risen late, unusual for him, but the lingering remnants of a winter cold he'd been trying to shake off was still sapping his strength.

He had dressed quickly, kissed his family goodbye and grabbed his heavy briefcase before stumbling from their apartment. His day ahead was busy. Not only his work at the bank, dealing with new clients and filing the paperwork at the accounts section, but today he was tasked with leaving a message at a discreet location which was a part of his secret work.

He didn't regard himself as a spy, merely as a conduit in the battle against a greater foe. He had started his career for the British during the war, when he'd been recruited to set up a network in occupied Holland. He'd been dropped in blind by Lysander and was lucky to escape when he discovered that the German intelligence apparatus had effectively gained control of the Dutch resistance. Willem had managed to smuggle himself out of the country and received a medal for his trouble, spending the remainder of the war working as an interrogator for military intelligence, interviewing captured prisoners of war.

To his chagrin, he'd been the spy that never was.

At the end of the war, he returned to his native Holland and began to carve a career in the banking industry; first for a Dutch commercial bank and later, after being headhunted, he relocated to Zurich to work in the established firm of the AGIG Banking House. He'd married his secretary, Ingrid, and they now had a wonderful daughter he doted on. His life was complete and he was happy.

Then one day, several years ago, he'd been approached for a meeting at one of Zurich's finest restaurants by what he thought was a new client, looking to invest some money. The client had turned out to be a funny little chubby fellow, who called himself 'Porter' and was very keen for Mr. De Veen to take up a rather well paid 'consultancy contract' with his former wartime comrades.

"But what would you want me to consult *on*, Mr. Porter?" he had asked in confusion.

The chubby fellow had dabbed at the corners of his mouth with his napkin, wiping away the excesses of the trout he'd devoured for lunch. "How's about we call it wrong footing the red's over the border, working a little mischief in their general direction. How does that grab you?"

De Veen had almost choked with laughter. "It almost sounds as if you want me to get involved in a little cloak and dagger work."

The chubby man, Porter, had been effusive to the extreme. "No buggering about Willem, that's *exactly* what I want you to do. I want you to step up and return to the role you sadly missed out on during the war. You're keen for it, I can tell by the crafty look in your eye – or are you happy just whiling away your days, salting money away for Swiss millionaires?"

By the end of the luncheon, Willem had accepted the enigmatic Porter's proposal. He had thrived over the years, oh, how he'd thrived, and it had all been so simple to set up. A recommendation from another supposed agent doubling for the British, a little flirting with the Russians and he'd been whisked away for the weekend for several KGB intelligence officers to have a look at him. Evidently they liked what they found – a willing agent, with access to Swiss banking and IMF liaison – because by the end of the following month he'd been 'in play', as Porter liked to say.

He was a double for the British, passing all kinds of doctored material to his KGB contacts in the hope that they believed him. At any moment in those first few months, he'd expected to be exposed. He'd worried over what the retribution from the Russians would be; a shot to the back of the neck, or poison in his drink? The thought made him shudder and Willem had to admit to himself, there were more than a few nights when he'd barely slept. Such is the stress of the spy.

But the bullet and the cyanide never came. In fact, it was quite the reverse. The spy work had started to take on a life of its own, quite distinct from his normal life. He separated them quite comfortably into various boxes; Box One was home and family and work, Box Two was the British, and Box Three was the KGB facade.

Willem glanced at his watch as he hurried down the street. 7.45 am. *Dammit, I'm going to be late,* he thought, picking up his pace. He'd missed the last tram and decided to try to find a taxi along his usual route, but with nothing on the street he decided to continue on foot. He didn't notice the large delivery wagon ambling distantly in the background, slowly crawling along. Nor did he notice the tall figure who was less than ten yards behind him. Why should he? The plans he had for the day were repeating in his mind as he approached the curb to cross the road.

Willem felt a push, although in those last few seconds if he'd had time to correct himself, he would have considered it more of a blast – a force impacting between his shoulder blades and throwing him forward onto the road. His briefcase skittered across the cobblestones and he landed on his knees. One trouser leg was torn and his spectacles had gotten dislodged and balanced precariously on the end of his nose.

He was about to turn and give whoever had jostled him a piece of his mind, when he heard the roar, the gunning of a motor and the squeal of the tires as an engine reached its peak.

Willem had just enough time to move his eyes to the left, before the impact of the truck's bumper smashed directly into the side of his skull. He experienced a dull pain before his body was dragged under the vehicle's heavy wheels. In a haze of semi-consciousness, it felt as if

Willem was being thrown around inside a huge washing machine, his body bouncing off the cobblestones and being ripped, then crushed by the heavy rubber tires and undercarriage of the truck.

On the far side of the street, the only witness to the accident was the octogenarian Alberto Fricke, the tobacconist, who was completing his morning routine of stocking shelves and straightening packets. He was up on his rickety stepladder when he heard the roar of a heavy engine and the squeal of tires.

He wasn't meant to be working that morning, it was supposed to be his rest day, but his angry wife had informed him she was visiting friends and as for his lazy great lump of a son... so it was work for Herr Fricke instead of what he should have been doing; enjoying the newspapers over a cafe crème in his favorite chair.

It was the dull thud which made him look. He twisted his head around in time to see the man being dragged under the delivery truck like a rag-doll. Later, Fricke would swear that he'd heard the man's bones, crunching and grinding beneath the wheels of the vehicle.

Herr Fricke flung himself down from his step ladder, no easy feat at his age, and hurried to the shop window to get a better look. He peered through the roller blind which would remain closed until opening time. The truck had stopped twenty feet further on, and the man, the poor wretched man lying on the street was spread-eagled, his limbs placed at unnatural angles.

Oh my God, an accident, a terrible accident, thought Fricke.

Then something strange happened. Actually, two strange things happened as he would later tell the police. The truck crunched its gears into reverse and accelerated back at high speed, once more trampling over the body. This time there was no crunching of bones, merely a squelching and popping noise as the man's head and internal organs collapsed, and then just as quickly, the truck moved off again, driving over the body for a third time before racing off down the street. The body looked like a scarecrow which had its stuffing removed, then been coated in red paint.

With a hand clutched to his mouth in horror, Fricke noticed the second strange event. A man was standing watching the events. A single man – why hadn't he noticed this man before? He was tall, dark of complexion, and with a trilby hat pulled down to cover his face. Was that a hint of grey streaks at his temples, creating two little horns above his ears?

The man had watched the whole thing, hadn't moved in fact, from the one spot. He'd remained standing on the pavement, exactly where the dead man had fallen onto the road… Herr Fricke's eyes widened in horror. Had this man… had he *pushed* the poor man into the truck's path! No, no surely not! This was Zurich after all, not some crime-ridden backstreet in Berlin or Paris.

The man in the trilby hat appeared to examine the corpse from a distance, before he casually turned and walked away, never once looking back.

Unknown to Herr Fricke, the first legitimate agent of the Constellation network, *ORION*, had been officially terminated.

Chapter Seven

The meeting between the operational team that made up MACE and the controller of the Constellation network took place in 'The Eyrie'. It was a small, two-roomed office, positioned at the top of one of the many obscure buildings behind Whitehall, which the Secret Intelligence Service maintained for discreet meetings between its officers.

A visit to Headquarters at Broadway would have been unthinkable. Redaction Unit members were always briefed and debriefed at an off-site secure location, and because of the nature of their work they seemed to have acquired a reputation for 'worrying' the regular officers.

So, Operation MACE; a mace like a weapon, hard and blunt and heavy. A weight to crush an enemy! It was what the Redaction Unit did best.

It was decided that the teams would be split into two. First, there was the 'Fire-Team', with Jack Grant as the Field Controller on the ground who, through experience and seniority, would have overall command. He would answer directly to Masterman at Redaction in Pimlico. Nicole Quayle would be the spotter used to ID the enemy targets, as well as providing surveillance and logistics support to Grant.

The second team would be the 'Trackers', who would be led by a young officer who'd only been introduced to them that very morning, although within the corridors of the Service he had an outstanding reputation, one that belied his youthful looks.

Toby Burrows resembled an undergraduate at one of the better universities. Tall, thin, impossibly young, tousled hair, bespectacled, and with a sense of dress that indicated he regarded his wardrobe requirements as something of a chore, rather than a necessity.

He was pleasant but aloof to his colleagues and regarded the vital meetings senior officers craved on a daily basis to be a distraction from the real work which was the lifeblood to him; that of catching spies.

His private life was a mystery to the others in the Service, and yet if they had scratched the surface they would have discovered he had a pretty wife, two adorable children and lived a contented life in Islington. His reputation had been earned in the Service's new counter-intelligence section, where he had a knack for tracking down enemy agents and playing them back against the enemy.

His nickname, the 'Burrower', fit him well. While other spies and agents favored the silenced pistol, high-tech surveillance equipment and all manner of bizarre gadgets, the 'Burrower's' Cold War weapons were his desk-bound secure telephone lines, access to the SIS Registry files and a wide range of contacts in friendly intelligence and police forces across the globe. His tenacity, a nose for a lead, and the ability to pull together any number of fragmented pieces of intelligence into one tangible picture, made him a much sought after counter-intelligence officer within SIS. While Grant and Nicole would be the physical part of Operation MACE, Toby and his team of assistants would undoubtedly be the brains.

They settled themselves into 'The Eyrie'. The room was laid out like a classroom, with Masterman and Porter sharing the main desk at the head of the room and Grant, Nicole and Burrows each at an individual desk. While Masterman was the team's direct controller, it was Porter who took the center stage chair and ran the briefing. Masterman leaned back in his own chair and gazed out at the rain covering all of Whitehall. "Are we all up to date on the background to the case?" asked Porter, opening the proceedings.

They were. They had had the files in the morning and had spent the past few hours reading and re-reading the background. A day with the files would have been better, but they were limited on time, so a morning would have to do.

"Well, I think we should start with Nicole's account of the two suspected CIA men. How did you come to I.D. our two lovelies... where was it again... the Caribbean? Why don't you talk us through it in detail, Nicole, tell us exactly how it happened," said Porter.

* * *

It is Ciudad Trujillo, Dominican Republic. It is night, it is hot and there is an air of unreality about the proceedings. By the end of the day the news that President Trujillo has been assassinated on a quiet country road will reach the rest of the world. El Benefactor has ridden the tiger and now the tiger has chosen to eat him whole it seems.

Nicole is having a drink at the Hotel Rafael, the local watering hole where all the Europeans hang out. Her host is Clive, the Deputy Head of Station. Clive is thin and tired and forty. Recently divorced, he has done his best to flirt, but as most Englishmen of a certain breed tend to, he is making a hash of being both seductive and romantic and is instead coming over as a lecher.

She had been invited for "drinks so that we can relax and perhaps have an informal chat about station business," which Nicole deciphers as being code for Clive wanting to seduce her. She fears Clive will be disappointed and knowing Clive's reputation, she will be in his bad books for the rest of her tour.

The Rafael's bar is pleasantly full with a mixture of journalists, local business impresarios loyal to the Trujillo government, and a hotchpotch of Latin American elite. Europeans are in the minority here. Everyone is trying their best to be relaxed and cultured, but the signs of tension around their eyes says otherwise. News is coming in regarding gunfire in various parts of the city. Clive's attempts at illuminating conversation are starting to run out of steam, and Nicole is doing her best to appear interested and courteous. She toys with her rum and in another fifteen minutes she will feign a migraine and ask if Clive can arrange for a car to take her back to her apartment.

Five minutes in, several sips of rum and a couple of Clive's clichés later, the moment happens, a man enters the bar. Whoever he is, he walks with a smooth, gliding motion and the confidence of an executive car salesman. He is tall and broad, his suit jacket draped lazily over one arm, and he reminds Nicole of a Roman General officiating at his own Triumph. His gaze wanders over the patrons of the bar as he strides toward a table in the corner. His eyes lock temporarily on to Clive's and the two conduct a covert nod of recognition before the Roman General turns his back on them and nurses his scotch.

"A friend of yours Clive?" asks Nicole.

For once Clive is reticent to part with information, and instead his response is clipped and scarce on detail. "Let's just say professional acquaintance, rather than a friend. He's the Cousin's man over here, sort of my opposite number. I see him at the monthly liaison meetings. He's in charge of the Americans ops in the region," replied Clive, trying not very successfully to hide his pang of jealousy at Nicole's interest in the other spy.

"Well, he seems very sure of himself," observed Nicole.

"Aren't all Americans like that? Name of Tanner. Excuse me for a moment; I'd better just chew the fat." And so Clive disentangles himself from his chair and heads over to the American.

The American by contrast, is less than pleased to be approached in a bar by a British intelligence officer, no matter how casual or innocent it might seem, but to his credit he display's none of this irritation overtly. Instead, he offers a glad hand to Clive and a friendly slap on the back before the two men incline heads towards one another and conduct a whispered conversation. The quiet dialogue continues for several minutes more, in fact long enough for Nicole to finish her drink and ready her purse to leave Clive and his American friend to it, when two obvious Europeans enter and head directly towards where the American is standing. One is tall and spare and distinguished the other squat like a bullet with a scar on his cheek.

Tanner turns to his guests, and addresses them directly. Then, Nicole notes, he turns to Clive and says something directly to him. Nicole imagines that it is the equivalent of a short, sharp directive to go forth and multiply. Whatever was said, Clive returns to his table red-faced at the American's comment.

"What was all that about?" asks Nicole.

"Tanner is a bloody arse, that's what. Meeting with a couple of his privateers," replies Clive, the florid color slowly disappearing from his cheeks.

"Privateers? Do you mean pirates, Clive?"

"Don't be so silly. Covert ops people, mercenaries, cutthroats probably. You know how the Americans are fond of using all kinds of scum like that."

"I didn't to be honest. What are they doing here?"

Clive laughs at her naivety. "Oh the Yanks are up to all kinds of mischief in the Caribbean. Stay around here long enough and you'll soon find that out. Wouldn't surprise me if they have a big op going on as we speak; and when you start to involve outside killers, well that usually means that it's regime change time. Still, none of our business is it, another drink?"

* * *

"And then what did the CIA man do?" asked Porter.

Nicole stared at him for a moment before she responded. She took a second to recall that she was no longer in the heat of the Caribbean, but instead returned to the drizzle of her present daily life. "They huddled in the corner for about twenty minutes talking, the American patted the taller man on the shoulder several times as if he was congratulating him, and then both parties went their separate ways."

"So why couldn't this Deputy Head of Station ID them? Why only you?" Burrows questioned, holding a pencil at the ready to scribble down any intelligence.

"He did, we both did. To be honest, at the time we didn't think much about it. We assumed they were CIA agents, which it seems they were, and wrote it up in the Operations Diary when we returned to base."

"You had no camera with you?" asked Grant, flicking through his file.

Nicole shook her head. "No, we were out having a drink, letting off some steam. It was only later when we found out that these two fitted the description of CIA contract agents on several possible murders."

"So how come Clive isn't sitting here and you are?" Porter asked.

Nicole paused, looked out of the window and took a deep breath. "Clive shot himself six weeks later. It seems his divorce had hit him harder than he liked to admit. He wasn't a bad man, just lonely."

Porter nodded, accepting the reality. "So you're the only living witness from our side that we know of. And now, after all this time you're sure you could recognize them?"

She nodded. "Believe me. They do tend to stick in the mind. When I see them, I'll know them."

"What happened after that? Any further sightings?" Burrows queried, writing furiously.

"Of the two mercenaries or whatever they are, no. The rest as they say is history. The killing of Trujillo took the whole of the country into hell. Mass arrests by the *Cascos Blancos*, the secret police, of anyone even suspected of involvement in the assassination. Widespread torture at La Cuarenta prison, death squads, and massacres, you name it. It's all in the station's files."

"And you. What happened to you?" Grant questioned.

Nicole shrugged. "All non-essential personnel were told to leave. I was out of the country by the end of the week and on a flight back to London. I was reassigned the very next day."

There was a pause in the flow of the conversation as the MACE team digested Nicole's story. The only sound was the patter of rain on the window and the imperceptible scribbling of pens on paper as notes were made.

It was Jack Grant who broke the silence. "I do have one question. These other agents – Soviet admittedly – what do we do about them?"

Porter grimaced. "We do nothing. It's just tough luck, Jack, they're on their own. Our priority is Constellation and its agents. If we're lucky, this CIA-backed action team will bugger up somewhere along the line, whether it's our agents or, if there is such a thing, innocent Soviet spies! If it slows them down so much the better, that way you'll be there to mop them up while they're looking the other way."

"And we definitely can't move our people, or throw a protective cordon around them? Or at the very least, alert them?" pushed Grant.

Porter sank into a Buddha-like pose. When his head rose, his face was grave. "No, no movement, no security, nothing out of the ordinary. Understood?"

"Sorry, Jack, you're it, I'm afraid. Keep it low key, and if at all possible, keep contact with the Constellation agents to a minimum," said Masterman.

"There's no chance of having a quiet word in the Americans' ears? 'Hey lads you're buggering about with our agents and would you please mind backing off'?" Grant pressed.

Porter shook his head. "The word from the top is that the Chief wants this situation to go away. He wants the Americans to be none the wiser about who these agents are actually working for, he wants this assassination operation dismantled by putting a fucking bullet in their heads, and finally, he wants the status quo to remain in place regarding the relationship with the American Service."

* * *

The rain had eased as Masterman and Grant walked back towards Westminster Bridge, headed for the Embankment. Pretty girls in short dresses were walking home with their fiancés, men in bowler hats had finished their day in the corridors of power, and buses took workers home to enjoy the weekend.

"So what's our license like for this?" Grant asked.

"The same as normal. You can have whatever you need; within rea-son, of course," replied Masterman. "Do whatever you need to get the job done. We'll back you to the hilt, with the caveat that if you get cor-nered, you better fucking shoot your way out or you're on your own."

"Thanks."

"Look, Jack, it's a difficult job. That's why it was given to you. I've got enough to worry about with the Vice-Chief on my back like a randy monkey. He's chasing me for every little detail on this, and I'm trying to keep him at bay for as long as I can. The man suddenly thinks he's a field agent."

Grant knew that Masterman despised Barton, as much as Barton despised the Head of the Redaction Unit. They came from two oppo-site ends of the spectrum; Barton was the man of backroom deals and meetings, Masterman was the man of action.

"And there's no chance that we can't up the manpower? I mean there's only two of us, and we've got a hell of a lot of ground to cover," said Grant.

"I know what you're saying, Jack, but the Redaction Unit is stretched as it is. Trench is in the Middle East working a job there, Spence is still tied up in that training program in Hong Kong and the rest are on assorted operations in the less inviting parts of the world. Aside from the European surveillance teams from the various stations, you're on your own."

Grant frowned. He'd known the answer before Masterman spelled it out, but he had to ask. "Alright," he said.

"Besides," continued Masterman as they approached the steps lead-ing to the lower levels of the embankment. "One team is more mobile – faster, quicker, and you're not beholden to anyone else. I learned that in the War. Get in, hit them, get out. You're more than capable of accomplishing the goal. So what do you want to do next?"

Grant turned to face him. "I need to get down to the tool shed and see what I can scavenge for this job."

The 'tool shed' referred to the Service's resources and technical sec-tion, which held all the necessary pieces of equipment an agent might need in the field – everything from disguises to surveillance devices and weapons, and while Broadway had an excellent range of kit buried deep in its cellars, the Redaction Unit had its own bespoke operation located in Battersea.

"Scavenge nothing," said Masterman. "This has the green light from the top floor; take whatever you need and if they give you any trouble, refer them straight to me."

Chapter Eight

Marquez and Gioradze met at the bar in Orly airport. It had been several weeks since they had last seen each other and in the intervening time they'd both separately been planning for the next phase of the operation. Each looked healthy and fit and to the casual observer, they could have been taken for two travelling sales representatives, wearing business suits, winter coats and carrying briefcases.

Their strategy had worked perfectly. Take out the less noticeable Russian agents first; in this case a junior diplomat of no regard, a banker with no profile and a businessman hardly anyone was aware of, so that they could move relatively unhindered against the most prominent targets.

Over the past few weeks neither had returned to their home addresses, instead preferring to stay in out of the way hotels. With the survivor's inbred instinct, they had decided not to take the risk of an enemy picking up their scent and following the trail back to their 'other' lives. The two men sat at a quiet corner table and watched planes take off and land with military precision.

"No problems in Hamburg. I read the news report," Gioradze said.

"No, it was simple; a slight wound to my hand during the kill, but it's healing well." Marquez flexed his hand, remembering how the garrote had accidently cut into his skin during the murder. "And you, no problems?"

Gioradze took a sip of his beer and shook his head. "It went like a dream. A good clean kill, the only hiccup was a witness who spotted me. Nothing to worry about, I wore a disguise and he only saw me for a brief moment."

Marquez nodded, satisfied. The trick was to reduce the risk as much as possible, whilst recognizing that this happened during all jobs and was inevitable.

"What about the money? Any news?" asked Gioradze.

"The payments for the first three contracts have been paid in full. When I spoke to him, the American was very happy," said Marquez.

Gioradze relaxed. Now that the money for the first contracts had been paid, he felt as though he could concentrate on the next part of the job. "What time is your flight to Marseilles?"

"In an hour. Yours?"

"I've got the evening flight, which means I get to hang around the bar and talk bullshit for three hours with all the other stiffs in suits," complained Gioradze.

As standard procedure, they would travel separately, just in case of unexpected eventualities such as a stop and search, or an arrest whilst passing through customs. That way, at least one of them would be free to carry out the remainder of the contracts.

"And the German?" asked Marquez.

"He will meet us in Marseilles, as agreed," Gioradze confirmed.

"Are we sure we can trust him?"

"He did okay for us in Zurich with driving the truck. Besides, we always knew we'd need an extra pair of hands. He'll be fine; leave him to me."

Marquez downed the rest of his drink, still unconvinced.

"And even if he isn't, he won't be surviving the full term of the operation anyway. That was the agreement, wasn't it?" said Gioradze.

"Loose ends," smiled Marquez.

"Exactly, loose ends," Gioradze reassured his partner.

Marquez made his way to the flight gate without ceremony. An hour later and travelling on a Dutch passport in the name of Vincent Joosen, he boarded the Air France flight which would take him south to Marseilles.

* * *

Kronos Engineering Ltd was located on a quiet industrial estate in Battersea. It was enclosed by a ten-foot-high perimeter fence topped with barbed wire, which could only be accessed through a manned security gate where dark eyes peered at unannounced visitors from the watchman's hut. With no appointment or clearance came no access and you would be gently discouraged from making further enquiries.

Kronos itself took up a large warehouse space comprising metal workshops, storage facilities, a draughtsman's office, canteen, garage and four delivery vans. To the casual observer, it was the same as any engineering workshop anywhere in the country. That was until you scratched the surface of the company – and then it was something very different indeed.

"Arnie's expecting you. The kettle *is* on," said the blousy-looking girl at the front desk, before handing Grant a chit authorizing him access to the secure area. Grant moved past the opening in the counter and made his way along the short corridor to an office which had 'FOREMAN' etched into the glass door.

A brief knock and Grant let himself in. The office was a monument to clutter; a cup full of stale tea bags was next to a set of receipts stuck onto a pending spike, and boxes of unpacked assorted mysteries made up a mini Berlin Wall across one side of the small office.

Grant was sure there was a desk in there somewhere, but underneath the avalanche of documents, files and outdated newspapers, he couldn't make out where it began or how big it was.

The man who sat behind the desk was a human version of the room. Dirty and unkempt, with a pencil behind his ear and overall pockets bulging with screwdrivers and spanners, but with the natural *joie de vivre* of a big man living a happy life. Various types of grime and oil permeated most sections of his skin most days of the week. He was sitting at his desk with the component parts of a dismantled semi-automatic pistol in front of him, a cloth in one hand and a can of gun oil in the other. When the door opened he looked up and beamed. "Well, Jack Grant, as I live and breathe. How you doing, you old bugger?" came the booming voice.

"Fine, thanks Arnie, just fine," said Grant, smiling in spite of himself.

"I heard you had been confined to barracks on the boss's orders. Needed some time off, I heard. Fancy a cuppa? The kettle's just boiled." The tea was Arnold Schwartz's usual fair, builder's tea; strong and sweet and thick enough to stand your teaspoon up in it. It came in the most enormous mug Grant had seen and he doubted he would ever finish it. They settled down in the rickety desk chairs.

"So how's life in the tool shed?" asked Grant, trying to make out the type of pistol on the desk. *A Colt,* he thought. *An old one.*

Schwartz shrugged. "Oh, you know they keep my boys busy. It's been better since the Colonel took over the tough guys, better funding. He's certainly fought for our corner, resources-wise. I remember in the old days; they'd expect us to take on the whole Cold War on a budget that the head office boys would use to buy lunch at their posh clubs. Shocking, I call it."

Grant smiled. Since Masterman had been appointed Head of Redaction, he had used his influence among the politicians, the War Office and the Treasury to gain a bigger slice of the secret operations' financial pie. His proposal was simple and cost effective; give Redaction the means to do what needs to be done and we can make it happen for you. Don't, and you get the level of operation that you pay for.

"'Course some of the lads still want some daft bloody things. Pens that can fire bullets or even guns with knives attached! I mean, what's the use in that; bloody comical if you ask me," said Schwartz, shaking his head at the shocking state of affairs he had to put up with.

Grant knew that Arnie Schwartz could take any every day, innocuous item and turn it into a lethal weapon, whether it was a knife, firearm or bludgeon. It was his trademark skill.

"So what can I do for you this fine morning, Jack?"

Grant took a slug of his tea and grimaced. "The usual. Off on a jaunt to Europe tomorrow, not sure for how long, so it'll be best to have a bit of everything."

Schwartz pondered the request. "Okay, I've got a couple of new directional mikes that you might find useful, very handy for static surveillance work. You just point and listen. How's that sound, if you'll pardon my pun?"

"Good. I'll need some standard gear as well; a couple of listening units and recorders, covert cameras, binoculars... just in case."

"Okay. Anything else?"

"Just my shooter. The usual one, the '39," said Grant.

"Ha, ha... now you're talking!"

And with that, Arnie Schwartz jumped to his feet, snatching up a large ring of keys in the process and seemingly transformed himself into an ad hoc tour guide of his little fiefdom. The pair made their way along the corridor, down a set of steps to a large steel door. A guard sat in front of it, reading that day's *Guardian*, barring the way to anyone unfortunate enough to make it this far. "You haven't seen the place since we had it tarted up, have you Jack? This is Arthur, give him your chit. Finished that crossword yet, young man?"

Arthur seemed not to hear, but instead simply inspected Grant's chit, stored it in his boiler suit pocket and opened up the door to the armory. They moved down another corridor of grey walls and poorly lit rooms, the only sounds their footsteps on the stone floor and the occasional report of a weapon being fired behind closed doors. "That's Trevor and Stan test firing a new American assault rifle, state of the art, so the Yanks tell me. Still only a prototype at the minute though," explained Arnie.

Eventually they reached the far end of the corridor and Arnie opened up the last steel door with a key from his set. "We've put in a new range, new targets on remote control bobbers. It's all very high-tech. We even have a makeshift close quarter battle house now with moveable walls. All soundproofed of course, don't want to upset the locals do we?"

Grant looked over the Redaction Unit's armory. The room was lined with storage racks containing a variety of unopened crates stenciled with 'ASSAULT RIFLES' and 'ASSORTED PISTOLS'" across their sides. At the far end of the room stood a large metal security cabinet the size of a grown man. Another key from Arnie's keychain was used and it clanked open to reveal a treasure trove of small arms; pistols, revolvers, magazines and ammunition.

Grant stood off to one side as the armorer delved into the depths of the cabinet, muttering and complaining as he rummaged through its contents of deniable handguns; Beretta's, Colt's, Browning's, Walther's. "Ah, here we go," he said as he removed a small metal case and brought it over to the display table. "Now no one's touched it, as per your instructions. It's been cleaned and oiled so it's ready to go."

Grant flicked open the case to reveal his weapon of choice, a 9mm Smith & Wesson Model 39 semi-automatic pistol. Similar in design to the 1911 Colt, it was however, a small framed and more compact weapon that suited Grant's shooting style perfectly. He had received the weapon from an American agent when he'd been working in Berlin many years ago. Grant had saved the American's life on an almost suicidal operation and had been given the weapon as a token of gratitude.

He had loved the '39 ever since and had given instructions that he was donating the weapon to the Redaction Unit's armory, on the clear understanding that only he and he alone was allowed to use it operationally. The only other person who was allowed to handle it was Arnie Schwartz and the first thing that Arnie had recommended had been the addition of a "bloody decent noise suppressor."

Redactors operated in a world of covert killing and stealth operations, and as such, this was reflected in an agent's weaponry. Silenced pistols, garrotes, knives, even unarmed killing skills such as neck breaks and strangulation were all part of the Redactors' armory. Grant's personal skill was in close range firearms work and the man who could make it happen for him silently, was Arnie Schwartz.

Arnie had taken the pistol to the Kronos workshop, and replaced the standard issue barrel with one that was an inch longer so that it extended beyond the front of the slide.

The end of the barrel was then threaded on the extended portion to accept the silencer and with the suppressor attached, it increased the weapon's length to just shy of twelve inches. It had been Grant's weapon of choice for operations now for the past five years. It was both his calling card and his good luck totem.

He picked it up; removed the magazine and pulled back the slide to check that it was empty. Satisfied, he placed the gun carefully on the table before turning his attention to the rest of the contents of the case. A spare magazine, bespoke suppressor, covert-style holster, spare magazine pouch and a small cleaning kit; everything he would need for this job. "Ammunition?" he asked.

"How much do you want?" said Schwartz.

"Can you sort me out with four for now? If I need any more I'll put in an overseas request," said Grant. Four boxes, at twenty-five rounds in a box should be more than enough for this operation; still it was always handy to have more than you needed rather than not enough. After all, he wasn't planning on engaging in skillful close combat with these contractors, he wanted to take them out as quickly as possible. "Oh, almost forgot, I'll need a personal protection weapon for my team mate on this. Nothing too complicated, small caliber, small gun."

Arnie pulled a contemptuous face. He was always an advocate of large caliber, so anyone that went for the little pop guns clearly didn't know what they were doing and instantly earned his contempt. "Small caliber, not complicated! What, you think this is a bloody toy shop! Who is he, another one of those Nancy-boys from Broadway that you're babysitting?"

Grant laughed, which seemed to make the armorer even more annoyed. "Actually, he's a *she* and it's more as a precaution, in case she bumps into some rough types."

Arnie shook his head, at near boiling point now. "Don't know what's going on in Head Office these days, sending the fairer sex off on these missions. Bloody ridiculous! In my day the girls were happy to stay at home with the kids – now I know I'm old fashioned, but it worked. Take my Maggie; we've been married nearly 30 years and—"

Grant thought it better to kill the flow of the conversation and interrupt before Arnie turned his attention to a diatribe on the negatives of women's rights and equality in the workplace. "Arnie I'm on the clock here. So what have you got for my partner? What would you say would be ideal for her?"

Schwartz knew when he was being told to shut up, even if it was done nicely. Plus, Grant was a friend. He thought for a moment. "I've recently acquired a very nice Walther PPK-L. It's small, lightweight, 7.65mm so it will hurt whoever a bullet hits on the way down. That fella in the movies is using a similar one at the moment. Not one I'd recommend to you lads, but it will do as a lady's gun."

Grant nodded with approval. He had no idea how much firearms training Nicole had, but he guessed not much, so he needed something that wouldn't scare the living daylights out of her if she had to use it for real. "Okay, good. Could you box it all up for me and ship it over to Pimlico?"

Arnie Schwartz nodded and reached for his clipboard. "Leave it with me, I'll get on to it straight away. Sign this just to confirm it all. Got to keep the paperwork in place for Head Office, haven't we now."

That very afternoon Arnie would box, bag and load everything into a large, commercially available suitcase which would then be transferred in a 'KRONOS ENGINEERING' van over to Pimlico. From there it would be sealed and packed as part of the Diplomatic Baggage, with its recipient officially being the British Embassy in Paris or more accurately, the SIS Station Head there.

"I've got a spare box of 9mm here. Do you fancy a quick practice, just to keep your eye in?" teased Arnie, stowing away the clipboard and waggling the box of ammunition in front of Grant.

Grant looked over at the big man and smiled. "Why not?" he said.

* * *

He stood in the glare of a single spotlight, the rest of the room encased in darkness and menace. He was calm, collected, his heart rate barely ticking over. He was the Gorilla now.

That's how he thought of himself when he was in this arena. Jack D. Grant, intelligence officer and former soldier, had been put to one side, discarded, like a snake shedding its skin. Somewhere between entering the firing range and picking up the weapon, he had transformed. Gorilla was at the forefront now, a different creature entirely; cold, brutal and someone to whom the normal rules didn't apply.

He stood with his suit jacket unbuttoned, his arms folded across his chest as though he was standing and considering a mesmerizing piece of artwork in a portrait gallery. One arm lay horizontally on top of the other, one tucked casually under his left armpit. He was at ease and relaxed.

The klaxon emanating from the speaker system sparked him back into life; his heart rate taking an involuntary jump. A movement to his left caught in his peripheral vision. He turned in one fluid motion; bending his knees and twisting in the direction of the threat. No hurried motion, no exotic stances, it was a movement of minimal, but effective, proportions.

At the same time, his hands detached themselves from their static position across his chest and both arms were instantly pumped outwards, towards the target that was fast approaching on the electric ceiling runner. A simple, quick draw; hand to gun, up, align on target and *Phut, phut! Double tap to the head, target finished,* thought Gorilla. The sound muffled by the suppressor was virtually non-existent, a testament to Schwartz's talents.

Another movement came at him from behind! He didn't spin, instead he simply stomped his right leg towards the next threat, and detached the hand holding his gun in a two handed grip and fired one handed right... ,Phut...Phut...Phut! One to the chest, two to the head!

The target down, and he remained alert for the next one... and almost as he finished thinking this, he was aware of a noise coming from behind him once more... *No time to move,* Gorilla thought. Instead, he pivoted from the hip, twisting his body round, and raised his left arm instinctively to protect his head while firing from a short hip position; the pistol clamped to his right hip and... *Phut, Phut, Phut!* The bullets moved up the paper target's body mass in a sewing machine stitch; starting at the sternum and ending in the middle of the forehead. Target down.

He scanned the darkness of the close quarter battle room for more targets. Nothing he was sure, but as was his habit, he kept the pistol in a low ready position in case the exercise was still in play.

The howl of the klaxon confirmed the drill was over. The smoke cleared, though the acrid smell of cordite remained, and the lights on the shooting range were activated, bathing the rubber coated room in harsh fluorescent light. The entire drill had taken no more than twenty seconds. Gorilla was that fast.

"Nice shooting, all finished off with two shots to the head. You still got it then, eh?" said Arnie Schwartz's disembodied voice from behind the safety wall.

Gorilla stripped the magazine from the weapon, checked that the chamber was empty, and then began to unscrew the suppressor from the barrel. Did he still have 'it' – that lightning quick ability to ruthlessly kill should the occasion require it? It was beyond instinctive, certainly. He didn't know how he could do it, merely that he could take this piece of machined metal, which effectively threw small metal balls in a straight line, and be quick and lethal with it.

He had trained with dozens of men in close quarter pistol work over the years and he could never quite see the problem some of them were having with shooting. He had seen them sweating, flinching from the report, all fingers and thumbs when loading or reloading; or the bad ones, who couldn't hit a barn door when it was standing right in front of them!

To him it was nothing even remotely extraordinary; no great soul searching, no extra time spent on the range to get marginally better, no knowing the ins and outs of every piece of shooting-related literature or the, to him, boring specifications of the latest gadget. No, no, no. It was just something that he could do to an almost superhuman level. It was why he was one of the best Redactors in the business.

Gorilla's tools of his trade were his '39, which he only carried on operations – and a gleaming, stainless steel cut-throat razor that he carried always. The pistol was a gift from his time in the military, the razor a gift from his time running with the street gangs. Both, in his opinion, complimented each other perfectly.

Oh, he still had it alright, but he could never quite figure out in his own mind whether this 'ability' of his was a blessing or a curse.

* * *

As was his routine when he was due to be away on operations for any length of time, Jack Grant always called home one last time before leaving. In his case 'home' was his sister's house.

He rarely saw his sister, in fact, it had been three years since they last met, but he sent money out of his monthly wage to the little terraced house in the tiny village nestled on the shore of Loch Lomond. The village was his safe haven; three terraced streets, a post office and a pub. It was, ironically, the one place that he hadn't been able to go for the past few years. Enemies had a way of tracking down those you loved the most and the risk of leading them to the banks of the Loch was just too great.

He heard the phone ringing and ringing; she was probably running around doing the housework, or clearing up. Eventually he heard a click as the receiver was picked up. "It's me," he said without preamble. He waited through the pause from the other end of the line.

"Well, hello *me*, long, long time. Did ye forget the number?" Her voice was hard and stern, as if she had no time for frivolities. It didn't matter who he was now and where he had been, he was always berated by his older sister. It was a tradition that went back to childhood.

"No, I've been busy, been away."

"Good for you, somewhere nice I hope? The postcard never appeared!"

"You know I can't say."

"Of course not, you cannie say much about anything, can ye? You seem to have the market in not saying things or talking about things or visiting things. Jack Grant, the master of eternal understatement."

"It's for the best. For everybody's sake," he said. He could hear his accent altering as he spoke, his emotions starting to run high and he could detect the burr returning to his voice, the one that he'd tried to smother over the years. Berlin, London and Beirut hadn't been able to totally eradicate it.

"Well, there ye go, same old Jack," he heard her say. The silent pause hung in the air and the tension filtered along the phone lines. His guilt and her anger at him. Family, why did bloody family always bring this uncertainty out in him?

"So to what do we owe the pleasure of this phone call? I've the tea on and don't want it to ruin."

"I'm going away again, very soon, tomorrow in fact. I don't know how long for. It'll be a couple of months at least."

"And you just wanted to let us know, make sure we're alright. Is that it?"

"Yes."

"Well, that's what families are for aren't they? Making sure we're alright... She's fine, by the way, thanks for asking."

"I was... I was going to ask... how she is, I mean," he said feebly.

"I just said she's fine, didn't I! Missing you obviously, but then you'd expect that. That's women for you Jack. No taste when it comes to you. Their brains go out the window."

"Does she need anything? I can send more money or—"

"No, we don't need any more! It's not yer money she needs. She was ill last month, it was touch and go at one stage, but Dr. Bremner helped her through. She's a fighter. She asks after you every day."

"I know. I'm sorry. I didn't want it to be like this, I know this is bloody hard—"

"Mind yer language! I will not have obscenities filling up my ears! I don't know what type of habits you've picked up in London, but don't apply them here, young man!"

There she goes again, he thought, *playing the puritanical elder sister once more.* "Sorry. When I get back, I'll try to arrange something about coming up if they'll let me."

"Aye, we'll see," she said, but her tone told him she didn't believe a word of it.

"Look, I need to go; I've things to do."

"The other one," she blurted out desperately, as if this was her final opportunity to mention it. "Have you *any* news on the other one?"

He sighed. He had been half expecting the question. "Look its best that you don't ask, it'll only be harder if you keep thinking about it."

"I have to know Jack; *she'll* have to know soon. There must be something. Someone must have heard something!"

He didn't know what to say. It was like a cancer, eating away at the remains of his family. The unspoken rule that they'd forced themselves to have; do not mention the *other* one. "I'm sorry, there's nothing. No news, no information. Nothing," he said.

He heard the anger and the venom leave her with a weary sigh. "Jack. Just be careful. You're still ma baby brother. Just… come back."

He knew that once he put down the phone and ended the conversation, the people in Loch Lomond would be forgotten. He was cruel like that. He was always like that on operations. He would touch base with the family, then step on a plane and they would be removed from his mind completely. He could afford no distractions from the job at hand. It was one of the greatest skills he had; the ability to detach from real life and focus solely on his task. He would put Jack Grant to one side and pick up the persona of Gorilla.

"I'll tell her that you called. I'll give her a kiss from you… she'll like that," she said and then he heard the phone click dead in his hand, leaving an empty line; but before that he was sure – not certain, but sure – that he'd heard the tremble in her voice as her harsh facade crumbled.

Chapter Nine

Paris - February 1965

Get to Paris and dig in, Masterman had told them. Sitting in his office, he'd briefed them both about the tactical advantages of being based in the City of Light. "It's the perfect jump off point for Operation MACE; anonymous, central for reaching the rest of Europe and the one place we know this renegade hit team will have to visit at some point. Plus, SIS has a vast range of assets in Paris which you can call on at a moment's notice."

They had purposefully kept the conversation on the BOAC flight to Orly light and frivolous. Not only because they couldn't conceivably talk about operational matters in an enclosed environment surrounded by their fellow passengers, but also because it gave them a brief opportunity to relax and talk nonsense before the tension of the mission began.

For their travel into the theatre of operations, Grant and Nicole had decided to go in covertly, travelling on passports in the assumed names of Mr. and Mrs. Martin Ronsom of Spalding, Kent. The Ronsoms were on a Europe-wide travelling honeymoon and could provide a recently issued marriage certificate to prove it. Would people have put them together as a couple very much in love: he, short and gruff, she tall and elegant? Probably not, but the Ronsoms were not intending to socialize with people who might ask such questions. In fact, once they had been collected from the airport, the Ronsom cover would cease to exist.

They arrived in the late afternoon, cleared customs quickly and were collected by a tame Citroën that was on hand to take them to their base of operations. The driver, actually the Deputy Head of the Paris Station, whisked them through the city with all the aplomb of an experienced Parisian taxi driver.

"I'm Ronnie. Douglas sends his apologies, work and all that. But he'll be with you later today, to see if you've settled in and if we can do anything for you young lovebirds while you're here," he said, as he negotiated the roads. In the distance, the Eiffel Tower loomed like a watchtower across the city as they headed towards the river and out of the grandeur of central Paris.

"We've got you a nice apartment. Bit off the beaten track, but close to everything you'll need while you're here. Don't worry about the lady who owns the building, she's one of ours going back before the war. She knows to keep an eye out for odd-bods and not to ask too many questions," said Ronnie, as the car cruised across the Seine.

As they drove through the famous streets, Nicole reflected on her previous visits to Paris with her father when she was a child and how it had hardly changed at all. But scratch beneath the cultural surface and the Paris of the 1960's had taken a bit of a nosedive as the center of all things vogue. That honor, unjustly in her opinion, was being given to 'swinging' London, which had stolen a march on its rival. Music, movies, fashion were all being played out across vibrant London.

Their car pulled up outside what was to be their base of operations for the next few weeks. The base was actually a third story apartment above a men's fashion store on the Rue des Rennes in Montparnasse. The former Bohemian enclave situated on the left bank was a shadow of its former self, with the elitist intellectuals and artists now dwindled to almost nothing. Instead, Montparnasse had become a haven for run-of-the-mill cafes and bars, indistinguishable from any other area in Paris. It had become a cemetery for failed poets and bitter, post-war political exiles.

Grant and Nicole got out, each holding a small suitcase. Nicole imagined they looked like a couple of orphans who had been pushed out onto the streets. Ronnie wound down his window and handed them a set of door keys. "Here you go, the big one's for the front door, small one's for the apartment on the third floor, Number 308. Make yourselves comfortable. The boss will be here later tonight to officially welcome you . Good luck."

They climbed the stairs to the third floor and let themselves into 308. It was a large two-bedroom apartment which overlooked the main street. It smelled of damp, had bare floorboards, and aging cobwebs hung from the ceiling.

"Hardly first class is it?" Nicole commented.

Grant shrugged; it was one of dozens of safe-houses that SIS had access to, all over the world. Most of them were owned and run by former agents, who were happy to have visiting officers stay over or use them as bases for operations. For Grant, it was neither here nor there. In his time, he had slept in billets, trenches and dosshouses. By those standards, this was a palace.

"People do tend to believe the myth that we always have penthouse suites when we're on operations," he said. "Unfortunately, it's just that: a myth. It's the movies, I suppose. It will do us just fine, so settle in."

Waiting for them in the lounge were two large suitcases, which had been posted in the diplomatic pouch to the Paris Station. Grant opened them up and found the personal weapons, communications kit and surveillance equipment. The first thing to do was to stash the weapons out of sight, in case they had their door busted in by the French security services. It was unlikely, but you never knew.

He went into the bathroom and searched around until he found what he was looking for. Carefully peeling back the linoleum, he used his foot to press down until he found a loose floorboard.

He got a hit on the first go and with the help of a butter knife from the kitchen, he pressed back the loose board. Next he wrapped the handguns, spare ammo, silencer and holsters in a series of cloths and stashed them in his new weapons cache. A quick replacement of the floorboard, folding back the lino and it was as good as new.

The weapons would only be removed when he was out of the apartment and operational, it was safer that way and better tradecraft. In the unlikely event that they were attacked in the apartment – well, he still had his cold steel razor. And he knew he could do a hell of a lot of damage with it.

That evening, they were visited by the Head of the Paris Station, a career intelligence officer by the name of Douglas Consterdine. Consterdine had cut his teeth in Malaya with military intelligence, hunting communist terrorists and had transferred over to SIS when his military service had ended. Within the Service he was considered a high-flyer, hence his prestigious posting to Paris.

Grant hated him on sight. Consterdine was a lean and dandyish man who favored the designer suits and gaudy silk ties that seemed to be the current fashion in France. A bright pink carnation burst forth from his lapel button and his hair was slicked sideways in a faux Clark Gable look. But the most irritating thing in Grant's opinion, was the way that the Head of Station talked down to everyone who hadn't been graced by God with a place at Oxford.

"So you're the bloody fire-team," he said, shaking Grant and Nicole's hands firmly. "How's London these days. Is Head Office still as divisive as ever?"

Grant, who knew little and cared less about the internal politics of Broadway's power-players, remained non-committal. That and the fact that Redaction agents weren't allowed within spitting distance of headquarters ruled out his interest in what he regarded as the 'fops' who held high office within SIS. "I doubt there's been much in the way of change since you were last there, Dougy" he said.

"Please don't call me that, there's a good chap. Douglas is the name my mama gave me and that's the one we'll stick to, if it's all the same to you," scolded Consterdine. "And the club? You get down to the club much these days?"

Grant's confused look turned to mischief. "What, White's? They wouldn't let me in there, *Douglas,*" he said, his tongue firmly in his cheek.

"Not White's, oh heavens' me, no. Didn't think for a moment you'd be on their roll of honor Jack, only the Chief could get an invite to join there. No offence. No, the spy club, Knightsbridge, haven't been there in an age," said Consterdine.

Grant had been to the Special Forces Club several times with Masterman. He had climbed its staircase to the first floor bar, nodded to several members from operations gone by and sat quietly in the corner, a glass of wine for Masterman and a beer for himself. He regarded the 'club' as one of the few places where he could relax and talk through this job, or that job, without fear of compromise. While in truth, he preferred the lower-rent underbelly drinking clubs of London, there was still a fondness for the collegial atmosphere of a truly elite private club that he yearned for on occasion. Grant shook his head. "Not recently. Never seem to have the time these days."

Consterdine seemed to accept that with a frown and then changed the subject. "Oh, and here's the keys to some wheels parked around the corner. Nothing too flash, but it will get you around while you're here." He threw a key fob over to Nicole, who caught it and gently placed it on the table in front of her. They had become the proud owners of an old Renault.

"I won't take you out to dinner at La Truite," said Consterdine. "I know that you Redaction people like to keep yourself to yourselves, so I won't intrude."

"Fair enough," growled Grant, who was growing tired of Consterdine at a rapid pace.

"If you need anything of a practical nature; pass a message to Broadway, secure encryption, bit of cash, a sneaky car, you know the sort of thing I mean – don't hesitate to give me a shout. Just promise me one thing."

"Name it," said Nicole.

"Do try and keep out of trouble on my patch. I have enough of a stormy relationship with the French Secret Service to last me a lifetime, so I could well do without you Redaction mob clunking around in your size nines."

Grant smiled, what he suspected was his most condescending, shit-eating grin. "Dougy, you won't even know we're here."

"Excellent," said Consterdine, who was either unaware of Grant's acid-tongued response or simply didn't care. "Well, the kitchen's stocked up to see you through for a day or two and there's a very nice bottle of Sancerre courtesy of the Station. *Au revoir.*"

They heard Consterdine's footsteps as he made his way down the staircase, he was humming something, to Nicole it sounded like a show tune.

"Prick," mumbled Grant. They stood silent for a moment, each taking in the other.

"So what do we do now?" asked Nicole. She had decided to take the lead from Grant, it was her first operational assignment after all and she thought it best to let him set the pace.

He looked at her, confused, and then seemed to make up his mind. "Can you cook?" he asked her.

"Of course," said the fledgling field agent.

"Good. Then food… we need to eat. Plus, we can crack open that bottle of wine. The mission can wait until tomorrow."

* * *

Back in London, the MACE Intelligence Requirement Team, or the 'Burrowers' as they were unofficially known in honor of their leader, were based on the third floor in a small office space annex of SIS's new headquarters in Lambeth.

The transition between Broadway and Century House was still very much a work in progress, but at C's insistence, the MACE team were to be housed in a quiet little corner of Century and afforded every resource that Broadway could offer them.

For his part, Toby worked tirelessly and had even set up a camp bed in the corner of the annex. He feared that his family wouldn't be seeing much of him over the coming weeks. Several telephone and telex lines had been hastily run in and desks and filing cabinets which had been languishing in a limbo between Broadway and Century were quickly delivered. A list was compiled of files that were required from Registry, and over the next two days they were moved across by a fleet of SIS's vans. There was a further day spent organizing the office and then the MACE team had everything they would need to conduct an international manhunt.

The Burrowers themselves were three strong and were there to decipher and correlate the limited intelligence picture that had been gleaned from the 'Dobos' recording and transcripts. Aside from Toby as the intelligence coordinator, the rest of the seconded team was made up of a 'Legman' and an 'Archivist'.

Roger, the Legman, was a former Special Branch officer who had completed a stint in the Security Service ("catching pesky spy's young master Toby") before being seconded over to Broadway's counter-intelligence section. Toby had worked with him before on several cases, and knew him to be a good ex-copper, not averse to bending the rules to get the job done.

The Archivist was Nora, a middle aged debutante who had been recruited into the Service at the end of the war. Her first overseas posting had been to Palestine. She had been unlucky enough to have been working at the King David Hotel, the main administrative base for the British Forces, when it was bombed by the Irgun in 1946. She'd been trapped for several hours until she had been dug out by rescue forces and she still wore a scar on her face from where she'd been blasted by a glass window.

As a team they complemented each other perfectly; Nora with her nose for finding even the most obscure detail in a mountain of files; Roger, with his nose for tracking down a lead like a bloodhound, and finally Toby as their seer, ready to guide them through the fog to a clear conclusion. It was no accident that they had nicknamed him the 'Oracle'. Roger and Nora were the Watsons, to Toby's Sherlock Holmes.

Roger, the hard bitten ex-street copper, looked around at his colleagues. *Look at you both,* he thought. *You're as fresh faced as a bunch of primary school children on their first day, all eager and full of hope and possibilities.* Little did Toby and Nora know that by the end of this manhunt, they would have physically aged, suffer from stomach ulcers, have bags under their eyes from a lack of sleep and permanent wind from all the coffee and tea they'd have drunk to keep them all going.

Toby came around and sat perched on the front of his desk, his somber black tie tucked neatly down his V neck jumper. "Alright, it's day one. So where do we start?" he said.

They started where they always started – by discussing what they already knew as 'fact'. The Burrowers began. They made notes, they threw around ideas, and they conferred as all good detectives must do if they want a successful result. There were no raised voices or talking over each other, like some of the rougher elements of SIS; instead they were composed and in control of what they were about to do and how they would achieve it. By the end of the first morning, they each had a task list with their own unique responsibilities.

The consensus was that being a CIA operation, it was bound to be well funded, that was for certain. Knowing the way the Americans operated, Toby assumed that they would be doing everything on a grand scale; the tactics, the time frame, even the weapons used to kill their targets.

"So the first thing we have to do, before we start giving out too much information to our allies overseas – no matter how much we may trust them – is to ensure that no word of this gets to Langley. If that happens, we're dead in the water and the fire-team could find itself in danger. Operational security is paramount," Toby warned.

Nora would begin the eye-straining detailed searches through the requested files, looking for anything related to contract killers or international mercenaries. Roger would start 'knocking on the doors' of his former workmates in Special Branch and the overseas police liaison offices in several European countries, and Toby would do similar with the overseas SIS stations and friendly European intelligence services.

"But don't give anything away too early," he told them. "Just a gentle tap on the door, to let them know we're in business and that we might need something over the coming weeks. But play it low-key for the moment. Remember, we have a timeframe to work to, but, if we want to have a hope in hell of finding these assassins, then patience and consistency are key."

The team's initial focus was on discovering the identity of the contract assassin. Once they had a name, all the other pieces of the puzzle would fall into place, they were certain. "Once we have a name, we can track him and see where he leads," Toby kept drumming into them.

"Surely he's operated in this line of work in the past? At least that's what the tape seems to imply, hence his recruitment," said Roger.

Toby agreed. "Well, if that's the case, he must have left a trail on a previous operation. He can't operate in a vacuum, can he? Right Nora, start searching for high level assassinations over the past five years; senior politicians, business tycoons, that sort of target. This chap isn't into kneecappings; he plays big and for big money, otherwise why else would the CIA make use of him?"

So far they had three confirmed deaths. The Chairman of a Lichtenstein shipping company who had been targeted by an anti-tank missile and fitted the profile of the 'Quartermaster', and the 'Diplomat', who appeared to be a junior British Embassy official in Hamburg, recently garroted in an apparent 'sex-murder'. The only clues had been from eye witnesses who described a tall, dark swarthy man in Hamburg and a short stocky, bearded man in Liechtenstein. The only Constellation agent killed so far was agent *ORION*, who had been involved in a hit and run in Zurich. Again, a witness had reported a tall, dark, well-dressed man at the scene.

So while the fire-team in Paris trod water, Toby and the rest of his team did what they did best. They dug and searched and checked. By the end of day three, they were beginning to hit brick walls. The liaison leads were coming in slowly and the *'Urgent –Trace'* on the identities of the assassins obviously wasn't a priority for SIS's overseas stations.

It was on the last day of the working week, during a bounce around session in which ideas would be batted forward and backwards that the team had an inspired notion and the first Toby knew about it was when the little-mouse, Nora, meekly raised her hand to make a point.

"Nor', you don't need to put your hand up; we're not in school you know, just shout it out," he said, not unkindly.

Nora played with the bracelet on her wrist, a sign of nerves, and cleared her throat before she spoke. "Well, it's just occurred to me that we might be attacking this from the wrong direction."

Roger and Toby shared a glance, eager to discover where she was going with this. "Okay, go on."

"Well, we're so keen on identifying this killer, going for the knock-out punch in one go and if you'll excuse me for saying so, we're getting nowhere yet. I wonder if perhaps we're missing a more realistic lead. Something that we do have a hope of locating."

"Come on Nora just get to the point, we haven't got all day," said Roger.

"The Forger," she blurted out, gaining confidence. "He mentions on page… yes, here we are, page seven of the transcript. He says 'a man in Antwerp'. This man has used the services of a forger in Belgium previously, we have to assume over the past few years, and there can't be that many forgers who have the expert knowledge needed to provide documentation for a top level criminal."

Roger glanced over at Toby; his head was down, in deep thought and he nodded. "She's right, it must be a very small group, probably no more than a handful."

Toby pushed away from his desk and walked to the chalkboard. He picked up a piece of chalk and started writing whatever was coming into his head. "Okay. So we follow the seam and see where it leads. We put in a new request to Belgian intelligence and police, asking for a trace on any known or suspected documentation forgers. But there's just one thing."

Both Nora and Roger looked at him eagerly, waiting to see if he had spotted a flaw in Nora's theory. The sound of the chalk hitting the board came to a stop.

"It's the forger himself," said Toby. "Just because we find him, it doesn't automatically equate that we'll gain any useful information. This killer has been operating for the past few weeks, probably months. He'll have all of his false papers already."

Nora, her fingers now entwined in her bracelet, nodded, giving Toby his moment. "True, but the forger will have photographs, a list of cover names he used, maybe even false papers he's used in the past. Who knows, perhaps he keeps them hidden away as a kind of insurance policy in case his clients cut up rough."

"But what makes you think he'll spill to the Belgian police or security service?" said Roger, playing the ex-copper.

"He won't. He's probably got a good lawyer to plead his legal rights," countered Nora.

"So I still don't see—"

"But he hasn't got any legal protection from Redaction. We send Gorilla in. He'll scare him into talking."

Roger burst out laughing. "Bloody brilliant," he said.

Toby had to admit, the thought of getting a visit from the little Redaction agent on a dark and lonely night would terrify the life out of him, also. He nodded approvingly. "Alright, let's go with it. Run a check to see if we have anybody on our files already, we don't want to use the Belgians unless we have to. If not, then we make a formal approach to Belgian Intelligence; we'll say that it's part of an ongoing investigation into diamond smuggling in the Congo or some such nonsense. Check, check and check again, let's get those names confirmed before we hand them over to the Redaction team."

"You know what that means, don't you, Nora love," said Roger, lighting his pipe.

"What?" she asked, confused.

"You've just got our weekend cancelled. Well done, old girl."

* * *

Nicole had slept well and awoke early, keen to start the operation running at a fast pace, she was determined to make a good impression with her field commander. Although in truth, she doubted that *anyone* could make a good impression on him.

The previous night after they'd eaten, she had watched as Grant unpacked the rest of the equipment cases before gruffly stating that he was "hitting the sack." He had risen from bed at ten the following morning and staggered his way to the small kitchenette, rubbing the sleep from his reddened eyes with the heel of his hand and tightening the belt of his dressing gown around him.

"Relax," he told her as his eyes focused on his first coffee of the day. It was good, hot, strong and sweet. "There's no point jumping up and down and running around just yet, at least not until we get something concrete from London. Take it easy, and for God's sake get me another cup of coffee."

They decided to use the waiting time wisely and get out and "get the lay of the land," as Grant put it. "We need to live out our cover story. Honeymooners doing the tourist thing, visiting sites and landmarks, plus it gives us a good excuse to get the pulse of the city and reconnoiter a few routes in and out to the airport, train station, that sort of thing. We never know when we'll have to move quickly."

"Wouldn't honeymooners spend most of their time in bed," she teased.

"Not on this trip they won't," he replied shortly.

"Why Mr. Ronsom, I do believe I've made you blush," she said going in for the kill.

They spent the next few days visiting Paris's notable landmarks, of which there were many. Some days they drove, and for variety, sometimes they took the old pre-war buses which serviced the city. They visited the Sacré-Cœur Basilica, walked along the Seine, and spent an hour or two being amused by the street and sketch artists of Montmartre. They gloried at the Arc de Triomphe and on a visit to the viewing platform at the top of the Eiffel Tower, Grant decided to give Nicole an impromptu lesson in the art of counter-surveillance.

"Remember that when you're trying to spot any type of hostile surveillance, you're looking for two things; repetition and anything that's out of the ordinary," he said. They stood looking into each other's eyes, but in reality, they were checking over each other's shoulders to practice their surveillance detection tactics. He gently stroked her ear, as a lover would whilst whispering.

"The man that you've spotted several times over a short period; the woman without a wedding ring pushing a pram, the couple who stop dead in the street and suddenly take an interest in a shop window when you do an about-face on a pavement. If you do find a tail, don't try to shake them off straight away – lead them a merry dance and drag them all over town if you have to. That'll wear them down and cause them to 'show out' and remember, the golden rule is to stay away from anywhere sensitive; dead letter drops, our base, agents, that sort of thing. They're all examples of classic surveillance techniques that you should be aware of."

She pulled her coat tighter around her, the high wind causing a chill at the top of the tower and looked at the city spread out. "You never did tell me about the woman in the photo," she said, hoping to catch him unawares.

He cocked a suspicious eye at her. "There's not much to tell and it's better that you don't know."

"Why, was she someone close?"

He sighed. What was it with a certain type of woman? They always want to dig deeper and push the boundaries of what they needed to know. "It was a long time ago, Nicole. We were running agents in Berlin; this was before the wall went up. It was a really wild time; shootings and kidnappings on the streets from both sides of the spy network; them and us. There were traitors everywhere and double and triple crosses were the norm."

She was unsure if she should continue, but then she found her feet. "And she was one of your agents."

"She's one of the 'lost ones' who never came back. She's in the past, forgotten about now by pretty much everyone," he said, his voice void of emotion.

"I'm sorry; I didn't mean to intrude."

"I told you that it's better that you don't know… it's fine, don't worry about it."

But Nicole saw that brief moment of melancholy in his eyes. She knew he was lying. *No, not lying,* she corrected herself. Not lying directly, he was, she was sure, just not telling her the whole story. Sensing that she had overreached with her inquisitiveness, she cannily backed off.

"So what about you?" asked Grant.

She was surprised that he'd chosen to carry on with a subject she thought was to be closed. "What about me, Mr. Ronsom," she teased, using his cover name.

"Is there anyone special out there for you?" he asked, flicking a glance out over Paris.

Nicole smiled and considered his question. "There's a boy I grew up with, we've known each other forever. We're friends more than anything. He's a local G.P., not far from the village where I lived. Dad always hoped that we'd end up getting hitched."

"And will you?"

"Maybe, who knows? But not yet. He's a lovely man, gentle, kind, good husband material, but I'm still working out if this is what I want to do for the rest of my life, or if I want to give it up to be a wife to a village doctor."

"There are worse things in the world than living a normal life. This business begins to take its toll on you after a while," he said bitterly.

She turned the question back at him. "Is that you speaking from experience?"

"Just an observation," he countered. "Sometimes we cross bridges we don't know we've crossed, until we cross them." He started to move toward the stairwell. "It's time we moved. Come on, that's enough sightseeing for today, we've got work to do."

They headed back to the apartment, but not before Grant, ever the field man, insisted that they check in with the Paris Station to see if there was any news that had come through while they were out.

"You should check the park," said the anonymous voice from the Paris Station after he'd called from a payphone and gone through the endless code numbers to verify who he was. "Boat seven on the west side. We've left a present for you." The voice hung up abruptly.

Grant headed back to where Nicole was parked in the Renault, its engine ticking over. "Anything?" she asked, checking the mirrors for anyone watching.

He nodded. "London has sent something through to the dead letter box drop. You go back to the apartment and I'll go and collect it."

She turned to him sharply. "Now wait a minute, I could come with you, be of help."

"No it's better this way, more secure. There's no need for both of us to be compromised if it's under surveillance. Head home and I'll get back as soon as I can."

The dead letter box connecting the MACE fire-team and the Paris Station was behind a bush, to the rear of the seventh park bench along the main path overlooking the lake in the notorious Bois de Boulogne. Grant waited until dusk before doing a run through and then finally chanced his arm. A quick walk past, a grab into the base of the bush and then the sealed envelope was in his pocket.

He spent the next thirty minutes running counter-surveillance drills before he decided he was clean and took a taxi which dropped him off on a street corner, five minutes' walk from the apartment. Nicole was waiting for him at the door when he arrived. "I was worried, I thought something had happened," she said, her arms crossed over her chest.

He nodded, understanding. It was always this way for new field agents, they tended to jump at shadows and see the enemy every-where. "I was just taking precautions, took the long route home in case I'd picked up some chancer taking an interest."

She looked doubtful. "Is that really necessary, all that doubling back and taking random routes? I mean, it's only Paris."

He shrugged. "We do the basics and then we're covered. We take our eye off the ball and something goes wrong, it usually means we end up in a stone hotel."

"Stone hotel?"

"Prison… or worse," he said, taking off his coat and throwing it over the chair.

Nicole took a moment to take in what he was saying. "So what is it?" she asked, pointing at the package he had recovered.

He ripped it open and muttered, "Number code, give me a few minutes." He sat at the table and set about deciphering the message hidden inside the single sheet of paper. Fifteen minutes later, when he'd double checked, he gave her the answer. "It seems London have come up with a lead. Seems a bit vague at the minute, but who knows, these things have a way of blowing open the whole case. They want us to track down the forger who was mentioned in the transcript."

She thought back to the briefing in London. "Antwerp, correct?" she said. "Where are we going to start?"

"*We* aren't going to start anywhere. *You* are going to man the base here and see if anything else comes in from London. Check in by public telephones to the Paris Station for the moment, unless it's really sensitive information. I'll call in if anything crops up."

She nodded, accepting his authority. He was the senior agent after all, but it still didn't mean she had to like being left behind. "Alright, seeing as I'm not coming, where are *you* going to start?"

"Forged documents. The Burrowers have given me a list of three Belgium-based forgers. That's my start point; I'll be gone for several days. I'll leave in the morning."

Chapter Ten

Jules Dumont had done well over the past five years. His good looks, attire, manner and luxury house spoke of his success. For as well as being a passionate collector and seller of rare books and works of art, he was also the foremost document forger in Belgium.

Passports, work papers, driving licenses, identification cards – all fell within the remit of his craft. Business was thriving and he had the respect, and protection, of the higher echelons of the Belgian underworld. He thought himself untouchable. He knew how to reproduce authentic watermarks and signatures, he knew the difference between the various bonded papers needed for official documentation, the fonts and inks required, and he knew the tricks – had even invented some himself – that were used for photographic identification, and while there were many competitors in his field, he rated himself the first among equals.

He had been apprenticed in his youth to Uncle Amos himself, a talented artist and professional lithographer who had worked for the resistance escape lines during the war. His expertise had been providing downed airmen with Swiss passports, which would move them down the escape and evasion rat line to Spain.

After the war Uncle Amos had indulged in a fling with the widow Dumont and had been 'persuaded' to take on young Jules as his assistant/apprentice. With Uncle Amos's retirement, and having no such moral qualms, Dumont had immediately gone into business as a passport engraver and forger to the Belgian underworld. His most recent client, with whom he'd met tonight, was a diamond smuggler who wished to move some 'rocks' between Europe and the USA.

Jules Dumont had been dining out for the evening, a rare treat these days, at the exclusive Minerva Hotel, one of his favorite establishments. It had been a fine night of good food, good company and excellent beer. He had flirted mercilessly with both his hostess and the waitresses, and he was feeling happy and buoyant. Life was good. But now he needed to rest. He had a busy day tomorrow, back to his little office and his work desk.

He unlocked the front door to his four story house on the fashionable Leescorfstraat located on the outskirts of the city, and entered. He took in the stylish hallway of marble floor tiles, the polished, mahogany-lined walls resplendent with leather bound books and the ornate lamp that gave an elegant glow through the passageway to the lounge. He flicked the light switch to the lounge and... nothing. No light, only darkness.

He flicked it again. Damn, he thought the bulb must have blown and he began to move across to open the heavy curtains to let in some light from the street lamps outside. He swished the curtains back to their respective sides and immediately his lounge was bathed in sepia tones; shadows from the trees swayed across the fireplace and dark patches seemed to move as car headlights passed by, animating them.

With startling speed one of the shadows moved, except it didn't just move, it glided like a ghost at a rapid pace. Not deviating in any way from its course, aiming directly at him...

With this revelation still fresh in his mind, he felt his legs kicked out from under him, his subsequent crash to the floor, a thump on his head when he caught it on the corner of his desk, then he felt the flow of blood from a cut to his temple. A hard, bony knee pressed deep into the small of his back, pinning him to the floor, and the unmistakable sensation of a pistol's cold steel was shoved hard against the nape of his neck.

"Don't fight. Don't struggle – you'll die. You've got a chance to live – take it." The voice was French, but with a trace of an accent. English? American?

"How?" cried Dumont. Because of his face being pushed into the carpet, it actually came out as "HEOWWHH!" But the shadow, whatever it was, seemed to get the general idea of his agonized plea and eased up the pressure on his neck before replying.

"By telling me everything I want to know."

* * *

Gorilla worked quickly, manipulating, pushing and pulling, until five minutes later the Belgian was handcuffed to a high-backed, ornate wooden chair in the center of his own dining room. A set of handcuffs locked the forger's wrists to the rear of the chair and an improvised gag of duct tape sealed his mouth. He quickly closed the heavy curtains and set about replacing the missing bulb from the room's light. A flick of the switch and the scene was lit.

The Belgian blinked, adjusting his eyes to the harsh light, blinked again and stared, eyes agog, beads of sweat running down into the creases of his shirt collar, his breathing rapid and heavy. Gorilla moved in close and whispered in Dumont's ear. "I'm going to remove the tape now. Don't scream. If you do, I'll have to hurt you. Okay? Do we have a deal?"

Dumont looked into Gorilla's eyes, noted the determination in them and nodded. The tape was ripped off in one smooth and practiced motion, allowing Dumont to breathe more easily.

"W-wh-what do you want?"

Gorilla mimed putting a finger to his lips and uttered a gentle "Ssshhhh." He picked up a small Gladstone bag and placed it on the table in front of him. He stared at the man, betraying no emotion, his face a blank canvas – a dentist ready to extract a small child's rotten tooth would have looked the same.

The forger stared back, watching Gorilla as he slowly started to pace across the room, thinking, musing how he was going to approach this task. It was a chore that needed resolving quickly.

"Please, my friend, please don't hurt me. I have money, please, take what you want. You are a robber, yes, a burglar? No matter," cried Dumont.

Gorilla paced back and forth across the small dining room, resembling a clockwork soldier. He shook his head.

"Then I have offended you in some way, some slight that I am unaware of, tell me what it is, give me the opportunity to calm the waters and apologize. Was it a woman?"

Once again the pacing and once again a shaking of his head from the small man. The Belgian's brow furrowed, his eyes narrowed, cunning appeared in them. He spoke slowly, his confidence returning. "Then you are from the underworld? You perhaps work for that cunt, Piette, eh? He has finally grown a pair of balls and wants to rub out his biggest competitor, eh?"

Luc Piette was the second most successful forger in the Belgian underworld. He had hounded Dumont's operation for the past two years. But still the small man paced, slowly shaking his head.

Dumont tried again. "Listen to me, *listen to me!* Do you know who *I am*? Do you know who you are *dealing* with?" His face was flushed red and spittle burst forth from his mouth with barely contained fury. His body was rocking in the chair, almost tipping it up with each outburst.

Once again, he received the signal for silence from Gorilla, his finger to his lips.

Dumont took a breath, calmed himself and when he spoke, it was through gritted teeth. "I am connected. I have the patronage of the De Vos brothers. I am protected, you little fucking dwarf! You want to start a war with me, I'll have them cut your fucking balls off and dump you in the Scheldt!"

Gorilla smiled, turned, and pulled up a dining chair to sit down, so that both men were facing each other, only a few feet apart. He stared at his captive for a moment, as if undecided as to what to do, and then he reached under his suit jacket to his right hip, withdrew the Smith & Wesson 39 and the suppressor that fitted onto it. Slowly, he began to screw the two together, taking his time and playing out the piece of theatre to an agonizing degree. "You know, while I was sitting here in the dark, waiting for your return, I had the opportunity to admire the collection of paintings that you have on your wall. Genuine?"

Dumont shrugged. "Mostly... even top class forgeries can reach six figure sums these days."

Gorilla shook his head as if the mysteries of the art world troubled every day of his life. Still slowly screwing the suppressor onto the barrel of the automatic. "Well, they obviously pay well. I've never seen such a stylish and grand apartment. It's very nice, very tasteful. You must be doing well, so more power to your elbow. But now to business, I'm afraid."

He had finished attaching the suppressor, pulled back the slide to do a quick chamber check and confirmed the brass cartridge was in place before letting the slide run forward and flicking off the safety catch. "Oh, forgive me; I've forgotten the most important part."

He quickly jumped from the chair, making his way to the kitchen. He returned moments later with three crystal wine glasses of exquisite quality, and placed one on either arm of the chair the Belgian was tethered to.

The third one had pride of place sandwiched between his legs, touching his balls, on the cushioned seat of the chair. Like a satisfied magician preparing a trick, Gorilla nodded and returned to his own seat, aiming the automatic directly at the terrified man. "Sorry about that. Now we can begin," said Gorilla.

This man is a lunatic, thought Dumont. "What are you going to do to me?" his voice was brittle and shrill.

Gorilla smiled. "When you were a kid, did you ever go to the funfair and have a go at the shooting gallery, play Tin-Can Alley? Do you have that here?"

The forger nodded, afraid that he knew where this conversation was headed. "Yes... of course... what of it?"

"Well, for the purposes of this demonstration..."

"Yes."

"You're going to be one of the tin cans. Here's how it works. I ask a question, you answer. Agreed?" said Gorilla, the business end of his gun never wavering from its target.

* * *

The Belgian nodded, wondering where this bizarre interrogation was headed.

"Good. If I think you're lying to me, or holding something back, I start shooting. Now I've never done this before, so I might be a little off with my aim, so it's in your best interests to keep it accurate. The first two shots might be okay, a little bit of a scratch from the flying glass, but the third." Gorilla indicated the crystal wine glass resting between Dumont's legs and shrugged. "Well, that could go either way I'm afraid, and a bullet isn't very forgiving. Sorry."

Dumont gasped and involuntarily, his eyes flicked to the target next to his testicles.

"So you've got three lives as it were. After that I'm all out of ideas with you and I'll be forced to resort to extreme measures, the measures I don't want to have to carry out unless you force me to. Do you understand?"

Dumont nodded rapidly, his mind working in double time, looking for an escape. "Y-yes."

"Good. Okay. First question, an easy one for sure. Are you, Monsieur Jules Dumont, professional forger?"

The Belgian nodded frantically.

"Good. See, I told you it was easy. Okay, next question. Do you regularly provide documentation for all manner of criminals, mercenaries and general low life—"

"P-p-please, I don't know who the people who visit me are, or what they -

The shot came without warning, a mere flick of Gorilla's wrist and the glass to Dumont's left disappeared in an instant, the sound from the suppressed Smith & Wesson barely audible, a mere phut! A large shard of glass embedded itself in Dumont's left cheek and a trickle of blood slowly rolled down onto his expensive white silk shirt.

"Please do not interrupt me when I'm speaking. It makes me twitchy and it's caused you to lose one of your lives in our little game. Now what was I saying… ah, yes, general low-life scum. Oui?"

To his credit, Gorilla could see that Dumont was keeping his nerve. It was an effort for sure, but he was hanging in there, nonetheless.

"Yes, I provide forged documents for exclusive clientele. What of it?" said Dumont, the blood rolling across his chin.

Gorilla smiled. Now they were getting somewhere. "Good. Next question. I am looking for a particular man, a man who recently purchased several of your products, say, within the last month or so."

"No, that is not possible. I have had no clients since summer last year," said Dumont, hoping he had put enough emphasis into his lie.

Gorilla smiled. He knew the man was lying. He knew, because he'd already tracked down the other two notable forgers to the underworld of Belgium over the past few days. One knew nothing, because he was in a graveyard, having died of a heart attack the previous summer. The other had spilled his guts the moment Gorilla had stuck the barrel of his gun in his eye and threatened to remove his fingers with his straight razor. He too, had known nothing.

But this man was proving to be tougher than he'd expected. He had a certain attitude that Gorilla admired. That alone told him volumes about the likelihood of his professional integrity. *Well, we'll see if we can bend that integrity a little,* thought Gorilla. *Not too much, just enough to give me the names that the target was now using.* Gorilla gave an imperceptible flick of his wrist and a squeeze of the trigger. The glass on the right disappeared in a hail of shards. The forger flinched and gave out another mewl of fear.

"Monsieur Dumont why do you resist; you are fast running out of lives. Come, you have a nice life here, why spoil it for some client who would turn you in at the drop of a hat?" said Gorilla reasonably.

"Alright… alright… I just need time to think."

"He would have purchased several identities – I would imagine; you have done work for him before. Tall, dark, slim, well-dressed, possibly Spanish or Italian. You know whom I mean?" said Gorilla.

"Yes, I know who you mean. And you are correct, he did visit me recently, I simply forgot."

"Of course, of course," soothed Gorilla. *Don't kid a kidder,* he thought. "What did he buy from you?"

Dumont thought for a moment, flicking through his mental catalogue of services. "There were several sets of passports, six in all. Three for himself and three for a business colleague, plus driving licenses and assorted identifications," replied Dumont, the words coming out in rapid succession.

Gorilla considered this. He hadn't expected details of the second assassin to fall into his lap also. This could turn out to be an interesting interrogation. "Who is he?"

"I know him as Marquez. Only that, I swear."

Gorilla considered the possibility and reasoned that it seemed the most likely. "Alright, I assume that you have the details of the false I.D. on file somewhere, say here in your private office?"

Dumont shook his head. "Alas, I do not keep copies or details of private clients, I—"

Phut! The explosion between Dumont's legs made the base of the wine goblet shatter and sent the bowl spinning up into the air before landing on his lap. A smoking hole had miraculously appeared where the bullet had blasted through the velvet cushion. The noise this time from Dumont was not a mewl, but a full on scream of terror.

"I'm getting quite good at this, Monsieur Dumont. Unfortunately for you, we are out of glasses." Gorilla stared at him hard. "The next shot means that our conversation will be over, permanently. And you were doing so well."

The Belgian forger looked down at the smoking bullet hole, his face pale except for the river of blood streaming down his face. "So what now? Torture ? You're going to torture me, you pig!"

Gorilla shook his head. "Torture? No, not my style, not my style at all. It takes too long and it's far too noisy. I prefer the more direct approach."

Dumont's eyes began to widen, certain that his imminent death was fast approaching. He watched as his tormenter placed the pistol on the table next to him, close at hand, then reached inside the bag that he'd brought in with him and withdrew the item that was going to make Jules Dumont, eminent art dealer and forger to the criminal fraternity of Antwerp sing like a canary.

"Oh my God," said Dumont, his voice a hoarse whisper. His eyes widened because there, resting on the table in front of him, and recently removed from the man's Gladstone bag, was the biggest wad of American Dollars the Belgian had seen for a very, very long time...

* * *

Dumont glanced from the pile of money on the table to the man holding the silenced weapon. A trickle of sweat rolled down his upper lip, onto his dandyish pencil moustache. "You mean you aren't going to kill me?" he asked. The question held a tone of disbelief, as if he suspected this was another trick from the small blond enforcer.

Gorilla stared him straight in the eye. "That very much depends on you. The way I see it is, you're a business man and your business, like mine, is very secretive. But on occasions, we can come together to our mutual benefit to assist each other. I need some information, you require money. We can conduct our business covertly and go our separate ways with no outside parties the wiser. Agreed?"

The Belgian nodded, it was the way most of his business was conducted. Through trust and a mutual respect for each other's trade. The question was whether or not he was going to let a foolish sense of professional pride get in the way of an easy payday.

Gorilla stood and watched the terrified man. "Simply put, the choice is yours. You can have a bag full of cash for the information, or you can have a bullet through the head. Either way, I'll get the information I want sooner or later, whether you're dead or alive is of no consequence to me."

Dumont frowned. "The Mexicans call it silver or lead. Of course I agree, I'm no fool, but why this rather unorthodox way to initiate our… business?"

Gorilla shrugged. "Because I needed to establish my bona fides and get your attention. Time is of the essence, as is the truthfulness of your answers."

"I see – hence your pistol display."

"The money I'm authorized to give you will more than recompense you for any discomfort you suffer here tonight. But more importantly, I wanted to focus your mind, and a bullet fired at close range tends to do that," said Gorilla, the '39 still rock steady.

The forger shuddered, remembering the sensation of the bullet passing mere inches from his groin. That was too close.

Gorilla continued. "Plus, I don't want you to be in any doubt that if you do lead me down the garden path with false information, or you decide to tip off certain parties of mutual interest via a phone call, I will come back here, I will find you and I will, slowly, kill you by using you as target practice."

Dumont snorted derisively. "I wasn't kidding, my friend, when I said I was protected! I'm under the protection of one of the biggest criminal gangs in Europe. They take threats against their own very seriously; it is bad for both their business and reputation."

Gorilla smiled and shook his head sadly. "Not important to me. I operate on a much bigger stage than Belgium; global in fact. I can hit you or them whenever I wish and disappear. But then you and your protectors will be dead, and I will be without the information I require. As I say it's your choice; five thousand dollars, or a bullet that costs less than a buck to make. That's the facts."

Dumont stared at this strange, tough little man. He was hard and he was no doubt a resourceful operator, but there was also a fairness about him that Dumont instantly liked. He glanced from the silenced automatic to the pile of cash sitting on his dining table.

"Do we have a deal? My trigger finger is starting to get tired, and when it gets tired it gets a little twitchy," threatened Gorilla, pushing the forger one last time.

Dumont sagged in the chair. "Oh yes, we have a deal, an understanding, or whatever you wish to call it. But right now, I think I need a very large drink to steady my nerves!"

* * *

Ten minutes later, Dumont led Gorilla down into the cellar of his house, where the forger kept his state-of-the-art workshop. Dumont went down the steps first, with Gorilla clutching the scruff of the man's collar with one hand and pushing the '39 into the small of the Belgian's back with the other. Any false moves or any tricks and Gorilla was ready to blow his spine open.

"I normally meet new clients at a bar, initially. Once I've satisfied myself that they're genuine and have paid a deposit, I allow them here to the workshop once the product is complete," explained Dumont.

The cellar was furnished as one might expect a high end printer, or book binders would be. Workstations, printing presses of various ages. On one wall were a multitude of ink bottles, next to reams of various qualities of papers, and numerous solvents, glues, pens, and pencils. It was from here that Jules Dumont furnished high end criminals with the means to slip in and out of countries unhindered.

Gorilla noted that Dumont seemed to have recovered his composure. He guessed that the introduction of American dollars had brought him back down to earth and shook the fear from his mind.

Determined to keep the momentum on Dumont, Gorilla asked about his business relationship with this 'Marquez'.

"Oh yes, I had done work for him before, many years ago. I thought he had retired," Dumont explained.

"What was he after?"

"The usual; passports, visas, driving licenses; the same things everyone wants."

"Which means?"

"Which means he evidently wished to travel far and wide,without arousing suspicion."

"How many?" asked Gorilla.

"There were three sets of passports and driving licenses each. One was French, one German, the other Dutch. One of each for him, and one of each for his business acquaintance," he said.

"The acquaintance. Who was he?"

"I don't know, I only met with Marquez."

"How much did they pay?"

Dumont thought for a while. He decided that his best policy, and chance for survival, was to be honest. "In truth, they paid more than the normal going rate. Marquez wanted the material quickly, but he also wanted it to be of the highest quality. This requires a certain degree of craftsmanship, not to mention my costs which are incurred for papers, pickpockets who have to filch the genuine papers, and the inks – my God, the price of some of the inks alone!"

Dumont rifled through a filing cabinet until he found a key, hidden within one of the manila files. He took the key and made his way to a painting which hung on the wall. The forger lifted the painting, revealing that it was hinged on the left hand side and moved it sideways to reveal a safe. He inserted the key and quickly reached inside.

Gorilla tensed, ready to move his finger onto the trigger of the '39. He hoped Dumont wasn't going to be foolish enough to go for a weapon. It would be a bad mistake, as Gorilla would have to ventilate the back of the man's head. Instead, Dumont removed a ledger, old and battered. He flicked through the pages, murmured an "Ah, here we are", and passed the book over.

Gorilla scanned through the names listed in Dumont's ledger. On the first page were the false names Marquez was using:

Vincent Joosen - Dutch
Andre Delacroix - French
Ulf Bayer - West German

On the following page were the names that had been assigned to the as yet unnamed associate:

Donal Rattigan - Irish
Jonathon Pike - British
Julian Blattner - Swiss

Gorilla quickly ripped out the page containing the details, placed it in his coat pocket and then turned to Dumont. "What about the photographs they used in the passports?" he asked.

Dumont held up his hands. "He had taken care of the photos himself. He only gave them to me on the day so that I could glue them in, seal them up and run over the fake stamps onto the paperwork. I never saw any negatives or other copies. He was a very careful man, Monsieur."

That was annoying, thought Gorilla. He had hoped the false papers would have current photographs with them; instead he'd have to settle for the killer's real name and the aliases on his false documentation.

"Can I ask? Why do you want this man so badly?" Dumont questioned, closing up the files and placing them back in the cabinet.

"He owes me money," said Gorilla, not even trying to hide the lie.

Dumont frowned. "Monsieur, please, I have one question. Can you give me your word that this will never be traced back to me? It could ruin my reputation and my life if this Marquez ever discovered what I have told you."

Gorilla placed a fatherly hand on the shoulder of the other man. "Don't worry. It's a fair bet they won't be coming back this way again. Ever!"

"And I can trust you on this?"

"You'll have to," barked Gorilla. "But never mind. Now that we know each other professionally, this could be the beginning of a beautiful friendship."

Jules Dumont doubted that very much. And like one who can slowly feel the hangman's noose slipping tightly around his neck, he knew that this wouldn't be the last he would see of this devil.

* * *

Ten minutes later, the small man had packed up his belongings and told Jules Dumont to stay in his workshop for the next half an hour. "Don't try to follow me or call anyone. If you do, I'll take that as a breach of our agreement," Gorilla had told him.

And so the Belgian forger had sat in the darkness of his studio, his hands still shaking, and waited until his newly-discovered nemesis for the evening had long gone. Eventually he staggered up the stairs to his lounge in desperate need of a very large drink to steady his nerves. He glanced around the semi-darkness of the room and noted that his phone line had been cut, but everything else was in its place and un-damaged.

It was only when he turned to sit at the table and stare at the piles of dollar bills he'd just earned, when he noticed the small, shiny 9mm bullet which had been left for him. His hand started to shake again as he held up, and inspected, what was both a warning, and the calling card of a ghost in the darkness.

Book Four:
By Way of Deception

Chapter One

Following the successful interrogation, and the subsequent recruitment of the forger as an agent, the word from London, and more specifically Masterman, was for the fire-team to not rest on their laurels.

In the space of one evening Gorilla had successfully found the names, both real and false, of his future target and had also, albeit unwittingly, recruited Dumont as a potential source for the future. He'd burned the forger once; he could certainly do it again. Gorilla passed the man's details to the Head of Station in Brussels, who he was sure would be happy to have one of Europe's most successful forgers 'on the hook' as a confidential informant.

Gorilla's persuasive methods had yielded not only a list of the false passports, but also the name of the contractor who they'd listened to on the tape recording. Marquez!

The name was quickly run through the files at Broadway. With a name, the files soon spilled out the limited information SIS had about Juan Raul Marquez. His war record, interrogation after the war, the information he gave to the prosecutors at Nuremburg and after that, pathetically little. There were only passing references and rumors from friendly intelligence services and a blurred photo of him taken postwar during his internment, before he ratted out his fellow Nazi's.

"Get out there and start tracking down even the smallest clue. Find out what you can about this man – anything – no matter how small.

Better that, than you two sitting on your backsides enjoying the good life at the tax payer's expense," chided Masterman to the two Redaction agents. "But play it subtle, behind the curtains, no mention of a manhunt. If anybody asks, we're looking for him to offer him some work, nothing more – understood?"

The Burrowers dug deeper and more laterally. They checked through agents' reports that they hadn't previously considered; British mercenaries recently returned from the Congo were paid a visit and questioned by local SIS station officers, a number of European agents with underworld connections were also run to ground and discreetly interrogated. All provided snippets of rumors; a name here, a location there, but nothing which could help them nail the killer's location. The most likely, and plausible, source details were passed to the team in Paris, and over the following fortnight the MACE fire-team set about touring Europe in the hope of scrounging a lead or a piece of intelligence that might put them on the man's scent.

In Amsterdam, there was a onetime confidence trickster who had allegedly worked for Marquez on a smuggling job years ago. But the man hadn't seen him since the payoff. "He was a smooth operator," the conman told Gorilla as they sat having a drink in a bar. "If you're going to work with him, you won't go far wrong. He's not a man to cross, though. But if you see him, tell him that Remy was asking after him."

There was a similar story from a former art thief turned legitimate businessman, who was now based in Berlin. After hanging around all day, Gorilla and Nicole had managed to arrange a meeting with the man at his offices. The story they went with was that they had some 'merchandise', which may or may not have been diamonds, and they wanted to smuggle them out of Africa.

The man had greeted their story with a serious response. "Marquez is a top man. If you are coming to me looking for a reference, then I will certainly give it with pleasure. He has many talents, he is a born operator, which in our business is a rarity. He will go the full length of the rope for his clients, but I should warn you that if you attempt to double cross or cheat him... well... let's just say he has a reputation for revenge."

"And how do we get in touch with him?" Nicole had asked.

The art thief shrugged. "The last I heard, he had moved to Luxembourg, but that was years ago. Besides, Marquez is the type of man who finds you, not the other way around. I understand he takes his privacy very seriously and is an expert at disappearing."

In Madrid, there lived a cancer-ridden, former SS intelligence officer by the name of Helf, who had known Marquez in Paris when he had been an agent of the SD. Gorilla and Nicole had phoned ahead to see the old man. Their cover story was that they were conducting background checks on a certain Marquez, whom SIS were interested in recruiting for an operation, and would Señor Helf be interested in answering a few questions about his experience of the man?

"I still occasionally have a use for your service here in Madrid," said Helf. "I pass them the odd piece of intelligence. Titbits, really. Tamzin, Oscar, come to heel, damn you!" Two Dobermans sat on either side of the old man's chair, resembling lions bookending a royal throne. The house was humbly decorated; a photo of a much younger Helf, taken on his wedding day, took pride of place on a stone fireplace. Next to it was a dust-covered urn.

"I shall tell you a story about Marquez that will, perhaps, help you understand what kind of man he is. He was working for us in Paris as an active agent – no matter what he said later, he was in it up to his neck. He would run sources for us, conduct surveillance on possible resistance leaders and yes, he did a little throat-slitting for us when the occasion was called for. Anyway, Marquez had a lover, a young man. We all knew Marquez was queer, but he didn't like to admit it openly. He got into a relationship with this young married man, who was obviously conflicted about his sexuality. Marquez became more and more obsessed with his lover and despite his pleas for this young man to leave his wife, the man wouldn't. As I understand it, this went on for quite some time, until one day, the wife and her children were shipped off to the Avenue Foch for interrogation. It seems that the wife had been helping the resistance in Paris. She had been informed upon and arrested."

"Was there any proof against her?" asked Nicole, thinking of her own mother suffering a similar fate at the hands of the Nazi's. It sent a chill down her spine.

The former SS man shook his head. "No, but the arresting officer was Marquez. We let the senior agents do that sort of thing for us from time to time. It saved us from getting our hands dirty when there were willing agents to act as proxy."

"What happened to her?"

Helf shrugged. "She died under questioning. Tortured, sodomized – until eventually her heart gave out. I understand the interrogator was very, how shall we say – *exuberant* in his methods."

Gorilla frowned. "Don't tell me, the interrogator was…"

The old man nodded. "That's right – Marquez. He had eliminated his love rival, had her children thrown into an orphanage and all because of his lust for another man. He is both ruthless and cold."

"What happened to the husband?" asked Gorilla.

"As far as I remember, he was found murdered a few weeks later, with a bullet to the back of the head, execution style."

Both Nicole and Gorilla dropped their gaze to their feet. The old man's implication was obvious. Had Marquez argued with, or simply grown tired of his lover after all?

Then, as an afterthought Helf said, "Are you really going to use him operationally?"

Gorilla looked at Nicole and then back to the old man. He shook his head. "No."

Helf thought about this and nodded. "Good. I hope you find him, for whatever it is that's going to happen to him. He's a psychopath. I think you people should remember that if it wasn't for willing agents like Marquez and others, we would never have been able to do the things we ended up doing."

* * *

Two days later, Nicole and Gorilla were back in their Paris apartment, exhausted after a fortnight of travelling. That night, they sat in the lounge, each nursing a glass of wine as they went over everything they'd learned about the man they were hunting.

"Do we chance a visit to Luxembourg?" asked Nicole. "It could be that he's returning between the contracts."

Gorilla considered this. It would be tempting to get close to where this man lived, but operationally, they would be better staying in Paris, ready to jump when the false passports were finally flagged as being used in a different country. "No, it's better if we stay here. We'll get the Luxembourg Station to run a trace."

So they put in a request, via London, for SIS Luxembourg to run a search for the man. The answer came back within a day. Gorilla made his regular visit to one of his tame telephone boxes and called direct to Consterdine in the Paris Station.

"By all accounts, he's a respectable businessman, at least in Luxembourg he is," said Consterdine. "SIS Luxembourg's contact with the local police said that as far as he was concerned, the man was not known to them."

"What about his home address?" asked Gorilla, scribbling notes on his pocket pad with a worn-down pencil.

"Actually, it's both his home and business address: a shop at the front and an apartment at the back. Marquez runs a fine art and antique business, does quite well by all accounts. Keeps himself to himself and is there most days."

"Most days?"

"The neighbors say that he occasionally goes away on business, for anything up to a week at a time, like now. The shop's been closed for the past month or so, which they admit is a tad unusual."

Gorilla wrote down the address in Luxembourg, thanked Consterdine and hung up. He stared at the notes. The man was definitely 'active' and was loose somewhere in Europe, either laying low or getting ready to go after the next target. Time was a factor. Unless they got a lead on their whereabouts soon – say in the next few days – the

MACE fire-team would have to uproot and go and sit on the shoulder of the next possible target on the hit list. Keeping at a distance and staying well back, hoping they'd picked the right agent to protect, and remaining in the shadows waiting for the assassins to make a move. It would be an unenviable task, too much to go wrong and too risky for both the protectors and the protected.

So it would be here in Paris, head to Italy, or back to England. It was a gamble and in truth, it would very much be guesswork as to which one to pick. Gorilla needed a lucky break and he reasoned that the only way to trace the hit-team was to catch them during what the spy-catchers called 'transitions'. Moving from one place to another, it meant catching them when they were most at risk and most vulnerable as they left one country and entered another. This option involved travel, and travel meant that you had to have passports, flight tickets, train tickets, car hire vouchers, and all the things that left a trail, no matter how well you tried to hide or disguise them.

Now that London had the names on the false travel documents, it was only a matter of time before they turned up somewhere. The question was though; would his fire-team be able to move quickly enough to intercept them? He hoped so, because at the moment the sand in the hourglass was quickly draining away.

* * *

In the end it was the Burrowers who got a 'hit' on the flagged passports.

The 'flagging' of the airport watch lists was a slow, grinding process and the French authorities had missed the 'Joosen' passport by several days. The call had gone out from SIS to friendly intelligence and police agencies, that the British were looking for a couple of suspected 'couriers' working for the Bulgarians. At least, that was the story fed to the liaison offices across Europe.

Toby and his Burrowers insisted on an 'Observe and Report Order', which was jargon for 'watch them and let us know where they go'.

They had sat around the office and sweated over the past week, waiting, praying and hoping that they hadn't been too late and missed the quarry.

The breakthrough came in early March, when a tired and overworked intelligence officer of the French Security Service, the DST, was backtracking through the airport watch-lists. Late at night and armed with only a ruler and a pencil, his job was to match the passenger lists from every airline which came in or out of France to the ever growing 'watch-list' of suspected terrorists, spies and international organized crime figures.

He moved the ruler carefully down the printout list, lest he should miss his place, and then would tick off the name if it wasn't flagged. He was well into his second hour, with still another thirty minutes before his next break, when he noted the name of a passenger who had travelled from Orly to Marseilles a week earlier, a Dutch citizen by the name of Vincent Joosen.

His eye flicked over the watch list. He looked away and then looked back. A rub of his eyes to make sure that he had a match. Vincent Joosen. The same!

The intelligence officer flicked through the operations order file to see what his response should be. He ran his finger down to the 'J's' and noted the Observe and Report Order, confirming he should immediately contact an officer of the British Secret Intelligence Service by the name of Tobias Burrows at Century House, London.

Chapter Two

Marseilles – March 1965

The German was perched on the end of the bed; his fingers interlocked with barely contained fury and frustration as he stared at his two 'senior employers'. He was large, well-built, greying at the temples and sweating, due to a combination of the Mediterranean temperature and the woolen suit he wore. Suppressed fury riddled his face; the glower seemingly a permanent feature.

Their base was a series of connected rooms on the top floor of the Hotel Azure, overlooking the old port of Marseilles. The rooms were serviceable, at best. In fact, they were disgusting and no doubt more suited for clients who wanted to bang the *putain's* these Corsican pimps peddled.

The only thing in its favor, was that as well as access to the main part of the hotel, they also had a separate entrance via an external staircase to the rear, meaning they could come and go without interfering with the 'business' at the front of house.

The hotel was part illegal gambling den and part brothel, used exclusively by the Capo's soldiers. It was considered a safe-house, as it was under the protection of the Guerini Clan, which ran the prostitution, vice, protection rackets, and drug trade for Southern France. The hotel offered discretion, anonymity and security, so that the team could discuss their next target.

The German pondered – as a man with much regret and wasted time in his life is often known to do – about how he came to be reduced to working for these two cutthroats. They had no honor, no sense of duty, and he trusted them about as far as he could throw them.

After all, it was not so very long ago when one of these men would undoubtedly have been one of his informants, and as for the other, the German and his team would have been hunting him down, interrogating him before dragging him out into the forests and emptying a magazine into him. Assuming he had survived the interrogation methods the German was infamous for… and not many did.

The German's name was Alfred Nadel. It was not the name on his current travelling papers, but it was the one he'd been born with and the one he held dear. He had, over recent years, been a Muller, a Bonson and a Mobert, and even if he had to swap and change identities in order to keep his liberty and survive in this hostile, post-war world that he despised, it was a small price he was happy to pay.

He had started his career working for one of the top men in the Sicherheitendienst, rising quickly and he'd been one of the prime architects in the plot to kidnap two British Intelligence men on the Czech border. Several weeks later, war had been declared and once again his career in the intelligence world had flourished.

He had run a small team of hunters, whose specialty had been the tracking and elimination of the various 'terrorist' and underground groups. He'd wanted to take his team to the ultimate hunting ground – Paris. He had been given Holland instead. He fumed, pushed his team harder and it had worked, earning him the reputation as one of the most feared SS officers in the Low Countries.

The extermination of Partisans on the Russian Front had been his finest hour, hunting down the Russians like rats. It had been good while it lasted, but by 1945, and with the tide of the war turning, it hadn't been long until the roles had been reversed and he became the hunted.

He had finally been captured not long after the fall of Berlin by the Americans and was set to be tried at Nuremburg, until one night he'd seized the opportunity to escape. He had strangled his guard with his bare hands and fled into the night. For the following decade, he'd remained on the run, living in the shadows, being hidden and aided by his former colleagues of the SS in their underground organizations: a bit of money here, false papers there and for a while, never sleeping in the same location for more than a few nights at a time.

He had travelled and hidden in South America, Spain, and Africa, and he found all of them to be shitholes. Instead, he yearned to return to his homeland. He had earned a living as everything from mercenary to a barman, from a garbage collector to a paid killer. All the while dodging the police forces holding warrants for his arrest, as well as an endless stream of Mossad agents determined to liquidate him and his former comrades.

He had met the Georgian through a mutual arms dealer contact years ago, when he had been hired as part of a team tasked to remove the arms dealer's 'rival' in Antwerp. The job had gone well and they had, sporadically, kept in touch. Of late though, the work began to dry up. His age was going against him, he knew, plus there were just too many operators for too few contracts. His last job had been working as an enforcer for a smuggling gang based out of the Spanish Costas. It was demeaning, and if he was honest with himself, he could probably have made more working as a waiter.

So when the Georgian had sought him out for a long-term contract, he'd snapped the little man's hand off. But the fact that he was a sub-contractor and not a main player in the job still ate away at him. He unclasped his fingers and turned his attention back to the Catalan and the Georgian. The subject at hand was who was to be the primary agent on the next hit.

"Can I just interject?" said Nadel. They both turned to look at him, one with amusement and one with indignation.

"Of course, Alfred," said Marquez.

"As I see it," said the German, "so far I've taken all the risk and done the main bulk of the work."

There, it was out there and to his mind, it needed to be said. The last hit on the most recent Soviet agent on the team's list had been handled by Nadel. It had been a relatively simple task really, driving, nothing more. The only difference was that it was at high speed directly at the victim, but still, it was just driving and was not his usual method of dispatching a 'mark'.

"That's not strictly true, is it? We were both involved in the operation in Zurich, and I personally took on the job in Hamburg," said Marquez.

Nadel snorted with derision. Of course the Catalan had taken sole responsibility for the hit on the Diplomat, he'd been a queer and knowing of Marquez's tastes, it had no doubt been part business and part pleasure for him.

"Did I say something wrong?" asked Marquez. He was starting to get annoyed with this German's infernal mood swings.

"No, no, it's just... never mind. Forget it." In truth, Nadel had been in a bad mood since they arrived here in Marseilles. He hated these stinking Corsicans with their *pastis*, bouillabaisse and arrogance. The majority of the milieu 'foot soldiers' were nothing more than glorified pimps, muscle in suits. Not even the whores who had been supplied to him by his hosts had improved his mood. "And why do we have to stay holed up in this filthy hotel? It stinks of sewage and as for these Corsicans..."

Marquez frowned. He had negotiated the terms of their stay personally with one of the senior lieutenants of the Guerini Clan. For an exorbitant fee, they had been given access to a secure floor of the hotel, food and drink, and enjoyed the added advantage of the hotel being protected by a number of Guerini toughs from the milieu.

The Georgian interjected. "You know why; we've been over all of this. We did three hits in northern Europe – the best place to hide out, re-group and plan is south. The Corsicans offered us safe haven so we can get the plumbing in place for the rest of the operation."

"We should have gone straight to the next target country, it would have been quicker," blustered Nadel.

Marquez, the leader, came over and stared down at him. When he spoke, his voice was calm and reasonable. "Yes, it would. Are you in a hurry, Alfred? You have somewhere else to be, perhaps? We take our time, we do it right, we go careful, yes. We let the dust settle. We are still within the timeframe of the contract we have been given."

Nadel waved his hand in a dismissive gesture. "Ahh… give me a gun, and I'll go to the next job and finish it myself… *quickly!* Why all this shitting about… we should be splitting up, hitting targets separately!"

"No. We are more effective as a team. We split, too many things can go wrong," said Gioradze.

"You did the Hamburg hit on your own," Nadel countered, talking directly to Marquez.

Marquez shrugged. "That's because I was the best, and besides, I don't think that you would have liked that young man's sexual tastes. Or is that it? Did I 'queer your pitch', as the English say?"

The innuendo was not wasted on Nadel, who reacted the way Marquez knew he would. "Fuck you, you—"

"Hey, that's enough!" said Gioradze, standing, arms ready to launch at the German like an attack dog in case he made a play for his master, and his fingers edged nearer to the concealed weapon in the waistband of his suit trousers.

"And fuck you, too," ranted the German.

But the steam had started to go out of Nadel's tirade; violence and aggression were not the best tactics to be used in a confined space such as this, especially with two experienced killers. "I'm going out… I need to walk." He stood and moved his bulk quickly to the door.

"Be back by four, we have much work to do," ordered Marquez, before returning to the maps and intelligence papers he was working on.

Nadel slammed the door on the way out, his point made. During the afternoons he had taken to walking along to the harbor and stopping at a small cafe to rest and take a drink, anything to escape the stifling confines of the hotel suite. Today he would need that fresh air more than ever.

At the lobby, he nodded reluctantly to the two toughs who 'minded' the door and made his way out into the glare of the afternoon sun. He was rounding the corner heading down to the Old Port when he heard Gioradze's voice. "Alfred, wait, we need to talk..."

* * *

The afternoon sun bathed the Old Port of Marseilles, turning the walls of its buildings a dazzling white and giving the reflection of the water the look of black glass. The smell of seafood, garlic and aniseed wafted in and out of the doorways and windows of the bars and cafes, and on the water, the boats rocked gently to a rhythm of their own making. The seafront was an idyll of beautiful women, mysterious men and the promise of adventure.

But that was only the veneer of the Mediterranean port. Beneath its surface Marseilles was 'run' by the organized crime gangs of the Corsican Mafia. The preeminent organized crime bosses in Marseilles were the Guerinis', and like their Sicilian cousins, they had graduated from a small island, in this case Corsica, to the mainland in 1912 and set about, through tough tactics and bloody vendettas, revolutionizing the criminal underworld in Marseilles.

Aside from the usual illegal gambling, prostitution and protection rackets, the Guerini brothers had cornered the market in both heroin production and smuggling. As well as the obvious benefits of this affluent trade, the Corsicans also bought political power and influence which was so necessary in order to keep the supply chain of narcotics flowing across the Mediterranean and into Asia. Marseilles was their choke point and everything related to the Guerinis' criminal empire was run through that harbor port. They were masters of all they surveyed.

The Georgian knew that Marquez had worked as a 'freelancer' for the Guerinis' on numerous occasions; usually on contracts that the Corsicans were unable to commit themselves or had trouble fulfilling. The Corsicans were fine pulling a trigger in a gangland feud on their own turf, but planning out an assassination in areas where they were not so well acquainted was definitely the preserve of an experienced assassin, an assassin like Juan Marquez.

This relationship with the Corsicans had allowed the team a chance to set up base and think through their next move – for a price, of course, because the Corsicans were nothing if not ruthless business-men, and the 'rent' for their stay in one of the Guerinis' safe-houses was, by most standards, astronomical.

But as Marquez had told them, it was a worthwhile cost. "We run into any trouble, it's good to have the milieu on hand. They're tough boys and don't take too kindly to anyone pissing on their patch. Be-sides, the cost will be put in as expenses to the CIA, it won't affect our remittance at all."

Gioradze just hoped they didn't end up going to war with the Guerini Clan because this stupid German ended up insulting them over an imagined slight. War – no, it wouldn't come to that, he knew. Marquez would take the German for a boat ride and only the Catalan killer would end up returning. They walked quickly, heading down to the harbor, Nadel walking at a pace to work his frustration out of his system, Gioradze to catch up with him.

"So what is it then, Alfred?" asked Gioradze.

"What?"

"You fucking know what. You're acting like we owe you a fucking living, complaining, moaning about the slightest thing. Is this how it was in the SS? No wonder you fuckers lost."

"Fuck you, Magyar pig!"

The Georgian grabbed the bigger man by the arm and dragged him back to a halt. He raised his sunglasses and placed them on top of his head, all the better to look the big German directly in the eyes. "You know, for a broken down old man without a pot to piss in, you're acting like some kind of prima donna here."

"I was a respected soldier; I fought against terrorists, I was an in-telligence officer in the SD, I—"

"Oh please, that's ancient history, a long time ago, Alfred. This is our contract and you work for us. It's as simple as that, and the sooner you wake up to that fact, the better. We say jump on this contract and you say how high!"

The German was fuming, but as if to show that he wasn't frightened of the bigger, older man, the Georgian craned his neck up to meet the other man's face, until they were almost nose-to-nose. "Listen, Alfred, you're a fucking beggar in this game, understand? If you don't like it, you can piss off back to hide under that rock where I found you... *understand!*"

The German knew there was no going back in this game. You weren't allowed to walk away from a job of this magnitude halfway through; you completed the full terms, or you ended up dead. The only question was, who was going to eliminate you – the people you were working against, or the people you were working with.

"Look. I think we both need to calm down," Gioradze said. "This is a good number for you and Marquez is a good operator. The word I have, is that if we do this right, there's more work on the way. And let's face it, none of us are getting any younger. It would make a nice little retirement plan, eh?" Gioradze watched the German's face carefully. His placating seemed to be doing the trick, and he watched as Nadel calmed himself down, rationalizing it out in his own head.

"Okay, okay... maybe if you included me in the planning more."

Gioradze threw up his hands in exasperation and smiled. "Of course, Alfred, of course. We'll include you all you like. Just as long as you re-member that we pay the bills and our word is final. Now have your walk, maybe grab a *pastis*, then straighten your head out and get your ass back to the Azure. We have a fucking job to plan out." The Georgian started to walk away, but only took a couple of steps before he stopped and turned. "Oh, and Alfred? This is your last chance. You understand me?"

Nadel watched Gioradze as he walked away, disappearing into the maze of streets. The threat was clear. He noticed his hands were shaking imperceptibly, and he was sure that a drink at his favorite cafe along the shoreline would settle him.

* * *

They had been in Marseilles for less than a week.

Following the lead that had been 'coerced' from the forger in Belgium and given to Toby and his team back in London, Grant and Nicole had settled back into an operational hibernation in Paris. They were good days; Nicole had the opportunity to enjoy the city she'd fallen in love with as a teenager when she visited with her father, whilst Grant had packed them each an overnight bag, just in case, and taken to pacing the floor to an irritating degree.

Several days later the call came from London which once again spurred them into action. "It's Marseilles," declared Toby, down the telephone. "The names of Vincent Joosen and Donal Rattigan were flagged as having both travelled separately to Marseille Provence Airport, that's the main airport which services the Old Port. Both were on connecting flights from Orly."

"So we can assume they originated from Paris?" said Grant.

"Well, one did, certainly, but the Joosen name shows up as travelling in from Germany a day earlier. From there he flew Orly to Marseilles. After that, we assume he took a taxi to his final destination, but what that final destination actually is we don't know. Nothing has shown up yet."

"And that's all we've got to go on?" asked Grant.

"For the moment I'm afraid, yes. Counter-intelligence is not an exact science, we deal with the obtuse," said Toby, defending his chosen trade stoically.

"You can say that again, sunshine." Grant, for all his careful planning still preferred the simple and direct approach; it had kept him alive for many years. He knew that it was only when things began to get complicated or abstract that problems started to occur for the operatives in the intelligence world.

"My advice is to get yourselves down to Marseilles double quick, at least that way, you're on the ground should something crop up. We'll keep going through the latest travel information that comes in. As soon as we know, you'll know," Toby announced.

They moved quickly and had immediately taken the first train from Gare du Nord, Paris to Gare Saint-Charles in Marseilles. The journey was a combined blur of exotic seascapes and arid, dry fields peppered with the occasional rundown farm buildings. The conversation was kept light and away from business.

"So his name's Lenin? Why did he name himself after Lenin? What is he, a communist?" asked Grant, only half serious.

"No," said Nicole, rolling her eyes at him in exasperation. "Not Lenin. *Lenn-on!*"

"Oh…"

"He's the lead singer. He plays the guitar."

Grant shook his head in wonderment. "And the others are Paul, George and… wait, let me get this right… Ringo! Honestly… Ringo?"

"What's wrong with Ringo?"

"If you have to ask… And these lads are a musical group called The Beatle Band, is that right?"

"No, Jack, The Beatles, they're just called *The* Beatles. Where have you been for the past eighteen months? Living in a cave?"

In truth, Grant had little time for 'modern' music, and only limited interest in music of any kind. He had been born at the tail end of the depression era and had experienced destitution, poverty and squalor. There was little time for the luxury of entertainment, no matter how much it was needed. His formative adult years had been built around surviving the austerity and hardship of the post-war era, where once again, circumstances had dictated that his attentions be geared more to survival than relaxation.

Now movies, that was a different matter. He loved movies. He could revel for hours in the wonders of Chaplin, John Ford, De Mille and Welles.

And so the conversations had gone between them on the train with both trying to keep the topics light and carefree, both pushing to the back of their minds – even just for a few hours – the potential threat and danger that awaited them.

They had arrived in Marseille that very same evening. An apartment had been hastily arranged for them on a month-by-month contract through an SIS 'front company', which specialized in such matters. They settled into a three bedroom, first floor apartment in a quiet block in the 6th Arrondissement on the edge of the city. The Marseilles apartment was better than the squalid Paris base, but not by much. *SIS seemed to have the monopoly on picking rundown accommodation for their undercover officers,* thought Nicole. It had that dilapidated look that her Dad would have said belonged to a retired, aging pimp; rundown, dry, and smelling of desperation.

They had a bedroom each with the third being used as their ad hoc operations room, and while it wasn't as cosmopolitan as their initial base in Paris, it did have the added advantage of having its own telephone line, which was vital in case they had to react quickly to a lead from London. They lived frugally and ventured out only when necessary, once again playing the cover role of newlyweds, so the rarity of leaving the apartment fitted their story well.

After securing the apartment and setting up their base and equipment, they had nothing to do but wait for the Burrowers back in London to give them a tip-off; something, anything that could point them in the right direction and spur them into action. So they waited.

By day five, the London team realized they were searching for a needle in a haystack and settled in for the long haul, both mentally and physically. The Burrowers had alerted their contacts with the police and intelligence informants in France, but so far, cast-iron information was proving to be scarce. The killers weren't registered in any of the main hotels, nothing appeared for car hires or flights out of the country – at least, not yet – and there was always the possibility that they'd taken a train to another destination. So the search continued, relentlessly.

By day six, Grant was bouncing off the walls, and he could see that the confinement was taking its toll on Nicole, also. He made an executive decision, more for his own sanity rather than for operational reasons. "Okay, we need to scout the area, get our bearings," Grant had said. "If they're here, we'll find them."

"True," agreed Nicole, toweling her hair dry after another shower – anything to kill the time. "And we're not going to find them sitting around here. Besides, I've never been to Marseilles and I'd like to see a bit more than these four walls and the view of the street outside."

Grant nodded. "Alright, some ground rules. We have to be careful not to draw attention to ourselves, the local police are riddled with informers for the Corsican gangs and we don't want to step on the toes of the local underworld. We'll see what comes back from London's police contacts before we start getting in too deep."

They dressed well, as honeymooners would. Nicole in a stylish cream shift dress with a short red jacket, her hair tied back in a carefree manner. Grant wore a lightweight summer suit and a light blue shirt, open at the neck. Nicole had picked it out for him.

"There," she pronounced inspecting them both in the wardrobe mirror. "We look fabulous enough for you to take me to lunch."

"We are meant to be at work, you know," he grumbled, but didn't sound as if he meant it.

She smiled, sensing she'd scored a victory point in their pretend marriage. *Teasing Grant was no challenge,* she decided. He was such easy fodder.

His one operational insistence, however, was the carrying of their weapons. His was secured in the leather inside-the-waistband holster that sat on his right hip. Nicole compromised and placed her weapon at the bottom of her handbag. She hated the thing.

They had strolled into town and enjoyed the warm and relaxing atmosphere of the Mediterranean sun. If it hadn't been for the fact that they were holding hands or linking arms, the casual observer could have been forgiven for thinking that Nicole was the plaything of a rich businessman and the smaller man at her side was her hired thug of a bodyguard. The crueler observers might have made the assumption that he was, in fact, the young lady's 'bit of rough'.

They found a small cafe on the outskirts of town and dined on pan fried duck and vegetables, complimenting it with a good, robust red wine. After lunch, they decided to take a stroll down to the busy Old Port.

"Time to switch back on," said Grant. "Keep your eyes peeled and see if you can spot our two mugs. Holiday time is over."

Her eyes were constantly moving as they walked, flicking from one face to another, registering and then dismissing them.

A few possible suspects; men with suntanned skins, jet black hair swept back, a certain walk or swagger, found Nicole digging deep into her memory of that night in the Dominican Republic for the faces of two killers she'd seen for only a matter of minutes. The streets, cafes, cars and pedestrians swept by as they walked the streets of Marseille, but so far, nothing.

The next day, they repeated the process with the exception of choosing a different family-run restaurant on the opposite side of town. They were due to meet with the local SIS officer at the consulate on the Avenue Prado at two o'clock.

"It's a shame we have to go back to work," Nicole said, enjoying the sun on her bare back. "I could quite get used to this."

Grant considered her comment for a moment. Really, his meeting with the local station officer was a formality, just a courtesy call to let the Head of Station know they were in town. "I'll go, there's no need for us both to be there, and it's only a welcome-to-town chat. Enjoy the afternoon and I'll meet you back at the apartment around three. If there's a problem, phone the apartment directly and I'll come and get you."

So Nicole had wandered, quite often catching the eye of swarthy, handsome men, bathing in the multitude of accents and dialects and living the life, at least in her eyes, of a spy in a foreign city.

Chapter Three

There are times in almost every intelligence operation, where fate intervenes and hands the agents on the ground a great big bouquet of good, old-fashioned luck. There's no rhyme or reason as to when it arrives, just that on the occasions when everything seems at its gloomiest, and with all hope lost, the patron saint of spies seems to hand out the clue, the picture, the source or the information that everyone is waiting for.

In the case of Operation MACE, it was given to Nicole Quayle, fledgling field agent. She had the good fortune to stop and browse at a small boutique, which advertised the season's latest designer fashion wear. The breeze had strengthened along the coast, making the air cooler and the walk along the storefronts selling dresses, make up and fashionable jewelry had given her a sense of reality again. This is what she would be doing back home in London; how fabulous that she was able to do it here as part of her job.

Her eyes stopped, moved away, before once again returning to two men, one middle aged, the other a few years younger –no more than twenty feet away across the square. The older, big and powerful, the younger, smaller and hard-looking. *Arguing by all accounts*, she thought, as she watched the gesticulation of fingers increasing at a rapid pace. Then the smaller, younger man ripped off his sunglasses and thrust his head forward so that he was virtually touching the other man's nose.

It couldn't be, could it? Then there it was, the confirmation she'd been scanning for; the scar. If she'd suspected it was a trick of the light before, that slash confirmed it. In that moment, she was whisked back in her mind's eye to a drinking hole in the Caribbean and the image of the two mercenaries talking with the American spy.

She realized that she was standing, stock still, staring at them with her mouth open. *You'll look like you're mad,* she thought, and quickly turned away, putting her sunglasses on and checking that she hadn't been spotted by the two men. She moved along the boutiques, casually glancing and all the time keeping the image of the two men's reflections in the windows of the stores. *What to do? Okay, keep calm,* she thought. *Remember your training, Agent Quayle!*

First thing, had she been 'made', as the American police shows called it. No, seemingly all clear. Next, could she confirm his ID? She could certainly get a bit nearer, but judging from the distance they had been from each other, taking into account the build of the man, and the scar – yes – she was ninety-nine percent certain that he was one of the men.

Finally, don't lose them... Oh bloody hell! She turned in time to see the shorter man, *her* man, walking off into the warren-like streets of Marseilles. She would never catch up with him at that speed.

Grant is going to kill me, she thought. *He never truly wanted me on this operation, he voiced it loudly enough, and now I've only gone and given him the ammunition he needs to have me returned to London. Damn, damn, bloody damn!*

But all was not lost and in those few moments of clarity, she saw a way back. It wasn't perfect, but it was a start, and while she didn't have the location of *her* man, she did have the next best thing. She had a wonderful 'live' target in her sights, a target who she could follow and watch and who would hopefully lead her to the two killers they had travelled so very far to find.

* * *

It was just after three and she decided to risk that Grant had returned to the apartment. She pumped the *jeton* into the machine and as soon as the receiver was picked up on the other end, she blurted out; "Jack, I've seen them!"

"Who?"

"Our men. Well, at least one of them. The smaller of the two. Short hair, scar on his face. He was talking to an older, larger man down by the harbor."

"You're sure?" Grant questioned.

"I'm certain. No, no, I'm positive."

Grant nodded to himself. Whilst he was eager to get into the game, he wanted to be sure they weren't jumping at shadows. He'd been back an hour from the meeting with the local SIS officer when the telephone in their apartment rang. The meeting had been a non-starter, a total waste of time with a Nothing Recorded Against and no news as of yet. The killers hadn't checked into anywhere 'legitimate'. In truth, they could have left Marseilles as soon as they'd arrived.

Grant refocused on Nicole. "Talk me through it. What did you see?"

Nicole took a breath, calmed herself and concentrated on the memory. This was the main reason she had been brought into this operation; to ID the two killers. Now that she had achieved that, she wanted to be sure she had every detail correct. "Two men down by the harbor; one tall and well built, one shorter and tough looking. It was only when the shorter man removed his sunglasses that I spotted the scar on his face. It was him; I'd stake my life on it."

"Let's hope you don't have to. What happened next?"

She thought some more, trying to keep the excitement out of her voice and the conversation as brief as possible. "They seemed to be arguing, it was getting quite heated at one point, and then the shorter man turned and walked away. He was gone in seconds; I'd never have caught him."

"What about the other man, the taller of the two, was that the other man you saw in the Caribbean?" he asked, hoping that both of his targets were here.

She clutched the handset of the payphone tightly, concentrating and trying to remember every detail. "No. This one is big, bigger in the shoulders, hard-looking, plus he's a lot older. The man in the Caribbean was younger, thinner and looked... cold."

Grant let the conversation pause. Nicole seemed convinced she'd seen at least one of the killers, and he knew from living and working with her over the past few weeks that she wasn't given to flights of fancy or wishful thinking.

"If what you say is true, it means they're still here in Marseilles for some reason," murmured Grant.

"Is one of the targets due to visit here soon?"

"Not according to our intelligence, no. They're all still in their own locales. It could be that they're using this as a temporary base, ready to move off to the next hit. Good work, Nicole, at least we've confirmed that they're still in Marseilles."

Nicole smiled to herself. Gorilla gave out praise sparingly, so she knew she'd done well.

"Right, get yourself back to the apartment, we can pick them up again, maybe see what the local informants can come up with."

"That's just it, Jack. The other man is seated at a bar across the courtyard from where I'm making this call! He's been here for the past fifteen minutes," she said, the excitement clear in her voice.

"What! You stay put, that's an order! I have seniority on this operation and you don't go anywhere until I come and get you!"

"What if he moves, damn it?"

"Do not follow, do you understand? Now where are you?"

She gave him the address of a small family cafe in the courtyard. She would sit outside, have a drink and read a magazine. It gave her a perfect view across the small square to where the sullen-looking man was sitting, nursing his drink and appearing like a man at the end of his tether.

The standoff went on for the next fifteen minutes, with Nicole tensing every time the man moved. They were having their own little Cold War standoff, played out against the cafe society of Marseilles. The watcher and the target engaged in an unwitting chess game of inactivity. *Come on Jack! Where are you, you should be here by now!* Nicole fretted.

She glanced up from her magazine and saw the big man was reaching into his jacket to retrieve some money; he threw the cash onto the table, gave a brief wave to the barman inside, stretched, and began to move away. She stared unashamedly in his direction as his stride grew longer. The conflict in her was palpable. Grant had given her a specific order, she knew. She also knew he would go mad at her for disobeying his instructions, but more importantly, for putting herself at risk.

To let him go would mean they were effectively back at the beginning again, with no leads and the possibility of losing their quarry forever. *Sorry Jack, but I'm not letting the only lead we've had for weeks wander off into the back streets of Marseilles.* So with a stubbornness her father would have recognized instantly, she set off after her target.

Nicole tried to remember as much as she could of her training in surveillance, limited though it was. There were rules for static, foot and vehicle surveillance which she had been taught by the instructors on the training days around London and the Home Counties.

In the end, the only things that remained in her mind from those long-ago training sessions was never to 'show out'. The wisdom was that it was better to lose them than give the game away, and never point at a target when explaining the target to another team member. The rest was a confused overload of information.

Nicole decided she would just act natural, keep her distance and live her cover of a tourist wandering through the Old Port of Marseilles. She turned off the main thoroughfare and onto the quieter Quai de Rive Neuve. There were less people and more doorways which didn't offer their wares to the passing tourist. These streets ran at a slower pace than the main roads, more solemn and weary. She kept a steady pace, not moving too keenly, the man's back always in her sights. He didn't falter; he didn't glance in shop windows or peruse cafe menus. He just walked, oblivious to what was going on around him.

The amble carried on down more back streets until, not ten feet in front of her, the man stopped, turned and looked straight at her. She blushed and composed a halfhearted smile, that in her mind, came out more like a grimace. She took in his hard face, the grey hair, the direct stare, and knew she had what her instructors on the one-day street surveillance refresher called 'showed out'. Her Dad would have called it having a 'bit of a dither'.

She did a shuffle with her feet, to carry on walking or to turn and feign an interest in the nearest shop window, unsure which option to choose before her instincts and training took over and she carried on crossing over the street so as to avoid risking another bout of eye contact. She just hoped it was enough. For today, she would have to cut her losses and abort the surveillance of the hard-looking man with the grey hair.

She spent the next fifteen minutes backtracking, and hoping that she'd covered her tracks. Better to lose the target for a day than to be completely made, is what her instructors would have said. There is always another day. Another day – maybe she could wear a disguise, maybe let Gorilla take over tomorrow or bring in a watcher from the local station, anything to pick up the target again.

Gorilla! Damn him, she could almost hear him now, telling her not to go back, it was too soon with too greater risk of being spotted. She knew he was right, but she had her mother's stubbornness. Her father would quite often, rather politely, call her willful. 'I told you so' is sometimes the one phrase we don't want to hear, even if it's true.

She turned onto a side street, one that would eventually take her back to the main road leading to the harbor. It was then, seemingly from nowhere, when she felt the presence of another human being beside her right shoulder, in her blind spot. A voice whispered, almost lovingly; "You shouldn't have smiled. No women smile at me, especially not ones as pretty as you. That was your mistake, my dear…"

* * *

264

Gorilla had calmed down, composed himself and gone to bring her back. He knew where the cafe was and he just hoped she hadn't been spotted. He would drag her back, kicking and screaming if he had too. He had seniority on this operation and he was damned if he was going to be dictated to by a novice.

He grabbed his weapon, slung on his jacket and rushed from the apartment into the street. From their apartment to the Old Port would take him about twenty minutes on foot, quicker if he could hail a taxi. He moved at a brisk pace. He was a businessman, enjoying an afternoon walk, perhaps on his way to meet an acquaintance and not wanting to be late. He knew where she was, plus she also had a distinctive red coat which made her visually easy to find. Follow little red riding hood.

He arrived at the cafe out of breath, expecting to see her. Nothing. He scanned left, right – still nothing, so he moved further along the street. He knew she'd disobey a direct order, that stupid bloody girl. *Keep calm and look,* he told himself. He did a full rotation and to his relief spotted her moving off down the far end of the street, dodging the busy traffic as she crossed the road. Thank God for that red coat. As visual markers went, it was bloody perfect.

Now that he had her in his sights he did what he did best; kept his distance and blended in. There was a definite art to the task of stalking a target, especially through the busy thoroughfares of one of Europe's major cities. It wasn't a science that could be studied quickly on a training course, nor was it something that could be learned by rote; instead it was something much more intangible that certain agents were not attuned to, while for others, it came as naturally as breathing. A good 'watcher' needed three things; a cool nerve, the ability to blend in to their surroundings and finally, luck – always luck.

For Gorilla, he certainly had the first two in abundance. As a hardened field agent, he'd earned his spurs in the melting pot that was post-war Berlin and had done his share of street work, but very rarely had he needed to follow a watcher who was following a target. Even for him that was something new, so he kept his distance and followed her into the warren-like streets.

* * *

The quick violence of the man's attack shocked her. No, it was more than that; it sent her into a spin of confusion. One moment she was backtracking, desperately trying to find a way back to the Old Port by cutting down a side street and into an alleyway between two buildings, and the next she was confronted by the big man and his hands roughly grabbed her and almost lifted her off her feet, half-carrying, half-dragging her.

There was no scream, she was far too terrified for that, but just for insurance, the big man had clamped a large, meaty hand over her mouth as he continued to drag her further down the alleyway and into its dark recesses. They were no more than fifteen feet from the alley's opening, nothing really, but it might have been the far side of the moon as far as anyone seeing them and coming to her rescue. She found herself lung back into an alcove covered in rubbish, animal waste and rat droppings. Then the man pressed against her; his forearm holding her chest and his other hand covering her mouth until she was pinned and silent.

"Don't scream, or I'll snap your neck like a twig," he said in a rumbling whisper, his breath smothering her.

She looked into his weather-lined face, noted his head of grey hair, and took in the piercing coldness of his blue eyes. He spoke in French, but the accent was definitely German.

"*Who* are you! Why have you been following me for the past fifteen minutes?" he demanded.

The question was barked at her, like a prison guard ordering a prisoner. He saw the fear in her eyes; and she knew in that moment that *he* knew that *she* knew that *she* had been following him. No pretense, no subterfuge; the guilty look in her eyes confirmed it for him in an instant. He glanced behind him briefly. "Are you alone?"

Nicole gave nothing away. Silence was her best ally. She knew she'd fallen for one of the oldest tricks in the book; she'd been 'made' and then lured to a choke point and then... this. She felt a fool.

The German changed his grip and moved his hand from across her mouth, instead clamping it tightly around her throat. She gulped in air, getting as much into her mouth as she could before he shut off her windpipe completely. The German moved his head in closer until his mouth was almost touching her ear. "Are you Israeli? A Jew? Are you and your people hunting me still?"

"Get off me, let me go, just let me go," she spluttered for something to say, something that would stay his hand of execution for a few moments longer. "Or... or my team will come and get me!"

He laughed, not a harsh laugh, but a pitying laugh; as a parent might find amusing the lies of a child. "No, little Jew-girl, I don't think that's the case, I don't think anyone's coming to get you. I think it's just you and me and this back alley. I think you are out of your depth; solo surveillance on a subject is notoriously hard to do."

She knew then that she would never make it out of here alive unless she fought. She tried to move against his weight, wriggle out, plead for mercy, anything – but his strength was too much and was backed up by a gentle squeeze of her delicate throat, like a vice holding an eggshell.

"Shhh, don't fight," he cooed. "It will go worse for you; better to stay calm, you are in good hands."

She looked into his eyes; they were alive, dancing like fire. She felt him swap arms, his left forearm now pinning her to the wall, leaving his right hand to move under her dress and up the length of her thigh. She felt his fingers begin to scrape away at the lining of her underwear and she shuddered. *No, God, please don't let it be like this,* she thought.

"I don't think I've ever fucked a girl as pretty as you before." His voice was deep with anticipation.

Nicole's reality had condensed and slowed and consisted of the man's heavy breath pumping into the side of her neck and his fingers fumbling under her dress. She could feel his hardness pressing against her stomach, felt him move his hand down and free himself from the confines of his trousers as he pushed himself upwards in the hope of consummating his attack.

She started to cry, more out of shame than fear or pain, and that weakness hurt her more than any physical assault could ever have done. Do something, anything, her Dad would have said. And in those few moments the fear of never seeing her papa's face again was too much to bear. *Move! Now!*

Her right arm had become free when the German had unzipped his fly, and his head was leaning to one side, exposing the left side of his face. It was a glorious target. She did the only thing she knew how to do, one of the few things she'd learned on the new intakes un-armed combat course. It wasn't terribly amazing, exotic or even useful in most situations. But right here, right now it was all she had and all she needed.

She bunched her small delicate hand into a fist, extended her thumb with one beautifully manicured nail protruding from the end like a talon, and thrust it deep into the corner of the man's eye, dragging the thumb deeply from left to right across the surface of the eyeball. She felt cold liquid running down her thumb, and for a brief moment, caught the sight of blood oozing from the man's eye socket.

And in that moment, she wasn't certain what was sweeter; the release of pressure across her chest, allowing her to breath, or the virulent howl of pain from the animal in front of her.

* * *

If it hadn't been for the howl of pain which echoed around the brick-lined alleyways, Gorilla would have moved onto the next street and missed them completely. He was lost, had no visual marker on either Nicole or the man she'd been following, and the backstreets had suddenly turned into a maze which snaked out in multiple directions.

His mind was whirling frantically, his eyes constantly searching out the most likely route Nicole, or indeed the man she was following, could have taken. He felt like a parent who temporarily loses a tod-dler in a department store; panic-ridden and bewildered with a kalei-doscope of nightmarish scenarios playing through his mind.

But the scream – a man's scream of pure agony – had brought him back. He slowly retraced his steps along the small side street, no more than twenty feet from the alleyway he knew had to be the place. *Bloody hell, I nearly missed it,* he thought. It was then that he saw it; a shoe, one perfect woman's high heeled shoe in fawn, half hidden among the boxes which had been dumped out for garbage collection. It was Nicole's shoe. He heard a raised voice in German; someone was being called a *ficken fotze* and in that moment, he knew he had only seconds left to find her.

He raced down the alleyway, spotting another shoe before he turned a corner and there, with his hands around her delicate throat, was a man, a huge man, attempting and possibly succeeding in strangling Nicole. Her face was contorted with the pressure and the color was draining from her fast.

No time for the gun, Gorilla decided, *too noisy and the last thing he needed was witnesses.* He needed to act fast. Gorilla finally got to do what he was both paid to do and what he was good at, and as the German belatedly became aware of a presence behind him and started turning to face the potential threat, Gorilla set his mind to very care-fully, and very precisely, killing the other man.

* * *

Alfred Nadel had once strangled a member of the Dutch Resistance to death with the man's own belt. True, the victim had been tied to a chair and was unable to move or resist, thus making the physical act of strangulation that much easier, but he had never shied away from the immense physical effort needed. In fact, he relished it far more than using a machine gun or a blunt instrument on his targets.

Over the years, he had fashioned himself a number of garrotes and ligatures, and on more than one occasion, in a professional capacity, he'd chosen the art of garroting as his chosen method of assassination. No such luxury was available here, though. It was to be his bare hands for the elimination, never murder, of this female he'd spotted tailing him for the past half an hour. He had no idea who she was, possibly police or possibly one of the teams of Israeli agents from Mossad, who still hunted men like him.

Whoever she was, he'd spotted her clumsy attempts at surveillance straight away. It was embarrassing, actually. He had been a hunted man for virtually all his adult life; been followed by policeman, soldiers and spies, so he knew the signs of what to look for and he also knew the signs of amateur surveillance, especially by one person.

When he'd turned the tables on his watcher and made eye contact on the street, he knew instantly that it wasn't just his imagination. Her eyes had said one word to him; guilty. The rest was simple. Trail the bait and lead them into an isolated location with no witnesses; after that, well, he could do as he pleased.

He was a big, powerful man, and despite his age, was more than capable of dealing with amateurs, especially where violence was to be used.

So it had surprised him – shocked would be a better word – that she'd fought back. She was, to his eyes, a frightened slip of a girl, almost stick thin and yet she'd taken his eye from him with a ruthlessness which belied her small frame. He'd experienced the searing pain in his eye and knew then that his 'fun' would no longer be an option – but her death definitely would be.

He slapped her across the face, sending her sprawling to the ground – fucking bitch – then he lifted her to her feet and slowly began to squeeze at her throat. An eye for an eye, wasn't that one of the Israeli's mottos? How very apt. But now, as he began to deal out his chosen method of murder, he was aware in his heightened state of something, or someone, coming up behind him.

* * *

270

Gorilla had been on all manner of unarmed combat courses during his time in the Army and with the Service. Most of them, in his opinion, were next to useless. Overcomplicated and unnecessary techniques designed to trip, sweep or put someone in a wristlock weren't like anything he'd ever encountered during his more 'active' assignments.

He thought them bullshit.

As a boy, he'd been taught by his uncle about the harsh reality of street fighting. Fists, boots, elbows, knees and head-butts had been the order of the day, especially for the small-framed new lad with the funny accent, growing up on the terraced streets besides the docks. Thus far – and Gorilla himself would be the first to admit that he was no sportsman or world class athlete – they had never let him down. He trusted them, knew how to use them, and despite his small build, could generate enough power into his punches to fell a mule. And a punch, or more accurately, a hook punch from the rear was what he used now against Nicole's attacker.

He moved fast, grabbing the collar of the big man with his left hand and throwing a hook punch right into the man's jaw line; once, twice, three times – each time sending the man further down and onto the ground. A kick to the man's face made Gorilla feel that little bit better. The man was down, but certainly not out.

Gorilla moved over to Nicole and sat her up. The finger marks on her throat were starting to bruise and the slap mark across her face was glowing red. "Nicole, Nicole, talk to me. Come on, love."

Slowly, she began to come round. She opened her eyes and looked at him, blinked once and then came the tears; of relief, joy, fear or shame, even she didn't know, but they came nonetheless. "Jack, I'm sorry, I'm so sorry... I should never have... *Jack!*"

Her warning had come a fraction too late. As she came around, she was aware of Gorilla kneeling over her and then a blurry movement from behind his left shoulder as the German's foot arched towards and then crashed into the side of Gorilla's head, sending him colliding into the wall. The kick was good, but not powerful enough to completely finish Gorilla, only stun him, and then both men were jumping to their feet, ready to fight again.

Nadel charged and slammed Gorilla back into the wall, sending a blast of air out of the smaller man's lungs, winding him. Gorilla, for his part, more out of survival instinct than having a clear shot, was desperately trying to head butt the German's nose, in the hope of disrupting his attack. But Nadel was twice Gorilla's size, both in build and weight, and simply spun the smaller man until his back was facing the German's front. The German resembled a grizzly bear hugging a small child.

The German's arms changed position, coiling around Gorilla's neck like a boa constrictor, ready to tighten and strangle; something that Alfred Nadel was very accomplished at. Gorilla felt the rear strangle go on, one meaty forearm across his windpipe and the other running across the back of his neck to tighten everything up, and he made a move for the pistol on his right hip.

Just as his fingers touched the base of the pistol's handle, Nadel also became aware of the surreptitious movement, assumed that a weapon was about to be brought into play and simply crushed his opponent against the wall, pinning Gorilla's weapon arm and rendering the weapon useless. Gorilla knew from experience that once a committed choke was applied, it was only a matter of seconds before unconsciousness and death came knocking on the door. With his firearm beyond reach, and with only seconds to spare, he used the last of his energy in the only way that he could; by slamming his heel into the German's instep and flinging his head back in the hope of smashing the man's face, anything to give him some leverage or room to breathe.

Both were in vain and slowly, ever so gradually, Gorilla began to feel the big man's powerful arms tighten up and then the inevitable blackness started to envelop him.

* * *

Nicole aimed for the German's back, and fired twice. The first round had hit the wall and skidded off down the alley, but the second shot caught the German's upper arm. A spray of blood emerged as did another cry of pain from the big man. Two shots, one miss, one hit.

She had seen Gorilla taken by the monster of a man, and even from her prone position on the floor, she knew he wouldn't be able to survive against the German. The man was just too big, too strong and too adept at killing with his hands. They were both simply outmatched.

She put her hand down to the ground to try and lift herself to her feet; maybe escape, call for help, anything, and there at the touch of her fingertips among the filth and rubbish, was the answer to her prayers. The handbag… her handbag, with the pistol inside.

Nicole ripped open the bag, rummaged inside and pulled out the Walther. Gorilla's tutorial at the Paris base during their less than active moments came back to her with breathtaking clarity. "Make sure the magazine is seated properly… pull back the slide and let it run forward… flick off the safety… point, aim and…"

The noise in the confines of the brick alcove startled her, so much so that she dropped the weapon after the second shot and tucked herself into the corner, her knees drawn up, face covered. Nicole closed her eyes, blotting out the violence. She heard the two men grunt and breathe and fight in the intimate noises of combat. Then she heard a barrage of shots ring out, heard a body slump to the floor with a groan and then silence.

* * *

With his imminent death approaching, Gorilla was pleasantly surprised to hear the distant report of a firearm being discharged, and even in his semi-unconscious state, he recognized that it was the bark of a small caliber weapon. The girl, it had to be the girl.

He smelt the charge from the weapon that was released into the air, smelt the metallic tang of blood, was even more aware of a cry of pain, and was relieved to feel the pressure on his throat loosen. He gulped in a breath through his swollen throat. His mind began to clear and he knew in that instant that he needed to act quickly if he wanted to survive the encounter. He felt the big man's single arm still attached to the collar of his jacket, so Gorilla spun his body around until they were face-to-face, or more accurately, chest-to-face, and grabbed hold of his opponent around the waist with his left arm, hugging him.

Gorilla's right hand snaked down to the concealed holster on his right hip, a quick grasp, a pull, and the weapon was up and out and jammed onto his hip in what was known in the trade as the retention position. The muzzle of the weapon had barely cleared the holster when he fired upwards in rapid succession, hitting the bigger man four times along the sternum. Gorilla felt the man tense, cry out and then drop to the ground.

Nicole slowly raised her eyes and there, to her relief, stood Gorilla; battered and bruised for sure, but alive and holding the pistol that was his calling card – and at the little man's feet lay the dead body of the monster who had very recently tried to kill them both.

Chapter Four

Their escape from the alley and back to the apartment base was both tense and seemingly endless, with Grant insisting on running a series of discreet counter-surveillance drills to ensure they hadn't been seen or followed. They arrived back at the apartment almost an hour and a half later, just as dusk was starting to cover the city.

Following the shooting of the German, Grant had searched the body and found a number of items which might be useful. He stored them safely in his jacket pocket. He would look at them later, when matters were less pressing. He'd dragged the big man to the far end of the alleyway before concealing the body underneath the recess of some stone steps leading up to the next level of *Le Panier*. He covered the front of the recess with a series of boxes, crates and assorted rubbish. Judging by the amount of trash which had accumulated in the alleyway, it wasn't cleaned on a regular basis and would hopefully keep the body hidden long enough to aid their escape.

He collected the spent bullet casings and pocketed them, before finally dragging Nicole to her feet, brushing her down, returning her lost shoes and making it very clear to her that they had to 'bloody well get out of here'. She had moved slowly at first, with Grant almost having to drag her, but soon she was keeping pace with him as they endeavored to put as much distance as possible between themselves and the killing ground. A walk, a taxi, a walk again, followed by a bus, until finally, they reached the corner of their apartment building.

Nicole had immediately showered and remained in her room, keeping the door shut. Grant, sensing the trauma she was going through, thought it best to leave her to rest and hopefully sleep it off. He changed his clothes, washed out his cuts and bruises, made them both some food and set about dismantling the '39 at the dining table. Halfway through the dismantling procedure, he noticed that his hand was shaking.

"Shouldn't we get out of Marseilles, just in case someone has seen us? Isn't that standard procedure?" Nicole was standing in the doorway. Her voice was barely a whisper and lacked her usual vitality.

Grant looked up from the table, where he was cleaning and oiling his gun. She had been in her room for the past hour, he assumed to rest, but now she was wrapped in a thick jumper and looked pale and fragile in his eyes. He shook his head and spoke gently. "That might apply to the mainstream of SIS operations, but Redaction officers are built of sterner stuff. Until we hear differently, we stay put."

Later that night, Grant removed the items he'd taken from the dead German from his pocket. They were interesting, to say the least. He laid them out on the floor and sat looking down at them from above. In the grand scheme of things, they were trivial; a book of matches and a passport, which was more than likely a fake. The passport was registered in the name of Anton Melton. It did, however, give enough physical details about the man that the Burrowers back home might be able to track down who he really was.

But it was the book of matches which really caught his eye; the sort of thing that could quite often be found on the bar or tables of a nightclub for free. The cover had the silhouette of a bright blue hotel emblazoned across the front and gave the name and address of the Hotel Azure in Marseilles.

Grant smiled. Some might say that it was nothing, only a book of matches. But no, he thought this was one big bloody clue and so far, the most tangible lead in tracking down the scar-faced killer Nicole had seen.

James Quinn

* * *

They had brought an MK. 123 radio set with them to Marseilles, which was to be their emergency communications source for passing information to London. It was old and heavy and just about fitted inside the suitcases they had brought with them, but it worked when it needed to.

Grant unpacked the MK. 123, connected the power pack and assembled the ancillaries. He checked his watch – 10.35pm – at that time of night only the duty communications clerk would be working, but the 'eyes only' would ensure Masterman was contacted sooner rather than later.

He then spent the next hour laboriously writing out his message in number code, a code which only the SIS communications desk and Masterman had the key to. Satisfied that he hadn't made an error, he sat before the radio pack, stretched out his fingers and began, slowly at first, and then with more competence to tap on the Morse code key. He sent it to Masterman's work name; SENTINEL – URGENT/EYES ONLY.

In truth, he hated the task of encoding and decoding, he hated the job of sending it through via Morse also. It made his head swim with boredom. But with Nicole, in her role as communications officer, temporarily out of action he had been forced to take over. So he tapped away; tap, tap, taaappp, tap, tap… *Anything but this,* he thought after another hour; *give me a brush past or a dead drop any day of the week, at least it's quick.*

When he'd finally finished, he sat back and rubbed the tiredness from his eyes. Now all he had to do was wait and see if headquarters would act quickly. Knowing Masterman's temperament for decisive action, he didn't doubt that SIS's considerable assets would be brought into play over the next twenty-four hours. He just hoped things moved quickly enough to trap his targets here in Marseilles, rather than them being alerted and escaping. That was the worst case scenario; having to up sticks and start all over again tracking them across Europe, hoping to stop them before the next killing happened.

The scream from Nicole's bedroom startled him. He turned, undecided as to whether or not to go to her. Then the noise abated, turning into a whimper, then silence. He sat for a while, listening, not daring to move, but there was no further repetition. It seemed that somewhere in the deep of her mind, Nicole was facing down her demons.

* * *

The message was received minutes later by the radio listeners at the Government Communications Headquarters in Cheltenham. It was passed as A Grade and then 'bounced' over to the resident communications clerk at Broadway. The SIS clerk took in the 'Eyes Only' and looked up the name of SENTINEL in the officers' cryptonym book. He noted the name of the Head of the Redaction section and then printed out the sheet.

TO SENTINEL:
UNIT CAME UNDER ATTACK. FIRST REDACTION
TAKEN PLACE. NOT. REPEAT. NOT OUR INITIAL
TARGETS. BELIEVED TO BE AN ASSOCIATE OR
SUB-CONTRACTOR. REDACTION TEAM SAFE AND
NOT COMPROMISED. MACE STILL A GO. REPEAT
MACE STILL A GO.
INDIVIDUAL A GERMAN AGED 45-60. LARGE WELL
BUILT. GREY HAIR. BLUE EYES. POSSIBLY ON
ISRAELI WANTED LIST SO THEREFORE COULD BE
SS OR WAR CRIMINAL. TRAVELLING ON BELGIAN
PASSPORT NAMED ANTON MELTON.
HAVE CONFIRMED THAT OUR TARGETS ARE STILL
RESIDING IN MARSEILLES. SCARFACE POSI-
TIVELY IDENTIFIED. NEED BURROWERS TO CHECK
DETAILS OF HOTEL AZURE/MARSEILLES. POSSI-

BLE THAT TARGETS ARE LOCATED THERE. NEED
MORE INFORMATION BEFORE WE CAN ACT. SUGGEST
'HAWKEYE' TEAM IS PUT ON STANDBY.
IF CONFIRMED WOULD LIKE TO CARRY OUT REDAC-
TION AT THEIR LOCATION. RETRIEVE ANY USE-
ABLE INTELLLIGENCE. WE MAY BE ABLE TO NIP
THIS THING IN THE BUD AT SOURCE.
2308

The communications clerk checked for any errors and finding none, sealed the printout in a secure envelope which would then be hand delivered to the desk of the Head of Redaction.

* * *

The next morning, Nicole emerged from her bedroom to find Grant stacking up her luggage in the lounge. The mark on her face had cooled and she had disguised the bruising on her throat with make-up. "What's going on?" she asked.

Grant took in her haunted hollow eyes. He guessed she'd had a troubled night's sleep. "I thought it for the best," he said simply.

Her eyes moved from him to the suitcase, a moment of confusion passed over her face and then came the dawning realization of what he was planning to do. "Oh, so that's it, is it? I've outlived my usefulness have I! You've got your confirmed ID's and I'm off the operation!"

Grant stared at the floor, hoping his meek manner would make her see sense. But he hadn't bargained with the steel inside the young woman who was his partner.

"Typical bloody selfish men, well don't you dare, don't you bloody dare! It's my problem, my body and my life and I'm going to finish this job!" she yelled at him.

"Look, the rules state that when an agent gets attacked in the field, it's an immediate return to home ground and—"

"Oh, what absolute rubbish! Since when did you care about rules and regulations? Don't start getting all sanctimonious on me, you, you... you... bloody *gorilla*!"

She had searched for an epithet to make her point; not finding one suitable she'd resorted to blurting out the first abusive remark that sprang to mind. She saw that it hurt him. Not so much the using of his cryptonym in a derogatory manner, but with the amount of venom it was delivered with. He stood, chastised, ashamed, like an adulterer who had been caught out. She knew she needed to maintain the momentum, had to stand her ground if she had any chance of remaining on this operation. "Have you cabled Masterman?"

He nodded. "Yes."

She crossed her arms over her chest. "About me? About what happened to me?"

"No, I haven't, not yet anyway. I just gave him the bare bones, the German, the hotel. Nothing about what happened. I just said we were both fine."

Well, that was something. She was still in with a fighting chance. If Masterman had been informed, her feet wouldn't have touched the ground and she would have been on the first flight home. In truth, she had thought about packing her things and heading back to London herself, more than a dozen times last night. Her frailty and vulnerability had almost been too much to bear.

But somewhere near when dawn had broken through the windows, she'd found some inner strength, perhaps some abject stubbornness that made her want to stay. She imagined the voices raised back in London, could almost hear them now. "Oh yes, young slip of a girl – Quayle gave her a shot at field operations. Sadly, she crumbled when the pressure was on; we sent her back to the typing pool. It's safer for everyone in the long run."

In time, she knew her name would be forgotten and the old and the bold would simply refer to her as a generic woman. Nicole... Sarah... Madeline... something, something. All women would be tarred with the same brush, and *that* she could not allow. Nicole decided there and

then that she would leave this operation when and how *she* decided to, and she wouldn't be dictated to by the British Secret Service. She turned her full gaze on Grant. "Then listen to me, you don't tell them anything. This is as much my operation now as it is yours. I'm not in the habit of quitting anything halfway through."

"Nicole, look you've been through hell—"

"*Yes!*" she shouted at him, probably far more severely than she'd meant to. "I have, but I'm here and I'm still fighting."

They settled into a truce for the next day and kept to their own space, only coming together to eat at meal times or for Grant to report that nothing had come in from London. He knew she needed time to heal and he was determined to give her as much as he could. His only concern was that they might have to throw themselves back into the field at a moment's notice, and he wasn't sure she was up to it... yet.

But with time comes healing and both Grant and Nicole soon relaxed, albeit temporarily, into the idyll of each other's company. "You up for doing some work?" he asked.

She was reading a magazine on the couch, her feet tucked under her legs. "Of course, what do you need?"

"Can you man the radio set; Masterman should be checking in soon. I want to have a look at this Hotel Azure, get a feel for the place."

She put down the magazine and stood up, ready to get started. "Okay. But isn't that a bit risky? Why don't we just let the Hawkeye team take over when they arrive?"

"Oh, I will, don't worry, it's just that Hawkeye teams look for patterns, evidence, clues. I need to look it over with my own eyes. I'm looking for something different. I'm looking for things they might not notice or even be aware of." He noticed a cloud pass across her face. Was it the thought of getting back into action that worried her? The possibility of new violence, perhaps, or the gravity of the mission they had to cope with? "How are you? You look better," he said, breaking the silence.

She ran a hand across her face self-consciously. She was still shaken by the whole experience, she knew, but the bad dreams weren't as intense and had grown more diluted. "I feel better. Thanks. I'm alright, I just want to get on with the job and see it through."

"Good. I'm glad you're staying." The silence returned again before he said quietly, "Thank you."

She was taken aback. "What for?"

"Well, if you hadn't used your gun, I'd be dead by now."

"It wasn't much of a shot, I'm afraid. It scared the life out of me."

"It was enough. You learned a valuable lesson, something that no training course could teach you – that when you face off against a bigger opponent and you draw a gun, you damn well better be ready to use it, otherwise you'll put everyone at risk. You meant to kill him to save me; the rest is just down to practice."

The tears began to well in her eyes and she brushed them away. "I just feel like a bloody fool. If I hadn't gone off on my own and got trapped... I hate the thought of having to kill another human being, no matter how repulsive they are, but when I saw what he was going to do to you... I just got angry."

Nicole stared down at her hands, and Grant couldn't tell if there was still rage inside of her or if she was ashamed. "Let's forget it. It's done. We'll call it even," he said and wondered, if for the second time in their relationship, he hadn't completely misjudged her.

* * *

Later that day, the radio chattered into life. Nicole sat down in front of it at the dining room table, picked up a pencil, placed the head-phones on her head and began to note down the strange rhythm of the code.

```
TO:  2308
SITUATION NOTED.
AZURE IS KNOWN TO LOCAL POLICE. RECOGNISED
AS AN ORGANISED CRIME BROTHEL/SAFE-HOUSE
BELONGING TO GUERINI UNDERWORLD CLAN.
```

PLEASE BE ADVISED EXTREMELY DANGEROUS OP-
ERATION.
HAWKEYE TEAM WILL BE WITH YOU TOMORROW.
ALSO A GIFT WILL BE SENT TO YOU IN THE
COMING DAYS. ENJOY IT AND USE IT WISELY.
HOPE IT HELPS. SENTINEL

Chapter Five

The Hawkeye team arrived in Marseilles less than two days after Grant's initial communiqué to Broadway. There was no fanfare, no notifying of local SIS, and the only time they would meet their man on the ground, who went by the cryptonym Gorilla, was when they had finished their surveillance operation and had something to report.

A base was set up on the outskirts of the city, vehicles were hired, equipment was unpacked and a routine was organized. They were self-reliant and very much left to their own devices as they were used to. All were ordinary, spoke fluent French and were experts at blending into their environment. The men and women of Hawkeye set up a static position in a hotel adjacent to the Hotel Azure, camper vans were parked opposite it and roving teams of Hawkeye operatives walked the route in relays when a suspected ID on a subject was needed. All had covert cameras, binoculars and superb eyesight for observing their targets.

The team had also considered a surreptitious entry to the pent-houses, but after a brief reconnaissance they decided it was wiser not to try. It was too heavily guarded and not worth the risk. Instead, they had to settle for a discreet listening device planted on the underside of the concierge's desk by a lost delivery man asking for directions and the usual long range photographs of people leaving and entering the building.

On the third day, they believed they'd struck gold. One of the Hawk-eye footmen snapped their two targets together, leaving the rear of the building from the penthouse exterior staircase. There was no time for a clear camera shot, but the description given by the Hawkeye team member gave them the best evidence that the targets were there and on the ground.

With confirmation of the targets in place, the team turned the rest of their attention to the layout of the building. If Redaction were involved, it usually meant that violence was going to be initiated at some point, something that was anathema to Hawkeye operators, and as such, they would need the most accurate information about the layout and security of the building. By the end of the job, the Hawkeye team had gathered a mountain of diagrams, plans, photo ID's and possible entry points for the Redaction fire-team.

At their base, the Hawkeye team leader looked over what his people had managed to achieve in the short space of five days and nodded. "Good, considering what he had to deal. I think I better meet with this Gorilla, then," he said.

* * *

The leader of the Hawkeye team arrived just after dusk had settled. He was a dour Yorkshire man in his thirties, called Johnson. They had agreed to meet in one of the evening bars, not far from the harbor.

"So, my boys and girls had a field day with this one. A nice easy job by comparison to some of the ones we get, normally we get to freeze our balls off trailing Russians in Norway or some such thing, so a lovely trip to the south of France made my team's week," he said.

Gorilla liked him immediately. He sensed that they would have both preferred to discuss this over a pint of bitter in their local pub. But then, Gorilla always did have an affinity for people who worked the front line of operations like himself.

"I don't know what you've got in mind, but what you're looking at taking down is basically a knocking shop on the go there. A lot of tough-looking punters make use of it; gangsters no doubt and from what my boys have shown me, they're mostly packing some sort of weapons," said Johnson pretending to like the glass of *vin rouge* he was sipping from unenthusiastically. "But that's not all," he continued. "Security is quite tight. A lot of muscle on play, again, probably packing weapons, there to make sure the place isn't raided by the local vice squad. The people you're after seem to have control of the top floor, the penthouse level."

Johnson passed across a photo of a tall, slim, dark-haired man standing on the penthouse balcony, smoking. The picture was fuzzy, as if it had been taken from a distance by a long range camera. "It's effectively four floors up and is serviced by a VIP lift and the main staircase. Obviously, we haven't been able to get up that far, but we can assume there's a decent level of security on the top floor."

Gorilla nodded and took the thick envelope that Johnson passed across. His reading matter for the next day.

"Can I give my tuppence worth?" said Johnson.

Gorilla nodded. "If you think it will help, sure."

"I don't know what you're hoping to do in there, and I don't want to. Redactors and Hawks are a bit like 'never the twain shall meet' in that respect, aren't they? But what I will tell you for free is that there will be no happy ending going in there on your own. It will be a bloody blood bath old mate, a bloody blood bath. Is there more of you?"

Gorilla shook his head. "No, it's just me and the girl at the moment. We're on our own."

Johnson raised an eyebrow, shrugged and took a gulp of his red wine. He winced. "Well then... Jesus, this stuff's rough on the palate... maybe it's better that you live to fight for another day rather than going on a suicide mission."

* * *

286

He had enjoyed the stroll back from the Old Port. The night was cool and the stickiness of the day's heat had disappeared. He'd turned the corner to the apartment building and glanced up at their windows.

What he saw had him taking a sharp intake of breath. A figure passed by in silhouette – a man. Gorilla moved into the nearest doorway to conceal himself and continued to watch. Moments later, the figure moved back again as if he was pacing in the lounge.

They've found us, he thought. *The hit-team has somehow tracked us back to base. How? Was there a leak in SIS? A leak in the local police?*

He made his way to the front door of the apartment and entered. He took the stairs as quietly and as quickly as he could. When he reached their apartment door, he removed the '39 from the holster on his hip, quickly attached the silencer and flicked off the safety. He let the weapon rest in his right hand. Then he slowly turned the handle and burst in at full speed. *Fuck subtlety,* he thought. *There's a time and a place for being covert, but tonight isn't it.*

He moved along the wall, weapon raised and ready to shoot down the intruder. Nothing was disrupted and he could see no signs of a struggle. He moved along the hall to the living room and pushed open the main double doors and there stood Nicole, her arms crossed firmly over her chest and scowling like a wife ready to spray down vitriol on an errant husband.

"Where is he, are you alright?" he garbled, his mind whirling, trying to figure out where the intruder was. He scanned left and right.

"Jack, I'm fine," was all she managed to say before she was interrupted by a voice emanating from the bathroom.

"You still toting that bloody Smith & Wesson from years ago?"

Gorilla would recognize that voice anywhere. It was like cut glass; harsh and brittle with an unashamed touch of arrogance and disdain. "Trench," was all Gorilla could feebly manage before the immaculate figure emerged from the bathroom, drying his hands on a towel.

"Indeed it is. Just scraping a bit of the muck off from my recent travels, I hope you don't mind. The girl said it was alright."

Ah, that was why Nicole looked furious, thought Gorilla as he lowered the '39. Trench had a reputation for not sparing the rod with the 'fairer sex' as he called them. Most women couldn't stand to be in Trench's company for five minutes, let alone a whole evening.

Gorilla looked over at Nicole again. She had one eyebrow cocked, and a cold look in her eye which said 'He's your friend – you deal with him!'"

Great, he thought, *I've just been promoted to peacemaker between a misogynist and a feminist.*

"Don't look so confused," said Trench. "I'm your little gift from Masterman, here to lend a hand. So, what's the job, old boy?"

Chapter Six

Frank Trench, the Iago of the Redaction Unit. Always plotting, always scheming, and always looking for the next high profile operation, the next promotion or the next advancement up the career ladder at SIS.

Grant's desk at Pimlico was situated opposite Trench's and he knew that the man had, in his opinion, delusions of grandeur. Trench was medium height and build with a military moustache and aged somewhere in his mid-forties. He was always dressed in well-cut suits from Saville Row and spoke with the sort of clipped accent beloved of British Army officers of a certain class.

But Grant knew it was bullshit. The man was nothing more than a spiv. Trench was no officer, had, in fact, not risen above the rank of Lance Corporal during his time with the Royal Engineers, first in Europe and latterly in Palestine. Trench had spent the postwar years hunting down terrorists in the Middle East after volunteering for one of the 'special units' which had been formed to curb the spread of Zionist terror gangs. He had a reputation for always getting his man and bringing him back; dead or alive. It was this ruthlessness which had made him perfect for the newly-formed Redaction Unit in the late 1950's.

Grant had found Trench was an acquired taste; people either tolerated him, or loathed him. There was no middle ground, and no one in recent memory could be said to be friends with the man. Yet despite all of his personality failings, he was considered to be a first class operator and was one of the legends of the Redaction Unit's covert war. He got the job done.

Grant settled Trench in to the apartment and it was decided that Nicole would keep her room and the two men would share. Then he set about bringing his colleague up to speed on recent events; the killing of the German and of the surveillance intelligence acquired by the Hawkeye team.

"So these chaps are holed up there, then," said Trench. He was lazing in the lounge, his feet draped carelessly over the arm of a chair and puffing on a cigarillo.

Grant nodded as he casually looked out through the window and onto the darkened street. "It seems that way. They don't come out unless they absolutely need to, even more so since their German friend disappeared on them."

Trench considered their options. "So if they're not coming out, we'll have to go in." He was fiddling with a piece of tobacco stuck in his teeth. He moved it around his gums before grabbing it between his fingers and flicking it onto the carpet.

Nicole frowned furiously and set off to the kitchen to make a pot of coffee. In her opinion, they had suddenly become a repertory company of spies. Of Trench, well, to say she detested him was a bit strong. Disliked certainly, trusted not at all and with all things being equal she didn't think there was much difference between him and the man she'd shot in the alley. In her own mind, she thought that the devil had come to stay.

She returned five minutes later, playing the little housekeeper with coffee pot and cups, to find both men stood over the dining table, making notes on a piece of paper; a rough sketch of a building lay at its center.

"If we play it right, we can make it look like a rival gang hit on the hotel, rather than a targeted Redaction on the hit-team. It wouldn't take much, a bit of shouting in French, threats to the Guerinis, that sort of thing," said Grant.

"It sounds feasible. Crash and bash, or stealth?" asked Trench.

"Stealth as much as we can, we want to catch these killers unawares. If they're as professional as we think they are, we want to take them on our terms and not theirs. Ideally, I'd like another few people on our team, but we'll just have to make do among us. Did you bring any tools with you?"

Trench stood and straightened his back, causing it to give a loud click. "I've brought a very nice piece with me that will be more than suitable for this operation. Silenced. Good for the covert approach. Bolt action, I'm afraid, but nothing we can't work with."

Grant nodded. "And are you up for this? Are you ready after your last job?" he asked.

Trench waved a hand dismissively. "Oh, Libya was such a bore. No challenge really. Besides, you know me old boy, always happy to be in at a kill. When do we go?"

"Tomorrow night."

* * *

Nicole awoke early the next morning to find that Grant had already left the apartment. A note he'd left for her said that he was going to give the target location one last scout, in case of any last minute changes or problems. Nicole thought it was just a way of giving himself a bit of space, away from the confines of the apartment.

Trench was sitting at the dining table in his shirt sleeves. The curtains had been drawn and he was cleaning the component parts of a rifle, which had obviously been concealed in what she thought was the kind of bag her father used for carrying his fishing rods. Evidently, it contained something much more lethal. Trench had the parts laid out carefully on the table before him. The magazine and the bolt had been removed and he was working some type of oil into the breech with an old rag that had definitely seen better days.

The weapon was a .45 caliber De Lisle Carbine, a stubby-looking rifle that had been built during the war for the sabotage service as an assassination weapon. The De Lisle was said to be the quietest carbine available, a testimony to the bulbous end of the rifle, which on a traditional weapon would consist of the barrel, but on this weapon, housed the integral silencer as a one-piece unit. It also had a folding stock and pistol grip to make it easier to conceal underneath a long coat and it was ideal for using at close quarters.

Trench had been using it on his last job with good results, and rather than hand it back to the local SIS Station, he'd chosen to bring it with him. Far behind him on the North African plains, lay a missing Libyan intelligence chief with a single bullet hole to his head, courtesy of Frank Trench and the De Lisle. He loaded the bolt back into its housing, working it a few times to ensure its smoothness, brought the weapon up to his shoulder and pulled the trigger. It gave a satisfying, dry fire *click*.

"It suits you," said Nicole.

"Does it indeed," said Trench, keeping one eye looking down the iron sights.

"Are you any good with it?"

He laughed. "Bloody awful, actually. But on a good day, if the wind is blowing in the right direction I can just about hit a barn door, maybe even kill a chap if I'm lucky."

"And is Jack... I mean Gorilla... is he any good?"

"Ah yes, well, Grant is a bit of a special case," said Trench smoothly, his tongue firmly in his cheek.

"In what way?"

Trench placed the weapon carefully down onto the table. He turned to look at her. "Grant is born for this kind of work. He's a natural. In fact, he's the best I've ever seen with a pistol. He's almost superhuman when it comes to close quarter shooting. He's got a few dead-eyes to his credit."

Nicole thought back to the conversations she'd had with Masterman and the gossip around SIS. They spoke of Gorilla's shooting skills with an almost reverence. "What *is* a dead-eye?"

Trench laughed. "Hasn't he brought you up to speed on our terminology? What *have* you two been doing all this while? A dead-eye is what we, unofficially, call our targets. Sort of a sick joke, I suppose. Once a Redaction contract has been formalized, the dead-eye is a corpse that just hasn't lain down."

She shuddered, remembering the fight in Marseilles. The violence, the blood. "It just seems so cold."

"Bloody hell, girl, it is cold. It's meant to be. Stone cold killers, that's us."

She didn't like the way the conversation was going and decided to change the subject. "Where did he get the name Gorilla?"

"Did you ask him? You seem like the type that would," he said. Trench fixed her with a glare and let the silence hang.

She relented. "He wouldn't tell me. I assume it's something to do with his past."

Trench had finished loading the bullets into several magazines, dried off his hands on the cloth and turned to her. He stepped toward her, his manner and voice becoming brooding. "Grant's past is a bit of a mystery, a bit murky so I'm led to believe, so I won't tell you either."

She took a step away from him and he smiled. "Got the hots for him, have you? I wouldn't have thought he was your type." His upper class cavalry officer accent had slipped, she noted, and had been replaced with a twang. Northern definitely… possibly Liverpool or Manchester and the sudden change in accent also gave him an even more sinister tone.

"No… not at all. I just wondered," she said, not wholly convincing herself.

"Fancy a bit of rough, do you? Grant's certainly that, alright. Gorilla by name, Gorilla by nature."

Nicole felt herself blushing, but still fixed a glare on Trench. God, he was loathsome.

"If you've got an itch that you can't scratch, I might be able to help you out old girl. A quick tumble perhaps, while the boss is away. It happens all the time, only natural. It could just be our little secret."

Nicole turned away from him and headed back to the kitchen. "You're disgusting, Trench. Just stay out of my way," she said.

Trench smiled, a smile which hid nothing of his malicious thoughts. The cavalry officer had returned once more. "Well, if you don't ask and all that..." she heard him say, as she slammed the door to the kitchen.

Chapter Seven

The night-time hit on the Hotel Azure, which left eight men dead, would later be generally accredited with being the spark which began the Corsican Mafia war in the spring of 1965.

The two main rivals in the war, the Guerini and Francisci Clans, had long been bitter rivals, each jockeying for position and power. The Guerinis had the power the Franciscis wanted. It was only a matter of time before something started the fire. The Guerini-owned and controlled Hotel Azure was a three story building overlooking the Old Port, and while it was generally referred to as a hotel, it was in reality a brothel and gambling den for the soldiers of the Guerinis.

On the ground floor was the bar/restaurant and reception areas, together with a back room where the gamblers could while away the hours doing what they enjoyed best. Upstairs consisted of twelve 'guest rooms' where visitors could be entertained by the girls who operated from those rooms, while its top floor consisted of two penthouse apartments, where special guests could stay or discreet business meetings could be held. The front of the hotel housed the main entrance, whilst to the rear was a more discreet, privately-accessed entrance, complete with external staircase for the patrons of the penthouse apartments. All were guarded on rotation by a number of armed Corsican underworld soldiers.

The attack began at the front of the hotel, when a small explosive charge blew out the front windows. Not a large explosion by any means, but one that provided enough of a bang, coupled with enough smoke and debris to make everyone in the vicinity come rushing to see what the commotion was. Which, in the grand scheme of things, is exactly what a decoy is meant to do.

* * *

They moved as a unit, a well-organized team, smoothly, quickly and efficiently. Gorilla was leading the way, the silenced '39 up and ready to use, with Trench, tight on his shoulder, bringing up the rear, the De Lisle poised and ready to take down any threat.

The main corridor was in semi-darkness, thanks to Trench's sabotaging of the electricity supply, causing shadows to loom and great patches of blackness to bear down on the narrow corridor. They had already killed a guard pacing the exterior of the building. He'd been smoking, perhaps on his break, when Gorilla had approached him, asking, "*Phillipe, est que vous?*"

The man had turned, the cigarette dangling from his lips, to see a small figure approaching in the darkness of the alley. As he was about to answer, Gorilla brought up the silenced pistol in a one-handed draw from beneath his black coat and fired twice. Head shots. The first target was down.

The stashing of the body and the picking of the rear door lock took no more than a minute and then Gorilla and Trench were inside. Both men were already dressed in dark clothes, to keep their visible profile down, but now they put on balaclava hoods to prevent them from being identified.

On the other side of the building, they could hear the panic and confusion caused by the detonation of the explosive decoy. The main priority now was to reach and ascend the rear staircase as quickly as possible. Gorilla just hoped they were in time to catch the hit-team in their base.

He noticed a movement coming from the doorway leading to the staircase; a large, grossly overweight man holding a revolver. Gorilla was quick, but Trench must have seen him first and fired the silenced carbine. Gorilla felt the wind as the bullet passed by his ear and watched as the man dropped to the ground, dead. The noise of the bullet entering his head had sounded like someone throwing a rotten tomato at a wall; an underwhelming splat.

They made their way along and down to the left, moving as one and reacting to whatever the darkness threw at them. There were figures running in panic from the whorehouse's various rooms, the noise and heat almost a physical entity. The Redaction team's minds were digesting the information as quickly as their eyes and senses detected it, at times it almost seemed as if there was a telepathic bond between the two men.

Shoot that one: *phut, phut, phut.* Target down. Don't shoot that one: it's one of the girls.

Gorilla was moving first and firing, and then Trench pepper-potting forward and eliminating the next. The only sounds were the metallic 'clacks' as Gorilla changed a magazine or Trench cycled the action on the carbine.

Gorilla saw a man take a bullet, one of Trench's, through the eye... another who had opened the door to his room, shotgun at the ready, had taken two rounds to the chest, causing it to explode... while a third had almost walked into Gorilla's silencer and was rewarded with a *phut* to the temple. To Gorilla it was like dropping an army of ghastly ghouls, in some horrific funfair arcade.

And still they moved forward in silence, taking out hostiles, pushing bystanders out of the way, Trench screaming in French for them all to "Descendre, descendre," and scanning for the targets of their mission. By the time they'd reached the flight of stairs leading to the penthouse level, Gorilla judged that they'd taken down a round dozen armed Corsican soldiers, who had either been clients seeing their favorite girls or strong-arm men brought in to provide security.

The whole thing from top to bottom had taken Gorilla and Trench no more than several minutes.

Gorilla knew it wouldn't be long before the Corsicans would start to re-organize and bring in reinforcements. They were so near, only a flight of stairs away from completing their mission and time was of the essence now, more than ever. He motioned to his partner to take a look, to see if he could spot any more targets. Trench raised himself up on the foot of the lower step and craned his neck. A nod and two fingers were held up, indicating how many targets he could see. Bodyguard's, probably, there to make sure that the VIP's hadn't been disturbed. Whoever they were, they must have some pull with the Corsican gangs to afford this level of protection.

Gorilla frowned. Two that Trench could see… but how many more that he couldn't? They would all be armed now, thanks to the explosion and screaming. The final push would be difficult. Fighting from a lower position was never an enviable place to be.

As if sensing his unease, Trench pointed to Gorilla and made the motion of putting his fingers in his ears. When the smaller man had done this, Trench stepped forward so that the penthouse floor landing was directly above him. He reached inside his coat pocket and withdrew a small, tennis ball shaped object. He pulled the pin and gently tossed it over his head, with just enough effort to ensure that it hit its mark. Trench moved back and also jammed his fingers into his ears and waited for the inevitable explosion.

* * *

"We should help them," said Gioradze.

"No," said Marquez. "It's their problem. Let the Corsicans solve it, that's what we pay them for. Our priority is to get out and stay out until it's resolved. Grab the pistols, the cash and the passports, just in case."

"What about the papers?"

Marquez shook his head. "Leave them, they're safer here. No one will be interested in them. The Guerinis will have whatever is going on dealt with soon enough and then we can come back and retrieve them."

They had both been relaxing when the lights had gone out, less than five minutes ago. They had been discussing the disappearance of the German, Nadel. He'd been gone for almost a week and the conclusion both men came to was that he'd simply decided to quit in a fit of pique. Marquez had asked the Corsicans to keep an eye out for him in Marseilles, but so far, no one had seen him. Gioradze, by contrast, vowed to cut his balls off, literally, when he caught up with the aging Nazi mercenary.

Then there had been the sound of a distant bang from below, followed by all the power being cut; the inevitable screams and shouts and confusion had followed. Gioradze had looked out the window and saw several half-dressed men and women leaving by the front entrance.

The first thing which occurred to Marquez was that it was a hit by one of the rival clans. It was no secret that the Corsican Capo Guerini was in a constant battle with rival clans, keen to remove the head of the Marseilles underworld from his throne. It was just bad luck that they happened to be caught up in the middle of it all.

"We'll have to use the main staircase. With the power out the lifts won't be working," said Marquez. The two men gathered their essential escape kit and weapons and ran for the apartment door. Gioradze had just about reached the handle when the explosion rocked them, knocking them both to the floor. It sounded as if someone had smashed the door with a sledgehammer, a shockwave of sound and energy. The air was filled with the smell of fire and dust.

Gioradze was the first to compose himself and managed to look through the gaping wound of what was once the door to their rooms. It was carnage. The two bodyguards had been eviscerated by the grenade and lay sprawled at unnatural angles on the landing, their blood flung across the art deco wallpaper.

He heard voices shouting from the floor below, and knew that whoever had lobbed that grenade would soon be following it up to finish off what they had started. He grabbed Marquez, who was shaking his head, trying to clear the ringing from his ears.

"Juan, we... we have to go... NOW! The windows, they're our only chance to escape!"

* * *

Gorilla had chamber-checked the '39 again, making sure that the bullet was seated properly and wouldn't misfire. Satisfied, he gave the thumbs up to Trench who had also completed a reload. Both men were standing to the side of the staircase, poised, waiting in the natural blind spot under the upper level.

The grenade had done its job; Gorilla was sure of that. Now it would be a simple mopping up operation for them.

He gave the 'go' signal, a short, chopping motion with his hand, and the two men launched themselves at the stairs, weapons up and ready to fire. The seven steps opened up onto what had recently been an expensively furnished penthouse landing; now it was a charnel house complete with debris, smoke and human remains scattered across the floor. Two doors, the doors to the penthouse suites, stood before them. Separating both rooms was the unusable elevator, with the upside down body of a Corsican barring entry to its broken doors.

"*Je Vais a gauche,*" Trench shouted to Gorilla as he centered the carbine on the left hand door and moved towards it at speed. Gorilla nodded and took the right side, booting in the door, dropping to one knee and scanning the interior of the hotel suite.

It was empty. No targets. Only a recently-used bed and a small suitcase propped against a chair. He made his way inside, covering his arcs of fire, until he reached the only other possible hiding place; the bathroom. He flung open the door, expecting to find his target holed up, but was rewarded only with an empty, luxurious marble bath. Nothing.

It was then that he heard the gunfire from the adjacent penthouse suite.

* * *

Trench had followed the exact same routine as Gorilla: kicked the door open, dropped to a knee and raised the De Lisle ready to scan and attack. He was greeted with the sight of two men, one small and balding and the other tall and dark, clambering out of the window and onto what he assumed would be a balcony terrace.

The smaller man seemed to be protecting his bigger compatriot, half pushing him and half pulling him out of the escape route.

Trench raised his weapon to get a clear aim and in that moment, almost as if there'd been some kind of ingrained survival instinct at play, the smaller man turned in one fluid motion and fired.

The rounds from the handgun came rapidly in a sustained volley and had the desired effect of making Trench flinch and driving him back behind the cover of the doorframe and into the hallway. But not for long and Trench was soon on his feet, and both he and Gorilla raced to the window, hoping to get a shot at the two fugitives.

They led with their weapons, in case the killers had decided to stage an ambush. Trench looked first. "Clear!" he shouted. Weapons raised, they peered out into the darkness. The only sights which greeted them were a crowd gathering outside of the hotel and the flashing beacons of a fire truck. Their quarry had flown.

"Shit," said Trench. "They must have hopped over to the next balcony and down, then across to the next building. We've no chance of catching up with them now."

Gorilla pulled off the balaclava hood, his short white hair spiked up from the heat and sweat was running down his brow. He took in a deep breath to cool himself. The aftershock of the past few minutes had gone and stillness settled over the building, the only sound being the distant repetition of a record player needle stuck on a loop; a crooner telling his love that it was over. Gorilla looked around the room while Trench guarded the door, ready and waiting to drop anyone who made it up the stairway.

Gorilla scanned the desk, the bed and the furnishings, which were covered with papers and files. He looked at each item carefully. It was a treasure trove of information, consisting of documents, notes and maps. They had obviously found their intended targets, right in the middle of planning the next hit, and even from this cursory glance, Gorilla was convinced there was enough real time intelligence contained in the scattered pages to keep Toby and his team going for weeks. He began to gather it up, quickly stuffing as much as he could into his jacket pockets.

"Anything?" Trench asked from over his shoulder. His eyes never left the threat of the smoldering staircase. His finger still rested dangerously close to the trigger.

"You could say that," said Gorilla, as he folded up a map and crammed it into his pocket.

"That's great. But before we bugger off, can I just make a suggestion? We need to burn the place down. They're gone, so it seems, but if they come back and find their papers and files missing, they'll instantly suspect foul play – or more accurately, foul play directed at them."

Gorilla considered this. The hit-team had vanished, they'd missed them by a whisker, but if they wanted any chance of catching up with them again, then this stash of operational intelligence was going to be the key.

"If they come back and find it all gone, the chances are they'll change their plans," said Trench. "We have to make them believe that any material belonging to them perished and hope they assume their security is still intact and carry on with the operation. Does that make sense?"

Gorilla nodded, loading a fresh magazine into the '39 before he pulled the balaclava back on. He was ready. "Frank?"

"Yes, Gorilla."

"I think we need one of your little firecrackers."

* * *

The fire, according to later reports from the Marseilles Fire Service, began in the upper floors of the now-lamented Hotel Azure. The blaze took over three hours to quell and had to be left overnight before it was considered safe enough to retrieve the dead bodies from inside.

In total, a dozen bodies were removed and the coroner's report would show that the victims had died from gunshot wounds, rather than from the effects of the fire.

In the immediate aftermath of the attack, no one noticed two figures climbing onto the roof and crossing to the neighboring property before scaling down the outer stairwell and then disappearing. Nor did anyone notice the small, rusting Renault which had been stolen earlier that day, ambling along and leaving the Port area at a slow pace.

The attack and subsequent burning down of the Azure were the final sparks in an already volatile tinderbox that was the Marseilles underworld. The results would be inevitable and when several Francisci Clan Underbosses were shot dead a week later, no one was surprised.

* * *

They had been sitting in the farthest, darkest corner of the old cinema for the past hour. They were watching *Une Femme Mariee* directed by Jean-Luc Goddard.

The audience was thinned and spread across the auditorium like island pockets, each isolated in their own little regions. They were mainly couples out on dates, enjoying some time together. Gioradze was convinced some of the men were less interested in the dialogue and were, in fact, getting sneaky hand jobs from their ladies.

The movie house had seemed the most natural place to hide. It was quiet, discreet and off the beaten track. It was the perfect place for them to re-group and analyze the violence of the past hour. Marquez and Gioradze kept their heads close together, their whispering voices lost among the volume of the film. Gioradze had his hand on the pistol concealed beneath his coat, in case they were about to be ambushed. "Could it have been the German after all? Has he sold us out?" he asked.

Marquez had considered this over the past hour, but after digesting the events of the night, had dismissed it. What did the German know? Very little, in fact; a few locations, but no specifics about the future targets. That information was on a need to know basis and only Gioradze and he knew the principals involved. "I think not. Nadel would have very little to gain from it, and loathe as I am to admit it, he is at least professional. Besides, I think he would want to settle it face-to-face with us," said Marquez.

"Then the police. Perhaps he ratted us out to *Les Flics*."

"For what purpose?"

"Who knows? Anger, revenge, jealousy, being a prick... whatever he did it for, he's a dead man when I get hold of him," snarled Gioradze.

Marquez shook his head. "David, those men weren't police. Did you see the weapons, the masks, the clothes? Besides, there were only two of them – if it was the police, they would have come mob handed."

"Two that we could see?"

"Alright, two that we could see, but they weren't there to arrest anyone, they were there to kill. Didn't you see the body count?"

Gioradze had to admit that even the Marseilles police, after years of having to deal with the violence of the Corsican milieu, wouldn't resort to murder. "Maybe it was the Barbouzes?" he said.

Marquez considered this. The *Barbouzes* – 'the bearded ones', – were the ruthless French Secret Service operators waging an underground war against the terrorist group, the OAS. They were certainly known for murder and execution. But he had never worked for the OAS and to his knowledge, neither had Gioradze, so he couldn't figure out why they would target them specifically. "Impossible. Why would the SDECE Action Groups wish to target us?"

"Okay, so what was it all about, then?"

Marquez sat silent for a moment or two, watching the film on the screen but not really taking in what was happening. Finally, he decided. "I think it was a spat, a very violent spat, between the Guerinis and a rival gang. We just got caught up in the middle of it all."

Gioradze tensed, his finger moving to the trigger. The couple three rows in front got up and shuffled their way to the exit. Either the film wasn't to their taste, or the young beau had finished with his girlfriend's ministrations. He settled back. "So what's our next move?" he asked.

Marquez considered it for a moment. There was no point returning to the Hotel Azure. As they'd been making their escape, he'd briefly turned back to see the building engulfed in flames. Fire poured from the top floor windows and he had no doubt that by now, the building would be all but destroyed along with the reminder of their belongings. *A good job that I have copies of the planning at the safe-house outside Paris,* he thought.

"We move. We take what we have and drive north. The south has become too exciting."

Outside, parked five hundred yards down from the cinema was a newly-acquired Citroën they'd appropriated from an unsuspecting driver an hour ago. The same unsuspecting driver was currently jammed into the boot of the car, a single bullet lodged in his forehead. The car had a full tank of petrol and would get them safely out of the area later that night.

"Okay," said Gioradze.

"We get back to the safe-house in Auvers-sur-Oise . We travel separately and rendezvous there. We'll have to alter our plans slightly, just in case someone *is* on our backs. Instead of attacking the targets geographically, I think we should be a bit more inventive and take the next few at random. You take the job in England. Once that's finished, I'll move on the target in Paris."

Chapter Eight

"That little operation you're running in Europe at the moment, Stephen, Operation MACE. It's getting a little loud, a little too noisy," said C.

They were sitting in the Chief's garden at his home in Tunbridge Wells. It was the Chief's one place of sanctuary, away from the machinations of Whitehall. It was a sultry day and the cool glasses of white wine made a refreshing respite as the two men sat on the garden terrace eating lunch. "I mean, we can't have chaps bombing and taking potshots at each other out in the open. It goes against the grain of covert intelligence work," continued C.

Masterman, who had been summoned to the Chief's private residence that very day, knew that when C was in full flow with his theorizing, it was better to let him lead and see where it ended up.

"So how's our batting average, Stephen? What's our score so far?"

"We've lost one confirmed agent from Constellation – *Orion*. Of the hit-team, we've gotten a one down and two-to-go ratio. So while not perfect, it's better than we expected," said Masterman. "Although if I'm honest, there's something about this whole CIA operation that's been nagging at me."

C poured them another glass each of wine each. "Well, go on. Don't leave me in suspense."

"There's something not right about it, something that doesn't quite ring true. It doesn't have the hallmarks of one of the Agency's normal missions. It's too rushed, a bit haphazard and since when did the Agency need to start using outside support such as forgers or armorers?" asked Masterman.

"I admit; it does sound a tad unusual. Carry on," prompted C.

"Firstly, why would the Americans use old, outside contractors for a kill list this size? Since Kennedy's assassination, the US Special Forces teams have taken over that type of operation. It doesn't add up. They're just taking a bigger risk of compromise by using outsiders."

C nodded. "Indeed, I'd had much the same thought myself. What are your conclusions?"

Masterman was unsure where his hypothesis was going, but decided to follow it to its natural conclusion. "It's false somehow. It could be a rogue operation, but it's certainly not mainstream CIA."

"Maybe it's time to declare our hand to the Americans," said the Spymaster.

Masterman turned to his Chief and frowned. "I thought the original aim was to keep it covert, without alerting the CIA. Surely that was the purpose of using Redaction for this."

"Oh, it's no reflection on you and your unit, Stephen. It's just that sometimes these things have to run their course and work themselves out. However, it seems that this time, we've gone as far as we can, and if the Americans do have a rogue element operating inside their organization, it's only proper that we alert them to it." C nibbled at his salad, dusted his lips and returned to his problem. "Perhaps it's time to bring the Americans up to speed. Nothing formal and certainly nothing official. Just a meeting between fellow officers and maybe a chat over a drink, to alert them to this problem – just to give them a nudge in the right direction."

Masterman didn't like the way the conversation was going. This could put his people at risk and being an ex-field agent himself, it was something he wasn't keen to encourage. "But won't that compromise my operation, not to mention the risk of exposing Constellation?"

"Constellation has always been the priority and if we do it correctly, it should be allowed to carry on unharmed. We'll simply say that we're aware of an attempted assassination plot against several Soviet agents. Let's see if we can embarrass the Agency a little, poke fun at their lack of operational security. Plus, if your team can remove these killers, we can also use it as leverage against the Agency to shut this silly operation down. We'll tell them we don't take too kindly to CIA-backed murder on British soil. After all, what intelligence service wants to be caught *in flagrante* by one of its allies? Certainly not the CIA, not after all its recent neutering by Congress. I'm sure we can count on their cooperation."

"And if they refuse?" asked Masterman.

C placed his glass on the table and rested his hands across his lap. "Well, if that happens – and I hope it won't come to that – we'll have a very interesting game on our hands, won't we? Do you know anyone on that side of the pond who we could have a quiet word with? An old friend perhaps, a compatriot, someone who appreciates the need for discretion and is part of the old boy network ?"

Masterman thought for a moment. He knew straight away who he would turn to. "There is a chap I used to know. Sort of my opposite number in the Agency in the bad old days, he was part of the CIA's covert action program in Berlin before they dismantled it all… well, after Kennedy and all that."

"I understand, I understand. And is he someone we could work with, perhaps pass a message to unofficially?"

Masterman nodded. "I believe so. We have an understanding, sir. Call it a line of communication between old comrades. The problem is, what do we tell him?"

C smiled and relaxed back in his wooden garden chair. "Fortunately, I have the answer to that one. We simply say that we appear to have stumbled across what we initially thought was a CIA operation to target Soviet intelligence agents in Europe, but that under closer scrutiny, we didn't think it actually was anything to do with the Agency. How does that sound?"

"What do I tell them about Operation MACE and the Redaction Unit?" Masterman questioned cautiously.

"You tell them nothing. That part, as agreed, is to remain closed to the Americans. Besides, your man appears to be well on the way to wiping out the contractors, isn't that right?" said C.

"What about Grant? Shall I recall him?"

"Oh no, dear boy, not at all! I do like to finish a job that's been started. No, he's to remain in place and track down the rest of these killers. He's done a fantastic job so far in this operation and he must continue to save the lives of the agents in Constellation, but now it's up to the Americans to do a bit of work and find out if one of their officers has gone off the reservation and decided to start fighting the Cold War on his own."

"Understood. I'll write up the information we have and pass it across to the CIA station here."

C frowned and leaned forward to rest an authoritative hand on the younger man's arm. "Ah, now I fear that may be a little too loud for what's required. Go personally to see your man, talk it through with him and give him the file of evidence that we have thus far."

"In America!"

"If that's where he is, why not? Nothing shows that you're acting in a matter of urgency better than a face-to-face meeting after travelling across an ocean. If anybody asks, simply tell them it's a routine liaison meeting. The file you give him – minus our involvement in tracking down the contractors, of course – may assist the cousins in finding out who the paymaster and the planner is behind all of this."

Masterman understood perfectly. His team were capable of handling the actual killing and removal of the assassins, but the CIA was in a much better position to narrow down who was behind them, the controllers, and the architects. "It's certainly been a most unusual operation, sir," said Masterman. "It's been particularly bloody from our point of view; the murder of *Orion* and the hit in Marseilles to name but two."

C snorted with laughter. It was a most vulgar show of emotion from a man who excelled at presenting a cool and calm veneer to his subordinates. "I do find it most amusing, and not a little irritating, when our masters in Whitehall and Parliament hark back to the glory days of fighting the Hun. It's rose-tinted spectacles time I'm afraid. They look at it as almost a boy's own adventure; commando raids in the dead of night, then back for hot chocolate and bacon sandwiches."

Masterman thought back to his own service during the war with the fledgling Special Forces; no hot chocolate, no bacon sandwiches, no romantic overtures. It had been three years stuck behind enemy lines, fearful of betrayal, short on food, short on equipment and short on help.

It had been bloody and murderous.

C continued. "And yet our Cold War is just as bloody and brutal as the fight against the Nazis ever was. In years to come, I suspect people will reminisce about this battle that we're fighting against Communism, and it will be a rose-tinted spectacles time again. Oh, the drama and romance of running spies behind the Iron Curtain. So gentlemanly, so clever, so cerebral. If I am still alive, I'll look them in the eye and tell them they're talking balderdash. The fight against the Russians and their agents is violent, torturous and more blood has been spilt in waging it, than the Germans could ever dream of during the six years of their little effort. The underground violence of the Cold War will be the benchmark that we're judged on by future members of our trade. If we're to survive it, and win it, we need resourceful and capable men like your good self, Stephen, and that man of yours. Remember that Stephen, always remember the greater good."

"I will sir, I will," said Masterman.

Chapter Nine

The Burrowers, over the past three months of being on duty for Operation MACE, had fallen into a weary slump, something which was instantly recognizable as the start of mission fatigue. They were tired, exhausted and not a little fraught with the possibility of the killers having slipped through their fingers.

Toby's team had also started to resemble a 'burrower' from the animal kingdom, such as a vole, weasel or mole. They were in to work early, stayed late into the night, and were constantly scurrying from one meeting to another, conducting covert trips to the new registry at Century House to clarify a new lead, or to plead a case to some unseen intelligence committee for extra resources. They were also rarely seen to speak to and the only evidence of their continued existence was the light in their office space, which burned late into the night.

For Toby, as the team's investigative lead, the stress of the operation was taking its toll too. Working hard, rarely seeing his family. It was a grind of travel to work, files, operations orders, work late into the night, travel back home, not see the kids, not eat properly and get a frosty reception from Caroline. Repeat, repeat, repeat.

So it came as a boost for the Burrowers, when three days after the unsuccessful hit on the hotel in Marseilles, a big fat parcel of intelligence was haughtily slammed down onto Toby's desk and gave the team a new lease of life. He sat at his desk, a half-finished cup of tea in his hand, and stared at the macabre jigsaw puzzle that lay before him.

The CIA had seemingly gone wild, a retired contract agent and killer on the loose, the murder of several people spread out across Europe, the use of 'outside' resources by the hit-team – and not to mention the breaking with known CIA operational protocols.

Plausible deniability was one thing, everybody did that to some degree, but this was unprecedented. It was almost as if the Agency had a bee in its bonnet about giving its operation *any* assistance, no matter how small. *No, something didn't fit right with this picture at all,* thought Toby. Masterman had touched on it fleetingly during the initial briefing and Toby as the lead desk officer and analyst of Operation MACE was inclined to agree with him.

The question was, what was it? What would cause the CIA to suddenly have a personality transplant and start what was the term the Americans used in the gangster movies – 'whacking' out the opposition? The relevant files to the case were laid out neatly before him, in the shape of a star. He knew he was missing something, and despite the treasure trove of information that the Redaction Agents Gorilla and Trench had managed to salvage from the attack in Marseilles, he suspected the real 'meat' of the intelligence was yet to be made available.

The trick now was to give a best estimate, a likely guess, as to which target the killers would be aiming at next. If Toby and his team deciphered the intelligence correctly, there was a very good chance the Redaction team could swoop on in there and halt the killers at the source. The Burrowers had checked their leads and read through the material brought back from Marseilles and on the face of it, certainly from a proximity viewpoint; the next target should have been in Paris. A quick drive or train journey from the south up to the north and take out the 'Soldier'.

There was even a growing cabal within the senior doors of SIS, led primarily by Barton the Vice-Chief, that wanted to send all their resources straight back to Paris to protect the agent known as *Cirius* and wait for the killers there. Sooner or later they would have to come out the woodwork, wouldn't they, argued the naysayers. It seemed like an open and shut case and a less experienced counter-intelligence officer might have easily put two and two together and come up with five.

But not Toby Burrow's.

Toby's mind, for all its academic traits had a streak of criminality about it. At times, it was as if he could put himself inside the mind of the person he was tracking. He'd been that way since childhood when he would reason out where his mum kept the chocolate biscuits which were his favorites. Not the biscuit barrel, that was far too obvious. He had made several false guesses – the pantry, behind the kettle, even on top of the cooker – until he'd finally figured it out. Not high up where little hands couldn't reach, but actually lower down were little minds wouldn't think of. The pots and pans cupboard under the cooker.

The rest had been a daring liberation of the said chocolate biscuits and happy indulgence… that is, until his mother had caught him, face smeared with chocolate and biscuit crumbs, and had sent him to his room without supper for the remainder of the night. Still, you live and learn.

The 'Marseilles Intelligence' gave references to a place called Scarrick Point in Cornwall. From reading the background files on the agents, Scarrick Point was the home of the man the killers knew as the 'Engineer', but who was better known to Toby by his codename of *Scorpius*. So they had a target and a location. Now they needed to know when and how the killers would get there.

The other piece of intelligence was a map with a circle around the Falmouth area and 'Scarrick Point' written in ink in large letters. There was a connecting line which stretched across the channel and stopped at another circled point somewhere around the Cherbourg region. It was headed by a word: 'March' and along the line the same hand had written 'Thamilia'.

But what exactly was Thamilia? Was it a codename? Perhaps the codename of a UK-based contract killer who the assassins were going to use?

But no, everything about what they'd done so far pointed to the fact that this hit-team was keeping the actual killing to themselves. They were using outside contractors for certain things; the German who Gorilla and Nicole had disposed of in Marseilles being a case in point. But on the whole, it was their show.

So how would they get to Scarrick Point, which wasn't the most accessible place from mainland France; boat, car or plane? It had to be one of those. Toby had quickly rung around his contacts in SIS's Naval Intelligence liaison, SIS Air Liaison and a contact of his in the port authorities' liaison office. He gave them all the same request: Find me something, anything that relates to the word 'Thamilia'.

Here he was the 'Ace-Detective' of the British Secret Service, hunter of spies and traitors, and he'd been confounded by a word he'd never heard before.

He had his answer the very next day, from Commander Rix, the SIS Naval Liaison. "Sorry we took our time on that one. We're all at sixes and sevens in the move over to Century from Broadway. Anyway, the 'Thamilia' is a French-registered vessel, a thirty-two-footer, no less. The owner is one Albert Verhoeven. The information came from my French navy contact. Well, you know the French are now in the counter-gun running business, stopping arms from Europe making their way to North Africa. It seems Verhoeven had been flagged as a possible gunrunner at some point over the past few years, but the French couldn't catch him in the act."

So a boat was the method of entry; the question was, where was it now? He'd put in a priority request to the French Desk, who in turn put in an order for the same Hawkeye team that had been so successful in Marseilles to take a trip down to the Cherbourg region and do some devilling about in the harbors and fishing ports, to see if they could track down the Thamilia.

The agents spread out across the area, operating under the cover of French holidaymakers exploring the coastal region and perhaps looking to hire a boat for a day or two of coastal exploration. For nearly a week, Toby heard nothing, and then a surprise phone call to his desk had spurred him into action. Not only had the Hawkeye agents managed to track down where the boat was moored, but they'd also been able to capture a few grainy, black and white photographs.

Johnson, the Hawkeye team leader, had phoned the Burrowers' office and relayed the information directly to Toby. "It's currently, as of this morning, moored in a small fishing village called Barfleur, which is about twenty-seven kilometers east of Cherbourg," said the dour surveillance expert.

"And it hasn't moved?" asked Toby.

"Not according to our man on the ground there. He's booked into a little hotel overlooking the harbor and he's got constant surveillance on it. There's been some coming and going over the past day or so, moving some type of equipment on board. Then yesterday, the skipper had a visit from a couple of hard cases. They went inside for a pow-wow, stayed an hour or so and then buggered off."

Toby's excitement was almost palpable. "If it moves, I need to know about it. We may only have a few hours to stop it."

The call finally came early on the Saturday morning. It was Roger who took it – it was his shift – but he immediately relayed it to Toby at home. "It's bloody well on the move. It's been kitted out with some kind of equipment, we have to assume relating to the hit, and it has four men on board; the Captain and the three hitters."

"Why three?" asked Toby, crunching down on a piece of toast. It had been a rare chance for a family breakfast together. That is, until the telephone rang.

"Who knows, maybe after Marseilles they're being overcautious," suggested Roger.

"What's their expected ETA in Falmouth?"

Toby heard the ruffling of papers from the other end of the line and then Roger said, "Best estimate if the conditions stay fair, they can make about eight knots in eight hours, twelve hours slowest. I've just checked the weather report and there's a bit of rough weather due in down there over the next day or so. I reckon they'll be there late tomorrow night. Obviously they're working to a deadline, or they'd just reschedule."

"Alright Rog', well done. I'm coming back into the office after I've notified Redaction. Have everything ready for me on my desk." Toby and his team had gone forward, gone backward and gone every which way. He had been sure it was Cornwall and the target was Scorpius and the intelligence had borne him out. Satisfied, he picked up the telephone and dialed the direct line for Masterman and got a "Yes?" almost at once.

"Sir, it's Toby Burrows. I think I have something." Toby briefed Masterman on the details of the material from Marseilles. Cornwall, the boat, the timeframe of the hit and the harbor they would sail from.

"Clever move on their part, that," said Masterman. "Going for the more abstract target, rather than one already in their neck of the woods. Even now, they're trying to wrong foot any potential trackers."

"I agree. The secret to good counter-intelligence work is to see a pattern within the madness, and by attacking the targets randomly, rather than geographically, it's making it harder for anyone to track them."

"Well, let's hope these fellows have a successful trip across the channel, then," said Masterman.

"Excuse me for speaking out of turn, Colonel, but couldn't we just send the Royal Navy to intercept them once they enter British waters? Cut them off?"

Masterman thought about whether to answer and then decided to give the young desk officer the full facts. He was, after all, responsible for tracing the boat and the targets. "Yes, we could Toby. Most certainly, we could. But you see, the rules of the game have changed slightly, it's suddenly become much more complex."

"So what are we going to do?"

"Why, that's simple. We're going to let them come to us. I'll need to get Gorilla back here on the first available flight."

Toby was about to say something to challenge his superior officer, something about calling in Special Branch to pick them up when they landed, but then thought better of it. As he listened down the telephone line, he was sure he heard a touch of pleasure in Masterman's voice. It was the sound of the huntsman starting to sniff out his quarry for the first time and sending the dogs in for the kill.

* * *

An hour earlier, *The Thamilia* had eased out of the small, crook-shaped harbor of Barfleur and gently ambled out to sea. Inside relaxing, David Gioradze and his two sub-contractors were playing poker for loose coins. It was to be a long journey, at least ten hours. The Captain, Verhoeven, had been told to take his time. No rushing to get there, just let the boat putter along at a gentle cruising speed. Gioradze wanted to hit the Cornish coast somewhere late on the Saturday night, the later the better.

Darkness was going to be their friend.

He gently moved the canvas bag at his feet and told one of the French sub-contractors to put it in the storage hold ready for arrival in English waters. Better to have things out of sight, just in case they happened to be boarded by either the French or British Royal Navy. After all, the bag contained their tools for this particular job; three fully loaded Israeli-made Uzi 9mm's with folding stocks.

The Israeli weapon had been chosen on purpose. Gioradze did like to have the very best weapons for his contracts, which in this case, was something short and powerful with a rapid rate of fire. The hope was that when the British authorities finally arrived on the scene and found the Uzis, they would assume that some Israeli hit-team had finally managed to track down another aging Nazi and handed out justice. Gioradze knew that if nothing else, it would buy them a little time to carry out the rest of the contracts on their list. While the British police were looking in one direction, they would be moving off in another. It was brilliantly planned. Something that Marquez excelled at.

Since the incident in Marseilles, they had moved quickly to keep the momentum going at the pace of the hits. Marquez had headed to the safe-house in Auvers sur-Oise while he'd made his way down the country to place the finishing touches on the 'Engineer' hit.

He looked at his hand of cards – a pair. Shit! *Better to fold,* he thought, and threw the cards down onto the table. The Frenchman across the table from him laughed, revealing a gold tooth, and swept the cards and the coins into a big meaty hand. "Not your day, eh David?" he said.

Gioradze shrugged. It was only a game of cards, fuck it; as long as it wasn't an omen for the coming night's events he would be fine. Yes, he would be fine.

Chapter Ten

As he stepped into the arrivals lounge of London Airport, Jack Grant was greeted by an army of faces and bodies jostling for position to be the first to spot their loved ones, families, business colleagues.

They were all a blur and through the exhaustion of recent events, not to mention the excursions to a host of European countries over the past few weeks, he was aware that his concentration levels were ebbing. He also recognized that he was starting to burn out, which for a man in his profession could be a dangerous flaw.

He started to lag behind the rest of his fellow passengers, hoping to buy himself some time, so as to spot someone he knew. Nothing, at least not visible, so with no other option, he decided to make his way outside and stand proudly in front of the terminal. In truth, he wasn't sure who would be waiting for him, some nameless staffer from headquarters who had been roped in to do an 'airport run' probably, so he was pleasantly surprised to feel a hand on his shoulder and see the familiar face of Masterman. *Christ, the man could move like a big cat when he had to,* thought Grant. Then he saw Masterman's serious expression and knew instantly there wasn't going to be a happy, welcome home party for him.

"You look like hell," said Masterman.

"Thanks. It comes from being awake for the past few days," said Grant, the tiredness evident in his voice.

"Rough, was it?"

"I've had worse. Had better also." If he had, he couldn't for the life of him remember when that was.

"Well, let's get you to the car, shall we? I've a flask of coffee to perk you up." Masterman's car, a sporty MK1 Triumph Spitfire in black, was parked at the farthest end of the small car park, facing a concrete wall.

The rain was tapping against the windscreen. *I've traded a wet, cold, miserable Paris for a wet, cold, miserable London,* thought Grant.

"What do you think of the car? It's new," asked Masterman as he settled into the driver's seat.

Grant nodded. "Very nice. Shift does it?"

"It pulls a little around the corners, but on the straight it's like a rocket. Elsa thinks it's far too young for me. She's probably right."

Elsa was Masterman's wife. Their marriage was one of the great romances of the Service's history. They had met in Cairo during the war and were completely devoted to each other. Legend has it she once faced down an Arab extremist in Palestine, who had broken into the house one night. She had been armed with a revolver, him with a knife. Really, it had been no contest and the fledgling terrorist had scarpered with his testicles still attached to the rest of him.

Masterman was pouring steaming hot black coffee from the flask into two metal cups. Grant accepted his, wrapping both hands around the cup, sniffed the aroma and then took an appreciative sip.

"How are the intelligence reports from the Burrower's going down?" asked Masterman.

"Well. Very well, in fact; for a young bloke he certainly knows his business. Tell him whatever he's doing to keep on doing it. At this rate, we'll have this team closed down in no time," said Grant.

Masterman raised an eyebrow at that. He knew from years past that praise from Grant was something of a rarity. "So you approve of the reports then? Clear, concise, accurate?"

"They seem to be."

"Good, because I've got another one for you. It's an urgent one, in fact."

"How urgent?"

"Like now urgent. That's why we've brought you back. We tracked them down again. You leave as soon as we've finished our little chat and you've had a look over this." Masterman pulled an envelope from the side pocket of the driver's door and handed it over.

Grant rubbed his eyes to draw away the tiredness and began to look through the briefing file. He skimmed it as usual, taking in the relevant points: Agent *Scorpius*, Cornwall, a boat called *The Thamilia* leaving from Barfleur, the window of opportunity over the next day to lure the killers into a trap; in fact, everything that was needed to complete the next phase of the operation.

"The bulk of the clues came from the intelligence you and Trench grabbed in Marseilles. It led us right to Scorpius as the next target," said Masterman.

Grant took another glance at the sheets and stuffed them into the glove compartment. "And there we were, thinking it was going to be Paris for the next hit."

Masterman nodded. "That's what they had all thought, except for young master Burrows. He had the foresight to think differently, which was confirmed by the movement of the vessel leaving Barfleur."

"What about weapons? I've none," said Grant. He had left his '39 back in the safe cache in the apartment in Paris. Following the shooting in the hotel, the Redaction team had evacuated the Marseilles base and quickly gone their separate ways. Grant and Nicole back to Paris and Trench separately to who knew where.

The standard procedure for overseas weapons carry was that Redaction agents didn't take firearms on commercial airline flights. This was partly for security reasons, but more practically so that the agents cover wasn't blown. Why would a businessman working for a firm of accountants have a revolver? Instead, weapons were sourced in country from contacts or delivered through the Embassy's diplomatic bag to the agent's dead drop. It wasn't a perfect system, but it worked.

"Don't worry. There's something useful secured in the boot for you. Not your normal tool of the trade, but the best I could get at short notice from the tool shed. There's a change of clothes also – oh, and I thought this might come in handy, on the off chance that you get the opportunity to have a quiet word with one of the targets." Masterman handed over a small, leather bound case similar to the type used as a gentleman's grooming bag, one that would normally hold scissors and nail clippers, comb and sewing kit.

"What is it?" asked Grant, unsure of just what the hell he was holding.

"We'll call it a modern version of the thumbscrews, shall we? Ironically, it's one of the test kits which has been given to us by the CIA; apparently, they rate these methods rather highly," said Masterman unconvincingly.

Grant unzipped the bag and took in its contents. Three syringes, a cannula, and an antiseptic cleaning kit. He quickly zipped it up again with disgust.

Masterman noted the other man's displeasure. "I know what you're thinking, Jack. I'm of the same mindset as you; it's not my thing either. I find it rather distasteful. But if it gives us the edge in this hunt, then use it."

Grant wiped away the condensation from the passenger side window and peered out at the grey airport terminal. He knew the case officers back at SIS hated the thought of using chemical interrogation methods. It went against their code. In truth, Grant was of a similar mind and found the idea abhorrent. But this was a unique situation and the one thing he didn't have was the luxury of time, time to slowly coerce a man in a skillful interrogation session, easing the information out in a calm and subtle way.

"Ideally, we'd like to haul these killers in and let the interrogation mob wear them down. Unfortunately, time is against us and this seems to be the most humane way of resolving the problem. Besides, it's an order, so get it done," said Masterman.

Grant placed the kit on top of the envelope and looked directly at Masterman, resigned to his orders. "Understood. So we let them come into the bay, luring them into a trap. What happens if the coastguard or police launches take an unhealthy interest in what they're doing?"

Masterman dismissed it as a minor issue. "Don't concern yourself with that. Just concentrate on getting the job done. SIS, as you know, has considerable influence in various quarters. We've had a quiet word with the local forces and coastguard. They've been told to look the other way and not to interfere with a boat called *The Thamilia.* It's officially down as a training exercise. They'll keep their noses out until we say so."

Grant could imagine the phone calls as Masterman pulled strings and called in favors. A request to SIS's Naval liaison officer, who would then call his opposite number in Naval Intelligence, who would then pass it directly to the Admiralty, who would then call the coastguard and so on and so forth.

SIS always made sure that the rules didn't apply to them. Masterman was setting the scene for a great big bear trap for the hit-team, and he didn't care who he had to manipulate to get what he wanted.

"What's the news on the American angle? Are we still playing against them?" asked Grant.

"For the moment, although I have orders to bring them into the fold soon. I'll wait until it's confirmed that you've removed the threat to Scorpius first, don't want to drop you in it, do I. But I think it's time that this stupid American enterprise was brought to a swift conclusion," said Masterman.

Grant looked doubtful. He knew that the Americans always insisted on having their own way. It seemed to be a national trait and he couldn't imagine some over-ambitious CIA operations officer taking any notice of Masterman, or anyone else.

"Think about it Jack, half of this hit-team will have been destroyed and if our intelligence is correct, there will only be one man left to carry out the remainder of the job. It would be impossible for him to continue effectively," said Masterman.

Grant had to admit that with the American operation out in the open and only one contractor left, then the odds of its continued success were diminishing with each new 'hit'. That was, unless the remaining contractor was something special or just damned lucky.

Masterman made a move to get out of the car. "I think a quiet word in the ear of the right person might let the Americans know that they've had their little piece of folly well and truly blown sky high. I'll leave you here and grab a taxi back to the office. Oh, and one more thing, please don't crash. I haven't run her in properly yet."

* * *

He set off in the dead of night. The streets of London, once busy and bustling were now deserted except for the occasional bus, lorry and police patrol car and he, for one of the few times in his life, enjoyed the solitude of driving on the streets of the nation's capital.

He had returned briefly to the toilets inside the airport terminal and changed into the clothes that Masterman had provided in a rucksack– a pair of dark, thick overalls, a stout pair of army boots, a heavy black duffel coat complete with gloves and an equally somber knitted cap. Masterman had picked well and knew that wherever Gorilla ended up, he might well have to approach the target both rurally and covertly.

The only other item in the boot was the weapon Masterman had provided: a Remington 870 pump-action shotgun, complete with a case containing a mixed bag of ammunition. The Remington was an excellent close quarter weapon and Masterman had chosen well.

The drive to Falmouth was a high-octane ride that passed in a blur of speed, noise, and darkness. With the burning lights of London soon behind him, he quickly entered a dream state of driving in the warmth and safety of the car, only mildly aware of the blanket of freezing fog which shrouded his route and soon even the high-pitched scream of the Spitfire's engine faded into the background.

Gorilla's exhaustion was pushed to one side now that he was operational again. He'd spent the past weeks chasing down leads and not coming up with very much, and he yearned for the call to arms again and the chance to bring down his targets. So all thoughts of sleep were eradicated and only his tenacity and iron hard will was keeping him going, pushing on through the darkness. The Spitfire handled well, it was a man's car and as such, Gorilla, ever the keen driver, drove it well. On the straights he floored the pedal, determined to make up speed as and when he could. On the corners and the bends, he threw it around proficiently, slow in and fast out.

He occasionally stopped in a layby, flicked on his hand torch and studied the road map that would take him nearer and nearer. Then it was the roar of the Spitfire's engine, the flare of the headlights and he was off again, pushing the car faster and faster.

The names on his route passed him by... Yeovil... then Exeter... Lauceston... Bodmin...

Then across the moors... Truro... Penryn... Falmouth... until the names of the villages and the road signs to his destination became more infrequent.

Finally, the road to Maenporth opened up and he was aware of the sea to his left as it crashed against the cliff face and the shoreline. He pulled the car over into a layby for one last check of his map and five minutes later, he found the gates to the property he was looking for. They were of substantial ornate ironwork with the words 'Scarrick Point' worked across the head, with a smaller, wooden signpost attached to the main bars warning visitors to 'Keep Out – Private Property'.

That was okay, thought Gorilla as he hefted the tools for the job over his shoulder. He wouldn't be going up the main path, just in case the man inside was nervous, or trigger happy, or both. He would be going over the wall further along and approach from an angle.

Better to flank and stay out of sight, until he was sure he was the first to arrive.

* * *

Scarrick Point had originally been a seventeenth century hunting and fishing lodge, which had once belonged to a local landowner who had a reputation for hanging poachers who dared to encroach on his land. It was reputed that he hanged them with their own bow strings.

It stood balanced on the edge of an eighty-foot-high cliff promontory, overlooking a cove near the town of Maenporth, and as its name implied, it looked as if it had been slashed, cutting a scar into the rock. During the summer months the cove was a haven for holidaymakers, there to enjoy its fine beach; but during the winter, it was a desolate place with the cliffs being exposed to the merciless battering of the elements.

The lodge was a simple three-bedroom affair and was unremarkable to the eye. However, it was its location that afforded it its grandeur, being set in five acres of land only accessible via a private road which led directly to the front door. Anyone approaching could be spotted almost at once. To its right stood the barred private road, to its left stood the sheer drop of the cliff and the brutal power of the waves. To all intents and purposes, it stood alone, isolated, unwelcoming and unapproachable to strangers.

In the 1950's Scarrick Point had been purchased, via a reputable property broker, on behalf of the Ministry of Defence as part of a resettlement package for one of their senior employees. The owner was one Albert Browning. Browning, a spry bachelor in his early sixties, was a respected engineer at the Rocket Propulsion Establishment, and every Monday morning he would take his small Austin A40 on the long journey from Falmouth to Buckinghamshire for the working week, only to make the return journey on the Friday afternoon. Scarrick Point was his safe haven, his place of comfort and solitude away from his past and his complicated life of deception and double cross.

His nearest neighbors were over a mile away in the village. The postmistress, a stern woman by the name of Mrs. Featherstone, when asked by the village gossips and outsiders from Truro about the lodge at Scarrick Point and its resident would simply say, "Ah well that's Mr. Browning. A very private gentleman. A bachelor who keeps his self to his self and always pays his bills on time. Which is more than can be said for some hereabouts."

"But where did he come from Fen? What's he doing up there in that lodge all by himself?" brave souls would ask, hoping not to incur the Featherstone wrath.

Fen Featherstone would fix them with a glare, a final warning to the downright insolent. "Well, he's worked away these past ten years or more, serving Queen and country I would imagine, but that's no one else's business but his and Her Majesty... now that'll be three and six, thank you very much."

And that would be the end of the conversation for any searchers of information. For Mrs. Fenella Featherstone, postmistress and widow of this parish, was Albert Browning's formidable verbal bodyguard and protector of his privacy. It was a duty that she took seriously, even more so as she was paid a regular monthly stipend by those nice gentlemen from the Ministry of Defense's Security Division in London to be their eyes and ears on the ground in Maenporth and to ensure that Senior Executive Engineer Albert Browning was left to his peace.

* * *

The old man filled the tin kettle and placed it on the decrepit cooker. He knew it would take an age to boil, so he sat at the worn kitchen table and waited. He knew patience. He had spent most of his life perfecting and controlling that particular discipline.

To the few neighbors who had met him over the past nine years, he was known as Albert Browning and he worked for the Ministry of Defense in a minor clerical role. That was the cover story he stuck to. He was never rude, he was always polite and courteous as befitted a man of his age.

In truth, he had been born over sixty years earlier in Dresden. His name, then, had been Walter Kauffman and during the years of the Nazi regime, he had been one of the top men in the creation of propulsion-based weapons and a contemporary of Wernher von Braun, the legendary aerospace engineer. In fact, the two men had worked together several times, developing the Nazi's V2 rocket system.

Kauffman had believed in the Nazi ideal, had watched as his country had grown powerful under Hitler, but as a scientist, he knew that his uniform would only ever be that of the lab coat and business suit instead of army fatigues. Following the fall of Berlin, he had escaped to his hometown and had quickly been arrested by allied military counter-intelligence officers, who were on the lookout for any of Hitler's former rocket scientists. Prison and interrogation followed, before he was judged to have sufficient knowledge and expertise in rocket systems to be classed as 'High-Value' to the Allies.

He had worked with the British scientific teams, who had, to his surprise, welcomed him with open arms and treated him with the utmost respect. A bond was forged in the mutual respect of engineering excellence. The British had wiped clean his past, furnished him with a new identity and given him a senior role in the secret Rocket Propulsion Establishment. He had made a new life, albeit one with some restrictions, but had integrated himself smoothly into his postwar life. And while he still loved Germany, it was now England that he considered his home.

Then ten years after he'd first set foot on English soil, he'd been called to Whitehall, seemingly for a standard security check, and had been whisked into a stuffy office on the fourth floor where he'd been approached by a stout little fellow by the name of Porter. The man looked like an Oxford Don, rather than a minion of the MOD.

"You don't need to know who I'm working for just yet, but you'd be doing your adopted country a great favor by taking part in a little bit of subterfuge," the man had said, as he heaved his bulk out of the chair. The subterfuge had, of course, been Porter's way of describing his future role as a double agent. "Trail your coat alongside the KGB, Walter, show them what you've got and where you work, then we give them just enough for them to take you seriously," the tubby agent-runner had said.

After the initial shock had worn off, Kauffman had flailed against the practicalities of his being a spy. "But what would be my motivation? No, no, no – they will never believe it. Not after all these years working for the British!"

But Porter had soothed him, setting out a plausible hypothesis. "'Course they will, they'll love you. A former Nazi who turned his coat against his colleagues and countrymen to work for their sworn enemy. Anyone who can do that once, can do it again! Who knows, maybe you're sick of England, maybe you're not being appreciated by your British paymasters, maybe you've found the ideology faulty after all these years and have finally decided to embrace communism. We'll find something and make it fit."

He dangled for a week before he decided to take up Porter's offer and so, as he approached his senior years, he'd decided that the role of a spy would be the next in a long line of experiences.

His double agent work didn't take up too much of his time, hardly any at all really; a weekend away occasionally to meet with his KGB contact, or a drive out to the Home Counties to leave a micro-dot at a dead letter drop beneath a beech tree in an isolated field, followed by regular meetings at his office at the RPE, where Porter would come in disguised as a cleaner or visiting personnel officer from the MOD. The risk to his life was a small price to pay for serving his adopted country and for being allowed to continue his life's work with people he'd grown fond of.

He heard the whistling of the kettle and stood up to remove it from the cooker. It was then that he heard the heavy knock on the wooden door. It startled him. He turned and stared at it for a long moment, disbelieving. In all the years he'd lived here, no one had ever come to visit uninvited. But now, here, on a stormy night, the impossible had happened. His stomach lurched and as he slowly approached the door, his legs began to shake with fear.

He reached out and pulled back the heavy wooden door, only a fraction at first, enough to have a conversation, but also to keep the howling wind and rain out. "Yes, who is it?" He could hear the tremor in his own voice and felt the cold of the night attack his face.

"Mr. Browning. My name is Jack. You need to let me in." The voice was quiet, but tinged with both urgency and authority.

"Jack. Jack, who? I know no Jacks. Please, I am very busy, it is late. Are you in trouble?"

The same quiet voice came back at him. "Your friends in London sent me. They send you their regards."

Doubt and confusion riddled the old man's mind. "Friends in London? But I have no friends in London either, young man. Now please I don't wish to telephone the local constabulary."

There was a sharp intake of breath from the disembodied voice outside, almost as if he'd realized an error in his introduction. "I'm sorry. My mistake, I apologize. If I said the name Scorpius to you, would that make a difference?"

The old man slammed the door shut. Through fear, shock or anger – even he wasn't sure. Then, only when he had regained his full composure did he unlock the bolt on the door, before slowly opening it to its widest aperture. The wind and rain hit him hard and there, illuminated by the kitchen light, stood a small, spare man dressed in a dockworker's black duffel coat, a knitted cap pulled down over his ears and what looked like a shotgun slung over his right shoulder. His face was pale but his eyes blazed with a furious urgency.

"Are you here to kill me?"

"No, Herr Kauffman, I am hopefully here to save you. But can we first start with you letting me in!"

And it was then that Agent Scorpius knew that things had gone very badly wrong indeed, with his career in espionage.

* * *

Scorpius sat at the wooden kitchen table, the heat from the cooker toasting his back, nursing his mug of tea. He was pondering the gravity of his situation whilst Gorilla quickly sauntered around the ground floor, checking if windows and doors were locked and covered. The Remington lay at an angle on the table, extra shotgun cartridges lined up next to it.

"So you are a spy, Herr Jack?" said Scorpius.

"Gorilla."

"Pardon?"

"You call me Gorilla. It's a nickname. Better than using real names."

Scorpius raised an eye at that. The espionage business was unusual, to say the least. You weren't anyone unless you had a codename. "Of course, I understand. So you are a spy, Herr Gorilla? Like me?"

The little man turned to him and shrugged. "In a way; I'm more of a specialist in certain areas."

"Like protecting elderly German engineers from… from what exactly? I am confused."

Gorilla was in the final stages of closing the curtains in the living area, before returning to the comforting warmth of the kitchen. He picked up his mug, drained the tea and steeled himself for the bad news he was about to deliver to the old man. "I'll tell you as much as I can, in the short time that we have."

Scorpius nodded, no less confused, but eager to hear why he'd been rousted late on a Saturday night.

"Your cover, so far, is still intact. You aren't blown, understand? You as an agent are still in play. That's the good news. The bad news, is that men are coming here to kill you tonight. I don't know exactly when they'll be here, but it will be soon. When I left London, I guessed that I had a four-hour head start on them, maybe. That's a conservative estimate," said Gorilla. His words were coming like rapid-fire, machine gun bullets. He just hoped the old man was alert enough to take in what was about to happen.

Scorpius looked down at his hands, reflecting upon what he'd just been told. "I see. Are they Russians? No, they can't be – you said my cover was intact. Why would the KGB kill me, if I am still working for them?"

Gorilla shook his head. "No, not Russians. All I can say is that these men will be here soon and we need to accept the reality of the situation. The less you know, the less you can betray later."

"How many are coming? Are they any good, Herr Gorilla?"

"They are professionals, so yes, they're good enough to kill one man on his own certainly. Numbers; more than one and no more than five. They have killed before and will continue, unless—"

"And can we not run to London or somewhere?" said Scorpius, hoping for an escape route.

"No. The plan is to sit it out and let them come to us."

"And then?"

"And then, we don't let them leave this place," Gorilla said simply.

Scorpius smiled. "Aha, then we capture them, Herr Gorilla. We call in your secret police and detain them in prison perhaps."

But Gorilla's face offered no warmth for a legal outcome. "No. They will not be arrested. They will not stand trial. If I do my job right, they'll disappear off the face of the earth here tonight."

Scorpius seemed to take in the gravity of his new protector's unspoken strategy. "I see, I see... and you are more than a match for these killers, Herr Gorilla? One man. You are experienced in such matters?"

"We'll find out by morning. Which leads me on to my next question; weapons? Do you have any weapons in the house? Guns, knives, coshes, tools; anything you could use to defend yourself with."

A wide smile spread across the old man's face. "I have my old Mauser from the war, that is all."

"Good. Do you have enough ammunition?"

Scorpius frowned. "Ah, there we may have a problem. Only a few rounds for the Mauser, I'm afraid."

The old man disappeared upstairs for a few moments. Gorilla could hear him moving furniture in one of the upstairs rooms. Moments later, he returned with an old and battered biscuit tin which he placed on the kitchen table. He lifted the lid to reveal the Mauser nestled inside, wrapped in an old dust cloth. The weapon had definitely seen better days; old and corroded, Gorilla estimated Scorpius would get two shots out of it before it seized up and misfired.

"It will suffice, Herr Gorilla?" asked Scorpius.

"It will have to. The Mauser, you know how to use it, yes? Then you keep it with you. That is your personal weapon. You may end up needing it, before the night is through."

They sat there in the dark for the next hour. Waiting and marking time. The faint embers of the fire keeping them warm. Then out in the distance, like a voice struggling to be heard on an untuned radio, came something that was of a different pitch and tone to the raging storm outside. As it came nearer, and even over the howl of the wind, Gorilla could make out the noise as clear as anything. *It was easy for the ear to pick things up, when you know what you're listening to,* he thought. A gentle burring that Gorilla knew from experience was the noise made by an inflatable, high speed motor boat.

"Herr Gorilla, I think, I think they are coming," said Scorpius, who had his head cocked to the side, listening.

"No," said Gorilla, picking up the Remington and racking the pump action of the shotgun with a satisfying click. "They're already here. *Move!*"

* * *

The killers moved like ghosts, they were practiced and experienced in such matters. It had been their lifelong career, and so they were experts at approaching a target building. The stormy night assisted them in their stealthy approach, hiding any noise from their movements, and the cloud cover dulled the moonlight which would have normally exposed them.

Ahead, they saw the lodge, an old, archaic building with a single lamplight dotted in the top bedroom window. They assumed the old man was in bed. He would die there.

The wind was coming in great gusts and now that they were within range to attack, the killers clutched their weapons tightly. What did they care, he was one old man on his own and caught unawares. He would be easy prey.

* * *

Scorpius huddled himself into the furthest reaches of the small bedroom, gripping the Mauser tightly. He looked down at his knuckles, noticing they were white with tension.

He'd been sitting in the top bedroom for the past twenty-five minutes. He'd been both dragged, then pushed up to the top floor of his house before being barked at to "stay put" by the little man who'd come to protect him. Scorpius wondered at that. Was the man's priority to protect his charge, or to kill the assassins who were sniffing at his door... perhaps a little of both.

He had been in this position only once before, when the Russians overran Berlin, slaughtering, raping, destroying and looting their way through the city. The fear then had been the reckless murder of both innocents and the not-so-innocents of the Nazi party. It was expected. Like a storm wave engulfing a coast, it takes all in its path indiscriminately. They would all fall together.

But this was something very different. The targeted murder of a man because of who he was, what he had become, made it personal by definition. He imagined the killers approaching; boots on cobbles, jackets snagging on bushes, then moving when the cloud covered the moon, edging nearer and nearer to his sanctuary, their fingers tense against the weapons that had been brought here to execute him.

The minutes ticked by. Thirty minutes, forty minutes and then heading towards an hour. And just as he had convinced himself it was all a false alarm, that someone in London was overreacting to an imagined threat, it was then that he heard a dull... *boom...* as a shotgun roared. It was in the cellar he would have guessed, judging by the muffled bark.

Then silence.

The lights went out throughout the house, leaving only moonlit shadows scattered across the floor… and then it got very, very noisy as the musical rhythm of semi-automatic gunfire began.

* * *

As soon as he'd heard the engine of the boat approaching from the distance, Gorilla had moved into action. Scorpius was to make his way to the top bedroom and lock the door. The killers would have to fight to the top of the building if they wanted to get to the target, and hopefully, Gorilla would be able to eliminate them before they got that far.

If they did get that far, well, let's hope those rounds in the old Mauser still worked and the old man was a decent shot, he thought.

Gorilla's plan was to use the top bedroom as bait, made even more obvious by it having the only light in it. For his part he would start in the basement, viewing through a hidden vantage point window to see how many were approaching and then work his way up behind the killer, or killers, to take them out of the game. Not the worst plan in the world, but not the best, either. In Redaction jobs, you worked with the hand you'd been dealt.

He'd opened the small floor window in the cellar. The floor window was level with the exterior grounds and looked out over the gravel courtyard. It was only the size of a tea tray, not anywhere near big enough to be able to crawl through, but was more than big enough to look through and see who was approaching the side of the house.

In the distance he now saw three men approaching, coming out of the misty rain, appearing like phantoms. Two large and one small, dressed in dark combat fatigues, each carrying a compact submachine gun of undetermined make. They seemed to melt out from the bushes that bordered the front lawn. *So they'd approached from the cliffs in a seaborne operation,* thought Gorilla.

They were at a distance of twenty feet when the smaller man barked out an order, lost to Gorilla's ears thanks to the driving winds. The small man was the one he wanted to keep alive. His body shape and size fitted one of the men they'd tagged in Marseilles. The others were bigger and bulkier, hulks and nothing more than sub-contracted hired guns, he was sure. They were therefore expendable.

The smaller man and the heavy man on his right branched off to make their way around to the main entrance. The other man kept on moving at a steady pace, heading towards the window. His body was slowly disappearing from view, but his legs were fast becoming the main focus through the window. Gorilla crouched down against the wall to the side of the window. He heard the crunch of gravel continue for a few more seconds and then it stopped. Gorilla glanced quickly and saw a pair of big-footed army boots, directly in front of his face.

Then he heard the grunt as the man began to crouch down to peer through the small open window, the muzzle of his weapon leading the way. The low level of the window meant he couldn't get a clear view, so he moved the weapon carelessly to his left hand and began to lower himself onto his knees. Sure that there was no threat, after all, it was only one old man who wasn't expecting company, the gunman crouched down on all fours to peer in through the gloomy cellar window. All he saw was the limited outline of a dark cellar.

It was then that Gorilla moved. He simply stepped from the side and jammed the shortened barrel of the shotgun against the glass and pulled the trigger.

The report inside the cellar was deafening and Gorilla's ears rang. The blast had hit the gunman square in the face. The heavy buckshot and glass had completely removed his features, leaving a mass of red, fleshy pulp and his body had buckled forward onto his knees. What remained of his head slumped forward, jamming itself onto the jagged shards of the now-fractured window pane.

With no time to admire the results of his work, Gorilla pumped another round into the chamber. In the distance somewhere above his head – the kitchen, he assumed – he was aware of the *rata-tat-tat* of gunfire. It seemed to be ripping apart the wooden door which led to the kitchen and was followed by a thump as the unmistakable sound of a boot kicked it open. More *rata-tat-tat, rata-tat-tat* as the gunman started shooting at shadows.

Amateur, thought Gorilla, *only shoot at something you can see, you must be almost out of ammunition by now.*

He flicked the switch to the power supply off covering the house in darkness. With these kinds of odds Gorilla needed all the help he could get, and prolonged darkness would help. He turned and ran at full pelt up the wooden cellar stairs, determined to get to the kitchen before the second gunman had a chance to reload. He was almost at the cellar door when it was flung open wide and a large, dark figure stood in silhouette at the top of the stairs.

Gorilla took the final step as a mighty jump, leaping forward and up. Both men clashed together, body weight hitting body weight. But Gorilla, ever the survivor of encounters like these, was determined to get the upper hand by smashing the butt of the shotgun pistol grip into the teeth of his opponent.

The man collapsed backwards against the wall in pain, his hands coming up to his face to try and stop what remained of his teeth from scattering into the darkness of the cellar. He needn't have bothered, as almost instantly, Gorilla had grabbed the man by the front of his tunic with one hand and was jamming the barrel of the shotgun up under his chin with the other.

The metal of the Remington cut into the second gunman's skin before... *boom...* another shot that ripped up into the intruder's head, and even in the murky darkness, Gorilla was aware of the combination of grey and red and tissue and bone as the brute of a man slid to the floor. At this kind of distance and with that kind of wound, there was no need for a second shot.

He reached into his coat pocket for new cartridges and pushed them into the feeding tube. One, two, three and then he pumped a new round into the chamber.

Gorilla flung back the cellar door and moved into the low light of the kitchen, his shotgun leading the way. Two down and one to go, except this time, his plan wasn't for killing the leader of the hit-team unless he had to, which made it all the more difficult. It was to be a capture.

He held tight to the shotgun and moved from the sanctuary of the cellar and into the foreboding darkness of the house.

* * *

Gioradze had heard the first muffled roar of a firearm from the side of the house, where Luc had gone to investigate, and then the crash of gunfire as Pierre had attacked the kitchen door to the rear of the building. He himself had swept quickly through the house, checking his angles and working his way across the rooms to the staircase.

Always the tricky part that – staircases. He knew to take them quickly and to leave the downstairs for Luc and Paul to deal with. Besides, he had seen the light on in the top room and knew that was where his target must be. He wanted to be the first one through the door for the kill. The boys could deal with anything downstairs.

He was almost at the top of the stairs now. Leading onto a landing, he moved forward carefully, slowly, the weapon up and ready. The door was illuminated by a thin seam of orange light at its edges. Gioradze smiled to himself, he was on the verge of taking out another target from the hit-list and looking forward to another payday. He bashed open the door with his shoulder and it flew back, hanging on, barely, by the bottom hinge after the top hinge shattered. His eyes quickly acclimatized to the gloom and he noticed the little candle lamp, emitting a sinister orange glow.

It was the bald head of the wizened old man that he noticed first, the orange light shining off his pate. Then, as he concentrated, he took in the outline of the man, sat crouched in the corner, his knees drawn up and what looked like the world's oldest pistol gripped between his hands and pointing directly at the door or more correctly, at whatever was coming through the door. Which on this occasion, was Gioradze.

Gioradze raised the Uzi and centered it on the figure in the corner. He saw the man tense and then shake with effort as he tried to pull the trigger on the Mauser and... *click*. Nothing. Dead. *An old man, holding an old gun and using old ammo,* thought Gioradze. This was like shooting fish in a barrel. He centered the Uzi back on the man's head. At this range, the bullets would simply decapitate him. Another one taken off Marquez's list—

He didn't hear the boom of the shotgun. He just felt a sharp pain shooting up the back of his legs, his aim wavering as he dropped the Uzi. He looked down and saw tissue and bone, all encased in a gelatinous mass of blood. He felt himself slowly sliding down the doorframe, before another round of heavy lead ripped through the other leg. He winced and his eyes watered. Soon the pain would come in great abundance, that he knew for sure. But first he might be able to get to the Uzi...

He saw the weapon kicked out of his reach and heard it clatter along the hallway.

The pain in his legs was coming now in intense waves. He turned his head, gasping for air, and looked up into the face of a small, blond-haired demon. The man's face was pale and set in a determined grimace. In his hands he held a pump-action shotgun with a shortened barrel.

The last thing Gioradze remembered was the small man raising the shotgun, rotating it around so that it resembled a club and then bringing down the heavy wooden butt of the weapon onto his skull. A white light shattered his mind and then there was only blackness.

Chapter Eleven

Gorilla carried the killer to the kitchen and sat him in a wooden chair. He tied both arms to the chair's armrests with rope from the cellar and rolled up the man's right sleeve, exposing his forearms. With the man secured, he set about inspecting the damage to the killer's lower legs.

The heavy shot had mangled the calf of one leg and almost totally eradicated the knee and the shin bone on the other. Unless he had surgery soon, the chances were that the man would bleed out and die and for what was about to come, Gorilla needed him very much alive. He padded out the wounds with tea towels and handkerchiefs culled from the old man's chest of drawers, before binding it all together with strips of bed sheet. Not ideal, but better than nothing under the present circumstances.

Gorilla switched off the kitchen light and instead lit a small oil lamp, which the old man probably used to visit the shed out in the dark. The darkness immediately engulfed the room, leaving only a red-tinged spotlight illuminating the small area where the killer was bound. To Gorilla, it looked like a scene from an old black and white movie-set, where the torturer has his victim exactly where he wanted him. It was both eerie and disturbing.

He squatted in front of the still-unconscious man and weighed up in his own mind how best to approach the forthcoming inquisition. Hard or soft? Kind or cruel? Physical or mental?

In truth, Gorilla had no idea which was the best option to take. He wasn't trained in interrogation methods and in the few times he had taken part in them, he'd simply gone with his instincts. So far, he had been quite successful – as to whether he would be as successful with this CIA contract killer was another matter; only time would tell.

He began to gently pat at the man's cheeks, to try to rouse him. With no response, he ever so slowly began to increase the force of the slap. The man gradually began to come around; a groan at first, followed by a confused turning of the head as he tried to get his bearings, and completed with a wince and a cry as the pain from his damaged legs finally registered. The man raised his head, a frown of fury and pain on his face, and glared up at his captor.

"Do you know who I am? Don't you remember me?" asked Gorilla

Gioradze squinted and tried his best to focus on the other man's face. "What do I care who you are? You look like a fucking Russian, if that's what you mean."

Gorilla smiled to himself. He could see what the other man meant, with his short white-blond hair, pugnacious manner and robust build he could very easily be mistaken for the archetypal KGB thug. Gorilla saw no reason to dissuade the killer of this assumption, in fact, if he played it right, it might actually be an asset in the forthcoming interrogation. "You should care about who I am. It could have life changing consequences for you. You need to be concerned, at the very least," said Gorilla.

Gioradze snorted. "Fuck you. Torture me all you want. You think this is the first time I've been tied to a chair and tortured?"

"Probably not," said Gorilla. "But this isn't the first time I've tied someone to a chair and interrogated them either, so on that score we're equal." He was thinking of his time spent with the forger in Belgium. But the one thing Gorilla was positive of was that, unlike the forger, this killer would not be walking away safely and with a suitcase full of cash.

In his role as faux KGB interrogator, Gorilla had decided to use that oldest and most dangerous of tactics first; honesty. Honesty to the subject, honesty about his potential fate, honesty leaves the subject with no place to hide and no maneuvering room. It spells it out for him in stark detail. You are here. I am here. These are the facts.

"I won't tell you a thing, you Russian pig," said Gioradze, as the anger started to rise in him.

Gorilla frowned. "Oh, I believe that *you* believe that. But there's one thing I can tell you from experience and that is, everyone talks, everyone has a breaking point. You just have to find the correct leverage. For some its pain, some people can't handle pain. However, in your case I think that you're such a tough man you could withstand it, I have no doubt."

The Georgian was breathing heavily now, gulping in huge lungsful of air, mentally bracing himself for what was about to come.

"Some people fear the danger that their loved ones might be targeted, but again, not applicable in your case," Gorilla continued.

Gioradze snorted with derision, as if the thought of using another human being as leverage over him would never have succeeded.

Gorilla knelt down so they were face-to-face. "What I think is, that in your case, it's simple. It's Biology. It's your own body. You're wounded, tired, under stress, so you're already weak, maybe even compliant, although you would never admit that. No, the one thing that's going to let you down here is your own body."

Gioradze looked down at his mangled legs. For the first time, the stunning realization that he was in pain, in a foreign country, isolated and about to be interrogated by a Russian operative, hit him.

"And you really don't remember me?" asked Gorilla, looking the man in the eye.

Gioradze shook his head violently. "I fucking told you – no!"

Gorilla brought his face closer, so that they almost touched, nose-to-nose, and then whispered through gritted teeth. "I'm the hitter from Marseilles. I'm back to haunt you, and you don't look pleased to see me at all, you miserable son-of-a-bitch!"

* * *

He was doing it by the book, exactly as the basic written instructions included in the sealed case advised him to. Gorilla unzipped the little leather case, exposing the syringe and two vials of the pre-mixed 'truth drug', known as Sodium Amytal.

With two complete vials, he had one to use now and a spare one should he need to extend the interrogation. He knew there was no such thing as a truth drug, but rather, it was a combination of certain powerful chemicals designed to make the subject more pliable and less resistant. He carefully inserted one of the vials into the syringe, ensured the needle was straight and pulled the plunger back to the stated dose. Finally, he firmly flicked the glass casing to make sure no air bubbles had found their way into the solution. Satisfied, he approached the man tied to the chair.

"Don't move and don't struggle, it won't do any good. If you do, I'll have to stop you," said Gorilla, inclining his head towards the shotgun standing nearby. A good 'crack' from the club handle would subdue an uncooperative subject.

Gorilla carefully injected half the chemical cocktail into the cannula attached to the man's arm in one continuous push of the plunger, and while the bound assassin didn't struggle following his warning, he did shout and curse at his captor.

Gorilla ignored the tirade and instead focused his mind on the upcoming interrogation. He knew it would take anywhere between ten to fifteen minutes, depending on the man's metabolism, before the drugs started to take effect and from then onwards, he would have anywhere between twenty to thirty minutes before the drug's effects began to dissipate.

Gorilla pulled up a chair and sat warming himself by the kitchen fire, occasionally glancing over as the little assassin slowly began to calm down and then eventually, quieten down. By the end of fifteen minutes, he'd slipped into a calm, semi-conscious drowse, his head lolling forward and occasionally snapping back up again as it regained control of itself. Gorilla thought the little man looked like a nodding dog, trying to stay awake after a busy day working out in the field.

Gorilla needed quick results from this interrogation. Time, as always on jobs like this, was of the essence. He started slowly, gently, keeping the questions simple at first and trying to create a rhythm so the prisoner would get into the habit of answering.

"Can you tell me your name?" It was said gently, like a parent talking to a drowsy child who was flitting in and out of sleep.

"Rrrr... Rogue." The voice was toneless, tired, exhausted.

"What is Rogue?"

"Codename, used for long, long time..."

"Okay, Rogue. Can you tell me the name you were born with? Your real name?"

"David."

"Okay David, good..."

"David Gioradze."

To Gorilla, the surname sounded as if it had come out of the man's mouth as "Jeee-yurr-addghee," probably a downside of the drugs. He looked like a dope fiend who'd succumbed to a huge hit of opium. "How did you get here, David? Car, boat, plane?"

"Boat from Barfleur. We moored off the coast, a small engine dingy to here... dumped on the beach... climbed the cliff track... hiked the last bit."

"And the others, David? Who were they?"

"Hired muscle... from the Legion... useless fuckers got shot... mmm."

"Who sent you here, David? Who's the paymaster? Where did the contract come from?" The man seemed not to notice the question; either that, or he chose not to commit to an answer. Gorilla pressed the remainder of the drug in the syringe into his bloodstream. He waited a few moments before Gioradze started speaking again.

"A man," he mumbled, his head rolling from side to side.

"Which man? What did he look like?" asked Gorilla, his voice comforting, willing the answers to flow.

"Never met him! Only know his name... Knight, Maurice Knight. American..."

So it was an American contract, thought Gorilla. The CIA had gotten itself involved in something way outside of their normal remit. It was time to refocus the interrogation. "Is there a code David? Do you have a code to send, confirming the hit has been carried out?"

A slurred "Yethhh" and the nodding dog head again.

"What is it?"

"Phone from here to a number in a village… outside Paris… Auvers-sur -Oise… code is Ciseaux… then hang up… mmm," he mumbled.

Ciseaux. *Scissors,* thought Gorilla. How very apt. A word code provided its own unique problems. He would have to listen carefully to this mercenary's accent to get it right. "What's the number? Can you remember it?"

Gioradze slurred out the number. Gorilla wrote it down, just to be certain. "Very good. Who is on the other end, David?"

Gioradze tried to lift his head up, but failed. "Partner… bad bastard… Marquez."

"And is that where he, Marquez, is based at the moment, David?"

Gioradze gave a nodding of the head once more. "Mmmm… but then he's gone."

"And does Marquez have a codename, David? A code name like yours?"

"Uh-huh… WIN."

"Pardon ?"

"The Yankees gave him the codename Q… J… WIN. Long, long time ago… before all this happened." He tried to wave a hand in a dismissive gesture, but because of his restraints, only succeeded in weakly waggling his fingers.

"Very good, David. Well done," soothed Gorilla. The man was beginning to slip in and out of consciousness, probably the combination of blood loss and the drugs.

Gorilla thought he knew the answer to the next question, but he wanted it from the man's mouth. "Who is the next one on your list, David? Who is the next pay-day? Is it Paris?"

"Uh-huh… military man… we flipped a coin for it. Heads the military man… tails… the old man… I got tails!"

Gorilla thought he sounded disappointed. "How's he going to do it, David?"

Gioradze shrugged his shoulders. "Dunno, how… gun suppose, maybe… his choice… on the bridge though. Pont Nerfff… the military man goes there every Sunday, takes a stroll, meets people… your people… bloody KGB… bloody."

The cocktail was wearing down. Gorilla waited again and then gently, quietly, he carried on with his questions. "David? You were telling me about the military man on the bridge."

"Uh-huh… Pont Nerfff."

"The Pont Neuf. That's right, on a Sunday. Is it this Sunday?"

"Uh-uh… not tomorrow… next Sunday… April… on the bridge. Give me time to finish here… then we take out the next one."

"How do you know he meets people there every Sunday?"

"The American… he told us… in the files he gave us."

So they certainly had some good cast iron intelligence, Gorilla thought. "And is there a rendezvous where you and Marquez are meant to meet up? David, stay with me."

Gioradze was slowly going under. It was going to be a race against the clock before he fell into a deep sleep. "No… call a bar in Florence. Leave my hotel number… Marquez finds me… finds me when his kill is done… more secure that way… mmmm."

Gorilla decided to change his line of questioning. He could find out from Porter when Cirius, the military man, met with the KGB. What he needed to know now, was how the rest of the assassination program was going to go down. "So the old man, then the military man? Who's next David, who is the next one?"

Gioradze gave a weak smile, as if he had half remembered something from his past. "*La plus e de grume.*"

Gorilla frowned. "Okay, the 'big vegetable' – who is that David? Can you tell me?"

"The bitch, the one we call the bitch... the woman politico... good looking... but still a bitch."

* * *

Gorilla picked up the remaining vial of drugs, filled the syringe and pumped the rest of it into the man's system. He knew what would happen and before too long, Gioradze slipped into a deep sleep. The problem now that he'd finished with squeezing the man for information, was what to do with him.

His orders were not to leave these killers alive if he found them. They had become too much of an embarrassment and a problem. He discounted simply shooting the man in the head. Gorilla, for all his Redactions, had never executed a man tied to a chair and he wasn't going to start now.

Bugger Constellation and its agents. Ideally, he would have liked another vial of drugs and let the man simply slip away from an overdose, but unfortunately, there was just enough to loosen the man's tongue and no more.

After much deliberation, he settled on what he considered the least distasteful way to go. He rummaged under the sink until he found what he was looking for. A medium-sized tin bucket. He placed it next to the chair so that it sat nestled underneath Gioradze's right arm. Then he took out his gleaming silver straight razor and flicked open the blade with his thumb.

Gorilla untied the rope holding the right arm in place and gently let it fall so that Gioradze's wrist was dangling directly over the tin bucket. Next, he placed the edge of the blade halfway along the man's right wrist, steadied his hand, and in one swift motion he dragged the blade sideways, opening up the vein. The cut was deep and true and at once, the blood began to seep from the man's wrist and down into the bucket.

Gorilla estimated it would take roughly five minutes before Gioradze would bleed out completely, maybe less if you counted in the amount of blood he'd already lost from the gunshot wounds. The blood flowed forth, spilling into both the bucket and dribbling onto the surrounding floor. In the dark of the room, it looked like a pool of shiny black oil.

Gorilla watched intently, he thought he owed the man that at least, and a few minutes later when the bucket was almost full, Gioradze slumped forward. He tensed momentarily and then the life left his body. Gorilla reached forward, closed the man's eyes and gently rested his head to one side. He opened the door and was met by the old man, sitting in the lounge. The old man's eyes were rheumy as if he'd been weeping.

"Don't touch anything. I'll be back in a minute," said Gorilla. He almost made it outside – almost – before the feeling got the better of him and he threw up the limited contents of his stomach onto the stone doorstep of the kitchen entrance.

* * *

Once he'd recovered, Gorilla set to work. His first task was to make the call to the number in France. He picked up the phone receiver in the living room and stared at the piece of paper with the phone number written on it.

This could go either way. He weighed up the options and reasoned that Gioradze had probably told the truth under interrogation, and even if he hadn't, what choice did he have now? Don't phone in the code and the operation is finished. Do phone it in and the man on the other end smells a rat and it's the same result. *Fuck it, let's just get on with it,* he thought.

He dialed for the operator, heard the click as she came online and read out the international number. He waited, clutching the receiver fiercely, the earpiece emitting a series of clicks and tones. It seemed like minutes passed, but he knew in fact, it was probably only a few seconds.

"Your call is about to be connected, caller," the operator announced. She sounded as if she was working from inside a metal chamber, her voice tinny and echoed.

"Oui," said a male voice from the earpiece. It was strong, and authoritative.

Gorilla remembered Gioradze's accent and tried his best to imitate it. It had been gruff and guttural and he knew that it was best to keep it brief in case the accent slipped. "Ciseaux."

There was a pause and then the voice said, "Merci" and hung up. The code was complete.

Gorilla gently placed the receiver back into the cradle. All he could do now was hope that the ruse had been successful. His next priority, he decided, was to conceal the bodies. There was one man outside in the grounds of the house, one in the cellar and Gioradze here in the kitchen. They had to be moved, and quickly, and then centralized in one location. The most obvious and unobtrusive place was the cellar.

Gorilla spent the next thirty minutes dragging and lifting the bodies and carefully laying them out on the cellar floor. He found an old tarpaulin and covered them. Finally, he made safe the Uzi's and then did a brief check around the outside of the property for any obvious damage that might be seen, once daylight came. When he'd finished, he made his way into the living room to talk to the old man who was wrapped in an old blanket and sat by the fire. He looked exhausted.

"What should I do now, Herr Gorilla?" said Scorpius, faintly.

Gorilla was busy packing away the Remington into its carry bag. "Nothing, just act like you normally would if tonight hadn't happened. Are you alright about the bodies in the cellar?"

Scorpius looked at the flames dancing in the hearth. "Herr Gorilla, I survived the horrors of Berlin after the fall of Hitler when the Soviet forces invaded. A few corpses of men sent to kill me... please, I will not even lose a wink of sleep."

But Gorilla didn't believe him for a minute. Corpses don't sit well with anyone, not even corpses who had recently made an effort to end your life. Gorilla thought it was just the old man trying to hide his fear and decided not to press him about it any further. "Good. I will leave in a few moments and you will never see me again. I was never here; do you understand?"

The old man nodded.

"In a few days, you will receive a call from a firm of builders, who will give you a date for when they will be coming to fix the windows, doors and to remove some old pipe work from the cellar. You understand?"

Again a nod. "I understand – pipe work. What if someone from the village enquires about my broken windows and doors in the meantime?"

"They won't. But if they do, simply tell them it was storm damage from tonight's gales, hence the need for the builders. The builders when they finish will leave your house in perfect condition."

Scorpius nodded. "And what will you do now, Herr Gorilla?"

"I have to finish cleaning up," said Gorilla, jerking a thumb towards the sea outside the rain spattered window.

* * *

Aldert Verhoeven sat in the galley of *The Thamilia* nursing a cup of scalding hot coffee laced with a slug of brandy. He checked his watch: 2.30 am. They were late, damn them! Gioradze had assured him that the whole thing would take no more than an hour. That had been just under two hours ago.

He would give them another thirty minutes, then he would scuttle out of here. They'd been lucky so far, having attracted no notice from either the coastguard or any passing ships on shipping lanes, probably due to both the stormy conditions and the lateness of the hour. He'd been monitoring Channel 16 on the radio, to see if *The Thamilia* had attracted any attention from other crafts and been reported to the coastguard station at Pendennis Head, but again, there had been nothing. For now.

But now he was sure his luck was running out and he didn't wish to tempt fate any further. *He who hides and runs away, gets to live another day,* was his smuggler's motto and one that had stood him in good stead over the past twenty years in his smuggling career. He glanced again at his watch. 2.45 am. Fifteen more minutes and then he was gone, back to Barfleur. Fuck Gioradze, fuck those French thugs and fuck the…

It was distant, but unmistakable; the noise he'd been straining to hear for the past few hours, the putt, putt, putt of a small engined boat. Verhoeven was an experienced smuggler and knew that darkness was the covert operator's friend. So no lights, no signals, nothing.

He made his way to the stern and saw the inflatable craft approaching. Fifty feet… thirty feet… twenty. They had been lucky, no coastguard or police launches in the vicinity, allowing them to have free reign. The small rubber boat covered the last fifteen feet and then the engine was cut, the craft smoothly and silently left to glide towards the mother ship.

Verhoeven waved his hand to guide the ship towards him; in the other he held a rope to tether the two crafts together. Through the darkness of the night he saw a small silhouette of a figure stand up. Judging by the man's size, he guessed it must have been Gioradze. "It's about time! You're late. Where are the others?"

He was answered with the blast of a shotgun. In the vastness of the ocean, it would have caused no more than a pop sound and the brief flash from the muzzle radiated out no more than a few feet. The round took Verhoeven in the head, killing him instantly. His body sagged back onto the deck.

To all intents and purposes, and with the last of the mercenary team killed, the attempted hit against an old man living on the coast of Cornwall might never have happened. Certainly, there were no living witnesses to argue otherwise.

* * *

An hour later, after returning to shore and destroying the inflatable, Gorilla made his way back to the concealed Spitfire in the nearby copse, packed away the shotgun into the boot and drove the mile to the nearest public telephone box on the outskirts of the village.

He checked his watch. It was just past 3.45 in the morning. *Good, a perfect time to wake Masterman up. It serves him right,* he thought. *Keep me up for days on end will you, Colonel? Well, two can play at that game.*

He dialed the secure number which he knew would be transferred to Masterman's private line at his house in Chelsea. Hearing the ringing tone, then the pips, he pumped in as much spare change as he could to feed the device.

"Yes." It was the familiar voice of Masterman. Rather annoyingly, he sounded wide awake, damn him, almost as if he'd been sitting waiting over the phone like a vulture ready to swoop on its prey.

"It's Gorilla."

"Of course it is, who else would be phoning at this time of night? How's my car? No scratches? Better hadn't be or I'll kick your backside all the way back to where I found you!"

"No, no scratches, a bit muddy, nothing a good hosepipe couldn't sort out."

"Well, make sure you clean it before you bring it back. How's our problem? Resolved, I hope," said Masterman, his mind diverted from the car.

Gorilla started his situation report. "The targets are down, Scorpius is safe and his cover is still intact. Minimal damage to the property, but we'll need to send a cleanup team in quickly, to remove the bodies and fix up some damage before the locals get wind of it."

"Fine, I'll sort that out today."

"Good. There's also a boat moored off the coastline, about a mile out, which will need to be hauled away."

"No problem. I'll have our tame coastguards confiscate it… and the captain?"

Gorilla glanced outside the phone box. It was silent and dark, the storm having long since subsided. "Unfortunately, he didn't make it. He decided to pay a visit to Davy Jones's locker."

Masterman didn't exactly burst into tears at the news. "Anything else?"

"Yes. I managed to take the team leader alive as instructed. I gave him the drug cocktail and ran with it. As much as I didn't like using it, I have to admit it was very effective. To cut a long story short, the next target is in Paris."

"So, Cirius, the soldier. How and when?" asked Masterman.

"Next Sunday. The man tonight was called David Gioradze, a mercenary who works with Marquez. It seems they were both contracted by an American called Mr. Maurice Knight. The plan was for Gioradze to send a simple code to their base just outside Paris. That would be the cue for Marquez to take out Cirius on the Pont Neuf, of all places. I've taken care of that, hopefully the false code worked."

"Ha, they're ambitious chaps, I'll give them that. Good work, Jack."

Gorilla nodded. "Thank you, sir, I'll write it up in more detail when I get back to London. At the very least, it's bought me a few days before I get back to Paris in time to cut off Marquez's head." Gorilla could hear Masterman breathing, thinking, weighing up the options. That's what made Masterman such a good leader of the Redaction Unit, his ability to improvise at a moment's notice and to take the strategic initiative away from his enemies. "Are you still there, sir?"

"Mmm," said Masterman. "Just thinking things out, seeing which way the wind blows. Get yourself back to London – quickly! We may have just come across a small window of opportunity to smoke out the last of the hit-team. How's your partner shaping up, by the way? Is she useful?"

Gorilla thought it better not to interrupt and tell Masterman that following the attack on Nicole, she'd more than justified her place at the operational top table. Instead, he decided to play the issue down. "She's done just fine. She wears skirts which are far too short and her legs have the male population gawping at her. So it can be a distraction when I need them looking at her, and not at me. Good and bad," he said.

"Good. She's going to get a chance to earn her wages."

"How so?"

"We can't move Cirius, at least not permanently, but we can move him into a position so we can drag this killer out into the open where he has to stick his nasty little head above the parapet. Then you can bloody well chop it off for him. Leave it to me; I'll need to move a few people around so that all my ducks are in a row. Oh, and Jack, do yourself a favor and buy a bloody big bouquet of flowers on your way back to London."

Gorilla was confused. "What for?" he asked.

"To say sorry to my good lady wife, for waking her up at such an ungodly hour as this!"

* * *

Gorilla made it back to London around lunchtime. There was a quick stop at the Pimlico office, to drop off the gear and to park Masterman's Spitfire. He changed back into his suit and left a note on his desk saying he would be on temporary leave for the next twenty-four hours and out of touch. His body was exhausted and all he wanted was to rest.

He made it back to his Maida Vale apartment, took off his clothes and flopped down onto the bed; covering himself with the sheets to block out the daylight. But sleep didn't come easy. That day and through into the night in the safety of his bed, Jack Grant dreamed of arms tied with rope, howling storms, a bone handled cut-throat razor dripping with blood, the slicing of flesh – but most of all, blood.

No, sleep didn't come easy for him that night at all.

Chapter Twelve

"Is it a coincidence, or something more?"

"You know as well as I that in this business, there is no such thing as coincidence, only enemy action."

The older man pulled a face of displeasure, his tone growing angry. "The bigger picture is that several of your agents from the *BEAR* network have been murdered."

They'd been walking for the past hour, battling through the snow-drift that had turned the pathway into a treacherous blanket of white ice. The snow clouds had receded, giving way to a bright clear day. Vladimir Krivitsky, KGB officer, had been forced to borrow a pair of snow boots from his host when he'd been told they would be going out for a walk to "discuss matters of some urgency." His host was General Yuri Sakharovsky, Chief of the First Chief Directorate, the KGB's overseas Intelligence arm, and his direct superior.

The recall from his *Rezidentura* in Istanbul to Moscow, he was sure, meant only one thing. He was either going to be promoted, or killed. And since he knew he'd done nothing out of the ordinary over the past year, that only left execution. What for, he had no idea. Normally, these sorts of things were due to a power struggle within the KGB, one faction fighting another for promotion or control of a Directorate. Then it would be trumped up charges, torture, the Gulag or a bullet to the back of the neck.

He'd been greeted from the Aeroflot flight by a non-descript car and whisked away from the city out into the countryside. The driver, a tough-looking Siberian hulk, had told him they would be travelling to a private Dacha outside Moscow, where he would be meeting General Sakharovsky.

When Krivitsky asked for what purpose he would be meeting the General, the Siberian simply glared at him before turning his attention back to the road. With no further information forthcoming, Krivitsky decided to sit back against the leather seats of the car and wait to see how it played out.

When they arrived, the General had been waiting at the foot of the steps to his hunting lodge. He'd been taciturn and simply waved Krivitsky inside. The General had poured them both a hearty glass of vodka and they'd toasted to each other's good health, Russian style. They decided to walk out on the forest path and stretch their legs, let the cold air awaken their brains and try to solve the mystery. They crunched along, Krivitsky in his borrowed snow boots and the General trying to keep pace with his furious junior officer.

Sakharovsky, for all his bullish and harsh manner had been a devout protector of Krivitsky, dating back before the Poland incident. He liked the man's ruthless and aggressive manner. "I didn't want to discuss this at the office. There are too many ears listening, and too many ambitious people plotting."

The General then gave Krivitsky the news no case officer ever wants to hear about his agents in the field. "Vladimir, it has come to our attention that over the past three months, several agents from your *BEAR* network have been murdered. *Sloth* has been butchered in an apparent sex-murder, *Giant* has been killed in a hit and run, and *Ursid* has been obliterated in an explosion caused by a warhead from an RPG! We want to know, from you, their senior controller, what is happening?"

Krivitsky had taken the news like an old boxer, reeling from a body blow. He bent his head down and for a few moments, he lost his balance. It was as if a shard of pure ice had penetrated his heart. He'd swayed, and the pain in his chest had been so intense, he thought he would never be able to breathe again.

But that had quickly given way to a venomous fury which turned his neck and face to a crimson red. The rage enveloped him; if he'd had a gun he would have killed any wild animals he could have found out here in the forest. Killed them and then ripped them apart with his bare hands... but no, never mind... he would vent his fury the next time he was back in Istanbul, he would work it out of his system as he had before. Buried in shallow graves were several prostitutes who he'd had his way with before dispatching them and concealing their bodies in the Turkish countryside. He would find a young one, one who would struggle; he liked it when they struggled...

The General was speaking to him. "I said, when was the last time you had a meeting with any of them?"

Krivitsky simply shook his head; he couldn't remember. He tried to clear his mind and focus on the news, looking for any clue as to how this had happened. He'd been the prime architect behind the *BEAR* network and he and his officers had worked hard to infiltrate the ranks of various western intelligence, military and government organizations over the past decade.

He ran through them all in his mind; *Kodiak*, the NATO officer in Paris; *Polar*, the engineer helping design state of the art rocket systems; *Sloth*, the British diplomat in Germany; *Giant*, the banker who moved secret operation money around for the KGB; *Grizzly*, the young GCHQ officer in the Middle East; *Ursid*, the covert arms dealer, and finally his crowning glory, *Nandi*, the aristocratic Italian politician who had a direct channel to the White House in Washington.

All provided him with secret intelligence, all keeping the KGB power-players off his back with up to date economic and military intelligence material. With the *BEAR* network in place, he was fireproof. Without it, he knew he would soon be pushed aside by any number of ruthless and power-hungry KGB officers, looking to oust the old guard.

His mind focused back on the General's question. "Personally? Not for several months. Most of the month-to-month running of the *BEAR* agents is left to my specially recruited officers in the individual *Rezidentura's*. I only visit a meeting if there is something of great importance to deal with."

"Then perhaps they have been careless? A security slip, by one of your agents or their case officers. I don't mean to be critical, it happens, it is normal. But the question should be, what we do to correct it?" pondered the General.

Krivitsky frowned. If his officers had been careless and jeopardized his team of agents, he would personally hang the whole bloody lot up on meat hooks and throttle them with his bare hands. "That is true. Mistakes can happen. But if what you say is correct, how all my agents could be targeted when they have no connection, no link and as far as I am aware, they have no knowledge of each other – is an enigma."

Neither one of them raised the possibility of a traitor within Russian intelligence, but then, really, neither one of them had to. In the espionage business it was always a real possibility, it hung over them all like a gypsy curse.

"Is it the émigré groups?" suggested Krivitsky, his mind racing around, searching out likely options.

The General looked doubtful. "I fear not. It is too targeted, too specific; besides the émigrés are too clumsy in their attempts; drunk on cheap vodka and schnapps most of them. This is different; it has an air of the professional about it."

Krivitsky stopped and turned. "Then a rival service, murdering our agents? But that is against all the rules. It is a violation, except under exceptional circumstances."

The General looked his colleague up and down and sneered. "I hardly think that you are in any position to judge anyone about that. Not after the scandal in Poland several years ago. Besides, we have a reputation within our service for encouraging assassination, don't you think?"

Krivitsky conceded the point. The General himself had a policy of using terrorist factions around the world to act as the KGB's defacto operational assassination arm. Not to mention his use of ruthlessly murdering anyone who stood in his way. "Is it connected, do you think? After all these years, are the Americans seeking revenge for Poland. Could they still organize something like this?"

"It is possible, Vladimir. The Americans can be brutal when they put their minds to it."

"But they must know that we will not sit back and let them hunt down KGB agents," Krivitsky growled.

"True. If left to fester, it could lead to an underground war on the streets and in the cities, on both sides of the Iron Curtain," said the General.

"From the sounds of it, it already has."

They carried on walking along the path, heads down, deep in thought. Eventually, it was the General who broke the silence. "I have decided to organize a team from the Directorate to investigate. To see if there are any hints, as to who is behind this."

Krivitsky's head snapped around. "General, if you let me run the investigation, it could benefit both my network and the Directorate as a whole—"

"Who is taking care of the investigation is not your concern. They are capable men, handpicked by myself. Your task – your only task – is to protect what's left of your network. How you do it is up to you, but whatever you decide upon, you must do it quickly, for the sake of the remaining agents."

Krivitsky was not an officer to shirk away from taking charge, nor was he one to delegate being the bearer of bad news to subordinates. He nodded to himself, at last sure of how to proceed. "I will go and meet with my agents directly."

"Is that wise?"

"It shows that we are taking the threat seriously. It is worth the risk."

"Where will you start?"

Krivitsky thought. He would travel to see his head agent in Paris. "I will travel to Paris, to see my oldest agent, the military man…"

* * *

It was the hammering at the door which brought him around from a deep sleep. It was constant, as if the person wasn't used to being kept waiting on the wrong side of doors.

Grant flicked a look at his alarm clock; two in the afternoon! Monday! Christ, he'd been asleep for over eighteen hours. He felt as if he'd been beaten around the head with a wet fish, his mouth was as dry as a boot and his stomach was a rumbling earthquake of hunger.

Still the banging on the door continued.

The 'thumper' seemed to have tired of rapping with the knuckles, and had now decided to use the bottom of the fist in a thumping motion. *I can't take much more of that,* thought Grant, and admitting defeat dragged himself out of bed, through the hall and pulled open the door.

"Ah, so you are in. I tried phoning. Got no answer, so decided to come calling. Bloody hell, Jack, at least put some clothes on." Masterman took in the apartment and aside from his semi-naked protégé, it was neat and tidy as befitted a bachelor pad which had been vacant for several weeks. The only evidence it had been used was the hint of a rumpled bed, peeking out from the next room.

And no booze on show, thought Masterman. That was a good sign that his man's mind was focused and still in the game. He made his way to the lounge and settled back on the leather sofa. "Well, while you've been catching up on your beauty sleep, the secret wheels of power at SIS have been grinding, ever so slowly forward."

Grant dragged a dressing gown from the bedroom and set off to make a pot of coffee. "So what's next?" he called from the kitchen.

"You leave on the evening flight to Paris," said Masterman. He heard Grant groan from the kitchen.

"Full circle."

"Full circle indeed, exactly back where you started."

"I'll need—"

"What you'll need has all been taken care of. Miss Quayle has all the immediate logistics in hand. She's quite a resourceful field agent. By now, she should be at your hotel in Paris, making a little home-away-from-home for you both. We've chucked the apartment, time for a change of scene for you two. Don't want people getting suspicious about your comings and goings. She has your flight details and will be ready to meet you with open arms at Orly," said Masterman.

Grant returned with two mugs of coffee and handed one to Masterman. "So it's Sunday. We know the hit was meant to be on Sunday? Is that still confirmed?"

Masterman nodded and took a sip of the coffee. "As confirmed as we can make it. Cirius is expected to meet his KGB control at the usual time and at the usual place; the Pont Neuf. He, of course, knows nothing about the expected assassination or the fact that we have you there, watching his back. Better that way."

Grant agreed. Cirius might be a very brave man, but the thought of walking into a killing zone was enough to spook even the bravest of soldiers.

"What we don't know of course, is where Marquez, the assassin, will attack from," said Masterman.

Grant had been thinking about that, playing it over in his mind. How would the assassin think? "He'll do it long range. In such a busy location, he won't want to get too close. He'll want to keep his distance."

"How do you know?"

"Because that's the way I'd do it. Is there anything on the telephone number in Auver-sur-Oise?" asked Grant.

"That was a good lead, excellent work on your part. Toby and his team traced the phone number to a privately-rented chalet. Paris Station had one of their agents take a trip up there. They did a little snooping around. It was empty. Cleaned out, spotless. Rented through a local letting agent. They'd paid cash for a six-month lease. This Marquez character must have left as soon as he'd received the code you telephoned through. The safe-house had served his purpose and he's abandoned it, which means he's somewhere in Paris, planning and plotting."

"He's a slippery fucker, isn't he? Any more information on him?"

Masterman shrugged, as if it was a matter of no consequence. "Aside from what we already have, nothing much. What we do know, is that he's obviously in the market for contract killing if the price is right. It seems he's been used by several different intelligence services over the past decade or so, most notably the Americans. There are rumors of hits in Africa, South America and the Caribbean, all against major targets. To be fair, as one professional to another, he's done remarkably well."

Grant grunted. Freelancers; you'd never catch him being a freelancer. Redaction was a pig of a job sometimes and the only thing that made the killing easier was the knowledge that you were serving a greater good. The greater good in this case, was the service of his country, but these cash bandits would whore themselves for the biggest pay-check. Never in this life, never him. No chance. "Anything further on what happened in Cornwall?" he asked, focusing his mind back to the events of the previous few days.

"The latest report I received this morning suggest that Scorpius is fine, considering what he went through. He is still in play. The cleanup crew will be finished by the end of today. You know how thorough those chaps are," replied Masterman.

Grant could well imagine. The cleanup unit was a specially recruited team of men, mainly drawn from former Royal Army Medical Corps, the Intelligence Corps, and ex-coppers, and were used to remove any evidence and to dispose of unwanted items from the scenes of SIS operations. The removal of anything from fingerprints to dead bodies all fell within their remit. They were grim-faced, dour men who spoke little and revealed almost nothing about their work.

"Who was Gioradze?" asked Grant, finishing the last of his coffee.

"It seems that he is, was, Marquez's long-term partner in crime. A Georgian émigré, mercenary and former bank robber. Last known address was a bar in Portugal."

Grant nodded. The image of the killer bleeding out was still fresh in his mind. He shuddered, as if to mentally erase the thought.

"So, you get yourself fed, washed and dressed. There's a ticket waiting for you at Pimlico for the 7 pm flight out. Everything else you'll need will be supplied, courtesy of the lovely Miss Quayle. And talking about flights," said Masterman, looking at his watch and starting to stand. "I too have a plane to catch."

"Are you going somewhere, sir?"

"A little trip away for a few days, nothing for you to worry about, Jack. I'll be back in time to welcome you home, victorious with this mercenary's head stuck to a pike."

Masterman let himself out and began to make his way down the communal staircase and out onto the street. No point in telling his operative that he was, in effect, going to open negotiations with the very people his man was actually working against. That would be extremely counterproductive for a Redaction agent in the field. No, it was better to leave Grant in blissful ignorance.

Need to know and compartmentalizing information was something he's learned well from C.

Book Five:
Black King, White Queen

Chapter One

The killer QJ/WIN sat perched in his room in the Hotel Henri IV on the Place Dauphine in Paris and surveyed the scene which lay before him. The open window let in a cool breeze, relaxing him and providing a portrait-framed shot of the Seine which was spread out in all its glory. The river ran like a snake up and away into the distance with the Pont Neuf Bridge intersecting it. He watched as the pedestrians hurried across, on their way to enjoy what was left of the weekend. It was a pleasantly normal Sunday afternoon in Paris.

Marquez had been sitting in his chair, leaning forward with his elbows resting on his knees and his hands linked loosely together, since before dawn. His body, through sheer force of will, was in splendid repose. He knew the target regularly made his way to the bridge every Sunday afternoon to meet up, or not, with his Russian Intelligence contact. Marquez thought it was sloppy tradecraft. After all, what fool would commit themselves to a regular meeting point in such a public location? It was a foolish mistake that would cost the Englishman.

He'd received the phone call code from his partner almost a week ago. The call meant that the target in Cornwall had been eliminated and Gioradze was on his way back to France to hide out and wait for the Catalan to complete the hit on the *Soldier*. With the phone call confirming the death of the man in England, Marquez had moved at once.

He'd retrieved the weapon for this particular hit from the cache underneath the floor of the old barn attached to the safe-house, cleaned and oiled it, then stored it safely away in the suitcase he would be travelling with.

He'd made a telephone booking, reserving a single room in the Hotel Henri IV overlooking the Seine. When he had arrived and checked in, he found the room he'd been given overlooked the river, rather than the bridge. Fortunately enough, the room that best suited his needs was free and a quick cash bribe to the hotel manager ensured he was swiftly relocated. The room itself was at best average; standard bed, two chairs, a small dresser, toilet and bathroom, totally unremarkable. But the view from the window was glorious.

Once he was settled, he moved quickly and expertly to set up his equipment. He assembled the photographer's telescopic tripod and clamped a pair of Zeiss binoculars to it, ensuring that the field of vision took in the expected killing zone the intelligence report had given him; the nearest quarter of the bridge in front of the statue of Henry IV.

Next he looked at the component parts of his weapon: a sniper rifle, but one that very few marksmen would have recognized.

The rifle consisted of three main groups; the firing group, the silencer group and the telescopic sight group. They each fitted snugly into his medium-sized valise, each wrapped separately inside an item of clothing to protect them from knocks or scrapes. Marquez fitted each of the pieces together, attaching the silencer section to the main frame of the rifle, twisting it into place a quarter turn until he heard a click that denoted it was secured. Next went the telescopic sight onto the top. Finally, he pushed into place the magazine loaded with eight 9mm Luger rounds.

He worked the 'butter knife' bolt handle and loaded a round into the firing chamber. Satisfied, he carefully placed the now-live weapon onto the bed in front of him and stared down at this extraordinary rifle. It looked like a normal bolt action rifle, with the exception that

---

where a standard rifle would have a long barrel protruding from the front, this weapon had a stubby silencer built in as part of the frame. The weapon itself was a lethal novelty and to Marquez it was both beautiful and unusual.

When Gioradze had returned from his 'shopping run' to the secret Gladio caches, Marquez had been expecting the usual pistols, submachine guns, ammunition, RPG's and explosives. So when David had pulled open a case containing this most unusual rifle, Marquez knew *he* had to be the one to fire it in Paris. He just had to. He imagined it was like a racing car driver having the opportunity, the once in a lifetime opportunity, to drive a state of the art supercar. It was impossible to pass up.

The weapon was the German made 9mm 'Gestapo' Silenced rifle. Marquez knew a little of its history. There was only a handful ever made and it had been the brainchild of a former Commander of the Nazi Security Service in Berlin in 1939. Count Wolf Von Helldorf had wanted a rifle that was powerful, compact, accurate, but above all else, completely silent. Rumor had it that it was to be used by Security Service agents to quietly eliminate opponents to the Nazi party in Berlin.

After the war, most of the weapons had been destroyed or damaged, but several had been found by US Army officers in Germany in 1945. They had then been passed over to the CIA who, it seemed, had decided to bury several for their European stay behind networks in weapons caches.

Marquez had tested the rifle in the woods near the safe-house in Auvers sur-Oise and he thought it was superb. He'd fired at a tree target on the other side of a small, wooded copse. The rifle had emitted no noise, only a slight *thwump* noise as the bullet hit home. It sounded as if someone had gently dropped a billiard ball into some soft soil. And while the distance from his shooting position to the expected killing zone was at the top end of the rifle's accepted range of one hundred yards, it would not be impossible to silently complete the contract. To Marquez, who prided himself on having the best tools for his profession, it was the ultimate assassination weapon.

With the rifle ready, Marquez had relaxed. He knew the target wouldn't be at the location until just after noon the following day, so he settled in for a light meal from his own supplies. He would not leave the room until after the killing had been completed.

And now on a clear Parisian day, he sat waiting patiently, with less than thirty minutes to go before his target walked into the killing zone. Aside from the occasional glance through the binoculars to confirm or dismiss a possible sighting, his eyes never wavered from that small piece of pathway on the Pont Neuf.

There was always the temptation to touch or manipulate the rifle, fiddle with the bolt action or triple check that the magazine was in place. But those would be the actions of an amateur. Instead, Marquez simply stared down at its unorthodox beauty, where it lay on a pillow on the floor. It was near his hands, it was armed and it was ready to be used when he required it.

Many times over the past few hours, he'd watched the coming and goings of the people crossing the bridge, traipsing backwards and forwards like ants, to and fro. More than once, he'd toyed with the idea of what it would be like to sit here in his sniper position and ruthlessly start shooting at the innocent and unwary on the streets of Paris. Would they scream? Would they flee? How many, he wondered, would rush to help their fellow citizens? It was a banal fantasy to help him pass the time, nothing more. An amateur would glory in causing a massacre, a professional – like himself – would only commit to a targeted killing shot.

He checked his watch and looked once more at the kill zone. At first, there was nothing and then he saw the tall Englishman, the *Soldier*, whom he knew from the photograph. The man ambled his way over the bridge. He looked as if he was in no hurry as he carefully negotiated the pedestrians coming from the opposite direction. Marquez picked up the rifle and settled it in place against his shoulder and cheek, moving the rifle carefully, trying not to dislodge the telescopic sight's tracking.

He saw the Englishmen tense for a moment, halt in his step, and confusion filtered across his face, before he regained his composure and carried on walking. What had made him falter? Marquez tracked across to the opposite side of the bridge. It had to be the contact, the KGB contact. That's who he was meeting here. But the Englishman met his controller here regularly, so why the pause? To the casual observer on the bridge, it wouldn't have been noticed. But through the magnified scope, the expression on the Englishman's face was vivid.

Marquez scanned the other faces; beautiful women, beautiful men, children, priests, but nothing...

Then he saw him in clear, magnified detail. The squat body, the ill-fitting suit, the toad-like appearance all matched the description and fuzzy photograph he'd been given. He looked again. It was him! The KGB network controller! The one Mr. Knight called the 'Prime Target'. The one who the American had told him trumped all other targets. Marquez had been given an open kill policy on the Russian. In any city, in any country, if he was seen meeting with any of the agents on the hit-list, then the orders were to eliminate the Russian on sight first.

He felt the heat from his own body, the perspiration soaking his hand. He squeezed the discomfort from his mind. And with his quarry in view, he carefully moved his eye to the scope, centered on his target, squeezed the grip safety to arm the rifle, took up the pressure on the trigger and began to close in for the kill.

* * *

Major Edward Barrington rose slightly later than normal that Sunday, permitting himself an extra thirty minutes in bed before finally rising at 7.30. He showered, breakfasted on his usual cup of *cafe au lait* and croissant, read yesterday's copy of *Le Monde*, before dressing in his usual weekend wear of slacks, casual jacket, shirt and sturdy walking shoes.

It was a normal weekend for him. A normal Sunday, that involved a 'crash' meeting with his KGB case officer. Every Sunday, come fair weather or foul, he took the long walk from his apartment which was a stone's throw from NATO headquarters on the Palais de Challot and walked along the banks of the Seine. Then when he reached the Pont Neuf, he would open up the small bag of breadcrumbs from his stale baguettes and casually scatter them to the wind, watching as they floated down onto the flowing river below.

Occasionally, as was his want, and if the opportunity presented itself, he would engage in some unremarkable conversation with a passing Parisian pensioner engaged in the same activity, or even, if fate had decreed it, a lovely French mademoiselle, for even though the Major was now well into his late fifties, he still had an eye for ladies half his age.

His French colleagues and friends thought it one of his uniquely British eccentricities. And so he would walk the route, taking in his surroundings, enjoying the views and chatting amiably with the people passing him. But the Pont Neuf was the key, the end result of the whole charade of the Sunday walks. To meet with the enemy.

The protocol was simple. They passed each other on the bridge. If the Russian case officer stopped and mentioned the weather, as strangers sometimes do, it was safe and he hadn't been the subject of hostile surveillance. With the all clear in place, they would make their way over to the far side of the bridge separately, take a bench along the embankment and conduct their business.

However, if the case officer carried on walking past and over to the other side of the bridge with no dialogue, then the meeting was aborted, for whatever reason, and they immediately went to the fallback plan. So far, in the years he'd been based in Paris, Barrington had never had an aborted meeting. He scattered the last of the bread crumbs out of the bag, admired the view and then made his way towards the statue across the bridge. It was when he was halfway there that he saw the Russian. It made him pause, jerk to a stop. He quickly confirmed the face in his head, to make sure he wasn't hallucinating and then, hesitantly, started to walk again.

It was the Russian, but not his regular Russian. It wasn't the normal *Rezidentura* flunky with the bad breath. No, not this time – this time it was the big man from Moscow, his original recruiter and controller of the network. The man known to him as 'Ivan', whom he knew was in fact, Vladimir Krivitsky. He was squat and vulgar in his manner and always wore a somber, baggy suit giving him the duck-like waddle that fat men have when they're rushing. To the fearful, he was a monster known as Svarog.

Krivitsky was old school KGB. He'd been earmarked for great things; a possible seat at KGB Director Semichastney's high table, it had been rumored. That was, until some scandal he'd been involved in several years ago in Poland, a shooting, the rumor mill said, but even now the details were sketchy.

Barrington smiled as his contact approached and just as they were almost shoulder-to-shoulder, preparing to pass each other, the Russian opened his mouth and began to speak, turning his body towards the Englishman. It was the Russian who started the recognition code which meant he had no surveillance on him, he was able to talk.

"My friend, the weather is good for…" said Krivitsky, in a deep rumble of a voice.

"Entertaining," said Barrington, completing the code.

They both stopped. Krivitsky glanced down at his watch, as if he was giving the time to a stranger. "My friend, there is grave news. The network has been betrayed, you must be cautious about your personal security. We—"

The sentence was left dead in the air as a bullet ripped into the Russian's head. A splatter of blood covered Barrington's face, momentarily blinding him. The Russian's head looked like a watermelon which had been hit with a ball hammer and his body fell forward, onto Barrington. Struggling to keep the dead man's weight upright, he quickly admitted defeat and lowered him to the ground.

* * *

They were walking alongside the Seine; honeymooners once again. Nicole and Gorilla had 'tagged' Agent Cirius as soon as he had left his apartment. They'd been in place for thirty minutes before Barrington emerged. They were ready, focused and armed. "We'll keep well back. We don't want to spook him," cautioned Gorilla.

They had trailed after him, ambling along, blending in and trying not to be seen. Thirty minutes into the walk, the crowds had started to increase and they relaxed a little more. It was better for cover and concealment and they watched the back of Cirius as he wandered towards his destination.

"You're not too tired?" said Gorilla, turning to Nicole. She had linked her arm through his and they were walking like lovers would. His hands were thrust deep into his coat pockets, his right hand resting against the weapon on his right hip.

"You just worry about yourself. Keep your eyes on the target and don't get distracted." She'd kept looking straight ahead, her eyes never wavering from their principal ahead of them. But the voice had been hard and cold. Gorilla raised an eyebrow at that.

Things had definitely changed in his brief absence. When Nicole had picked him up from the airport, there had been tiredness around her eyes and her manner was abrasive. "Get in, we're on the clock," she'd barked as he threw his overnight bag into the back seat of a new, but equally shabby, Renault before she gunned the engine and thundered away, driving Parisian style. He had seen that look before on agents just back from a long stretch in hostile territory; a hardness, an independence, a self-sufficiency which had manifested itself while he'd been away.

It had been a long operation for Nicole and he suspected she would have liked to return to England with him. She'd been living a vagabond lifestyle for the past few months and he knew even the briefest break from active operations could give a field agent a new zeal. But her pride and stubbornness wouldn't let her admit she was exhausted. She'd dug her heels in and set about moving their base of operations to the Hotel Peletier on the Rue le Peletier.

They were approaching the embankment leading to the bridge. They both knew that now was the most vulnerable time for *Cirius*. They gave each other a final look. In truth, they'd already discussed what their immediate action plan was going to be, once the attack on Barrington was initiated. For Gorilla, it was simply a case of being quicker to the draw than the hidden assassin and for Nicole, it was to get their agent out and away from the kill zone quickly.

Nicole took a breath as they walked up onto the entrance to the bridge. The bridge was busy and her eyes were scanning constantly. Men, women, children, pets. She had learned harsh lessons from her time in Marseilles, but now she was intent on searching out that one face, the one face she'd last seen years ago in the Caribbean.

Gorilla stopped and turned, embracing her as a lover would. "You see anything, any faces?" he whispered in her ear.

She shook her head and she felt his hand move out of his pocket, ready for the quick draw that would have to happen soon. They moved once again at a slower pace, a good thirty feet away from Barrington who was nearly at the statue. She saw him falter in his step and then he moved cautiously towards an ugly toad of a man who was undoubtedly his Russian contact. Nicole gave a brief look in Gorilla's direction. His eyes were everywhere, high and low and the effort of concentration was evident on his face

She looked over at the two men, saw them pause to casually speak to each other and then she saw the KGB man's head explode!

She knew then the honeymoon was over.

* * *

It was the screams of the couple passing the scene which first roused Barrington from his shock, and being a soldier who'd seen battle more than a few times, he immediately did what he was trained to do and found cover behind one of the stone alcoves dotted across the bridge.

Spat... Spat. He heard two more successive shots ricochet off the stonework, trying to pick him off behind his meagre cover position.

A sniper! A silenced weapon! A bolt action, hence the pause as the marksman took time to reload. Barrington peered around frantically. Where was the shooter? On the bridge? Not judging by the angles and distance.

Cars were slowing down to rubberneck at the commotion and people were running frantically in all directions. Fathers protecting their children, lovers in each other's arms, running in a crouch, all trying desperately to get away.

Spat... Spat; two more hit the stonework above his head.

The bugger's getting closer, he thought; *I've got to move and fast!* He'd spotted the near side of the bridge wall, which would provide better cover than the exposed position he was in. How far away though... twenty... thirty feet? Possible, even for an old duffer like him who was used to chairing meetings these days rather than running under fire.

Spat... Spat!

"Ahhh!" The second round ripped across his bicep. He felt the initial sting, then the slow burn of the metal churning up his flesh before he suffered excruciating pain. He clutched a hand over the wound, and blood oozed from between his fingers. It was a flesh wound, bad but bearable. *Move man, or you are going to die here!*

Just as he was about to launch himself once more into combat, two things happened almost simultaneously.

The first, was that he noticed a small, blond-haired man in a business suit and thick winter overcoat sprint at full speed across the bridge towards the opposite side. The man didn't look as if he was running away from the gunfire, far from it, in fact he looked as if he was running towards it. His legs were pounding like a man possessed, and his right hand seemed to be reaching beneath his heavy coat, either to hold something in place, or to draw it from his waist.

The second remarkable thing, in amongst the scene of chaos and bloodshed, was the hand that firmly grabbed him by the shoulder and was dragging him away from the imaginary security of the old bridge's stone viewing balcony. He looked up and saw the face of one of the prettiest girls he'd ever had the pleasure to see while he was being shot at. *"Come on, Major, move!"* she was yelling at him.

"What... who... get down girl, for heaven's sake, there's a sniper somewhere," he babbled.

The young woman fixed him with a grim look and shouted directly into his face, "Cirius, get on your feet *now* and *run!"*

* * *

Gorilla had spotted where the sniper was firing from almost at once. While everyone else was running for cover, his eyes followed the line of sight, tracing the bullet's path from the dead Russian to... where? A window in the hotel opposite the bridge, it had to be. Then he'd seen the fluttering of a curtain through the open window and the shape of a long, thick rifle barrel as it was retracted.

He set off at a sprint, determined to bust his way into the hotel and find the room if he had to. He'd reached the corner of Dauphine Square when he saw the man with a small suitcase leaving the hotel in a hurry. Not a run by any means, but at a pace which suggested he would rather be somewhere else right at that moment. And yes, it had to be the same man from Marseilles; same build, same height and the face held the same characteristics of the wartime photo he'd seen in the man's file.

Gorilla watched as the man strode quickly through the square and away. Gorilla bought a newspaper from a vendor, threw whatever change he had in his pockets at him, and began to hurry after the assassin. The newspaper was there to cover the pistol and silencer, which he would have to use very soon. After all a shootout in the middle of Paris was not the way to handle this Redaction. No, track the man, isolate him and then finish him off.

He was always amused by the movies when the hero would shout 'Freeze' or 'Don't move' or 'Put your hands up', and he supposed if the hero was a policeman, that would have been the correct thing to do. But Gorilla wasn't a policeman, he was a Redactor and Redactors shot first, without warning. To warn your enemy was to give him an advantage, an advantage which could be terminal.

They'd reached the entrance to the embankment leading off from the Quai des Grands Augustins. *Perfect,* Gorilla thought. The sloping slip road led down to the river. It was still busy down there, but he would have more of an opportunity to quietly deal with this Marquez and perhaps even get rid of the body in the water.

He looked left and right; people were strolling, a few artists with easels were painting the view of the river. He ducked into a shop doorway and quickly removed the pistol and silencer from the leather holster on his right hip. With his back turned to the street, he rapidly screwed the two pieces together; after a cursory chamber-check he concealed the weapon beneath the newspaper. If anybody had taken the time to notice him, they would have seen a man holding a rolled up newspaper across his body at waist height. All Gorilla would have to do was walk up alongside the assassin, and put two rounds into the man's spine. A lowering of the newspaper to his side and two more shots into the head as the man hit the floor would bring the operation to a swift conclusion. He just had to get within a few feet of Marquez and it would be game over. He'd lost the bastard once in Marseilles, this time he was going to have his pound of flesh.

He made his way back onto the street, following, edging closer and closer through the crowds. In the distance, he could hear the wail of sirens; the police and ambulances on their way to the scene at the Pont Neuf. The Sunday crowds were both a help and a hindrance. They were good for cover, but also made it slow going as he fought his way through them.

Marquez turned onto the quiet side street, the Rue des Grands Augustin. Gorilla increased his pace to catch up with the target. The more time Marquez was out of eye contact, the more the risk of his escape increased. Gorilla reached the corner and paused. Counted one, two, and three. Then he casually sauntered around the corner away from the busy main street, his newspaper still held at his waist.

What he saw caused his step to falter and he quickly moved into the doorway of a restaurant, trying his best to stay in the shadows. He risked another glance and saw the man, Marquez, standing at the driver's door of a Citroën DS19.

The door was open as if he was about to drive off, but was hampered by the fact that he'd been stopped by a young police constable of *La Surete Nationale*. Gorilla thought the copper looked like he was fresh faced and just out of police training, but to his credit, he was taking control of the situation and detaining Marquez in a random 'stop and search'.

Gorilla guessed the call had gone out quickly about the shooting further up the riverbank – that and the fact that his swarthy complexion could easily have Marquez down as a possible OAS terrorist, which would definitely make him a person of interest to the police.

The Sûreté constable was asking Marquez questions and gesticulating towards the small suitcase he was carrying. Marquez shrugged and offered a response that Gorilla couldn't make out. Marquez seemed to acquiesce and then handed over the suitcase, but just as the constable took the weight of the case, the bigger man leaped forward and gripped him by the throat with his left hand. At the same time, his other fished into his coat pocket, and with a flash of steel, a glinting switchblade sprung into life.

The policeman desperately tried to reach for the gun at his hip, but the bigger man's stiletto was fast moving and in constant motion as it pumped in, again and again, at the younger man's throat. A woman walking on the opposite side of the road had turned and witnessed the attack. Her scream caused Marquez to break off his knifing and he let the policeman slump to the ground, all life gone out of him as the blood cascaded over his uniform.

Marquez threw the case into the car and was about to climb into the driver's seat when he caught sight of Gorilla moving out of the shadows. They saw each other as only two people who are of the same ilk can, with a clarity and recognition of the breed they are.

Gorilla swung the newspaper up, a fast moving blur, and centered it on the man framed against the car. Almost instantly, Marquez ducked into the car, leaving only his hand resting on the roof as he tried to move his tall frame inside. Gorilla took the shot; the end of the newspaper snapped once as the bullet sped out from the barrel and blew two fingers from Marquez's hand.

Even before Marquez screamed with pain, Gorilla knew his shot had hit home. It was his skill after all, for even though the majority of his Redactions took place in close quarters, Gorilla still prided himself on being an expert shot for long distance pistol work.

Gorilla started to move forward slowly, taking his time and carefully placing his shots.

The bullets took out the passenger's side window and skimmed off the roof, and Gorilla cursed; going for the quick kill headshot had caused the bullets to bounce high. To his credit and despite the gunshot wound, Marquez was nimble enough to get the car moving, slowly at first and then faster as the engine reached a whining crescendo. The car lurched forward as its power increased, before speeding away, its door flapping open and closed until the car's momentum was strong enough to slam it shut.

Gorilla stood framed in the narrow street; the newspaper now abandoned and the '39 up and aimed as he carefully shot out the rear lights and splintered the back window... twenty-five feet... thirty feet... until the car careered away, swinging around the corner into the distant Rue Saint Andre des Arts.

Gorilla picked up the spent ammunition casings from the ground. He checked around. The few remaining witnesses were at the far end of the street and from this distance, wouldn't have a clear view of him. In the distance, the police sirens were getting closer.

The police would already be twitchy after the scene on the Pont Neuf and now with a secondary shooting less than half a mile away, the last thing he needed was for his description from two sets of witnesses to be relayed to the authorities. He knew he had to get out of the area and meet Nicole back at the emergency rendezvous. He turned and without looking back, quickly made his way back towards the river.

"I've seen you sunshine," he whispered to himself. "I've seen you now and I never forget a face."

* * *

Nicole had one hand stuffed into her handbag, clutching the Walther pistol, and one hand holding onto the upper bicep of her recently-acquired Agent *Cirius*, like a bodyguard moving a protected VIP out of danger.

They'd been hurrying along the Quai des Tuileries for a good ten minutes following the shooting when Barrington pulled her up. Nicole turned to him. The man looked ashen; partly through the injury and partly from shock.

"Wait… I need to rest," he said, panting.

"No, we have to keep moving, we have to put some distance between us and what happened back there," she said. They'd not long passed the entrance to the Louvre. There were crowds of people everywhere and each one of them could have been a threat. Who knew how many contractors these killers might have recruited? Nicole tightened her grip on the gun in her handbag. "A little further, then we can stop and talk."

"But I need answers… and… I don't feel well," said Barrington.

She put one arm under his and lifted him up. "Walk with me, put your arm around me and I'll hold you up. Pretend we're out for a stroll. Just a little further, until we can't hear the sirens or see the flashing lights anymore. Then we can stop."

Barrington allowed himself to be lifted and nodded. "Alright… alright… I could quite get used to this," he said, a flirtatious smile on his lips.

"Don't get too carried away, Major. If anyone tries to come at us, I want you to drop to the floor while I deal with them. You understand?"

"Young lady, you certainly have a way of killing a romantic moment."

They carried on walking for a further ten minutes, until they turned off the main route and onto the Avenue Dutuit which led them on to beautifully manicured parkland. They made their way to the side of the Petit Palais past its ornate facade, until they found the rather more drab service entrance to the rear. She pulled him into an inlet that was accessed by five steps and led down to a solid metal door. It would hide them, she decided, while she had to do what she had to do.

"Take off your jacket and let me see how bad it is," she ordered him.

Barrington carefully took off his casual jacket, wincing as he revealed the arm which had taken the shot. Nicole inspected it carefully. "It hasn't gone in, just a graze, a flesh wound. That Russian taking the shot probably saved your life. Do you have a handkerchief? A proper one, mind you, not that paper rubbish they use these days."

Barrington nodded and removed the handkerchief from his pocket. Nicole took it from him, ripped it down the center until it had two prongs and then carefully tied it around the open wound. "Now put your jacket back on. It's not perfect, but it will have to do for now."

"Who are you people? You and the other fellow?" asked Barrington, his senses and suspicion coming back to him.

"We've been sent here to watch over you *Cirius*. Porter sent us," she said simply.

"The Russian said I was in danger..."

Nicole nodded. "The Russian was right. There's been a big operation in play for the past few months. Someone's been trying to eliminate the network. We've been trying to stop them."

"You mean you and the chap you were with?"

She nodded. A moment of pride lit her up inside. Yes, *she* and her partner from the Redaction Unit, Gorilla; a team. Saving lives and stopping extremists. Wasn't that the truth of it all?

"How many of the agents have been killed. Where do I come on the list?" he asked. He'd slipped his jacket back on and some of the color had returned to his cheeks. Although the events of the last thirty minutes still seemed surreal, his mind was now returning to its usual sharp self.

"You don't need to know. It wouldn't do you any good, even if you did. All that should concern you right here, right now, is that you're still in play. Your cover is intact. As of this moment, as far as the Russians are concerned, you're still Major Edward Barrington, KGB spy inside NATO."

He was silent for a moment as he digested this information. "What should I do?"

She looked him square in the eye. "Play it for real. Get in touch with the Russians."

"What! How? My contact's just had his bloody head blown off!" He looked down at the smudges of dried blood which splattered his shirt. He brushed an involuntary hand over them, as if to shoo them away.

Nicole stood her full height and looked directly at him. She was the agent-runner now and the only thing that would bring this spy back to order was to speak to him with authority and confidence. She just hoped that *Cirius* fell for it. "There must be an emergency contact procedure, there always is. They'll want to talk to you sooner, rather than later, to find out what happened on the bridge. The best advice is to make contact with them first, tell them what happened and get your shot in, if you'll excuse the pun."

A smile came to Barrington's face. The good advice and humor had brought him back to reality. "Yes, yes of course. It's the logical thing to do," he said.

"Who knows, this might help strengthen your cover story with the Russians even more. Compose yourself, *Cirius,* and do what you've been told. We'll be in touch."

"When?"

"Soon. Don't worry, it will all work out." She glanced over her shoulder to make sure there were no witnesses and the coast was clear.

"How can I thank you?" It was all he could think of to say. A cliché, perhaps, but it was the best he could do.

She stared at him for a few moments, as if deciding what the best response would be; something witty or something blasé? In the end she opted for plain honesty. "By staying alive, *Cirius*. There's too much blood being shed to fail at this late stage of the game."

She looked at him a moment longer, then turned and climbed the steps.

* * *

Gorilla returned to their hotel at a little after eleven o clock that night. He'd been on the run for the past ten hours and a day of stress and exhaustion from running counter-surveillance drills had taken its toll on him. He just hoped Nicole had gotten away safely with *Cirius*.

He turned the key in the door and stepped into the hotel room. It was dark; the only ambient light came from the street lights outside. He heard the door click gently behind him and for the first time all day, he felt secure.

On the bed was a shape; Nicole, laying in repose. She was still wearing her clothes, coat and shoes. Her hands rested gently on her chest.

"You awake?" he whispered, as he lowered his body onto the bed next to her. A chasm of several inches lay between them, separating their bodies.

"Barely," he heard her reply.

Christ, she sounded as exhausted as he felt. He grunted in understanding. "Did *Cirius* get away?"

"He got away. I gave him his marching orders and set him off. He'll be fine," she said.

"And you? You get away alright?"

She had spent the afternoon covering her back; running counter-surveillance tactics, stopping for drinks, shopping, getting in and out of buses, taxis and trains.

Hours later and satisfied she hadn't been spotted or was being watched, she decided to risk it and make her way back to their hotel. She suspected Gorilla had been doing much the same for the majority of the day. "I wasn't followed, if that's what you mean. Did you get the dead-eye?"

He smiled to himself in the darkness. He liked the way she'd begun to pick up the *patois* of the Redaction team. "No… he escaped. I only wounded him."

He heard her groan. It was the sound of someone who had expected a better result from a superior officer and realizes that the work isn't finished just yet. "If it's any consolation, he won't be playing the violin anytime soon. Not with only a thumb and two fingers on one hand," he said.

She let the silence embrace them both while she pondered Gorilla's informal assessment of the day's action. Eventually, she turned her head and looked at him, the profile of his face stark against the exterior light of the window. "What will he do now?" she asked.

"He'll run and he'll run quickly. He'd be crazy to stay around. He's had his shot at *Cirius* and missed. He got the Russian, so he'll count that as a positive. His next stop will be Italy. It makes the most sense tactically, geographically and practically. He's got one final target to go for and he'll want to make his move soon."

"And what about us?"

He grunted. "We have to move too. We take the car and drive. It's probably safer that way. I'll contact Pimlico tomorrow and tell them what we need. Our dead-eye is wounded and under pressure to finish his contract. That could go in our favour; wounded and stressed equals mistakes. And we're going to be there to catch him when he drops the ball. But now, right now, we need to sleep."

She sighed and once more let silence fill the gap.

"Penny for them," he said. The quiet continued and at first, he thought she wasn't going to answer him.

"I was just thinking about being back in the bar at the Savoy; champagne and malt whisky. It seems a hundred years ago now. I wish we were back there."

"Do you regret it? Meeting me and then all this?" he said, waving an invisible arm in the darkness to illustrate the mayhem of the past few months.

She laughed, a harsh, bitter laugh. "Don't be so hard on yourself, Jack, you were wonderful. As for the rest of it, the mission, the killings, well, I'll just have to learn to live with it. Besides, it's my own fault for falling under the spell of the first spy who bought me a few drinks and then promised to take me on a top secret mission."

Despite the teasing, he could hear the drowsiness in her voice. He felt the warmth of the room and the comfort of the mattress and knew that sleep was beginning to take a hold of him.

Nicole draped a lazy arm over his chest and snuggled into his body, the rough material of his jacket brushing against her cheek. She didn't mind that though, it felt warm, safe and secure.

She tried to ask one more question; what it was going to be, even she wasn't sure. She never made it though, because moments later they were both asleep.

Chapter Two

"Yes."

"This is QJ/WIN," said Marquez into the telephone. The code was an old habit now, especially after all the reports they had conducted over the past few months. If Marquez announced himself as 'QJ/WIN', it meant he was operating freely. However, if he simply referred to himself as 'WIN', it meant he'd been captured and was speaking under duress. It was simple, but effective.

"Report," said Mr. Knight.

"The Paris job was compromised."

There was a sharp intake of breath from the American. "Compromised how?"

"A man and a woman came to the *Soldier*'s assistance."

"Good Samaritans?"

"No, the man was armed, a professional. He came after me, wounded me. The woman helped the soldier escape."

"Police, perhaps?"

"No, I don't think so. I think the operation must have been compromised."

Mr. Knight gave out a nervous laugh. "Impossible, our security has been excellent."

Marquez grunted. "And yet these people were at the same location as the targets, at exactly the same time. It could be that the Russians are aware of what we are doing."

Mr. Knight thought this eminently possible. You don't start killing Soviet agents without someone at the KGB becoming suspicious and starting to connect the dots. He'd hoped they would be further along with the operation before the KGB became aware of what was happening. Still, never mind. "What about the targets?" he asked.

"One confirmed kill. One escaped with a flesh wound," replied Marquez.

"Who was the kill?"

"It was the Russian, the prime target. Not the spy. The KGB officer."

There was silence down the phone. Then a murmur, as if Mr. Knight was whispering something. To Marquez, it sounded as if he was praying. "That is acceptable. I think my superiors can live with that."

Marquez thought he detected a hint of relief and pleasure in Mr. Knight's voice, which was very strange, very strange indeed. "There is one other thing," continued Marquez.

"Go on."

"It's WI/ROGUE. He hasn't checked in since the last job against the *Engineer*."

"Perhaps he's decided to keep a low profile. Perhaps he has a woman somewhere and is hiding out."

"No, it's not his style, especially when we're working. He doesn't break protocol. I received the phone code confirming the job had been completed, and then... nothing."

Marquez was disturbed. Things weren't adding up. It was almost as if there was a hidden force working against them, which in this case seemed to be a KGB team. On its own, these things probably meant nothing, but when you connected them, the disappearance of the German in Marseilles, the attack of the Hotel Azure, the missing Gioradze and now the interference of the man in Paris – no, things were definitely askew. Protocol dictated that if a contract was compromised, then the operator closed down the operation quickly and left the game.

"What do you want to do?" asked Mr. Knight, breaking the silence.

"I don't know… I need to think," said Marquez. The pain in his hand was excruciating and wasn't helped by the stress of having to make difficult decisions on the fly.

"You have done remarkably well, better than we could have imagined. There would be no shame in stopping now. The last target, we will get some time, somewhere," said the American.

"I said, I need to think. I will call back later today with my decision." Marquez put the phone down.

Following the shoot-out at the Pont Neuf he'd escaped from the area, thrown off the tracking of the small blond man, dumped the bullet-ridden car and hailed a taxi to take him to a hotel in Montmartre. He'd bandaged up his wounded left hand, the little finger and half the ring fingers were missing. The pain was unbearable, so he donned a pair of gloves and set out to find a backstreet pharmacist to buy some 'off the books' morphine.

He returned, took a dose of the morphine and for the rest of the day he lay on the bed in his little hotel room and flitted between sleeping and thinking. His mind was a whirlwind of possible outcomes and backtracking for clues. Where was the leak? Was it the Russians who were after them? If so, how long had they been there? Since Marseilles, or before that?

Finally, several hours later, he'd made up his mind and donned his current disguise from his small suitcase; a pair of sunglasses, an old sports coat and a beret. He needed to lose the rifle, dispose of it somehow, and the most likely way was to break down the unusual-looking weapon into its component parts and scatter it across the city.

An hour later the stock had been dropped into a nearby canal, the bolt action had been slipped down a manhole cover in another part of the city, the scope had been thrown into a garbage collection pile and the bullets had been thrown into the Seine. Afterwards, he wandered the streets of Paris, a city he'd once called home, feeling lost like a stranger, alone in his thoughts.

Marquez was pretty sure Gioradze had fallen somewhere between Cornwall and returning to France. There had been no contact, overt or covert on any of the communication lines. That wasn't like the Georgian. Not like him at all. Maybe the German had been killed in Marseilles, after all. Maybe he hadn't simply pulled out of the operation, but had instead been eliminated, perhaps as a result of the little blond man or one of his compatriots.

He found himself feeling melancholy for his former partner. Whilst Gioradze had simply been a colleague and a mercenary devoted only to money, Marquez realized he would miss the likeable 'Rogue'. Oh, they'd never been friends in the classic sense of the word, but they'd shared many experiences and adventures over the last five years. Marquez would see his woman right. He would send some money to the bar in Portugal where Gioradze had made his home. The rest of the stipend he would, of course, keep for himself. Now, as the sole contractor, it was only right that he should keep the lion's share of the contract fee.

Which brought him back to the current contract for the CIA: what should he do?

The easy option would be to cut his losses and walk away. But that didn't sit easy with him. He'd never quit a contract before and he wasn't going to start now. If he did, he feared he would never be employed again by the CIA. The Americans had a way of remembering little things like that; besides, his own integrity and stubbornness wouldn't let him quit. He was committed to seeing this through, even if it meant capture and death.

He walked back into the center of Montmartre and found a bar that was quiet, ordered himself a small glass of wine, drank it in one go and then made his way to the telephone booth near the back. He inserted a *jeton* and punched in the number. Almost at once, the handset was picked up. Mr. Knight must have been waiting, poised and ready for his call. "Yes."

"This is QJ/WIN. I have made a decision."

"I hope it's the right one."

"It is."

"In that case…"

"My answer is this. Watch the news over the coming weeks. I am going to shake the Russian intelligence network in Europe to its core. The contract is still on."

Chapter Three

It was late at night when the telephone rang at the private residence. A flicking of the study room light, a tightening of the dressing gown belt, a rub of the eyes and the man picked up the handset. "Hello!"

"This is SENTINEL."

The man paused to search his memory. A codename! Then he remembered. "Good to hear from you, it's been a while."

"Did I disturb you? What with it being the middle of the night?"

"Not at all, SENTINEL, I had to get up anyway, the phone was ringing." It was an old and terrible joke that had passed between them for years. "To what do I owe the pleasure at this godforsaken time?"

"I've a little present for you. Some information, unofficial at the moment, just between you and me, and I wondered if you could shed some light on it."

The man rubbed the sleep from his eyes and tried to focus. "If I can, sure. Anything for an old friend, even an unofficial one."

"It's about an operation your people are running in Europe."

"Is this line secured, SENTINEL?" The man knew that his private phone line was 'cleaned' and monitored daily to ensure no third party was using electronic measures to 'bug' the line. But he couldn't be sure his caller's line had the same integrity.

"No, it's not been cleaned. That's why I'd like to meet face to face. I'm in New York."

The man laughed. "And it couldn't have waited until morning? Jeez."

"What can I say; I was eager to speak to you. Would tomorrow morning be convenient? Say about eleven."

"Sure, just swing by the office."

"Ah, would it be possible to have a chat somewhere more neutral? I was thinking of 350 Fifth Avenue, on the eighty-sixth floor. You know where I mean, don't you? I've never been before and would relish the opportunity."

"How very theatrical, not like you."

"Well, at least there'll be no one in a building overlooking us. Plus, it makes it easier to spot anyone taking an unhealthy interest in two old friends having a chat."

"Yeah, plus we can always toss them over the side if we don't like the look of them!"

* * *

350 Fifth Avenue is better known by its more iconic title of the Empire State Building. The lower observation deck is situated on the eighty-sixth floor and it was here that Masterman stood at 10.55am.

His early arrival had nothing to do with the covert meeting and running a counter-surveillance assessment. Instead, he just wanted to spend some time enjoying the spectacular vista. It had been well worth both the cost in time and the extra expense as he took in the sprawling view of Manhattan.

"I'll say one thing for you Brits; you certainly do pick the most impressive meeting points."

Masterman turned and looked at the man walking towards him. It had been, what? Four, five years since they'd last worked together in the bad old days of Berlin. CIA officer Troy Dempsey was of a similar hue to Masterman. Tall, powerful in the shoulders, he looked like an American Football linebacker. The well-cut suit seemed to be molded to his body, his physical strength and the lilting Texas drawl belying a sharp and ruthless mind.

"Troy, it's good to see you again. Come, let's have a stroll and enjoy the view," said Masterman. They walked casually on; each man aware of the people around them and each checking for signs of people showing an interest.

"How's work these days? I hear your people closed down the old office," said Masterman.

Dempsey frowned. It had been a torrid few years for him at the CIA. After being one of the prime architects of the Executive Action department, the unit responsible for covert action and assassination, he had watched in horror as the CIA top floor and congress had essentially stripped Executive Action down to a shadow of its former self. Operations which had been months in the planning had been dismantled overnight, Grade 1 agents had been dropped and left out in the cold, and loyal officers had been thrown to the political wolves.

Dempsey had been lucky. He was too much of a valued CIA man to be let loose into the commercial world. Instead, he'd been moved sideways and given a lesser post, running operations against Iron Curtain assets at the United Nations. He shrugged as if it was just one of those things. "You know the brass; they always know best. Makes you wonder what we'd all do without them. So what's this all about, Stephen? Not that I'm not glad to see you again, you understand. It's just that coming all this way to see me, well, it's mighty intriguing."

Masterman smiled. "I hope that alone tells you how important my people consider this information. I mean, flying first class to New York, have you seen the price of airline tickets these days? It appears, and I admit it is a little unusual, but not without precedent, that we are on opposing sides on this occasion."

Dempsey's head snapped around, military style and he looked hard at Masterman, trying to read what the British intelligence officer was up to. "You're kidding?" he said.

They'd stopped and both men stared out across the Hudson River. The observation deck was growing busy with tourists and sightseers, so the two spies moved along several times until they found a spot where they wouldn't be disturbed. They spoke casually in a level tone; as old friends do when they're having a private conversation.

Masterman gave the CIA man the edited version of events; technical surveillance which had uncovered an American plot to kill British and European citizens, the assassins operating in Europe and even the possibility of attempting a hit on British soil. He gave just enough information to get Dempsey interested and laid out the evidence bit-by-bit to keep him hooked. He retained the active involvement of the British Redaction team, at least for the time being, for no intelligence officer likes to give away his ace too early. That would come soon enough, but at a tactical time of Masterman's choosing. Now it was time to twist the knife.

"So it seems that someone in the CIA has returned to their old ways and hired a bunch of killers to attack various targets across Europe. This team has had several scores – Hamburg, Zurich, Lichtenstein, if my reports are correct," said Masterman.

Dempsey's face filled with contempt. He'd heard some crazy shit in his time at the Agency, but this was off the wall. "Ummm... obviously I can neither confirm nor deny anything, but it does all sound rather unlikely. Impossible, in fact! The Agency would never target British citizens without consent from your offices first; besides, what makes you think it's a CIA operation? It could be another service, or even a criminal organization, taking it upon itself to get involved. What's the intel and where did you come by it?"

"I'd rather not say at the moment, but needless to say, we have it on the very best authority that Americans are involved."

"Bullshit! Besides, you know the agreement; no poaching on each other's turf!"

Masterman knew of the CIA/SIS agreement, certainly, but he also knew that it wouldn't count for much if some over-ambitious zealot wanted to change it on a whim. "Indeed. However, it appears that the message doesn't seem to have reached the ears of the contractors. If I were to say the codename QJ/WIN to you, would it mean anything?"

The question blindsided Dempsey, and for a fraction of a second, the shock of hearing the secret codename of a CIA contract agent had thrown him. Even in a secret organization like the CIA, people talk, and as Dempsey had been an active operations officer in the clandestine service, he more than anyone was aware of the 'legends' that certain contract agents had become, even if he didn't know their individual details.

Dempsey paused, his bright blue eyes taking in the Englishman's face, searching for any signs of deception. He knew he had to tread carefully. "Ummm, now you know I can't confirm nor deny anything. It sounds like bad fiction. That stuff just doesn't happen in the real world."

"Well then, it appears that the Agency has a bit of a mystery on its hands; namely, that someone out there is recruiting hired killers, former CIA contract agents, to actively murder people in the name of the American government. It sounds like you either have a bit of a leaky ship, or a bit of a rogue elephant," said Masterman.

Dempsey turned away for a moment, to collect his thoughts before looking back over his shoulder. "Then we've reached a bit of an impasse. Unless you can give me something more concrete, like evidence, I can't really approach anyone at the Agency about it. I'd get laughed out of Langley."

"I understand, Troy," said Masterman, reaching into his coat pocket and pulling out a sealed envelope. "That's as much as we can provide; it's not everything by any means, but it should get you started. A few names, dates, locations – you know the way these things work."

"Well, let's hope it's enough to keep the Director of Plans convinced," said Dempsey, still not certain that he was going to be able to sell this to his superiors.

"Ah, there we may have a problem. I'm sure the DP is a trustworthy chap, but the condition of this is that it goes directly to the top. The DCI only, I'm afraid," said Masterman. "Those are the conditions from my Chief."

Dempsey frowned. "The Director of Central Intelligence! Stephen, there is no way the DCI would see me, even if he did believe me. I'm an operations officer, in a relatively outlying intelligence post. The guy probably can't even remember me."

"Don't concern yourself too much. My Chief will be getting in touch with your DCI sometime over the next day or so. We'd like you to read and digest the information first. Who knows, it might be a lot of nonsense, it might even be explainable, or it might just be another scandal lurking around the corner for the CIA. At least this way, your people can chop the head off any rogue agents before they start a great big bloody war," said Masterman, gripping his friend's arm in what he hoped was a congenial manner.

Dempsey ruminated. He couldn't imagine the Agency killing its own agents. Pay them off or imprison them, yes. But killing a contractor would send shockwaves through the intelligence network. Word would soon get around that the Agency was free and easy about 'eliminating' its own contractors at the drop of a hat. They would never get anyone to work for them again! He turned to Masterman and spoke, not unkindly. "I don't know whether to thank you or punch you, Stephen."

Masterman laughed. "A little of both, I would imagine. But I hope that you'll see this as an opportunity to halt something very dangerous and to investigate to see if you have a rogue element working inside your organization."

The two men walked towards the elevator; the rain had started to come in, and their brief meeting was at an end. The tourists were remaining behind and a tour guide had started shouting out his pitch. Masterman pulled on his gloves and Dempsey stuffed the envelope inside his coat. As they made it into the elevator, Dempsey remembered something from their Berlin days.

"How's the little guy from Berlin? What was his name... ape... chimp... something like that? Protégé of yours wasn't he?"

"Gorilla."

Dempsey nodded. "Ah, Gorilla, the British Tom Horn. How is he these days?"

"You sound almost jealous. He's fine."

"I tell you, Stephen, I never saw anyone shoot like him. Maybe we should hire him to solve our rogue agent problem," said Dempsey in a startling moment of perception which sent shivers down Masterman's spine.

"Grant is fine. He's fast gaining a reputation as one of our best field agents. I'll give him your best, Troy."

* * *

Troy Dempsey hit the streets and walked away, heading back to his office in the Rockefeller Center. He was tempted to break out into a run, a run that would take him all the way back to Washington in a hunt for a possible infiltrator and a traitor.

He of course did not run. He was a seasoned officer and knew better than to show his hand to a 'Brit', even if they were old friends.

So he sauntered along the street, taking his time and acting like he didn't have a care in the world. But he had to admit that what he had now, in this moment, was a new sense of purpose and determination which he hadn't experienced for many a good year.

Chapter Four

CIA Headquarters, Langley, Virginia – April 1965

The return to Langley and the subsequent visit to the offices of the Director of Central Intelligence had been brief to say the least, thought Dempsey. An Agency car had collected him from the airport and driven him straight through to CIA headquarters. He was whisked upstairs, through the security gates and past the minimal amount of people necessary. The DCI, obviously a savvy operator, wanted to keep as many people out of the loop as possible.

He entered the inner sanctum and was greeted by an air of tension. A brief handshake and the DCI laid out the problem. "SIS have found something Troy, something that their Chief considers serious enough to pass on to us. They have asked for you personally; I understand that you worked with one of their senior men in the past. He has suggested you as the initial point of contact."

Dempsey gave the DCI a brief outline of his dealings with Masterman. "We devilled together in the bad old days," he said, as way of an explanation of why Masterman seemed to have chosen a washed up CIA officer.

"I understand that you have some investigation experience?" asked the DCI.

Dempsey nodded. "Yes, Mr. Director, I served with the Counter Intelligence Corps at the end of the war. Mainly rounding up Nazis and catching a few spies."

The DCI leaned back in his chair, secure in the knowledge that he had the right man for the job. "Excellent, well, I must say this dossier makes disturbing reading. If it's true, then we do have a problem, a rogue elephant problem."

Dempsey looked concerned and in truth, was unsure how best to approach his next statement. "So I take it that this operation we've stumbled upon is in no way a legitimate CIA operation. Can I just confirm that?"

The DCI had started drumming his fountain pen on the cover of the file, tapping out a tune Dempsey couldn't quite work out. "I can categorically state that this is not one of our operations. Furthermore, I will not be raked over the coals like my predecessor, in front of all kinds of god-awful committees and hearings because we're being blamed for some kind of false flag operation. If there is a problem, I want it stamped out or contained."

Dempsey knew the current DCI had been brought in to replace the mishandling of the Agency's affairs following the sacking of its previous incumbent. No one had liked the previous Director, who many at CIA considered way out of his depth both in terms of intelligence operations and as a leader of men.

"I want you to look under the blanket; find where this dossier from SIS leads us," continued the DCI. "You work directly for me and answer only to me. I want answers, but I want it done with discretion."

"What about the Office of Security, surely this is their department?" said Dempsey, who had no inclination to get embroiled in an internal turf war.

"At the moment, the OS is out of the loop. I want an initial investigation to see if this rumor has any credence. If not, then no one needs to be any the wiser. I'd like to keep the security people out of it as long as possible, at least until we have something more concrete," said the DCI.

Dempsey considered this. At least with the DCI at his back, he would have full Agency authority. "I'll need to look through any number of files and interrogate any number of leads. What if I hit a wall?"

The DCI picked up a sealed envelope which had been lying on his desk. It was made from good quality paper with the CIA crest on the flap. He handed it to Dempsey. "That's your keys to the kingdom, at least as far as the CIA is concerned. You hit a wall, you show them that. Boiled down, it basically says that you speak for me. If you want something, you get it or the officer involved will report to me shortly before he begins a new posting somewhere extreme, such as Outer Mongolia."

"I'll need help," said Dempsey.

"You can have one officer. Someone you trust, and an office down the corridor. If anyone asks, you're working on a special project for the Director's office."

The meeting ended as quickly as it had started. Another handshake and then the DCI was escorting him to the door of the office. Dempsey hadn't even had time to take in the view. As they reached the door, the DCI gave him one last parting shot. "Oh, and Troy, I have two simple rules; make it quick and don't fail!"

* * *

Dempsey decided to hit the ground running. He'd set up a temporary office in the east wing, somewhere quiet where he wouldn't be bothered. Then he made his way down to the Intelligence Division to see if he could find the man he was looking for.

Frank Wellings wasn't in his office, but he was down in the cafeteria enjoying a well-earned break and enjoying a cup of 'joe'.

"Holy shit! When did you get back in town? I thought you were hitting the bars down in Manhattan these days."

Wellings was a rangy forty-year-old who had worked with the anti-Castro movement down in Florida, prior to the Bay of Pigs. Dempsey had seconded him to several Executive Action operations prior to the

EA department being blown. These days, he was stuck assessing agent reports for the Northern Europe Section of the Intelligence Directorate. In his opinion, it sucked.

Dempsey knew him as a good man who knew how to keep a secret and was possessed with a good investigative mind. He deserved better than being stuck in a cubbyhole and moving paper around. He sat down at the table next to Wellings and sipped at his coffee. "Oh, I've been dragged back to run something. I've got something for you. You busy these days?"

"Oh yeah, sure, rushed off my feet. There are always paperclips that need putting away," said Wellings, loosening his tie.

"I need you to do some snooping around for me. Quiet and discreet. Nothing official, at least not yet, not until we have something concrete."

"And this comes from?"

For an answer Dempsey merely raised one finger and pointed it directly up into the sky. "God himself," he said.

Wellings leaned back in his chair and whistled. The DCI himself. It must be explosive. He stared back hard at Dempsey and then a wide grin spread across his face. "When do we start?"

* * *

A day later and the combined forces of Troy Dempsey and Frank Wellings were in full swing. They had an office, phone lines, access to files and the keys to Heaven from the DCI.

"Okay, we start with what we know, which is not a lot. The principals, let's begin with them. We start with the agents and see if it leads us back to the major players in this little drama," said Dempsey, grabbing an office notepad. He began to write:

INTELLGENCE   LEADS:
QJ/WIN
WI/ROGUE

MR. MAURICE KNIGHT – CIA?
HIT-LIST
EUROPE

The first point of call was to pull QJ/WIN's 201 file. A 201 file was a document held for every CIA agent or 'asset' which had been recruited by the Agency. Fundamentally, it gave a biography of the individual and how the case officer involved in the recruitment saw the running of the agent and how it should progress.

The file on Marquez was extensive. Dempsey had put in a 'Priority File Request' to the CIA's Registry and thirty minutes later it was delivered by one of the clerks. He signed for it and then flicked through the agent's file, noting the man's last known address; Luxembourg. *Well, that fits with the intelligence from SIS,* thought Dempsey. *So far so good.*

But it was the scale of operations that QJ/WIN had been involved in that amazed him. The agent had initially been part of the CIA's Soviet counter-espionage project, before being upgraded to work on several Executive Action assassination operations. There were no specific details in the files, but the names and locations stood out a mile; Lumumba/Congo, Trujillo/Dominican Republic, Castro/Cuba, Bolivia, Ecuador.

There was a mention of several operations being conducted with a fellow agent; WI/ROGUE. A call to the Registry and another thirty-minute wait before the knock came at the door and that file too, was dropped on his desk. He signed for it and then tossed the WI/ROGUE file over to Wellings. "Here, get up to speed on this," he said, before returning to the biography of Marquez.

The rest of the file contained numerous assessments by QJ/WIN's various case officers.

"Subject has many contacts within the European underworld and criminal class."

"He is a man who can rationalize his actions and can ruthlessly execute his orders."

"Discreet, cultured and a born intelligence operator."

And so on and so forth. The agent was highly thought of. So, what went wrong?

The last page of the file revealed all. In late 1963 QJ/WIN was 'terminated' as an agent and the reason was the assassination of John F. Kennedy. Since the start of the oversight committees following the Kennedy assassination, and Capital Hill's witch hunt within the American intelligence community – most notably the CIA – the Office of Covert Action had been depleted to almost an administrative section.

Under the leadership of its first Chief, it had a hand or organized roles in the covert world, mainly against high profile targets such as Castro, Lumumba and Trujillo. But once the senators and politicians had started delving deeper, it had been given a choice; toe the line and downsize, or we scatter the Agency to the winds. The new Director of Central Intelligence had capitulated and backed down.

A new Chief had been brought in to reorganize Covert Action; the old Chief moved sideways to a posting in Europe, and the responsibility for paramilitary action was being passed more and more to the mainstream Army and Navy, and less was being done by the civilian operators at the Agency. These days, the Office of Covert Action, or ORCA as it was known, was there only to assist with paperwork and pre-operational planning. ORCA had been neutered.

"So what do we have?" said Dempsey, once the files had been returned to the registry.

Wellings glanced up from his desk on the opposite side of the room and shrugged. "We have a couple of former contract agents who have been reactivated by someone claiming to be CIA. The reason seems to be to eliminate perceived KGB agents in Europe. Someone's definitely trying to screw up a network. The question is, why?"

"Usually it's money or revenge, that's if we take the professional reasons for this type of operation out of the equation. Seeing as this operation is well-funded, I guess we can rule out extortion and if we're to believe the DCI, then it only leaves us with one logical outcome – revenge."

"Someone certainly knew where to look to find those guys."

They both sat for a minute, digesting what they'd read. Then it hit Dempsey like a hammer. "Shit, that's it... get those files back up here. Call Registry and get them back now!"

The clerk from Registry came back, lugging both the files. He was barely through the door when Dempsey grabbed them from him. "Come on, come on," he said, his voice quickening with the thrill of excitement. Could it be the break that could open it up? He flicked through to the last page of the file that bore the title 'ACCESS LIST', the document every officer had to sign whenever they wished to read through a file.

He ran his finger down the line until he came to the dates. The penultimate date was January 1964 and was signed by the Chief of Registry prior to stamping it 'Terminated Agent'. The only other one was in September of 1964, followed by a signature and title.

Dempsey turned and did the same with the WI/ROGUE file. Once again, there was the January 1964 date, the Chief of Registry and the 'Terminated Agent' stamp. The final one on the list was the same date as the other agent; September 1964 and the same signature and title.

"What is it? *Who* is it?" asked Wellings.

Dempsey turned and stared. "Oh shit... it's the Assistant Director of Plans. It's Richard Higgins!"

Chapter Five

The investigation quickly gathered pace and if it was to go any further, Dempsey and Wellings would need access to the holiest of holies – officer's files direct from the personnel department of the Admin Division.

Filching and examining agent files was all very well, but for CIA officers to have access to their colleagues' personnel sleeves required the direct authorization from the DCI himself. After much wrangling and a few veiled threats by mentioning the DCI's office, the Director of Admin finally capitulated on the clear understanding that any files would have to be viewed in a secure room under the control of the Admin offices.

Wellings took on the role of assessing their new target's personnel file and armed with a notepad and pen he sat and began to dissect the file relating to one of the most senior men at the CIA.

"Find something out of the ordinary. I know that's not going to be easy, given Higgins' prolific role in having an overview of the Directorate of Plans operations. Trust your gut instinct, look for something askew, something that started out as one thing, but turned into something else completely," said Dempsey.

Higgins' file seemed to be that of the archetypal CIA man during the 1960's. Private money, OSS background during the war, moved over to the Office of Policy Co-ordination with Frank Wisner before it changed its name to CIA.

His career had been on a steady trajectory upwards in various locations around the world, before he'd made his place in the Plans Directorate. In his fifties now, he was riding high as the second in command of the operations arm of the CIA.

As the Assistant to the Director of Plans, his range was far and wide. He could intervene in an operation, had authority to alter or change a mission, and his seniority dictated that he was listened to. Wellings spent the next hour searching through his file, searching for that one lead. He noted several possibilities down, but then later discounted them as being average and not 'askew' or 'out of the ordinary' as Dempsey had stated.

By the end of the second hour, there were still three notations left on his pad. The first was in relation to a blackmail operation against a Bolivian diplomat; the man had been kidnapped by his own people and had simply disappeared off the face of the earth. *No*, thought Wellings. It was too vague and way off from any European-related operations that this case was a part of. He scrubbed it out with his pencil.

That left the final two. One was to do with a shooting in Poland several years ago, in which a network had been blown and a CIA case officer had been killed. Wellings vaguely remembered the talk around the office about it, but as Polish operations were light years away from the fighting down in Cuba, it had, to him, been nothing more than coffee break talk. It seems that Higgins had decided to open up an investigation into the killing and given himself the role of lead investigator in the case. Unusual for the ADP to get directly involved in such an investigation.

The other was in relation to a possible Russian Intelligence defector who had decided he wanted to come over to the West and live the good life. Higgins had seemingly become embroiled in the case and decided to overrule the defector team which had travelled to see if the man had any 'bones' to validate his claims. The defector team said he was an A Grade source, Higgins argued that after meeting him, he'd judged him to be an agent of disinformation and so on the ADP's orders, the case had been dropped. The Russian had later been found dead. *Well, that was interesting,* Wellings thought, - *decides to come over to us one day, then six feet under the next.*

Wellings circled the two notations on his pad and drew a straight line from one to the other. A connection; maybe? But what it was, he had no idea. Yet. He would need to dig deeper into the files again and look at a murder in Warsaw Zoo and the tragic life of a Russian Intelligence defector by the name of Anatoli Galerkin.

* * *

"Galerkin was one of the shrewdest operators who approached us in the Helsinki Station. When he got in touch, he definitely had his capitalist businessman's head on."

Troy Dempsey was drinking excellent coffee in the sixth floor offices of Renner & Stone Law of Chicago. His host was Joe Stanhope, junior partner and former CIA intelligence officer.

"Oh, don't get me wrong, he was a pain in the ass to deal with on a day-by-day basis. He was very high maintenance and if he'd lived, I could have imagined the debriefing team stateside getting a bit rough with him," continued Stanhope. "But the stuff that he was going to bring us was going to be top drawer, or so he insinuated."

"Top drawer how?" asked Dempsey.

Stanhope lifted his feet down from his desk, where he'd been laconically relaxing. He was young and smartly dressed; his only concession to a relaxed look was removing his jacket in his office. Stanhope, after a successful five years with the Agency, had decided to return to his first love, being a lawyer. The offers, the prospects and the money were just too good to ignore, especially after the way he and his colleagues working on the Galerkin case had been treated.

"Oh, we had snippets of the rundown of the local KGB Stations in the geographical area, which was nice, some material relating to the intentions of the Politburo towards the Scandinavian countries. Good stuff, just enough to whet the appetite and establish Galerkin's bona fides. Then of course, there was the shooting in Poland. You know about that, of course you do, otherwise you wouldn't be here. That's when Higgins got involved."

Dempsey smiled a 'gosh-shucks' kind of grin, as if he'd been found out. "Can I just ask, Joe, prior to the ADP being involved, how was the Galerkin case going?"

Stanhope nodded. "Just fine, perfect in fact. We were doing everything right running our agent and Galerkin was doing everything right in getting the best deal for himself that he could. Then he started getting the shivers and the nerves kicked in. He claimed people were watching him, his own people, and they were ready to grab him."

"And were they?"

"Who knows? Nobody knows for sure, but we hadn't seen anything of the kind. That's when the talk at our meetings turned from Galerkin being an agent in place, to wanting to defect overnight."

"So what did you do?"

"We stalled him, like we do with all defectors. Buy some time and give him the usual excuses; it will take some time, red tape, legal considerations. Anything to keep him hanging on in there for a while longer."

Dempsey had done similar with his own agents in the past, part bullying and part coercing them to remain active rather than wanting to jump ship because they'd gotten a little spooked.

"Then he started to take the information he claimed to have to another level. Big stuff, he said. That's when he began to talk about his knowledge of the shooting in Poland, plus one or two other pieces of intelligence that he thought would tempt us. We cabled Langley and asked for guidance." Stanhope told the rest at a staccato rapid fire pace. A cable back from Langley, someone from the Plans Directorate had an interest in the case, partly the shooting in Poland investigation and partly to see if Galerkin was worth taking seriously.

"The whole team was cock-a-hoop. Helsinki isn't exactly at the sharp end and yet we'd managed to get ourselves a genuine KGB defector who wanted to come over to us and who had a stash of hard information that he was going to bring out. Roll out the gravy train, or so we thought."

"Then what happened?" asked Dempsey. Wellings had already briefed him on what was in the files before he had stepped onto the flight to Chicago, but he wanted it direct from the former case officer's mouth.

Stanhope frowned. "What happened was that we gave Higgins one session with our guy, and the next thing we know, he's pulled the plug on the operation. We got a cable back from Higgins at Langley, saying that our guy was a fraud and we were to drop him like yesterday. We were pissed at that. So, Grimes, the Chief of Station, gets on the war drums and sends back a terse reply."

"Obviously it didn't work."

"No. Grimes was just letting off steam, we all were, but he was pro enough to know not to screw with headquarters once they'd issued a directive. Langley told us to watch our mouths and toe the party line. So we did what any team of CIA spies do when the going gets tough. We went out and got drunk. We all had a hell of a hangover the next day."

Dempsey smiled. He liked Stanhope, would have probably enjoyed working with him.

"It was a moot point, anyway. We'd been warned off by Higgins or the DCI or Langley as a whole and then we got the news."

"What news?" said Dempsey, although he imagined he knew what the other man meant.

"Galerkin had been found dead. Murdered in the same hotel room where we'd had our last meeting. FUBAR," said Stanhope grimly.

Dempsey stood and looked out at the mid-afternoon sun bathing the streets of Chicago. "Fucked Up Beyond All Recognition, indeed."

"After that, well, there really wasn't much to do. All the intel that Galerkin had passed to us was pretty much ditched. The analysis back from Langley was that it had all been fraudulent or scraps anyway, so no big deal. The fact that Galerkin had been killed just added more weight to the argument that he was probably a bit of a flake and un-reliable. We always assumed the KGB thugs had gotten him."

"Did you take it any further with Langley, about Galerkin being the real deal?" said Dempsey.

"I tried several times, but my messages were either ignored or just brushed aside as me being resentful. Finally, I got a warning from Higgins to stop. It was the usual series of veiled threats; bad for business, bad for my promotion, bad for Agency morale, so just shut up, Stanhope!"

"Maybe he was right. Maybe Galerkin was a bad egg." Dempsey let the thought hang in the air for a second or two before continuing. "Unless you have something else that could back up your hypothesis."

Stanhope twirled his office chair around and glared at Dempsey. "Can I just tell you something, Troy? I used to love the Agency. The people, the operations, the challenges. I felt at home there. I would have taken a bullet for any of the guys I worked with." He stood and walked across to Dempsey, so they were face-to-face. "But what I can't stand, is the fact that in those last few months, I spent more time fighting my own senior officers than I did the Russians. That kind of sticks in my throat."

Dempsey understood perfectly. "So I'll ask again, Joe. Is there anything else, or is this all just sour grapes on your part?"

Stanhope shook his head. Dempsey thought this was the way he would behave when he was giving a closing speech in court. "I don't work for the Agency anymore, Troy. I'm out and all the better for it. The most I have to deal with in the back-stabbing business is having the senior partners not invite me to all the client parties and functions, but that's nothing compared to having a bunch of CIA stiffs try and screw me over. Especially when I know that something doesn't add up. Besides, if I do give you what I think… sorry, know… then I don't want the strong arm of the CIA weighing down on me."

"Look, if you're concerned about your name being linked to this, or some senior people in the Directorate of Plans giving you a hard time, then don't. I have the ear of the DCI; this comes all the way from the top," said Dempsey reasonably.

Stanhope took in Dempsey's face for a moment longer, trying to read him. "Alright, here's what we'll do. As they say in the legal business, let's retire to my private chambers. Then we can talk."

* * *

Stanhope's private chamber was actually the roof of the building. *Clever,* thought Dempsey. *Hard to carry out surveillance on, nobody around and nobody to overhear them.*

He had barely made it to the top of the access stairs leading onto the roof when he felt the forceful push from behind. The blast sent him sprawling onto the gravel of the flat roof, and then he was yanked backwards so that he was facing the sky and felt the needle sharp tip of a knife pressed against the side of his throat. He froze; keeping his hands where Stanhope could see them, because the last thing he wanted was to have the former CIA man slit his throat through a misunderstanding.

"Don't move, Troy, keep still. It's not personal. I just need to be sure. Are you wearing a wire?" said Stanhope as he ran his hands over Dempsey's waist, up his chest and down the crease of his back.

"Don't be an asshole, Joe, of course not."

But Stanhope continued on with the search until he was satisfied that Dempsey wasn't hooked up. "Okay, you're clean, you can stand up," he said, slowly backing up and keeping the blade out front of him... just in case. "Now Troy, you're going to want to kick my ass, but let's not do this, okay. Friends?"

Dempsey stood up, dusted off his jacket and straightened his tie. He took a deep breath and looked over at Stanhope. Probably in his position he'd have done much the same thing. Better to be safe than sorry. "Where the fuck did you get a prison shiv from anyway, Joe? You're a member of the legal profession."

Stanhope tucked the blade back into his shoe where it had been concealed and smiled. "Hey, this is Chicago. Capone may be long gone, but it's still a rough place, even more so for lawyers. It pays to have a little bit of an equalizer handy from time to time."

Dempsey flung out his hands in exasperation and stared around at the Chicago skyline. "Well lookee here, I'm not wired and no one else knows that we're up here and I have authority from the top man at CIA himself. So can you please stop dicking around and tell me what you know?"

Stanhope nodded and motioned to the wall of a heating vent. Sit down, he seemed to be saying. Both men sat and watched as the late afternoon sun gave the city buildings a honey colored hue.

"It was the night following the meeting between Higgins and Galerkin. As I mentioned, the team were on a high. Galerkin was doing his stuff and all we needed was for Higgins to give us the green light and the cogs of the CIA would have kicked in to secure our defector in place operation. Grimes phoned Higgins' hotel and asked to speak to him. Nothing official, just to invite him for a drink that evening before he flew out the next day. We got no answer, so I decided to call around to the hotel and pick him up. You know how these things work; you get a boss in town from headquarters and you're expected to wine and dine him and show him a good time. Plus, the rest of the station was in a celebrating mood, so we thought why not."

Dempsey nodded. It seemed reasonable, but he still wasn't sure where Stanhope's story was going.

"Higgins was staying at a nice hotel over on Pohjoisesplanadi. I had his room number, so I made my way up and knocked on the door. No answer."

"Maybe he was asleep. Jet lag?" suggested Dempsey.

"That's what I thought, so I let myself in," said Stanhope, not a bit sheepishly. "I used my regulation lock-picks. I always had the knack with them."

"And?"

"Nothing. He wasn't there. Clothes, suitcase, bag; everything else was still in place, but no Higgins."

"Maybe he'd had the same idea as you and hit the bars?"

"That's what I thought... maybe. It's just that Higgins didn't seem the type. He's too much of a square, plus he didn't know the area. I went back down to reception and asked if Mr. Higgins in room 708 had left that evening. The night porter said that no one had passed him and he'd been on duty since late afternoon. Wherever Higgins was, he'd snuck out and hadn't handed his key in to reception."

"Maybe he'd decided to meet up with a woman," said Dempsey. Stanhope scowled. "Don't make me laugh. Something wasn't right. I was more worried that a senior CIA officer had gotten into some kind of trouble than anything else. I sat across from the hotel in the car until just after one in the morning. It was freezing and just as I was about to call it a night and raise the alarm at the Embassy that our visitor had gone missing, who should turn up, walking down the street, but Higgins, carrying an attaché case."

"Well, he'd obviously been somewhere. Perhaps someone else at the Embassy had hosted him?"

"That's what I thought at the time. The next day, I was due to pick him up and drive him to the airport. I mentioned that we'd tried to call him the previous night to invite him out for a meal with the station officers. He shrugged it aside."

"Where had he been?"

"Well now, that's the thing. He said he hadn't been anywhere. He reckoned he'd had a light supper and then turned in for an early night. Said he hadn't left the hotel at all," said Stanhope.

"Which is evidently not true, as confirmed by your brief spell of breaking and entering," said Dempsey.

"Exactly. A top CIA officer sneaks out from under the nose of a local station, disappears for several hours, turns up in the middle of the night carrying a briefcase and then says that he'd spent the night tucked up in bed. FUBAR!"

Dempsey considered Stanhope's version. "Okay, so he got up to something, but it's hardly a criminal offence."

Stanhope laughed. "Troy I would have agreed with you totally, if it hadn't been for the next forty-eight hours' worth of events, when we got our operation cancelled by the same man and then our agent turns up dead. Higgins was the last CIA man to see him alive."

Dempsey looked incredulous. "You're saying there's a connection. That's pretty wild, Joe. You're a man of the law, where's the proof of any of that?"

Stanhope shook his head, resigned to the fact that his theory would only ever be a theory. "That's the problem. Theories I have, actual proof I have none. But my guess is, that's why you're here. Something's happened back at Langley, something serious enough to have the Director send you in undercover and poking around. I don't know what that thing is, and I guess you're not going to give me the inside information about whatever it is you're investigating, but you've got to admit that what happened in Helsinki over those few days is certainly intriguing."

The sudden realization hit Dempsey like a shot from a heavyweight boxer. Higgins had deep sixed the proposed defection operation of Anatoli Galerkin.

His final report had claimed the KGB man was obviously a plant and untrustworthy, this despite the vehement protestations of the CIA case officers who had dealt with the man. That and the fact that the Russian showed up dead. Could it have just been coincidence, or was it something more? Was it murder? Had he been eliminated in order to keep him silenced?

Why would anyone, let alone a senior CIA officer, want to silence a potential defector in place from a rival service? Obvious really – the man was set to expose someone.

Was Higgins a traitor? A deep cover KGB spy? *But no, that didn't sit right*, thought Dempsey. If this was a run-of-the-mill double agent inside CIA type operation, then maybe. But this was something else, something new, a hybrid operation. If it wasn't to protect a source, then the only other reason could be that the man had useful intelligence he wanted to trade, intelligence that someone else wanted to get to first. Get to, and perhaps keep.

It was all mixed up in his head, he needed time to let it settle and then analyze it calmly. He turned his attention back to Stanhope, who was standing looking out at the traffic moving down below.

"So what did you do next?"

Stanhope shrugged. "Just what I told you. We fought against the decision about Galerkin for a while and demanded that the Directorate of Plans conduct a thorough investigation into how the operation was cancelled. But of course, by that time it was all over. Galerkin was dead and we were told to button it. I pushed for a few more weeks, but no one wanted to listen. Eventually I was getting lots of reprimands from Langley that weren't doing me any favors."

Stanhope spat onto the gravel roof in disgust. "By that time, I'd had enough, handed in my resignation, and worked my required time out. Two months later, I moved back here to join the family law firm. As for Galerkin, he was as tough as old shoe leather and all business. I'm not sure he did guilt as an emotion. He just wanted to get his wife and unborn child to the West."

Dempsey nodded in sympathy.

Stanhope looked at him. "The next thing to ask, would be what was Higgins doing in the unaccounted for hours of that night? Where had he been, who had he been meeting, and most importantly of all what was in that attaché case that he had clutched to his chest?"

Chapter Six

"So you came all this way to see me. I'm honored."

They were sitting in one of the standard Arc Deco hotels that ran along the front of Miami Beach. It was all pink and blue pastels. The bar was mostly empty, except for a few Cubans and their women. Evening dinner time was over and now the night animals had come out to play.

"Cut the crap, Paul, I'm here because I have to be, not because I want to be," said Dempsey. He was nursing some kind of cocktail that he had no intention of drinking. The thing looked like a garden in a glass with a multi-colored straw sticking out of it.

"Fair enough. So to what do I owe the pleasure, seeing as you're not actually a client," said the tall, blond haired man in the snappy business suit. Paul was Paul Koening; former CIA officer who had worked with the anti-Castroists before, during, and after the fuck up that was the Bay of Pigs. He'd been kicked out of the Agency in the shake-up following Kennedy's assassination. Rather than up sticks and head back to Washington, Koening had decided to set up shop as a Miami-based private investigator.

It evidently paid well, thought Dempsey, judging by the way Koening was flashing his cash. "You see many of the old team?" asked Dempsey. "Bump into anyone on a regular basis?"

Koening waved a vague hand. "Jeez, Troy, you throw a stick around here and you're practically guaranteed to hit someone who's visited

Langley. Miami's crawling with spooks. And as for the Cubans, it's like Havana down here. Do you know the Diaz brothers?"

Dempsey shook his head.

"Well," continued Koening, "they were part of the original hit-teams we trained up to take care of Raul Castro. Good operators, tough guys. They seem to have tired of being political and have gone into the murder for hire business. Drugs guys, mafia guys, anyone really. There's a lot of talent down here that we trained Troy. Not all of it is good."

Dempsey downed his drink in one. It was sweetly sickening, but with a hell of a kick at the end.

Koening let out a laugh. "Man, you've spent too long drinking Tom Collins in DC."

Dempsey pushed the glass to one side and returned to the conversation. "What about guys from DC, Paul? You run into any of those over the past few months, professionally speaking of course?"

For the first time, Koening's clubby persona had evaporated and was replaced by a look of mistrust. He shook his head. "No, no one that I'm aware of, Troy."

Dempsey let the silence linger and then gave Koening a look that said 'I can wait all day for you to join the dots'. He had a list of Higgins' travel details over the past few years. The man had been all over the world on Agency business, including a trip to Miami several months ago. There was nothing unusual in that. Except that when he was meant to be down here on CIA business, he had evidently been meeting with a former CIA officer turned scumbag private eye. The phone records from Higgins' internal line had shown that. Not the details of the conversation, of course, just that the phone line in Miami belonged to Koening.

Koening blinked first. "Okay, what's this about? You make an appointment to see me using an alias, you travel all this way, and when I arrive, I find not some swinging dick whose wife is humping one of our Cuban brothers, but a CIA man I haven't seen for three years. What gives?"

"I'm not hearing a no from you, Paul. Not hearing a yes to be fair, either. All that I'm hearing at the minute is a lot of stalling."

Koening held up his hands in mock surrender. "Hey, you know I can't discuss my clients, confidentiality and all that."

"Richard Higgins. That name ring a bell, Paul?"

"Hey, hey, hey... Don't even ask. Client confidentiality, you must be aware of that, Troy. They still have that in DC. I don't have to answer shit; I don't work for the Agency anymore. I'm freelance."

Dempsey leaned in close, threatening in his manner. "You listen to me, you dumbass. You never leave the Agency, even when you're buried six feet under you're still on the reserve list. You understand? Now Higgins – you've heard from him, yes?"

"You can't make it stick. I'm protected by a senior Agency official. I'm fireproof, Troy, so fuck you... arrrgghh!"

Dempsey had laughed and then jammed a big meaty hand into Koening's crotch. He grabbed, squeezed and most disturbingly, held on in a vice-like grip.

The color drained from Koening's face and he let out a low mewl, his breath coming in rapid pants like he was struggling to breathe underwater. "Now Paul, it might seem like you have the upper hand, but believe me when I say it only seems that way. You say you have the protection of a senior CIA man, well, who am I to doubt you? But you're not thinking straight, Paul, you don't have the whole picture, the big picture."

Dempsey squeezed again, to emphasize his point. He glanced around; no one was paying them any attention.

The Cubans were too busy fondling the asses of their girlfriends to care what two businessmen were up to. "I can beat your pair of aces hands down, especially as I have the DCI himself in my corner. Now you better start being co-operative double quick, or I might have to have the IRS come in and audit your books and check everything is above board, or maybe have the feds snoop around and raid your business premises. Maybe you fancy doing a little jail time, I'm sure we could make that happen. Don't worry about the crime, we can think of something. Of course, that's the official way. Perhaps I could arrange for those guys, the Diaz brothers, to make you disappear permanently."

Dempsey released his grip and watched as the other man sagged forward, relieved that the pain in his groin had disappeared. "I'm just going to the bar to get a real drink and when I get back, and hopefully your balls have stopped killing you, we're going to talk."

* * *

When Dempsey returned several minutes later carrying a bourbon, the color had returned to Koening's face. Dempsey took a sip and turned his gaze towards him.

"How do I know you're not bullshitting me, Troy?"

Dempsey laughed. "Paul, in all the years we've known each other, when have I ever bullshitted you? You know me, straight down the line. What I'm telling you is fact. You want to challenge that and take a risk, then you better start settling your affairs in this world."

"Alright, alright…"

"Now, you were telling me about Richard Higgins and how he initially made contact with you. What was it, a phone call?"

Koening settled himself in his seat, his balls still aching. "No, that would have been normal practice, right. I got a knock on the door of my apartment late on a Saturday night, about eight months ago and who's standing there but the Assistant Director of Plans. Shit, I thought the Agency was going to reinstate me."

"So what did he want, Paul? Obviously you're not back on the books. To come all this way to see you, it must have been important."

"Yeah, well at the minute everybody seems to be travelling across country to see me," said Koening. "He said that he was running an off-the-books op, something that was going to go down in Europe. They needed civilian personnel with no Agency connection. He said it made the op more secure that way."

"And what did you think?"

"I thought it was crap. I mean, since when did the Agency need to search out assets and staff in Europe? They're swimming with guys who will do jobs for them over there. But hey, Higgins was offering two thousand dollars for an introduction and some names. I'd be crazy to turn it down!"

"So what did he want specifically, Paul?"

"He wanted off-the-books people, residents in their own country who could provide a discreet 'surveillance capability' – they're his words, not mine. He wanted the names and contact details of private investigators in several countries. Guys who could do a little digging and poking around, ex-cops, ex-security people, that kind of thing."

"And you have these names?"

Koening nodded. "Sure, I'm part of a network of private investigators. We all swap numbers; you need a guy in Europe or the Middle East or Asia to do a little tracing or find a missing person, one of our guys will fit the bill."

Dempsey pondered on that. "What countries was he specifically looking for?"

"Britain, France, Italy, bits of Germany, Switzerland."

"Did he say why?"

"Nope, he didn't and I didn't ask. My own guess was to track some people, prior to pitching a recruitment offer. But in these crazy times, it could be anything."

It could be some research on some future assets, thought Dempsey. *Or some people, some potential Russian agents with a big red cross on their foreheads. Some targets, some dead targets.*

"So what happens now?" asked Koening, keen to discover his fate at the hands of the big Texan.

"Now you're going to give me the contact details of your PI network in Europe and then you're going to drop those memories of yours into a big black hole and forget that this ever happened. You understand?"

Koening nodded. He knew when to play the game and when to leave. "One thing I learned from working down here, Troy, is that Miami is the place to bury secrets.

* * *

The next morning Troy Dempsey presented himself at the offices of the Melmar Corporation, which had a series of buildings on the campus of the University of Miami.

What Melmar actually did, nobody knew.

It was in fact, the Miami-based CIA station operating under the codename of JM/WAVE and was there to provide a base for the continuing operations against Cuba. For Dempsey, none of that was of interest; he merely wanted a secure telephone and telex line so that he could pass back the information from Koening to Langley. He introduced himself to the Station's Comptroller and told him what he wanted. The office was small and quiet. Dempsey picked up a desk phone and punched in the number to Wellings' secure line at Langley.

"How's Miami?" asked Wellings.

"Swampy. Listen up, I got another piece of the jigsaw. I'm going to telex it through to the communications center, should be in about thirty minutes once I've figured out how this machine works."

"Okay. I'll put in an immediate access request for when it arrives."

"How about you? Anything turned up?"

Wellings sighed. "Nothing. I've spent the past few days searching through dozens and dozens of files that might turn something up. But as I'm not sure what I'm actually supposed to be looking for it's turning into a needle in a haystack situation."

Dempsey sympathized. "We always knew it was going to be the fine details that would break this investigation open."

"It doesn't help that Higgins' remit is to be a professional nosy-parker in other people's operations. I mean, that's what he's employed to do by the Director of Plans. Potentially, he could have accessed thousands of operations, everything from agent running, to technical, to defections. The list is endless."

"Keep at it. He's not in it alone, there has to be a partner, maybe even two or three. That's what we want now, the next man along. The best advice I can give you until I return is to try to put yourself in the operational commander's shoes. How would you set this type of operation up; what would you need? Remember, they have access to pretty much all of the Agency's logistical contacts. How would *you* put in the plumbing?" said Dempsey.

They had the theory that Higgins was up to no good; something involving the death of a defector, an investigation into a shooting in Poland and a fictitious operation across Europe. Separately, they didn't add up to much. What they needed were the finer details about where it was going to lead them and bring all the threads together.

Chapter Seven

"I think we've found something," said Wellings, recently returned from the Archives Section at Langley.

It was three days after Dempsey had returned from Miami and things were beginning to look bleak. He had the feeling that they were going around in circles. They needed a lucky break... and fast. "Okay, shoot – what you got for me?"

"How does an operation that never happened grab you? Operation KINO; a joint CIA and South Korean intelligence op from eight years ago. Its plan was to help infiltrate and then run a covert network in the North. According to what we have, it would have been run as a sabotage and insurrection task force in case the North decided to overrun the South."

"Never heard of it," shrugged Dempsey. "What happened to it?"

"Nothing, it never happened, that's what. The file says that it was an unacceptable risk and the project was killed dead before it went operational."

Nothing new there then. If Dempsey had a buck for every time a feasible op had been spiked by the brass, he would be living the high life in the Bahamas.

Wellings continued. "Except this time all the operational planning was already in place. They had a field commander, assets in place, resources, you name it. Hell, the agents were virtually in the plane and ready to be parachuted in when it was cancelled. But that's not the most interesting point, not by a long shot. You want to know the name– sorry, the cover name, of the field controller involved in running it?"

Dempsey sat up straighter in his chair; suddenly the temperature in the room had risen by an alarming degree.

Wellings let him hang for a moment more. "The Field Commander's name was one Maurice Knight. Canadian businessman cover. Aged fifty and resident of Ontario."

"Holy shit! You found him," said Dempsey, punching the air and nearly spilling out of his chair.

Wellings was smiling. "It wasn't easy. Korean ops come under the Near East/South Asia Division, but for some reason, reasons I can now guess, the shelved op reports were hidden away in Void Liaison Operations."

"So someone was trying to conceal a weak spot," said Dempsey. While it wouldn't have been possible to totally destroy all evidence of an authenticated file, it certainly would have been possible to conceal it somewhere else. Somewhere where no one would think to look. Void Liaison Operations was the black hole of the CIA's filing system; the place where aborted operations went to decompose. "What made you look in those files? It was a one in a million chance surely?"

"It was simply a process of elimination. We'd looked everywhere else, and that was one of the few places left to cover. So you want to see who Mr. Maurice Knight was in real life?" said Wellings. He lifted up the file and presented it to Dempsey with all the flourish of a stage magician.

Dempsey pressed the file down with the flat of his palms and peered closely at the typewritten report. He scanned it and then breathed out a long slow breath. A moment of clarity hit him. All this time he was wrong! Higgins wasn't the prime operator, Higgins was the inside man, the feeder of information and the fixer of resources. He used CIA assets and logistics to further an illegal operation – an assassination operation – for his principal 'Mr. Maurice Knight'.

And Maurice Knight, according to the slip of paper that lay before him now, was the one time work name of former CIA officer Charles 'Chuck' Ferrera.

* * *

They were walking up the hill track, the stones and mud squelching beneath their feet. *Not a bad day for a hike in the Vermont countryside,* thought Dempsey. Crisp and clear. The kind of day he'd have enjoyed taking the dog for a half day walk on his vacation time.

"It's about a mile up ahead. The track rises steadily," said Ralph Barr, Dempsey's guide, companion for the day and his latest informant in the search for the elusive Maurice Knight.

"Not a problem." Dempsey had worn his old jungle boots, from his time in CBI. They were comfortable and asked nothing from him. In the jungles of Asia, he'd climbed and fought in all manner of hills and mountains, so a medium-sized hill in Vermont wasn't going to be too much of a challenge.

"So you've been picked to re-examine the murder of one of my old case officers. Jeez, I thought that investigation had been shelved years ago. Didn't someone already look at that and decide there wasn't enough information to carry on with it?" asked Barr.

Dempsey looked over at Barr. He was like a tough gnome; rambunctious, no nonsense and settled in his retirement. Despite all that, Dempsey knew he had a good reputation at the CIA for being one of the ablest desk officers in the Soviet Satellites Division. "Oh, you know the way it is. New DCI comes in and wants to straighten the whole place out on his first watch. Soldiers, like you and me, we just do as we're told."

Barr grunted. "I suppose you've read up on the background to Black Orchestra?"

Dempsey nodded. He'd spent the past few days poring over everything in the files relating to the long term intelligence network that the CIA had worked so hard to maintain. He thought he had the gist of how it was run, what it had achieved and the theories of why it was blown. What he didn't have, was the information that never makes it into the files; the small details, the nuances and the hidden secrets.

"Then you know that as the network's Division Desk Officer, I had inherited a damned fine unit," said Barr. "Great people, first class agents in Poland, superb support staff. I'd been attached to it when I first joined the Agency way back when, so after touring around behind the Iron Curtain I was thrilled when I was given command of Black Orchestra."

They crunched along the path, Dempsey keeping a good pace, and Barr wheezing beside him. Barr caught his breath and continued. "The network had begun in 1946 with a bunch of former Nazi's and their informants. We'd turned them around and made them an offer; work for us or head for Nuremburg. Not surprisingly, they didn't fancy the thought of swinging from a rope. Over the next few years, the original agents made their way in the Polish government and ended up acting as informal spotters and recruiters. Consequently, we were able to recruit a whole new stable of agents. Within the space of a year or two, Black Orchestra had grown from a mom and pop operation to the equivalent of a multi-national. We had agents inside the local parliaments, the military forces, even some in the intelligence services. It was a good network, we ran it well and the team was committed."

"And then it all went wrong. Why?" asked Dempsey.

Barr shrugged. "Well, that's the million-dollar question in cases like these, isn't it? Who fucked up? Was it a deeper KGB conspiracy or had we been played all along? My gut tells me that it was something simple. No great conspiracy, no convoluted counter-espionage operation aimed against us. No, someone didn't follow something simple like security or counter-surveillance protocols and the whole network suffered because someone hadn't marked a lamppost or checked his back. After that, you catch one agent, stick him in the interrogation cells and he starts to talk, then you catch another two, three, until eventually some lucky Polish counter-intelligence officer has suddenly got himself a whole Western spy network in the bag."

They reached a fork in the path and headed to the right, rising further upwards. In the distance, Dempsey could see the sun glinting off the icy peaks of a mountain. It was beautiful.

"And the shooting in Warsaw Zoo, where did that fit into the whole thing?" asked Dempsey.

Barr frowned at that. "That's the most infuriating thing, Troy. By our calculations, the majority of Black Orchestra had been rolled up by then. The agents had gone silent and we were left pretty much blind. My guess is that the KGB wanted a real live Western intelligence officer to parade in front of the world. The people running the roll up of the network wanted to have their cake and eat it, all at the same time. Unfortunately for us, Dan paid the ultimate price."

Dempsey picked up on the bitterness and sadness in Barr's voice. *Better to turn it around,* he thought, and bring the story onto the principal characters. "What was he like?"

"Who, Dan? Oh, Daniel was a great guy. Everybody loved him. Charming, courteous, good at his job, you couldn't not like him. When we heard that the network had been rolled up and Dan had been killed, well, it just took the wind out of me. I was angry at first, then bitter and finally the sadness took over. I cried. I don't mind admitting that. No one deserves to be shot down like an animal and then have his body incinerated."

"Were there any clues as to who was behind the shooting?"

Barr shook his head. "Not much. It was a Polish security service operation to take down our network, but who the shooter was, we never knew. There were rumors of it being overseen by the KGB, but again, there was no concrete proof."

They had reached the top of the hilly track and came to a gate with a 'Private Road' sign on it. Dempsey thought that the private road led into an enclave of trees. They were nearing their destination.

"Ah, here we are," said Barr, as he unhooked the gate and escorted Dempsey through. They carried on walking through the shade of the evergreens.

"What about Dan's father, Charles – how did he take it?" asked Dempsey.

Barr grimaced, as if he'd experienced a taste of something bitter. "Do you know Chuck Ferrera?" he asked.

Dempsey shook his head. "Only by reputation, I never met the man."

"Let me tell you, Chuck Ferrera was one of the best officers the CIA ever had. We both served in the OSS and then transferred over to the Agency after the war. Chuck was one hard son-of-a-bitch when the mood took him; definitely old school OSS. I had a meeting with him following the destruction of Black Orchestra. As the senior officer responsible for the operation, he had every right to talk to me and find out what had happened, didn't he? It's about a ten minute walk up that way," said Barr, indicating a track over to his left.

"What did you tell him?"

"Not much, there wasn't a lot of info coming in at that time. Remember, it was only a matter of days after the shooting. Chuck walked into my office and sat down, Christ; I didn't even recognize him at first. I know the death of Daniel must have come as a shock, but he looked like a man ready for the grave himself. I talked to him, told him what we knew, but I'm not sure he was taking any of it in. You see, Dan was Chuck's world, he loved that boy like a father is *meant* to love a son; utterly and completely. But I think it was a bit more than that also."

"How do you mean?"

"You see, Chuck brought Dan into the Agency. I won't say he pulled a few strings, because he didn't need to, Dan would have made it on his own under any circumstances. But I know that Chuck certainly pushed CIA and Dan Ferrera together. I'm guessing that the feeling of guilt was the thing that was eating Chuck. The next time I saw him was at the memorial for Dan at Langley. It was a nice service, obviously Chuck couldn't have a funeral because there wasn't a body, but we did the best we could for him. Everyone said nice things and the Director handed Chuck Dan's Intelligence Star. I think Chuck just wanted to get through the day. After that, I lost track of him for a while. Compassionate leave for a few months, I heard."

"Did Chuck have family around him at this time?"

"I'm not sure, there was certainly no one close that I was aware of; distant cousins, perhaps. The person who Chuck relied on most was Dick Higgins. He was always close to hand."

A shiver went down Dempsey's spine. *Don't react,* he told himself. *Don't let the outer shell crack.* "Why Higgins? Were they close?"

Barr looked at him as though he was a dumb hick. "Why sure, they were family through marriage. Chuck Ferrera married Dick Higgins sister, Theresa. They'd known each other for years, been in the OSS together before moving over to CIA. Dick Higgins was Daniel Ferrera's godfather."

Dempsey analyzed the information quickly. Higgins was close to Chuck Ferrera, was godfather to Daniel Ferrera. If that wasn't motivation enough, then what was? Troy Dempsey had found what the old hand detectives would call an investigative chain of evidence.

"Of course, the problems for Chuck didn't go away. In fact, as soon as he returned to work, it just got worse. The drinking, not showing up for meetings, his appearance. Eventually, he got moved out of operations and shoved somewhere deep and dark where he wouldn't make a nuisance of himself; finance or something I heard," said Barr.

The path had cleared and the mass of the forest was starting to thin out. Dempsey could see what looked like the start of a man-made gravel path up ahead, the type which would lead the walker up to the front porch of a lodge.

Barr dug in his walking stick and lifted his body forward. "The booze was the main problem for Chuck, can't blame him, especially after what he'd been through. But I think the straw that broke the camel's back was when he started petitioning the DCI for permission to implement his wacko scheme to send a covert action snatch team into Europe."

"What?" Dempsey said, surprised by this information. *Well, that was new.*

"Yeah, don't tell me you haven't heard any of this before. It was all around Langley, Chuck had become a bit of a joke at CIA," said Barr.

"I've been pretty much away from Langley for the past few years, so the inside gossip has passed me by. Until I was appointed to this case, I very rarely got back to headquarters."

"That's okay," said Barr. "I'll tell you what I know, as long as it helps with your investigation. Don't want Langley to think I've been telling tales out of school."

Dempsey had looked through the files containing Charles Ferrera, the shooting in Warsaw and the Black Orchestra network and none of them gave any hint of Ferrera's actions. The drinking and his shabby appearance sure, even his bust up with the Director, but of planning a covert op; nothing.

"He kept trying to get into the Director's office with this plan of his. I think the DCI humored him for a while, and then quickly grew tired. He wanted CIA to drop in a special unit with the express aim of identifying and snatching numerous Russian agents in Europe before whisking them off to a secure location, one of the forts that we use in Malta for prepping special operations, and submitting them to interrogation," said Barr.

"You've got to be kidding. That's a crazy idea!"

Barr nodded, he'd said much the same himself. "Of course it is, and CIA would never run anything so plain ass dumb in a million years. It was too much to lose and not enough to gain. But you've got to remember, we were dealing with a grief-stricken man at the end of his tether. That and copious amounts of booze don't exactly make a good combination for clear and practical thinking."

"So how did it resolve itself? Did he get fired?"

"No. At least, not straight away and not in the way you're thinking. Chuck began to start yelling louder and louder about his 'special operation' and in the end, someone on the senior staff had to pull him in and give him some straight talking."

"Let me guess; Higgins," said Dempsey.

"That's what I heard. Higgins gave him a good talking to and several days later, Chuck Ferrera formally resigned from the Agency. I think there was a collective sigh of relief when it happened, for everyone's sake. He never showed up for his leaving party and meeting with the DCI. Probably for the best in the long run."

"What happened to him after he left the Agency?"

"This happened," said Barr, pointing to the rise of the hillock. What stood before them was the long since burnt remains of a typical Vermont family hunting lodge. In its time, it must have been quite a building, capable of sustaining several people over the course of a season. Dempsey thought it must have been beautiful in this location in the mountains. The two men stood among the ruins of the wooden building. Dempsey flicked the charred remains with the toe of his walking boot.

"I got a phone call from him, several months later. He said he'd pretty much sold up and moved to Vermont and was living here. Would I like to come up and visit for the weekend, do a bit of shooting and fishing? So that's exactly what I did," said Barr.

"How was he?"

"Better, much better in fact. He still had his demons, you could see that, but he was better than before. The isolation, the environment, the lack of whisky had obviously done wonders."

"How long had he been up here?"

"Oh, months. I'd come up and visit him every now and again; play some chess, do some hiking. In truth, I fell in love with the place. So much so that when I retired from the Agency last year, I bought a place a couple of miles down the road; Karen and I get up here whenever we can."

"So what happened here?" asked Dempsey, pointing at the remains of the lodge.

Barr turned around, inspecting the scene. "That's partly why I asked you up here. Don't get me wrong, I was glad to receive your call and I'm happy to help with your investigation, especially as it comes straight from the Director. But I wanted to see if you could help me."

Dempsey looked confused. "I don't understand Ralph. What happened?"

Barr sighed. "I came up here about a month before I retired. I hadn't heard from Chuck in a wee while and just decided on the spur of the moment to make a visit. It's a pain in the ass to get up here, but I was worried. When I arrived, I found this. The place had been deliberately torched and by all accounts, had gone up like an inferno."

"But no one inside?"

"No, sir, no bodies inside at the time. The local fire investigator said that a propellant had been used extensively inside. That's his way of saying that someone doused the place with petrol and then set it alight."

"And Ferrera?"

"Gone. Missing. No word, no letters, no contact numbers; a big fat zero. Everything from his life had been... disconnected."

Dempsey tried another tack. "What about Higgins, did you try him? Especially as you say that they were friends, family. Maybe he knows?"

"I tried Higgins, but he knew nothing. He said he'd been busy, hadn't seen Chuck in a while. I got the impression they weren't on speaking terms anymore."

Dempsey walked around the carcass of the property. An old kettle lay on its side, blackened by the heat, a chess piece had somehow survived and was hidden away among the broken wood. A clock, a picture frame, a metal chair leg...

Where had Chuck Ferrera gone and why? Wherever he was, he certainly wasn't dead if the theory of Mr. Knight's identity carried any weight. Ferrera had obviously made a pact with the Devil and decided literally to burn the bridge back to his old life.

"Is there anything else you want to see? It'll be getting dark soon," said Barr, looking at the sky.

Dempsey shook his head. "No thanks, Ralph, I think I've seen enough. You've been very helpful. I think it's time we made it back to the cars." Back to the cars and then back to Langley. Dempsey had a report to write.

* * *

It had taken Dempsey a week to compile his final report which would be shown to the DCI and when it was ready, and both he and Wellings were satisfied that they'd covered all the angles, Dempsey put in a call to the Director's office.

That very afternoon, Dempsey sat in front of the DCI as he read through the report. The only other person present was the Deputy Director of Central Intelligence, Royston Webster, the DCI's hatchet man. Taking his time, turning the pages carefully, occasionally turning back to remind himself of a passage in the eight-page report, the DCI began to devour the information. But it was the conclusion that the Director wanted to make himself conversant with.

OPERATION: TALLON
Subject - Internal Investigation;
Date - May 1965
CONCLUSION:
I BELIEVE THAT THE ILLEGAL ACTIONS OF TWO INTELLIGENCE OFFICERS FROM THIS AGENCY, AS WELL AS THEIR FRAUDULENT USE OF AGENCY LO-GISTICS AND RESOURCES, WAS CONDUCTED TO CARRY OUT AN ASSASSINATION OPERATION TO TARGET SOVIET INTELLIGENCE ASSETS THROUGH-OUT EUROPE. AS FAR AS WE KNOW, SEVERAL PEOPLE HAVE ALREADY BEEN MURDERED. WE HAVE NO REASON TO DOUBT THAT MANY MORE WILL ALSO BE KILLED.
FOLLOWING THE CONNECTION BETWEEN THE TER-MINATED AGENCY ASSETS QJ/WIN AND WI/ROGUE TO RICHARD HIGGINS AND FORMER CIA OFFICER CHARLES FERRERA, I BELIEVE WE HAVE A CLEAR CHAIN OF EVENTS; THE SHOOTING IN POLAND, THE MURDER OF ANATOLI GALERKIN, THE IN-SIDE INFORMATION OF HIGGINS TO THE COVER IDENTITY OF FERRERA AS 'KNIGHT'.

HOWEVER, AS THIS INVESTIGATION WAS ONLY A PRELIMINARY OPERATION, I FEEL THAT A MORE INDEPTH ENQUIRY SHOULD BE CARRIED OUT BY THE RELEVANT BODY WITHIN THE AGENCY, NAMELY INVESTIGATORS FROM THE OFFICE OF SECURITY. TROY DEMPSEY – OFFICER ASSIGNED.

The Director placed the file carefully down onto his desk and stared at it for a moment. "So it was for revenge, revenge for his son. I can quite understand that, even if I can't condone it."

Dempsey sat relaxed in the chair. "If I can just correct you a moment, Mr. Director, I don't think it was *all* done for his son."

The DCI frowned and turned to look directly at Dempsey. "Explain please, Troy."

"I think it started out that way, I mean what father wouldn't want to catch the person who cold bloodedly murdered a loved one. No, I think Chuck Ferrara's thirst for vengeance went much further than that. He set up this fake operation and network to track down the KGB man responsible certainly, something he achieved with ruthless efficiency."

The Director and the DDCI nodded. The CIA trained their operatives well it seemed, even retired ones.

"But," continued Dempsey. "I think it went much further than that. I believe he wanted to set a spark, a spark that would ignite a war between the CIA and the KGB, something that would engulf both agencies and possibly break down the fragile truce of the Cold War."

"But why? I mean revenge for the death of his son, yes, but all-out war… that's madness. Just insane!" said the DCI.

Dempsey nodded. "Probably by the end he was insane, we will never know. But look at it from his perspective. His son was murdered in the line of duty, something that is anathema in our profession; the killing of each other's officers. Added to which the unwillingness and inactivity of the previous DCI to at least try to find out what had happened to Daniel Ferrera on that operation in Poland. But I think the final tipping point was when he was fired from the Agency. It left him with no options, and for a man with little left to live for, that's a dangerous combination."

"And we're definitely sure that this Mr. Knight is Ferrera, are we?" said Webster, seated at his Master's left shoulder.

"As sure as we can be. It all leads back to him. We received a copy of the tape of Mr. Knight speaking in Luxembourg from SIS. We sent it down to Technical Services Division for voice recognition analysis. We had also managed to search out a recording of Chuck Ferrera, giving a lecture at the 'Farm' a few years ago."

"And what was the result?" asked the DCI.

"Ninety percent match on both voices. It was the same person." Dempsey could see that the DCI was deliberating, unsure if this was enough evidence to hang the former CIA man. He decided to force the issue and give his own opinion. "Mr. Director none of this would stand up in a court of law. A good defense lawyer would rip this investigation to shreds. My remit was to follow the seam and see where it led us. Unfortunately, we'll never get to know all the answers about why and what they did."

The DCI seemed satisfied with Dempsey's analysis. "Precisely, the last thing we'll be doing is dragging this to a court of law. It's the culprits that we want and not necessarily a prosecution. I have no desire to preside over our agents' details being dragged out into the public domain."

"So where are they now? Today, at this moment in time?" asked Webster.

"As I understand it, the Office of Security has conducted a preliminary interview with Assistant Director Higgins. They played it low-key, as per your instructions. Questions about his relationship with Chuck Ferrera, Ferrera's current whereabouts, his godson Daniel, the shooting in Poland. Details that don't implicate Higgins directly, but send a clear message that we know he was up to something without going as far as accusing him."

"So give him enough rope to hang himself. A good tactical move. So what has changed?"

Wellings spoke for the first time. "We've had a surveillance team on Higgins; the usual stuff, bugging his home phone and office line, surveillance units following him, and up until recently they had nothing. Then, following the interview with OS Investigators, Higgins was seen to leave Langley and drive into Downtown DC to make a call from a payphone. We traced the number back through the company phone records and found that it was an international call through to Mexico. When he did it again several days later, we were ready for him and the call was able to be recorded."

"Ferrera?" asked the DCI.

Dempsey nodded. "The Hotel San Domingo in Mexico City, room 533 is registered in the name of Maurice Knight. We've had Mexico Station keep a team on the comings and goings. So far, the elusive Mr. Knight hasn't left his room for the past week and probably not before that either."

"He's frightened of being snatched. Wise man," said Webster.

"But he can't stay there indefinitely. He'll have to come out, sooner, rather than later. I think we need to authorize a containment team to bring him back. Roy, can you arrange that with Mexico Station and the Mexican police?" said the DCI.

"Consider it done Mr. Director," and the DDCI pulled himself out of his chair and left the office to issue orders to his subordinates.

The DCI looked over at Dempsey and Wellings. "Gentlemen, you have performed superbly, a credit to the Agency. I think we can afford you some vacation time. How does that sound?"

They both looked at each other. Some vacation time sounded just what they needed – anything that didn't involve searching through files or surveillance logs.

"And after that, we'll look at perhaps a change of role for both of you. Something a bit more in line with what you're trained to do. Operations is a big place, I'm sure we can make use of your talents," said the DCI.

Dempsey smiled politely. He was no fool and knew exactly what the DCI was up to. He was both keeping them out of the loop for the next few weeks and bribing them with promotion. It was a game, and Dempsey was happy to play along with it. Carrot and stick, his old man would have called it, carrot and stick.

Book Six:
Shadow Moves

Chapter One

Charles 'Chuck' Ferrera, better known by his cryptonym of Mr. Maurice Knight, ran a hand through his close-cropped salt and pepper hair to calm himself and sighed.

The Hotel San Domingo was one of the best that Mexico City had to offer and aside from a few other venues scattered around Europe, it had been his main base of operations for the past year. He feared that his time as an honored guest of this fine hotel would soon be at an end.

His operation was slowly starting to unravel. He knew it would happen at some point, for no 'False Flag' operation can hide in the shadows indefinitely, but he'd hoped that with the Russian, Krivitsky dead, the hit-team would be able to concentrate on removing the rest of the target list. But the last time he'd spoken to his agent QJ/WIN, the normally composed Marquez had sounded shattered and stressed.

In fact, he sounded rattled, perhaps even scared.

It had been one of their routine check-in times that fluctuated between his hotel room telephone and the street telephone booths in the locale. Judging by what Marquez had told him, it would be the last time that they would speak. The news was not good. A shoot out in Paris! WI/ROGUE possibly dead! The Catalan killer wounded!

In truth, Ferrera thought the Catalan had done far better than he'd originally envisioned and had taken down more targets than he thought possible. Marquez was a useful action agent and his reputation had preceded him certainly, but his success on this operation was enviable. A true professional, he'd picked his contractor well. It was just a pity that he wouldn't be receiving the balance of his stipend.

That was the beauty of a double cross; they do all the work and expect a big payout at the end, you cut them off at the knees and leave them swinging in the wind.

It was a warm, sticky evening so Ferrara stripped off his clothes and lay naked on top of his bed, enjoying the coolness of the air conditioning. On the bed next to him, was a half-full bottle of Jack Daniels and a fully loaded .38 revolver. He was trying to decide which one he would choose to blow his brains out with. The .38 or the booze? One would make it permanent while the other would be temporary, at least until the hangover had dissipated and then he would have to endure the hell of real life again.

He closed his eyes and relaxed in the luxury that his plan, after months of preparation and scheming, had finally come to fruition. The murderer of his son had gotten his head blown off in Paris by an assassin's bullet, several Soviet agents had also been eliminated from active operations across Europe, causing a major blow to Russian Intelligence, and the CIA was going to be hung out to dry. Good job.

But what to do next? Front it out, or run and hide somewhere? He still had enough private money to make it happen, but for how long? And even his not inconsiderable wealth would run out at some point, and after that... what? Of course, there was the third way. The .38 way.

He traced his finger along the barrel of the revolver. Maybe, soon? It was long overdue, but not yet, he decided. He closed his eyes to help him review the events of the past few years, which had led him to be a will-o'-the-wisp flitting across the world, and ultimately to this luxury hotel room where he was contemplating suicide.

It had all been born of remorse and sadness certainly, but there had also been something invigorating and alive about working back in his old trade of subterfuge, running agents and planning covert operations in foreign countries. He enjoyed being, what the old intelligence hands called, 'back in the game'.

Despite all of this, the 'game' only really began with the murder of a young patriotic man in Poland and the subsequent shattered grief, remorse and love of a desperate father.

Chapter Two

The game that Ferrera had instigated, when it had finally played out to its lethal conclusion, would later be judged by the survivors and those on the sidelines to have effectively have been created out of a mere nugget of trivia, a kernel of information seemingly of no use to anyone.

Like most operations of the 'great game' it didn't come from a single source. Instead, it filtered down from a variety of avenues, like rice flung far and wide in the sky. Eventually, enough grains made up the meal upon the plate. A grain here, a grain there, none of them seemingly connected.

In a very real sense, the maelstrom began with the destruction of the CIA's Black Orchestra network in Poland. Black Orchestra was a long term intelligence-run network that had been born in the aftermath of the Second World War, when former Nazi's and anti-communist elements were played back against the encroaching threat of Russia. In time, and with many additions to its agent list, it had grown to become one of the foremost CIA networks behind the Iron Curtain.

Over the years, Black Orchestra had been handled by many case officers, most of whom had cut their teeth in the war against Germany. But over recent years, Langley had felt that a 'new breed' of CIA officer was needed to be the next ones to keep the flame alive and the network running smoothly. But as with most intelligence professionals, the case officers were routinely re-routed and moved on, either through age, retirement, or from having their accredited cover blown making them *persona non grata*.

There was also the relentless surveillance on the CIA's Polish Stations, which made it difficult for the station officers on the ground to operate on a day-to-day basis.

It was decided by the Soviet Operations desk at Langley that what was needed was a covert action team capable of operating outside of the Embassy and diplomatic protection channels. They would enter the various countries – Poland, Hungary, Czechoslovakia, Bulgaria – 'on the black' with no diplomatic immunity and would therefore be deniable. This specialist team of men and women would enter the target country under commercial or civilian cover, get in, meet their agents, empty a dead letter box and receive useable intelligence products from the informants, before getting out without anyone being the wiser.

These people would be self-sufficient, with impeccable cover stories and nerves of steel.

The Agency set out on a recruitment and training program, looking for people with the 'right stuff', before narrowing the recruits down to just twelve people; ten men and two women. They were to be the elite of the Agency's agent handling sections. All the candidates had some unique quality; languages, previous intelligence experience, a background in the commercial world.

Candidate number six was a tall, fit twenty-seven-year-old who had already been through the CIA's recruitment process. His name was Daniel Samuel Ferrera. He had been in and out of Poland several times to collect messages, meet contacts or to service a dead drop. This time was no different than before. A regular pick up at a dead drop site in Warsaw Zoo. It was business as usual.

* * *

Charles Ferrera had been at home, having breakfast when the call came. The voice was one he didn't recognize, someone from the Director's office, a woman who spoke in clipped tones and who was terse to the point of rudeness. "Chuck, don't come in today. Stay at home. You have a visitor coming to see you. Someone you'll know," the voice said.

Confused, he took off his suit jacket, folded it neatly and sat at the dining table to drink his coffee and read through that morning's paper. It was a habit he'd slowly fallen into, following the death of his wife Theresa.

The house was a sprawling six-bedroom affair in the Georgetown suburbs. Since Theresa had passed away several years before, and his son had moved out to start his own life, he'd almost felt swamped by the scale of the house. His plan had been to limit the rooms he used; kitchen, lounge, bathroom and master bedroom – that way he didn't feel as alone or like a pea rattling around in a tin can. In fact, at times it felt cozy. It worked.

He was a Senior Executive Officer in the Near East/South Asia Division of the Directorate of Plans. He had cut his teeth, like most of them, being dropped behind enemy lines during the war and had carried on when the OSS was dissolved and went through its various incarnations, until it had been reformed into the CIA.

He was halfway through an article regarding the crisis in Cuba, when he heard a car pull onto the drive. There were footsteps, a pause, and then a confident knock on the door. Ferrera downed the dregs of his coffee and made his way to the front door.

Before him, looking fit, tanned and successful, was his comrade, brother-in-law and friend, Richard Higgins. Higgins, the Assistant Director of Plans at CIA, was second only to the big man in the Plans Directorate, the Director of Plans. He was also Ferrera's direct superior and an old-school cold warrior, not known for backing down or pulling his punches.

And yet this morning, as his colleague and friend sat in his living room, Charles Ferrera sensed there was something more, something hidden going on behind the dark sunglasses. It was only when Higgins removed them, that it was revealed they were being worn not to diffuse the sun's glare, but to hide reddened and tearful eyes.

"Richard, what is it?" Ferrera said. His own voice sounded pensive and worried.

Higgins began to speak. "Chuck, I'm sorry to have to tell you this…"

Later, as he tried to review the conversation in his mind, Ferrera could only remember fragments of what his friend had told him. Daniel… A black operation in Poland… A confirmed fatality… The Polish network rolled up… The body disposed of by the KGB.

Daniel…

The noise which came from him had started as a mewling sound, and quickly degenerated into a desperate roar of pain. All pretense of control was gone; instead it was replaced by the noise of a wounded animal. He slipped to the floor, his hands ripping at his hair and his fists beating on the floor. Higgins held him for a while, both men curled up, trying to gain control of each other and failing.

He had wept at Theresa's bedside all those years ago when the cancer took her; he had been strong then, for the boy, for Daniel. But the wrenching away of his son, the suddenness, the brutality of it was too much to comprehend. *We never know,* thought Ferrara. *We never know that when we say goodbye to someone for even the most mundane of reasons, if we will ever see them again.*

As the moment passed, the two men wiped away the tears which had been streaming down their faces for the past twenty minutes, uncontrollable sobs which racked body and soul. They sat back and regarded each other, one the father, one the uncle.

"Tell me everything," said Ferrera.

* * *

Charles Ferrera always thought of his son in the moments before he slept and how God had given him a blessed life. He'd enjoyed an affluent lifestyle, a good career, and had a caring and loving wife. But it was his only child whom he prized, far above all these other things.

He was a second-generation Italian immigrant from Bologna. Grandfather Enzo Ferrera had been a shrewd businessman who had succeeded in taking his small import/export company specializing in a reciprocal trade between America and Italy, and turned it into something he was eventually able to float on the stock market.

The family had earned their wealth and were the new breed of immigrants to America. They were rich and successful. The money had paid for Enzo's grandson, Charles, to buy his way into Yale and establish the Ferrera family into the upper echelons of American society.

At the beginning of his first term, Charles Ferrera had been roomed up with a young man by the name of Richard Higgins. It was on their first spring break when Higgins invited his friend to spend a week with them at his family's home in Connecticut, where he'd been introduced to Higgins' sister, Theresa.

It had been love at first sight for both of them; he the tall, dark haired, good-looking Italian boy and she the willowy blonde debutante. Their courtship was brief and with university completed, they'd decided to marry as quickly as possible. Charles tried his hand at journalism – his grandfather and father had wanted him to take over the family business – but he felt commerce was too restricting. He had a world to explore and wanted to make his own mark upon it.

In 1935, their only son Daniel was born. Charles was actually in Europe at the time, reporting on the growing economic and military rumblings from Germany. He returned home two months later. His thoughts of work and the rest of the world were thrown aside as they dealt with the new addition to the Ferrera family. Having a son changed Chuck Ferrera. He'd seen a hint of the violence that was coming, violence that would engulf every nation on the planet, and he was determined to protect his son from it at all costs.

Seven years later, with the world at war and America's part in it becoming more prevalent, he was approached by his wife's father. Retired US Army Colonel William Higgins had heard, through his private old boys' network, of a new organization being built from the ground up and thought it would suit Charles perfectly. "Top secret at the moment and they're looking for bright young fellows with language skills. It's a lot safer than getting your head blown off in a trench," his father-in-law had said.

Unfortunately, that wasn't to be an accurate appraisal.

The organization Ferrera was recruited into was the Office of Strategic Services, and his first operational foray into the field was assisting the partisans in Yugoslavia. He'd been dropped behind enemy lines as part of a five-man team, there to liaise with Tito's forces and to recruit informants. Ferrera was the radio man. The team leader was Richard Higgins. It had been a bloody and frenetic operation, but both men, comrades in arms, had survived, thanks to the trust each had for the other.

The rest of the war had been a whirlwind for Ferrera and Higgins. Operations in Italy, Greece and eventually France in the lead up to D-Day had ensured the two men had become well embroiled in the secret war against the soon-to-be defeated Germany.

Not that their partnership had ended with the dropping of the bombs in Japan in 1945; far from it. They had immediately switched from the wartime intelligence organizations of the United States to the newly created civilian version. The two men were now secret warriors, through and through. They had acquired a taste for covert operations and neither relished the thought of returning to their pre-war occupations. They were, and would be forever more, post-war cold warriors.

The lifeblood of the Central Intelligence Agency ran through their veins.

* * *

To a son, a father can be a hero, and the irrefutable truth is that son's follow their father's footsteps, whether they admit it or not.

To Daniel Ferrera his 'pop' was the greatest living hero he'd ever known. He read comic books with his classmates, stories of cowboys, aviators, explorers and spacemen. With each new edition he would say to his pals; "Those guys are okay, but none of them stand up next to my Dad!"

Daniel knew his father was involved in *some* kind of secret work, what it involved he didn't know, but there was certainly a lot of travelling, working late and whispered telephone conversations. In a sense, not knowing what his father did made it all the more exciting and mysterious.

But the best times were when the two of them would travel up to their lodge in Vermont, on the rare times when Charles wasn't away on operations, and go hunting, fishing and walking in the mountains. It was their time together, time that allowed them to bond. On one of these occasions when he was fifteen, Daniel had asked his father: "Pop, are you a spy?"

Charles Ferrera had turned to his son as they walked the mountain paths and smiled. "No, I'm not a spy, I'm the guy who tells the spy what to do," he'd said. When Daniel had asked what his father meant, Charles simply shook his head and laughed. "All in good time, little man, all in good time. Let's get cleaned up for supper."

Ten years later, it was inevitable that Daniel would be drawn into the intelligence business, and while Charles hadn't exactly pushed Dan into applying for the Agency, he'd certainly made it sound like an attractive career prospect. He had done nothing to discourage him. Hell, he'd even opened a few doors for his son. Why the hell not? What was the point of being a senior operations officer at CIA, if you couldn't search out new talent?

And talent was what Daniel Ferrera had in spades. He was young, intelligent, good-looking and patriotic. He had also inherited his father's skill and courage for operating in the field. To Charles Ferrera, his son was the role model for a new generation of CIA officer: elite, resourceful and brave. With an army of men like that, the CIA would be a force to be reckoned with across the intelligence community.

But all that had ended with a bullet on a cold winter's day in Poland.

Chapter Three

Three months after the news of Daniel's death, and at the end of his compassionate leave, Charles Ferrera was moved from active operations to a desk job. The Agency 'shrink' had declared him fit for duty, but with the caveat that he be kept away from front-line operations for the foreseeable future.

For Ferrera, it had been another blow. Following the death of Daniel, he'd hit the booze. It had been hard going. His neighbors had tried to stand by him as best they could, but after finding him lying in the gutter outside the family home, covered in vomit and urine, they'd quickly distanced themselves from him. When he was finally sober enough to return to work, he'd been hit with the third hammer blow. A desk job! Not operational, for a man who had parachuted into Nazi-occupied Europe and run agents behind the Iron Curtain, was very much like having a thoroughbred racehorse pulling a milk-cart. It was purgatory.

So with his son murdered, his wife having long since passed away and now being tied to a desk in Langley, he'd hit the bourbon once more. He was a man lost.

And yet deep down inside in the pit of his stomach, he burned. Burned with a violent fury, burned with the frustration of a man unable to right a wrong, burned at the injustice of the way his child, his boy, had been ripped from him. His anger grew over how the great and powerful secret arm of the American government had been impotent in its reply to the Russians.

"Stan knew the risks, Chuck," sniveled the new Director of Central Intelligence at the 'welcome back to work' meeting he was required to attend six months ago. The new DCI had been brought in to shake up the Agency. Senior staff viewed him as an 'interferer' who knew little about intelligence operations. "We have to remain professional and not let our personal feelings – no matter how repugnant and distasteful we view the Russian Service's actions – cloud our judgement. Stan would have known that."

"It's *Dan*, Mr. Director." It came out as a whisper, barely audible over the Director's pep talk.

"We simply can't be seen to be using the Agency as a vehicle for personal vendetta's, and this talk of retribution, of us trying to close down possible Soviet networks that you seem to be encouraging. It's the stuff of fiction, not the responsible actions of one the best intelligence services in the world. Stan was one of our best young officers he would have gone far—"

"It's *Dan. Daniel*," Ferrera said in a flat statement, still with respect in his tone.

But the Director was in full flow. "...and no amount of cloak and dagger games will bring him back, Chuck. We have an exciting new job for you, not operational, you understand, but still interesting enough to keep you active. Risk assessment for our overseas stations – a very valuable job, lots to do, lots to get involved with."

The Director had risen from his desk and outstretched his hand, indicating that the meeting was drawing to a close. "Get your life back, Chuck, throw yourself into your work. It's what Stan would have wanted."

It was then that Ferrera's anger had spilled over. "*His fucking name was* Daniel, *you moron!*"

And that was that. He'd stormed from the Director's office, driven into Georgetown and hit the bars. Martinis and bar nuts filled the rest of his day.

The following months had been a lesson in mediocrity, boredom, inaction, and loneliness. When he wasn't at work, he was getting drunk, and when he wasn't getting drunk, he would look in the mirror and see the face of an old, broken man staring back at him.

His only respite, if it could be called pleasurable, was to stand and stare at the memorial wall in the main reception at Langley and occasionally he would move forward and trace his finger over the star on the plaque that represented his son. With no grave he could visit, that small gesture, if nothing else, gave him some comfort.

* * *

Thump, thump, thump!

It was a beautiful spring day, that much he knew. He could just about see the sunlight shining in, through the cracks in both the curtains and his eyelids. He could see his alarm clock. 1.53 in the afternoon.

Thump, thump, thump!

He groaned. He'd missed work again.

Thump, thump, thump!

The banging on the front door had awoken him from his stupor. A commotion, tinged with the potential for violence. He staggered from the bed, took one last slug of 'Jack', and made his way down the stairs to fling the door open.

"So, you haven't done it yet. That's good to know," said a very annoyed Assistant Director of Plans.

"Ugghh." That was as much of a speech that Ferrera, in his hungover state, could manage.

"Eloquently put, Chuck. Jeez, it stinks in here. How much sauce have you put away?" Higgins took in the room. The half-naked man in front of him, the empty bottles, the gun on the floor where it had dropped from its owner's grip during the night.

"Done what?" said Ferrera. He was still working his way through the questions in his scrambled thought process.

450

Higgins entered the room, closed the door and gently sat Ferrera back onto the nearest couch in the lounge. "Oh, I think you know what."

Ferrera slumped back onto the couch and groan softly.

"Oh, don't worry, I won't report it. I wasn't sure if I'd find you wrapped round some hooker or if I'd find your brains splattered all over the walls by the time I got here," snarled Higgins.

"Huh… wrong on both counts, *sir*," slurred Ferrera. He rolled his furry tongue around the inside of his mouth, trying to work up a modicum of fluid.

It was then that Higgins lost his temper. "Oh, cut the crap Chuck, and put some clothes on. You need to pull yourself together and quick. You're slowly drinking yourself to death, you look like shit and you're basically finished at the Agency. Not even I can stop that happening now."

Ferrera fixed the other man with a harsh, beady-eyed stare. "So why should I care, then, huh, *huh!* My boy's dead, family is finished, job's down the crapper. *What's left!*"

The slap, when it came, rocked Ferrera. It contained such contempt and together with the dismissive look on Higgins' face, Ferrera wasn't sure what had just happened. Then the tears came. He held his head in despair.

Higgins crouched down so that they were at eye level. When he spoke, his voice was soft, gentle and reasonable. "Chuck, you're sitting here in your own piss, contemplating suicide. All those things you once hung onto are finished and the sooner that registers, the better. Your life will never be the same again. But if you want to stand any chance of getting payback for your boy, for Daniel, then you need to shape up quickly."

"You said yourself I'm finished at the Agency, the DCI himself has deep-sixed the plans I drew up to attack those Soviet networks."

A slow nod from Higgins. "All that's true. But I've been thinking. I don't think the opportunity for justice is with the CIA. It's far too narrowly focused for that. The Agency have become a bunch of ass-kissers in Washington, headed I might say, by our revered, at least in his own mind, new Director of Central Intelligence."

Ferrera shook his head. He still wasn't connecting the dots; maybe it was the booze gripping him.

Higgins placed a gentle hand on his friend's head and caressed it. "Don't worry about it now. I'll explain in time. Even I'm not sure what I mean yet. The first thing we're going to do is get you well again, somewhere away from Washington. There are too many memories here, too many distractions and too much booze. Don't try and resist or I'll have the goons from the Office of Security drag you out of here."

Ferrera looked up and nodded his acquiescence. He'd cause no trouble. Higgins nodded, satisfied. "Then we're going to draft a letter, handing in your resignation on health grounds, which I'll take to the DCI personally; that way, you'll at least get a good resettlement package. Finally, I'm going to hide you somewhere remote, somewhere isolated, so we can dry you out and get your brain cells working again like they did in the old days."

"And then what?"

"Why, that's the simple part. Then we start planning," replied Higgins.

And it was then, on that day when he'd reached rock bottom, that Charles Ferrera experienced a moment of clarity. Not an epiphany, nothing so biblical or as all-encompassing as that, but he came to realize in the nexus of that moment that he had wasted too much time in mourning his own son, his Daniel.

He'd mourned, he'd cried, he'd indulged in self-pity and despair. He'd been a sham. What type of father simply sits back and lets a bigger aggressor snuff out the life of a child, without extracting some kind of retribution? His Italian ancestors would have demanded revenge so that honor could be restored. He lay back, relaxed and somewhere deep in his mind, he sought out a glimmer of hope.

A month later, on the day he was due to retire from the CIA, have lunch with the Director and receive his Certificate of Merit for long and faithful service, Charles Ferrera didn't show up for work again.

This time it had nothing to do with him being drunk; he was simply too disgusted with the establishment to which he had dedicated his working life.

* * *

The American Central Intelligence Agency, like any large government institution, is a bureaucracy and over recent years, there had been a growing culture of neat, tidy men with short haircuts and Brooks Brothers suits. They had a narrow focus and an even narrower mindset of the world. What had started out after the war as a sleek and lean organization, had grown and grown until it was like a fat man spilling out of his suit, and like most over-large, obese and unaccountable secret societies, it could, if you had the right insider knowledge and technical know-how, be quite easily manipulated.

This was Richard Higgins' beginnings of a plan.

Following the aborted Polish operation, Higgins had been put in charge of investigating what had gone wrong in Warsaw Zoo and the murder of Daniel Ferrera. Put in charge of it, hell, he had requested it vehemently. He would track down those responsible for the death of his nephew, come hell or high water.

Not that Higgins despised or hated his Agency, far from it. Oh sure, it was weak at times, ineffectual, overly-complex and always pandering to those jerk politicians. But despite all this, he loved the CIA, as a teenager who has loved his first girlfriend will later love and respect her as a wife. They had a history. Which in a sense made it all the harder for him to betray the trust he had afforded the CIA.

That summer, Higgins was the lion that didn't roar. He sat and waited, watching and brooding. He oversaw the Agency's operations as usual, but because of his seniority at the CIA, he was also able to observe and manipulate. He followed leads and noted sources and assets which could be beneficial.

"I've got the authority to investigate the Polish operation," he told Ferrera. "I'll follow the seam and see where it leads. See if I can find out who was behind it, who was the team leader, who was the gunman, but more importantly *why* Daniel was shot. You keep your head down and get yourself strong again."

For months, there had been nothing. Only what they knew from official sources. There had been a shooting of a Western spy as part of a Russian/Polish counter-intelligence operation. One confirmed kill, with the body being disposed of in a Warsaw funeral directors. The spy was there on the 'black', without diplomatic cover and was therefore deniable by the US, hence the CIA's distancing itself from the whole sorry mess.

For Higgins, the leads led nowhere, and he knew he was hitting a wall. Nothing was coming out of Soviet Operations; nothing from the CIA station in Warsaw and the death of a junior officer in the Directorate of Plans was fast losing momentum and fading fast. There was a war on and in war, there are always casualties. The young CIA man would receive a star on the CIA's memorial wall and the family would receive the sympathy of a grateful US government and nation. Besides, said the naysayers, Poland was a Cold War backwater. Now Vietnam, that was where the real cut and thrust of intelligence work was going to be over the next few years. Real fighting, a real war!

And then, just as both Higgins and Ferrera feared the trail had gone cold forever, they experienced a piece of luck that changed everything. It came in the shape of a disaffected Russian intelligence officer, who had made an offer to the CIA station in Helsinki.

Chapter Four

The report into the offer of intelligence by the KGB officer, Anatoli Galerkin, landed on the desk of the Director of Plans in early August of 1963. It was read, digested and the appropriate recommendations were made.

One of those on the distribution list was the DP's assistant, Richard Higgins. There was a cover note attached to the file that said '*MACAW – Thought this may interest you.*' MACAW was the codename for his ongoing, but so far sparse, investigation into the Warsaw Zoo shooting. The note was signed by the Deputy Division Chief of Soviet Ops, an old friend of Higgins' who he'd brought up through the ranks.

He had sat in his office, sipped at his morning coffee and skimmed through the papers. It was when he reached the fifth page that he stopped and asked his secretary to cancel his appointments for the next hour. He settled himself back at his desk and began to read through the report again in more detail. Maybe, just maybe, he had something here.

The CIA case officer responsible for the initial meeting with the possible future agent Galerkin, noted in his report;'Galerkin has a high pitched nasal whine that is not attractive to the ear, but fits his physical appearance. He is thin, pasty, shrew-like. He is a squealer and likes to make himself appear more important than he really is'.

Higgins had immediately cabled the Helsinki Station, pulled rank and booked onto the next flight out. On the plane, Higgins had read over the handwritten case notes he'd taken from the official files. Comrade Galerkin was proving to be an interesting customer.

The first agent meeting had taken place in a quiet back-street hotel in Helsinki, several weeks earlier. Security was tight around the defector and his family, just in case the Russians discovered his subterfuge. It was unlikely, but always a possibility. It had been at the end of the second meeting, when the CIA case officer had started to question him about Western penetration operations by the KGB. They had him running down his list of departments, Soviet policy and Russian intelligence effectiveness, before they started on the meat and potatoes of names and dates. What he'd told them showed that Galerkin had excellent access to good intelligence product.

But Galerkin, being no fool, wanted assurances that he and his family would be protected when the time came for him to 'come over'. He was holding back his treasure chest of A1 intelligence, until he was convinced of the American's intentions. In order to give up this intelligence, Galerkin had asked, no demanded, that he meet with senior officers from Langley.

Higgins saw an opportunity and it spurred him into action. A car from the Embassy was waiting for him when he landed. *Fuck hotels and sleep,* he thought. He told the driver, "Take me straight to see the Chief of Station."

It took three days of wrangling, calling in favors and not a little bullying of his junior officers, before Higgins was given permission to go and meet and assess the KGB man on the ground, face-to-face.

It had certainly ruffled a few feathers with the senior men at Soviet Ops; it was, after all, their territory and their agent, but Higgins had seniority over all of them and was a ruthless political fighter when he had to be.

The next day, Higgins was to meet Galerkin. The venue was the same small hotel near the park. The arrangements had been made by the local CIA station.

Same hotel, same room, same time – we keep the continuity, Higgins had told them. "But I want to meet with him alone. Just the two of us, with no outside interference. I'll know within one meeting if he has anything of use to say," he insisted to the case officers at the Helsinki Station. If the CIA men had any concerns about this unorthodox practice, they chose to keep it to themselves.

Higgins travelled alone and calmly made his way up to the room. Before giving a light tap at the door, Higgins pressed the record button on the body-worn tape recorder in his inside pocket. The door opened and the KGB man stood there.

The CIA case officer's description of Galerkin had been exact. He was small, thin and weasel-like, and had an irritating manner that instantly made people wince. The two men shook hands and settled down. Galerkin began the meeting nervously, but when he realized he was conferring with a Senior Executive Officer from Langley, he became much more open and animated.

Higgins began his pitch, seeking to find out just how much this man knew. "So, Anatoli. I'm here to assess whether it would be beneficial for us to work together. I hope so, as I understand that you have some information we're keen to look at. I wondered if you would be willing to meet with me over the next few days, while I'm in town?"

Galerkin began to protest, but Higgins cut him off. "Don't worry, these meetings won't last very long, an hour or so, nothing that would alert your people or arouse suspicions. Where do your people think you are now?"

Galerkin's fingers were scratching at his trouser legs, his nerves evident. "I have told them that I am attempting to recruit a clerk in the Finnish Ministry of the Interior. I do know of such a person, and we have met several times, but I have not recruited him as a spy," he declared proudly.

Higgins thought about it. Not a bad cover story actually, plausible certainly. "Anatoli, as I say, our time here is short and I'm hoping you can help me. This meeting is partly to establish your bona fides and partly to establish a level of trust between two professionals such as us."

Galerkin nodded and Higgins could see that he was winning him over. The Russian smiled. "Of course I am flattered that you came from Washington to see me. I hope that I can help. What is your question?"

Higgins craned forward on the edge of the bed and interlocked his fingers together, resting his chin on them. "I would like to hear about the shooting of one of my men, in the Warsaw Zoo."

* * *

Galerkin had started slowly and then as he found his own pace he began to speak with a flourish. "So you know about the spy with the codename Svarog? No? He is something of a legend inside KGB. His reputation is that of a man who is ruthless. Krivitsky is his real name, Vladimir Krivitsky, but Svarog fits him much better, it is the God of fire who rains down flame on its enemies."

Higgins nodded, eager for the KGB man to go on. He felt the tape turning in the body mike underneath his shirt, hoping Galerkin's words were coming through clear.

Galerkin continued. "He had fought bravely in the Great Patriotic War, where he had eliminated many Nazi agents. He had also been one of the first officers recruited to Russian Intelligence and had the favors of the KGB Director himself. This, I think, made him almost invulnerable inside the political infighting at the KGB. I first met him when I was attached to the Department of Western Operations. It had been a promotion for excellent work. I was very proud."

"Anatoli could you tell me what you were expected to do in this new position?" asked Higgins, trying to stop the Russian from getting distracted.

Galerkin nodded enthusiastically. "My new job was to create cover identities and to manage the production of intelligence from KGB agents working in Europe. It was a very interesting job, one that allowed me access to much classified material from the West. Within a matter of weeks, I was ordered to the office of a senior KGB case officer; Major Krivitsky. He had been recently seconded to Western

Operations following an aborted operation in Poland that had resulted
in the rolling up of a Western intelligence network. Apparently, someone had been killed as part of the operation... rumored to be a Western
spy, but I did not know the details... I was still attached to a different
department then."

Higgins was keen to ask about the shooting in Poland, but restraint
took over. He didn't want to disrupt the man's flow. He motioned for
Galerkin to carry on and the Russian continued.

"Anyway, I arrived promptly and was greeted by a man who looked
like an angry gargoyle. I apologize, but that is the best way I can describe him. I will not lie to you, Svarog frightened me. He was squat,
rough in manner. I sensed that I was dealing with a man of great feroc-
ity and presence. He bade me to sit down. His voice, while courteous,
was harsh, like an angry wolf. 'Galerkin, you are to be my right hand
for the next few weeks. I wish to use your skills. I have been appointed
personally by the Director to set up a new operation'. "

Higgins leaned in closer. "What about the shooting in Warsaw? Did
Svarog say anything about this? What happened that caused him to
fire at our man?"

Galerkin frowned and stood to stretch his legs.

He was building himself up to deliver bad news. "As I have said,
Major Krivitsky is a very violent man. It is stamped on his face. I was
under the impression that the plan to capture the CIA man had gotten
out of control and when your colleague tried to escape, Major Krivitsky ensured he would be put down. Major Krivitsky is a man who
does not like to lose face."

"But there is no doubt in your mind that Svarog – I mean Krivitsky
– was the one who pulled the trigger?" said Higgins.

Galerkin sat down again. "It was Krivitsky. He was not ashamed of
his act, in fact, quite the opposite. He was quite open about it to junior
officers. It added to his ferocious reputation and advanced him up the
ladder of promotion also."

Higgins smiled. "Okay, so what was this new secret operation?"

"He proceeded to lay out the details of his new operation. It involved several high-level traitors from the West. These spies, he assured me, were totally loyal to the cause of the Motherland, even though they were not Russian by birth. Several, he had recruited himself, whilst the rest had been 'grandfathered' to him from other case officers. Case officers who had either been blown or been transferred. Svarog said his network of spies had high strategic and intelligence value. He did not clarify, and I was not in a position to ask such details."

Higgins looked at his watch. They had been at it for nearly an hour. Tradecraft dictated that the meetings were to be kept short, in case the KGB man's absence was noticed. "Anatoli, I think that's enough for today. You've been very helpful. It's certainly given me plenty to think on—"

"There is one other thing," interrupted Galerkin. "I have a gift, a gift for your people. I can bring it with me tomorrow, if you can arrange for me to come out straight away?"

Higgins leaned back, looking doubtful. "I don't know if that's possible, Anatoli."

The Russian clasped his hands together like a penitent. "It would be worth your while."

"It would have to be exceptional material. Ideally, we would like you to carry on as you are. That's standard procedure. Better that way in the long run," said Higgins.

"I can give you Svarog's network in the West," blurted out the Russian. "His agents, their roles, how far deep they have infiltrated your systems. The whole thing; photos, contacts, written orders, meeting places. I have it hidden safe!"

Higgins knew that the chasm between what an agent says and what is truth can sometimes be as wide as an ocean, so he tested his new agent's mettle. "And you can get them for us, from Moscow, and bring them here to Helsinki?"

Galerkin shook his head, desperate now for the CIA man to hear him. "No, you misunderstand me. I do not have to go to Moscow, I have them here, copies, taken from KGB headquarters and brought with me to Finland. It is my price for resettlement in the West."

And in that moment, Higgins knew he'd found the goldmine of intelligence that could give them a way to strike back, not for the CIA, but for the private vengeance both he and Ferrera had decided to embark upon. A fortuitous turn of events and lucky break had given them exactly what they wanted.

"Tomorrow," said Higgins, quickly deciding upon a course of action from which he knew there was no going back. "You will bring it to me tomorrow."

Chapter Five

The next day, Galerkin returned to the hotel. The same rules, the same protocols, the same tape recorder inside Higgins' jacket pocket.

The only differences being that this meeting wasn't sanctioned by the Agency. The CIA station didn't know that Higgins was meeting Galerkin for a second time and it was strictly off the books; two spies hiding from their own sides for a brief period of time.

Galerkin had brought with him an attaché case, filled with raw intelligence material, purloined from the very heart of one of Russian Intelligence's most notorious case officers. Higgins looked at the case, his eyes constantly drawn back to it and the secrets that lay within. "Mr. Galerkin, have you told anyone else about this in the Agency?"

Galerkin looked offended. "I have not. They told me that you are a very important man and that you wished to talk to me in confidence about certain matters. The people from your Embassy said that I should discuss important matters with you and that you alone, had the power to bring me out."

Higgins nodded; that was good. As far as the Agency knew, it was only about the shooting in Poland. This mine of intelligence had, so far, slipped underneath their radar. "Then you must say nothing, Galerkin. This is a matter of national security. It is a closed door to everyone, but me. This comes from the very highest level of our government. Do you understand?"

Galerkin nodded his weasel-like head. "I do; I most certainly do."

It was a good bluff that had frightened the man to his core and Higgins had no doubt he would play ball. Unfortunately for Galerkin, the fact that he'd passed the information about the Warsaw shooting and the clues relating to Svarog's network of agents in the West, made him a liability.

There could – if Higgins and Ferrera's future plans to exact revenge stood any chance of success – be only one possible outcome for Anatoli Galerkin, KGB officer. He would have to be removed from the game and silenced.

Higgins had spent the previous night thinking it through, justifying his future actions to himself. Ideally, he would have liked to give the man an 'out' – a way of letting him live, while still handing over the intelligence. In truth, there was no other way of getting the information without alerting the mainstream CIA.

Higgins stood and held out his hand for the attaché case. Galerkin looked at him, doubtful for a moment and then handed over the case.

The CIA man flipped open the latch and rummaged briefly through the files; photos of the agents, contact procedure details, biographies. If it checked out, and judging by the look of it Higgins had no reason to doubt that it wasn't genuine, it would burst open a huge intelligence network. He closed up the attaché case and placed it carefully on the chair next to him. He turned to Galerkin, his face sporting a grim expression.

"I think our work here is done. I will let the local station handle the details, but from my point of view, I will be recommending we get you out of the country tonight, plus the usual retirement package in the USA. For now, I need you to stay in this room where you're safe," said Higgins and he held out his hand for the Russian to shake. It was a sign of trust for future comrades.

The Russian had barely gotten out a "Thank you," when Higgins stepped forward and punched the other man in the stomach, sending him to his knees in pain. Higgins knew he had to move fast, especially if he wanted to keep it quiet. He'd learned that during the war; the silent killing, the sentry removal. He clamped a hand over the man's mouth and dragged him into the small bathroom, throwing him into the large metal bath. Galerkin hit the back of his head on the taps and blood started to seep down the curvature of the bath.

Soon the Russian would regain his senses, the pain would start to ease and he would begin to scream or fight back. Higgins threw his own body weight on top of Galerkin and pushed a pure white towel down onto his mouth, making him gag. The Russian was starting to fight back and Higgins knew he had to end this quickly. He looked around the small bathroom, searching for anything that could be used as a weapon. The only thing in range was a heavy ceramic soap dish. He grabbed it, brought it up past his shoulder and brought it down on the top of the Russian's head; once, twice, three times – each time putting more power into the shots.

There was a cracking sound, like a delicate eggshell had been broken, followed by a crunch as the soap dish began to grind down the Russian's skull with each new blow. Galerkin's head was caved in on one side, like a football which has been deflated, and still Higgins pounded away with the soap dish, trying to make it quick for himself, as well as for Galerkin.

On the thirteenth blow he stopped, exhausted. Higgins looked around at the carnage. The bath and wall tiles were coated with blood and it dripped over the lip of the bath and onto the floor. He dropped the soap dish onto the lifeless body and stared at his hand. It looked like it had been dipped in red paint. He climbed carefully out of the bath, trying not to disturb the body and not looking at the man's face, the eyes. The eyes were just too much to take in. The lifeless eyes looked back at him and said 'betrayer' and 'murderer'." He quickly set about washing any blood off his hands and face.

He pulled the shower curtain across and closed the door to the bathroom. His body shook all over and it was several minutes more before he donned his hat, scarf, coat and gloves. He picked up the attaché case, pulled the scarf higher around his face to hide his identity and let himself out of the hotel room. He quickly moved down the stairs to the service entrance and let himself out the back. He passed no one.

Poor Galerkin, thought Higgins as he made his way out into the back alley of the hotel, hitting the streets. He had learned the hard way that sometimes it was necessary to eliminate pawns from the game in order to achieve exceptional results and that the end, did indeed, justify the means.

Chapter Six

Higgins arrived back in Washington two days later. He didn't even go home to his wife. Instead, the first thing he did was cable the Helsinki Station to say that in his opinion, Galerkin was an agent of penetration, designed by the Russians to try to infiltrate himself into the CIA's defector program and spread disinformation. The man had fluffed several of the questions and made a crude attempt to extort money from a senior officer from Langley. Higgins' recommendation was that Galerkin be dropped as soon as possible and no further contact should be made with him by CIA Helsinki.

The next thing he did was to go down to the Registry and look up the few details they had on a Russian intelligence officer by the name of Vladimir Krivitsky. There was precious little. A few postings when he had operated under diplomatic cover; Switzerland, Paris, Berlin, plus one grainy photograph that showed the man in profile. Higgins stared at the photo, imprinting the man's face in his memory.

Aside from a meeting with the Director of Plans, for the rest of the day he sat in his office, making notes in his personal ledger. The ledger he would take home with him to work on and to streamline the scribbling inside into a workable strategy. By late that afternoon, he was tired and suffering from being on the road for the past week.

"This just came in. It's from Helsinki in reply to your cable," said his secretary. He was on his way out the door, but waved his hand for her to pass it to him. Then he was going home to his wife, his home and his bed. The cable read:

```
RE: CABLE/CIA-HELSINKI
ACKNOWLEDGE YOUR CONCERNS OVER GALERKIN.
CIA STATION HAS ORDERS NOT TO APPROACH.
UNDERSTOOD. IT SEEMS WE CAN'T TRUST ANYONE
THESE DAYS.
FOR REFERENCE: A LOCAL NEWS REPORT STATES
THAT RUSSIAN EMBASSY OFFICIAL ANATOLI
GALERKIN HAS DISAPPEARED. RUSSIAN EMBASSY
HAS ALERTED LOCAL POLICE FORCES.
SEEMS YOU WERE RIGHT. OBVIOUSLY RUNNING
SCARED. SERVES HIM RIGHT.
```

Higgins had driven through the night to reach Vermont. Following his enforced retirement, Chuck Ferrera had been staying at the family-owned lodge in the mountains not far from Mount Mansfield.

The cabin was anything but modest, a five room hunting lodge in six acres of grounds, which had been bought by the Ferrera family for long weekend vacations. For now, though, it had a very different purpose. It was partly to rehabilitate Chuck, partly to settle his mind, but also to see if his desire for revenge was quenched in the calm stillness of the mountains.

That night following his return from Helsinki, Higgins had found Chuck Ferrera sitting in his reading chair by the fire, halfway through a book. There was no evidence of alcohol anywhere in the room.

Higgins took off his winter jacket, sat in the chair opposite his friend and whispered quietly, "I think we've found him."

Ferrera had put his book down calmly and said, "Good, then let's begin."

* * *

Over the coming weeks, Higgins would make a visit to the mountain lodge once a fortnight, landing at Burlington Municipal Airport and then taking a winding car journey through the mountains, ostensibly to visit a grieving friend, but in reality, to bring any intelligence he had managed to glean from CIA files and to plan out the next phase of their covert operation. They would sit drinking coffee and talking, late into the night. Their talk was operational. Do we target the man or the system? What about our escape plan? Is it deniable enough?

On a practical level, no operation can exist without the necessary funds and monies to make it happen, so Ferrera had, through intermediaries, liquidated all his assets; properties, shares, savings bond, pensions and his termination package from the Agency, which all went into the fund. He had the funds deposited into a Swiss bank account, as well as several smaller, satellite banks located throughout Europe. By the end of several weeks, he had a two-million-dollar bounty which would enable him to run his operation and resettle him somewhere outside of US jurisdiction when the job was over.

The final thing to do was to destroy any ID naming him as Charles Ferrera. He gathered together his passport, driving license and birth certificate and set fire to them outside the lodge on a clear and starry night. He watched as the embers finally burned away. They were inconsequential anyway, he had several sets of new ID's, which had been provided by one of Higgins' contacts that the CIA used.

It was a way of putting down his old life and taking up a new one.

And so on that night, Charles 'Chuck' Ferrera, former CIA officer, and soon-to-be traitor, dropped off the intelligence radar and officially ceased to exist.

* * *

"It means that Dan's unsolved murder has to be buried and the investigation cancelled. Especially if we have any hope of covering our tracks," said Higgins, at one of their regular meetings. They were sitting on the porch, enjoying the view of the mountains and the cool evening air.

"As long as we have that scum's head and his network destroyed, it will be worth it," said Ferrera bitterly.

"I've read through the Helsinki Station's reports into Galerkin. The Warsaw shooting, Krivitsky, his agents in the West. Only we have access to that list. If there's anything that could lead back to us, I'll see if a little judicious trimming of file details might be enough to throw them off the scent," said Higgins.

Ferrera looked concerned. *It might be easier said than done,* he thought. Altering a few biographical details would be enough to confuse most case officers, but he knew the Chief of Counter-Intelligence was a driven, some would say, zealot of a man who refused to take no for an answer. "What about Angleton?" he said.

"It's not a problem; I'll take care of Jim. I outrank him by a country mile, besides, he's gotten more than enough intelligence product to keep his little team happy for the next few years," said Higgins.

The plan had been simple. Identify Krivitsky's network of agents and start eliminating them, one by one. Let Krivitsky watch as his agents were picked off one at a time and then when he has no more network left, and the effectiveness of KGB operations in the West was almost decimated, they would wait for Svarog to come out into the open and then they would strike – chopping off the head of the hydra. Svarog was to be the ultimate target.

They had an impressive target list; a NATO liaison officer, propulsion engineer, bankers, diplomats, businessmen, political appointees. All Soviet agents and all easy targets. Of course, this couldn't be an official CIA-backed operation; no, not even the Assistant to the Director of Plans could swing that, and besides Ferrera had made an enemy of the current DCI. But what it could be, was a private enterprise between two old friends and comrades, determined to get revenge for the death of a loved one. They'd spent the night discussing various options, some good and some terrible.

Finally, they settled on a false flag operation as the one with the most realistic chance of succeeding. A false flag was a time-honored tradition in the intelligence world. You represented yourself as one thing, when in fact you were another. So a French Intelligence officer might pass himself off as an Italian spy, in the hope of recruiting an Italian citizen to pass him information. As long as the agent believed they were working for one side, usually out of patriotism, the concept would work well.

For Ferrara, he would be representing himself as a still-active CIA case officer. They'd put in the necessary 'plumbing', to use an old Agency phrase. Hired safe-houses, prepared false travel documents and where they needed on the ground intelligence about their targets, they set about hiring private detectives from the various target countries to provide them with addresses, car registration numbers, up-to-date surveillance photos or to track movements on a day-to-day basis. It was expensive, but money well spent in the long run.

By the end of September of 1963, they had a workable plan complete with an accurate target list, surveillance logs and a timeline for the operation to start. However, there had been a bigger concern as summer gave way to fall. There had been a blip in the running of the operation, just as everything had about to be launched.

The assassination of President John Fitzgerald Kennedy in Dallas in November of 1963 had shut everything down. Security was tight within the various branches of government, not least within the Agency, where there was a witch hunt going on.

"We need to close this down," Higgins had said. "Hoover and his boys are seeing reds under the beds everywhere at the minute. They're paranoid!"

"I agree," said Ferrera. "There's too much heat at the moment. We have everything in place, so the hard part is done. Besides, we don't want to get caught up in the assassination investigation. The worst case is that the FBI blunders into the fringes of our op, and the whole thing is blown sky high."

So they packed up the operation until the FBI hunters and Secret Service had begun to wind down their respective investigations. It was a long and painfully frustrating time for Ferrera, but as the operation's controller, he knew the wisdom of calling a temporary halt to proceedings.

But as a father out for vengeance, it was akin to going through the whole grieving process again. Had the targets moved? Would Svarog go further underground? Would the whole thing still be workable when it was finally launched? Would it lose momentum and if so, what could he do to get it back on track?

He had no definite answer to any of these imponderables, so he did the only thing he could; he stayed in Vermont and walked and read and hunted and planned. And when he'd finished planning, he planned some more in detail. He existed only in limbo, caught between the fine line of action and failure. Finally, the hiatus was at an end and he threw himself back into the heart of the operation, taking personal control of the next, crucial level.

They would, of course, need suitably qualified contractors to carry out their mission. Higgins had made time to rifle through the agent files of known 'contractors' who were capable of carrying out the job. Not that they would have an exhaustive list of contract killers, in fact the reverse was true, the list was anything but grand, it was downright miniscule. Following Kennedy's murder, the CIA had gone into freefall and ousted many of their contract personnel to avoid any kind of scandal. This meant that a number of agents with some very deniable skills were tossed out onto the garbage heap, which for a likely recruiter, would make it a buyer's market.

As part of the false flag ruse, they both felt it would be wise to choose agents who had been cut loose from the Agency and were no longer classed as 'active agents'. This would remove the risk of direct conflict of interests with current personnel, and reduce the risk of the agent betraying them to the CIA.

Instead, Higgins searched for contractors who had been deactivated, but who were still in the market to take on a freelance job if the conditions were favorable. Eventually, they short-listed three likely candidates.

The first was a retired US Special Forces Colonel who had liaised with the CIA during the 1950's, and had carried out several long-range sniper killings.

His credentials were impeccable. But after much thought, they ruled the man out. He was still an American citizen and therefore probably still had a lot of contacts within the military and intelligence services. They couldn't trust that he wouldn't betray the operation, especially one that was a false flag. The man might have seen it as being part of a traitorous operation against his own government. Besides, their contractor needed to be a bit more flexible in his approach to killing the targets they had acquired. Not everything could be solved with a rifle from half a mile away.

The second was a Ukrainian national who was living in Frankfurt. He'd completed several contract killings for the Ukrainian nationalist groups against informers and double agents, and had, in fact, been a very good operator by all accounts, even though he had only operated in Germany. Was he good enough to hit numerous targets across Europe, some of them high profile? He may be good at eliminating static ethnic groups, but Ferrera doubted he would be comfortable working this type of operation.

The third man was a former drug smuggler and international criminal who had been recruited into the CIA's Executive Action program to carry out, or be part of, several high profile assassinations the Agency had been involved in. Lumumba and Trujillo, to name but two.

"He seems perfect. I vaguely remember hearing about that operation. Not the details, of course, just that the Executive Action department had several very good men at their disposal," said Ferrera.

Higgins nodded agreement. "He certainly has the right temperament and qualifications. You'll need a cut-out man, someone to act as an initial go-between."

Ferrera shook his head. "No. There's no need. I can handle simple agent recruitments."

"No, *you're* wrong Chuck. Think about it. We have to make it look like a legitimate CIA operation and that means following agent recruitment protocols to the letter. These people will know how the Agency acts. If they see something out of the ordinary, they'll smell a rat."

Ferrera thought about it. Higgins was right, of course. Besides, a cut-out man would have other uses too, such as arranging security, safe-houses and the like. "Okay, who did you have in mind?"

Higgins pulled out a copied file. "This man. He's Hungarian, an intelligence peddler, but everyone uses him for small jobs. He's based out of Vienna. We use him, then we dispose of him."

* * *

Did they class themselves as traitors?

Higgins had mulled it over time and time again, and still his conclusions weren't as straightforward as he would have liked. He surmised that they weren't, in the classic sense of the word. They weren't actively betraying their country by selling secrets, or by trying to subvert the United States government. But still it didn't sit comfortably with either man, he was sure.

He understood Ferrera's motive, certainly. The former intelligence officer wanted nothing more than good old-fashioned revenge for what was the brutal gunning down of his only son. That motive was as old as time.

But his own was a little vaguer. Of course he also wanted revenge for the murder of one of his officers, even more so, because Daniel Ferrera had been his nephew, his sister's flesh and blood. He had known him since his first day, seen him grow and had been one of the people responsible for bringing him into the Agency.

But more than that, he wanted the chance, probably the final chance in his career, to inflict a grievous wound on his enemies. Turning, arresting or monitoring a Soviet espionage network was all very well, but at this late stage of the game, he wanted to make a stand and wound them deeply. He'd drawn a line in the sand and he was damned if he was going to cross it for the sake of job security.

And if it should all cave in, the operation blown and the Agency hunters on his tail? Well, it wouldn't take long for the investigation team to work out who had assisted Chuck Ferrera in his rogue operation. Chuck would hold out as long as he could, he knew that, but these days, the Agency had access to some very clever people and technical support, namely interrogation drugs, which could open up the mind of even the most resolute of prisoners.

He guessed – no, he knew, that his days at the Agency were numbered anyway. The old guard were out and the new intake, under the new broom of a DCI, were quickly being fast-tracked to senior positions.

And Ferrera? Even at this late stage of the operation, the ordering of the execution of these men didn't sit easy with his conscience. The thought of ordering the killing of men half a world away, like some kind of Roman Emperor, in normal times, would have been abhorrent to him. It went against every moral code he'd been exposed to; first in his Catholic upbringing, and then as a professional intelligence officer.

He wasn't a psychopath, he wasn't a monster, but he recognized he'd made a vow to the memory of his son, and honor had to be restored. So it came as no surprise that during one of their final planning meetings, that Higgins confronted him.

"Chuck, the question, after all these months of reflection and working through your grief, is whether or not you wish to take this further. There's no shame in stopping it dead right here and now. But this is the absolute last chance to abort. If we go on from here, we have to go all the way," he said.

Ferrera had pondered much the same thing over recent days in the lead up to the final planning stages. He looked back at Higgins. Greyness had invaded his pallor, he looked unwell. By contrast, Ferrera felt more and more invigorated and looked the picture of health. Something had happened in their relationship over the past few months. Their roles had reversed; whereas Higgins was once the leader, now

Ferrera, with his single mindedness, had assumed the figure of authority and command.

Ferrera placed a hand on Higgins' shoulder and smiled. "We go all the way, Richard, all the way until they are all dead."

Chapter Seven

Three months into the start of their unofficial operation, Charles Ferrera started to get 'the episodes', as he called them.

In truth, the headaches had been there for weeks, in the background and distant. But just recently, they had been growing stronger, blinding almost, so much so that at times he would take himself off to his room, close the curtains during the day and suffer through the intense pain.

At first he thought it was just a buildup of stress from the past year, or possibly a consequence of drying out from the booze. But as the weeks passed, he soon began to realize that this was no 'cold turkey' affliction and he would frequently throw up during these attacks. There was nausea, sickness, and the ever-returning headaches.

All the good work he'd done to attain physical fitness in Vermont was slowly being undone. In the end, he could bear it no longer and made an appointment to see a private physician in New York. The doctors had looked at his medical history, ran the standard tests, and submitted him to a thorough examination and biopsy. Then he was told to return in two weeks' time, when the results would be available.

He knew what it was before he boarded the flight back to New York, fourteen days later. What else could it have been? He'd sat in the doctor's office in Manhattan and listened; a brain tumor, inoperable. "I'm sorry Mr. Ferrera," said the specialist.

Ferrera brushed the platitudes aside. "How long do I have?"

"Less than a year certainly, but the treatment we have can make it comfortable for you, so maybe a little longer."

Damn. He'd planned on at least a good year to complete the operation, now he would be lucky to see Svarog's head on a spike. The thought of death didn't frighten him at all, but the thought of not completing his unfinished business terrified him to the core. He would have to move the operation along to hit a new deadline.

The doctor spoke of medication, treatment, hospices. Ferrera ignored all the man's advice. He knew what he had to do and how he was going to live out the rest of his life, and it wouldn't be bedridden and pumped full of drugs. He instantly decided on two courses of action. Firstly, he would not tell Higgins about what he'd just learned and secondly, he was even more determined to push ahead with this revenge operation.

Chuck Ferrera was a tough man and he would, through sheer force of will, stay alive long enough to see his son's killer and his agents dead in the gutter. *Besides,* he thought, *a walking dead man has nothing to lose and that made him a very dangerous adversary.*

The specialist made an appointment for him for the following week, to begin his treatment.

He never went back.

* * *

A week later, the man who boarded the morning flight from Washington to London had up until that morning, not officially existed. The name on his passport was Maurice Knight. He was in his early 60's, wore an expensive business suit and appeared to be a senior executive from one of the large corporations that were so vibrant in the States right now.

He was flying direct to London and then taking a connecting flight to Paris. A brief stopover in Paris overnight, before he flew to Vienna the next day. He looked relaxed and in control of his own destiny.

As the airliner made its way skyward across the Atlantic, Mr. Knight sat back in his business class seat, removed his leather wallet from his inside jacket pocket and took out a small, black and white photograph. It was the only concession to his old life.

The picture gave him focus and resolve. It was his compass which kept him going true north. The picture was that of a young boy sitting on a beach somewhere, perhaps on a family vacation. The boy looked to be around ten years old and was holding a catcher's mitt that was way too big for him.

Chapter Eight

Mexico City – May 1965

It was the phone ringing again that shook him from his reverie. He was once again back in his hotel suite in Mexico City with the heat, the sweat and the noise from the air conditioning. The memories of the past few months had quickly evaporated.

He knew it wasn't Marquez again so soon. The man knew not to break protocol, unless he had something to report. The only other person who had his number and who had been in touch constantly over the last few days, was Higgins. He picked up the handset, knowing who it was before he'd even heard the voice.

"It's me," said Higgins, down the notoriously bad Mexican telephone line.

"Has it exploded in our face?" asked Ferrera. He could feel the start of a headache, a dull, throbbing pain behind his eye.

"That's the understatement of the year. I can't talk long. There's a good chance they're monitoring my calls. I'm on a payphone."

"I understand. What have you heard?"

Higgins took a breath. "The Agency knows something. In fact, they know more than they're letting on. I've been hauled in by the goons from the Office of Security to answer questions about you, Dan, the shooting in Poland. I don't think it's quite at full-scale internal investigation level yet, but it soon will be."

"Perhaps they're just fishing, perhaps in truth they have nothing concrete yet?" suggested Ferrera.

"Chuck, they know it was you, they must do. My guess is that they're on their way to you as we speak. I figure you haven't got long before the local FBI man bursts in with some Mexican *Federales* and shackles you in chains."

"I'm going nowhere. I'm not running and I'm not hiding. I'm making my last stand here," said Ferrera.

"But—"

"But nothing. We achieved what we set out to do. We got Dan's murderer and fought the Cold War on our own terms. Mission accomplished. It's time for you to look after yourself, Richard."

"What will you do?"

"It's better that you don't know. Just look after yourself, deny everything and if they do get too close blame everything on me. Say I duped you into it. Hopefully, that will stop you from receiving any jail time," said Ferrera calmly.

Higgins held the handset close to his ear, thinking, weighing up the truth of the situation. "I understand, Chuck. Just go easy."

Ferrera gently replaced the handset. There was no time for sentiment or thanks. That had all been said the last time they'd met.

He would never be taken alive, he knew that. Not only for Higgins' sake, but also for the fact that it was time to leave this world. As the puppet-master of the ultimate game, he had played superbly. He had controlled his pawns, pieces and minions across the globe, tactically moving each into the optimum position to benefit his own ends.

Would he go to hell for his misdemeanors and underhanded practices; the manipulation of the weak and the shedding of blood – all in the name of revenge? He didn't truly know, but he did know he wouldn't have to wait long. He could already hear the screaming whine of the police vehicles in the distance. They could be for another incident nearby, but he doubted it.

He stood and looked out from his balcony. The street below was teeming with the flotsam and jetsam of the city. Everything appeared normal. But were they already here; the Agency watchers and the Bureau, with their surveillance vans, observation points and radios? And what was *their* final endgame; to take him alive, or eliminate him quietly? No, he was sure they would want to question him first, to find out as much as they could about his rogue operation. Only then would he be dropped down a deep hole, never to be seen again.

He knew how he would do it if the roles were reversed. A room service waiter to gain them access, then a four-man snatch team to storm the room and subdue him. He would then be drugged and extracted in a laundry trolley and whisked away to US territory.

Ferrera picked up the .38, thumbed back the hammer. Was this the way?

He had come this far and been ruthless; to kill himself seemed almost admitting defeat. He would never be taken, he knew that, but if he was going to leave the game, then he was certain he was going to take his hunters with him. He threw away the .38 and dressed quickly in his best suit.

Satisfied, he placed a number of items of importance in his inside jacket pocket. These would go with him, wherever he ended up after this adventure. The suitcase, the suitcase was next.

Ferrera lifted it up onto the bed. Inside the case, under a false panel, was what he termed his doomsday equipment. As well as the .38, it had contained several 'cakes' of plastic explosive, wires, detonators and electronic triggers. He had already 'primed' the room with enough plastic explosive to lift the floor off the building. It was sealed around the door and window frames and hidden behind the paintings and mirrors on the walls. It had been his first job, when he'd registered in the hotel suite.

Now it was the electronic trigger switch he removed from the suitcase. He flicked the switch and activated it, hearing a faint hum emanating from it. All that was left to do, was press the button when he was ready. He returned once again to the balcony, enjoying the sights of the city at night. He knew what he was looking for. The dark sedan that suddenly emits several men; men with purpose and uniformity and flanked by a small contingent of the Mexican police, resplendent in their fawn uniforms and their shiny side arm's tucked carelessly into worn leather holsters on the hip.

In his mind's eye, he could see the shapes of several figures running along the corridor of his hotel floor. They would remain covert for as long as possible and they would be armed. They could neither let him escape, or die. They wanted him to talk.

So it came as no surprise when the knock on the hotel room door came, less than five minutes later. He moved to a spot directly in front of the door, like an actor on a theatre stage, about to give a grand performance. His arms were outstretched at shoulder height to his sides; a Christ-like figure on the cross. He was ready and eager to leave this world. "The door's open," he called. "Let yourself in."

To hell with them all, he thought. The CIA, the KGB, and the politicians that run them. Hell, let them butcher one another. He hoped the Cold War would become a Hot War. Many times in the great game, the knight was sacrificed for a better tactical advantage, so why should this time be any different?

He waited for the pause, then slowly the handle turned and the door began to open on its arc, the barrel of an automatic pistol cautiously leading the way. He had enough time to see this before he pressed the button on the detonator and watched as the fizzle of the acid burned away and dropped the plunger into the plastic explosive.

The firestorm of light was almost biblical.

Chapter Nine

The Director of Central Intelligence was about to pack up his brief-case for the day and call for his driver to bring the car around when his personal line rang. It was his Deputy Director, Webster. "Mr. Director we've just had word from Mexico City. There's been an explosion. Eight confirmed dead, dozens more wounded."

"Ferrera?"

"Yes sir, he set off a bomb he'd rigged inside his hotel room. Took out himself, our snatch team and several Mexican police officers," said Webster.

The DCI swore under his breath. "Alright Roy, get up here, we need to manage this situation."

It was a god-awful mess. The DCI was a father himself, knew how he would have felt, and he certainly would have handled Ferrera's grief much better than his predecessor, who had frankly made the situation worse with his acid tongue and incompetence. However, this didn't make his problem any less tangible. Ferrera was dead now – that at least was a blessing – and even if he had left any evidence behind the Agency would simply make it disappear, or simply deny everything anyway.

No, the real problem now was Higgins. What to do with him? He certainly couldn't be let off. His actions were treasonous, after all. He'd broken a bond of trust that could never be repaired and to give him his liberty was opening the Agency up to possible extortion. And that would not happen, not during his tenure. Higgins was too dangerous to be kept alive and free. What was needed, was a subtle removal to a thorny problem.

Ten minutes later, Roy Webster entered the DCI's office. Both men sat down and looked at each other. Finally, it was the DCI who spoke. "I think we need to make this mess go away, Roy. Go away and trim off any loose ends."

"I take it you mean Higgins?"

The DCI nodded. "He's the one who holds the balance of power at the moment, the one who could destroy the Agency with a phone call."

Webster nodded. "I think that's a wise decision, Mr. Director. There's someone we know of who could deal with this problem for us. Quietly, discreetly."

The DCI was well aware of the gravity of issuing the order to kill an operative. It was both risky and morally askew. And while as a government employee, albeit a very powerful one, he could not sanction an assassination at a political level anymore thanks to the recent Executive Orders from the White House, there was a caveat that allowed him to interject at an operational level if necessary in extreme circumstances. Extreme circumstances like this. "Who, someone on staff?"

"No, it's… complicated. He's a freelancer, effectively. He's very good, exceptional in fact. His cryptonym is Caravaggio," said Webster.

The DCI raised an eyebrow. "Caravaggio, like the artist? I've heard of this fellow, rumor only, of course."

"Actually, he's informally known as the 'Master'. They say he's turned wet-work into an art form."

"Do we have control of him? As an asset, I mean?" asked the DCI.

"No, sir, he's not an agent in the classic sense of the word. He works only for very high rewards and even then, only if the 'job' interests or challenges him. He's been involved in several high-level intelligence operations for a variety of Western agencies, all of them successful. I think it's fair to say he's something of a legend within the intelligence community."

"Mmm," the Director mused. He didn't like the thought of not having a source under his control, it was too vague and unwieldy, but he had to admit his options were limited. The Assistant Director of Plans had left him in a precarious situation, both professionally and politically. He had been brought in to take a firm hold of the CIA following the retirement of the previous Director, and he was damned if he was going to be kicked out because one of his senior men had decided to be a part of some stupid revenge crusade. He needed this whole mess to disappear.

He had made up his mind, distasteful as it was, but sometimes ruthless decisions needed to be taken by honorable men. "Can you get in touch with this Caravaggio?"

"I'll try, sir. We can only ask, however, as I say, he only works for the highest bidder and for unique operations."

"There is no price ceiling on this one. How would it... happen?"

Webster shrugged. "Oh, these things always play out a certain way Mr. Director. We offer Higgins a choice; prosecution or early retirement. He'll fall into line and retire. We then cut him loose from the Agency and have him on a very long leash. In six months, or eight months, or even a year's time from now, just when everyone has forgotten about this affair, that's when our contractor makes his move."

The Director nodded, satisfied with the DDCI's hypothesis. "Tell him that, and I want it done quietly, an accident maybe."

"Perhaps a heart attack, sir, middle aged men, stressful job – it's not uncommon," suggested Webster.

The Director had no doubt that in a few months' time, following the enforced retirement of Richard Higgins, he would receive a report about the man's fate; drowning while swimming, a car accident, a fatal illness, a random shooting while out hunting. Really, the method was irrelevant, only the end result mattered.

Yes, it would be a report that he would read, digest and then burn in the fullness of time.

He could wait. He was a patient man.

Book Seven:
Endgame

Chapter One

Rome. The Eternal City. A place of culture, art, history and equally entwined in its lineage was a record of both murder and politics. *It was a beautiful day, in fact the perfect day to carry out the final contract of the mission,* thought Marquez.

He had been in Italy less than three days. He'd flown in to Rome's Fiumicino Airport using his final false passport in the name of Andre Delacroix, a Frenchman. In that time, he'd settled into a quiet hotel along the Tiber, purchased a small car and rented a garage, which he would use as a workshop to carry out the necessary planning.

His plan was to snatch her once she left her city apartment and he was certain from his systematic surveillance, that he had most of the details of her routine; out shopping during the day, stop for lunch with friends, meetings in the afternoons with what seemed to be senior officials from the various ministries of the Italian government, before returning to her apartment. In the evenings, she would normally be the dinner guest of wealthy Italian families who were keen to have her company, before returning home around midnight.

He knew she had been in Rome on vacation for the past week, he also knew he only had a window of another two days before she returned to New York and the United Nations. Therefore, he had to act tonight. It was simple really, probably the easiest of all the contracts he'd been asked to complete.

Pick her up after she left her apartment and was headed for her Alfa Romeo, get her in the car, take her somewhere remote, in this case the garage he'd rented on the outskirts of the city, drug her, tie her up in the passenger seat of her car and detonate it outside the Russian Embassy in Rome. He would finish this contract with a bang.

After the aborted shooting in Paris and the disappearance of Gioradze off the face of the earth, he had to assume the operation had been compromised in some way. Where the leak had come from, was anyone's guess. It could have been that one of his contacts had talked, possibly the German had felt slighted in Marseilles and had tipped off the Russians for some coin. He discounted the fact that Gioradze would have talked. The man was far too tough and the last person he would spill to would be the Russians. He hated them with a passion.

The Paris shooting had also injured him. The bullet from the short, blond-haired man had taken him in the left hand and while it had been painful, it had been bearable for a man of his constitution. Should he have continued with the contract? He'd given his word to the American certainly, and the CIA man himself had given him tacit approval to back out if he wished.

But Marquez was not a man who was easily dissuaded from risk, far from it. So the decision to carry on with the contract when all his professional nerves were signaling for him to cancel and abort came as no surprise. It was the challenge of the odds against him which kept him playing. Besides, Rome was his last job and after that, his false life would be dumped and he could return to his real identity.

All he had to do was kill one more target; a woman who wouldn't see him coming and who was, physically at least, no match for a determined abductor and killer.

* * *

Contessa Sophia Argento sat at her writing bureau and signed her name across a letter she had penned to her late husband's brother in Washington. It was a ritual she completed several times a year, to reassure her brother-in-law that she was in good health and doing well.

She looked in the mirror above her writing desk and took note of the face that stared back at her. She still had a delicate, elfin face, despite the odd line around the eyes, and thick, lustrous dark hair tumbled over her left shoulder showing only the odd fleck of grey. The elfin face had come from her mother, an English governess who worked for a rich family in Taranto, and the dark hair had been a gift from her father, an aristocratic Italian Count who had wooed the English governess over the course of a hot and passionate summer more than four decades before.

Her childhood had been one of happiness and love, and as her teenage years turned into adulthood, she had found a calling in helping her fellow Italians in their villages and communities. Her English mother's sense of fairness and her Italian father's drive had given Sophia a good grounding in connecting with people. She'd been a passionate representative of the people of Italy during the war, when she'd been an active member of one of the numerous Communist Party resistance groups, determined to remove the Nazi boot-heel from the face of Italy.

In 1946 she'd married Thomas Reynolds, whom she had first met when he'd been parachuted in as part of an SIS/OSS liaison team to help stir up resistance ahead of the impending invasion. Captain Tom Reynolds had been the archetypal all-American officer; strong, confident and handsome. The young Captain and his beautiful Italian resistant contact had inevitably grown close over the coming months, working together, moving from safe-house to safe-house, with Sophia acting as his interpreter and guide.

What had started as a bond forged by war, had grown into a full-on, passionate affair and with the war over, Sophia had thrown herself into rebuilding her country when she later stood as a Member of Parliament. Tom had also assisted, by using his contacts in the US government and they had both been part of a post-war project helping to invigorate Italy. They'd been happy years; helping the people, making a difference to Italy and finding their love for each other once again.

The couple had lived a blessed life working in Rome, holidaying in America and visiting her late mother's relatives in London. They were the glamour couple of Italian politics during the 1950's. Travel, success and good looks had made them a part of the international 'jet-set'. Her husband's contacts had also given her some political clout. The Reynolds brothers were keen supporters of a young, up-and-coming Democratic congressman from Massachusetts. Several times on their visits to Washington they had a chance to meet with the charismatic and handsome politician. "He's the future of America Soph'," Tom had said. "That Kennedy guy sure knows how to get things done."

Not that it had all been smooth sailing in the early years of her political career; the blustering fools of the collegial parliament had thought she'd been a Communist. She was not and never would be. It was just that the Italian Communist Party had held the best advantage of active measures and resistance against the Germans during the war, and it seemed like the best vehicle for motivating the peasants.

In time, her reputation for honesty and fairness grew among her colleagues and it became known that she was not open to corruption and bribes. She was wealthy enough in her own right, thanks to the inheritance left to her by her father. She owned land, farms, property and shares in various businesses and could not be persuaded to compromise herself for any expedient political opportunity that came along.

Sophia Argento transcended the traditional political classes of the right and the left and instead, was a calming influence within the bloody in-fighting of the Italian parliament. She later declared herself a moderate and joined the Christian Democrats, where it was rumored she had the ear of the soon-to-be Prime Minister Aldo Moro.

In 1959, Tom had been travelling back to their summer villa in Puglia when his car had been stopped one night by a cart upturned and its contents of straw strewn across the small back road. Tom had looked at his watch. 8.45. He was already late for their dinner party and Sophia would give him that fiery Italian look of hers that said 'Let me down at your peril!' To drive back down onto the main road would add another fifteen minutes to his journey. But if he could move the abandoned cart onto the side of the road… So he did what anyone would do. He stepped out of his car and into the warmth of a summer night to clear the debris. That was to be a fatal mistake. A figure in the darkness rose from behind a wall and opened up with a sub-machine gun. A short clatter of gunfire later, and Thomas Reynolds was thrown back onto the hood of his own vehicle.

His body was found later that night by a search party from the villa, who went looking for their errant host. On his chest was pinned a note, claiming that he had been assassinated by the local brigade of the Italian Communist Revolutionary Party. His crime, so the message said, was for his continuing support of the puppet regime in Rome.

She had grieved for over a year, had dressed in a traditional black mourning dress and shroud and had shut herself away, either in her villa in Puglia or on the occasional visits to Rome in her apartment. She did not socialize, shunned publicity from the press and to all intents and purposes, had become a recluse. Then, as season gave way to season, she'd grown stronger, less fragile and more determined not to be a victim.

Following Thomas' death, she'd reverted back to her maiden name of Argento, and as she hadn't been able to have children, she decided she would dedicate the rest of her working life to helping the poor and impoverished, not only in Italy, but across the globe.

Her reputation had quickly seen her head-hunted by the newly appointed U.N. Secretary-General, who had admired her work in the Italian government and wanted her knowledge and wisdom to assist him with running a 'new U.N. for a new generation'. A move to New York and a position of trust as an Executive Assistant to the Secretary-General had given her a new lease of life, in the years following Tom's death.

Of course, there was also her secret work which she had elected to become involved in, and it was during these years that she'd been approached by two ruthless spies: the mercurial Porter from the British Secret Service and the intense Krivitsky from the KGB. It was a high-wire act of nerve and danger, and just as she loved Porter for his mind, his passion for his cause and his unwavering battle against his enemy, she also loathed and detested Krivitsky for his narrow-mindedness, murderous intent and morally corrupt ideology.

She had been in New York at the U.N. for barely a month, when she'd been contacted by a short, chubby man with a mop of unruly hair, who claimed to be a representative of an organization called 'The Phoenix Society'.

"We aim to help the people who really need help in some of the poorest countries in the world," the Englishman had said when he handed over a business card. "Perhaps I could buy you lunch, there's a very good place I know uptown."

The place was the restaurant in the Hotel St. Moritz and once the plates and glasses had been cleared away, the meeting had taken a distinctly surreal twist. The man, Porter, had braced his fingers together and leaned forward, conspiracy gleaming in his eyes. He told her, calmly and in detail, her life up until that point in time. He told her he respected her socialist leanings, her love of peoples, not just Italian, but all those who were downtrodden and had no voice to speak up for them.

"What are you?" she had asked, not believing any of his make believe story so far.

He had looked at her, bewildered, as if it was a nonsensical question. "Why I'm a spy, my love, pure and simple."

Her first reaction on hearing this had been to roar at him, make a show of him in front of the guests at the restaurant and then storm out. But the English man, no, the English *spy*, had soothed and calmed her. So she had put aside her temper and tapped into the cool logic that was her mother's discipline.

"Sophia you are one of us, we know how you assisted our agents during the war. We're on the same side and we always have been. Think of it as stopping the madness, bringing about a better future for both of our peoples. Together we can lift the veil and let the people see that the Communists are *lying* to the people," said Porter.

Oh, she had wanted to do that and more, she had said as a rebuke. But above all else, she wanted some kind of revenge for Tom. She knew the Englishman was manipulating her emotions regarding the circumstances surrounding Tom's death, of course he was. But in truth, she didn't care, she was happy to be used if it meant that some kind of justice was handed out for the murder of her husband. If it would stop another 'revolutionary' picking up a gun and killing another good and innocent man, then she would spy on the devil himself.

She rationalized it, by convincing herself she was using the intelligence services, just as much as they were using her. Porter convinced her that she was perfect for her future role as a double agent. She had a good pedigree; English mother, aristocratic Italian father. She had fought against the Germans during the war, had been a member of the Socialist party, had assisted the agents dropped behind the lines and post-war, rather than living a feckless life living off her father's money, she'd devoted herself to public life and become a respected member of the Italian Parliament.

Her initial 'pitch' to the resident KGB man in New York had been a nerve-wracking experience. She'd offered the cover story that she had long been a secret Communist, had recognized the weakness and folly of the capitalist system and was now, at this point in her life, determined to make a difference to the people of the world. She believed, she said, that the most effective way to do that was through a Communist system.

The KGB man had noted down her comments and promised he would be in touch. When he'd gone, she'd stood shaking in the middle of her hotel room, sweat running down the small of her back. She was a fraud, a liar; she would fail and be exposed as a sham. She knew it, the KGB man knew it, and then the whole world would know it.

A week later, she had her first agent-to-agent contact with her KGB recruiter and controller, the fearsome Krivitsky. She thrived and had taken to her new role with a relish, and so at the age of forty-seven,

Sophia Argento had dipped her toes into the festering pond of double agent intelligence work.

The star of LYRA had risen and shone.

Chapter Two

Sophia Argento's apartment was on the fourth floor, a three-bedroom exclusive domicile on the fashionable Via Margutta, an area that was the preserve of the wealthy and the famous.

In recent years, she had seen Sophia Loren and the film director Fellini in the neighborhood. It was her private sanctuary when she was in Rome and the one place where she could relax. Her regular annual vacation back to Rome also gave her the chance to indulge in the secret part of her life that her family and friends had no idea about. She had met with her KGB contact at Piazza San Pietro, pretending she was just another tourist visiting the Vatican.

However, this time her contact was not the usual Russian, the vile little man who leered at her through his butcher's eyes. For some reason, he hadn't been able to attend and had been replaced by a nervous young officer. The man had stuttered in appalling Italian that there was a crisis and that her usual contact would not be able to make it.

"Should I be concerned?" she'd asked.

The man had shaken his head. "We will be in touch; but you should be aware of your personal security. This is a dangerous business."

No details, no idea what form this 'danger' would manifest itself in, no advice and no help. So she had returned to her apartment, eaten a light lunch and then set about writing a letter to her brother-in-law in Washington.

It was only when she'd finished the letter and signed her name that she heard the gentle knock on her apartment door. Sophia turned in her chair and looked for a long, cool moment at the door at the far end of the hallway. It couldn't be any of her neighbors in the other apartments; she knew that instantly, that wasn't the way it worked on the Via Margutta.

At that moment, the words of the KGB contact came back to her – something about it being a dangerous business.

* * *

She opened the door and was greeted not by a hard-faced assassin, but by a young lady, a beautiful young lady. *A touch of a young Katherine Hepburn,* thought Sophia. Except for the eyes, the eyes held a recently acquired hardness. "Si?" said Sophia, a questioning look on her face.

The young woman took a step forward into the apartment and spoke. "Might I have a word with you in private? No, don't speak, please, and forgive my awful trampling of your language. My name is Nicole. We have a mutual acquaintance, it seems, a Mr. Porter, an English gentleman. You know whom I mean?"

Sophia shook her head, living her cover. "I'm sorry, I have no idea..."

But the young woman was not dissuaded and carried on, taking another step forward so that her whole body was now in the doorway. "He regrets he couldn't come himself, but he thought I would be an acceptable replacement. He asked me to ask you how his 'Lyra' is. And does she still miss the British winters?"

Sophia Argento gasped as she recognized the truth of what this young woman was saying and she wondered if the truth was something she wanted to hear.

* * *

Fifteen minutes later, they were sitting in the drawing room, face-to-face. The young woman, Nicole, had switched off the light, drawn all the curtains and then turned the light switch in the room back on. Then she'd given the older woman a brief appraisal of the situation that was developing that night in Rome.

"What should I do? Should I go to the British Embassy?" Sophia had asked.

"No! Absolutely not! Your cover is still intact, and besides, they know nothing about this mission. Best bet is to disappear. Don't contact anyone. You have to leave now. My senior officer is waiting for you downstairs. He'll take you somewhere secure. You'll go out through the rear of the property, there's less chance of the killer having surveillance there. Take nothing with you," said Nicole.

Sophia nodded. It was all happening so fast that her mind was whirling with the gravity and scale of it all.

"My boss's name is Gorilla. Don't worry, he's house trained." Nicole smiled, trying to lighten the mood and put the older woman at ease. "Give me the keys to your car. I'll go out the front. If we're lucky, I'll be able to draw him away from your home. At night, and at a distance, we could easily pass for each other."

Sophia smiled, "Oh, I wish I had your youthful looks, my dear." But this English intelligence agent was right. The height, build, hair color and sense of dress were passable. Perhaps with a headscarf and darkened glasses it could work.

"I'll keep up your routine for the next few hours, until you've disappeared," said Nicole.

"And then?"

"Then I'll dump your car and meet up with you at our apartment later tonight. Don't worry, we'll keep you safe. Now go," said Nicole, pushing Agent LYRA out of the door.

Sophia scurried down the staircase, her heels clicking on the elegant stone steps that spiraled towards the main hallway. She passed the third floor, praying that she didn't meet Signora Fausti who lived below her, well-meaning though she was, the Signora could talk until the end of days or even more awkward would be bumping into Dottore Abbate, who would want to know every little detail of what she had been up to during her visit to Rome this time.

But good fortune was with her. The stairway and landings were empty and the residents of the rest of the apartments were safely ensconced inside. She increased her pace, one hand lightly brushing the banister rail while all the time her feet were working in perfect synchronicity to reach the bottom of the stairs.

The hallway was in semi-darkness; someone had turned off several of the hall lights. Probably the English spy or her partner. She looked out towards the front doors, expecting to see the young woman's partner. But instead all she was treated to was a foreboding heavy oak door which was locked against the chill night. Then she remembered. The young woman had said that she would be leaving by the rear entrance, which would take her past the shed where the gardener kept his work tools, along the secret garden at the rear of the property and out into the side street on the Via del Babuino.

Sophia began to turn when a voice spoke. "Lyra," said the voice from the dark recess of the hallway. A man stepped forward, giving a physical form to the voice.

"Yes… you are Gorilla?" she said. It was a question, not a statement. She looked doubtfully at the man in front of her. He was well presented, a good suit, quality overcoat, expensive shoes.

But it was the face; short cropped blond hair, a scowl and hard eyes. The face of a thug. He looked more like a London gangster, such as she had seen in the newspapers, than an intelligence operative.

The man nodded and held out a hand. "Please come with me. We haven't far to travel and my car is just down the street." She took his hand and let him lead her into the darkness. "Be brave," he said. "We have to be alert. There is danger on every street corner."

Chapter Three

Gorilla and Nicole had been alerted by the Burrowers that one of the 'flagged' passports that Marquez was using – Delacroix – had shown up and that they needed to get to Rome fast. They had arrived less than a day and a half ago and were secreted in another one of SIS's tame safe-houses, this time in a small apartment block off the Piazza Navona, which like its predecessors in Paris and Marseilles, was functional but nothing more. They had run to the same routine they'd used in the past, and why not, it worked!

Their ID covers were clean and despite the shootings in France, there was no evidence to confirm that anyone was looking for them. So once again, they were the Ronsom's, the travelling honeymoon couple who stayed in safe-houses provided by the local SIS Stations and travelled around in cheap, disposable cars that were destined for the scrap yard once their operation was finished.

Nicole gave the Contessa a good twenty minutes to get clear of the apartment building before she decided to leave. The dark glasses, the scarf wrapped tightly around her head and the elegant suede coat would do enough to hide the subterfuge to the casual passersby. *And hopefully, a trained killer also,* she thought.

She glanced out into the dark street to see if she could spot any possible surveillance. A few cars, a few people walking quickly in an attempt to dodge the rain, but nothing untoward, nothing that set off any alarm bells. *But then there wouldn't be would there,* she thought.

If he's as professional as we think he is, he wouldn't leave any signs of surveillance. Nicole gave herself a final inspection in the mirror. Satisfied, she grabbed the keys to the Alfa Romeo from the little ashtray and left, carefully closing the door behind her.

When she made it to ground level, she noted that the hallway was poorly lit. *That's Gorilla, taking care of business,* she thought. With limited illumination, the darkness of the hallway would also help with her disguise. She pulled open the heavy front door and stood stock still, seemingly adjusting her coat and gloves, but in reality to give any surveillance watchers the opportunity to see her and take the bait.

Nicole looked out at the rain, the drizzle had turned to a downpour, but nevertheless she was determined to keep herself on show as long as possible. She turned, pulled the main door shut, then began the fifty yard walk to the car.

Behind the dark glasses her eyes were on the alert, looking left and right, but noting no sign of a threat or danger. *Maybe he's not in place,* she thought. *Or maybe he's called the hit off, perhaps having spotted us!*

She made it safely all the way into the Alfa Romeo, a 1964 Giulia Sprint GTC in gleaming red. She inserted the key into the lock and turned. She quickly climbed into the leather seat, eager to be out of the pouring rain. The engine purred into life and she gently revved the accelerator to get a feel for the car's power. She checked the rear view mirror, ready to move away and was confronted with a dark spectre looming over her from the rear passenger seat.

A hand clamped down firmly on her right shoulder and she felt the unmistakable coldness of a pistol barrel pushed into the small gap between her ear and the headscarf. Nicole let out an involuntary yelp. The pistol ground in deeper, as if in warning. There would be no missed shots at this range she knew; the bullet would simply blow a hole in her skull.

She risked a glance once more into the rear view mirror. The man's face was dark, hidden in shadows. She could make out the long profile of the face, the slicked back dark hair and blazing eyes. The last time she'd seen this face was in a bar years ago in the Caribbean, and yes, she wasn't that far off with her memory, a little older and a little greyer certainly, but still the same.

"Good evening, Contessa," said the voice, thick and cultured. "My Italian is poor, so just in case there is any misunderstanding, I will converse in English. Is that acceptable?"

Nicole gently nodded her head forward, being careful not to make any sudden movements and reinforced it with a "Si."

"Excellent, then please drive and don't try anything foolish. It would be a shame to ruin the inside of your car with blood."

* * *

Marquez had been lucky when he'd snatched his target. The Via Margutta had been quiet at that time of night, that and the fact that the rain had kept most people off the streets had also worked in his favor. He had plenty of time to 'pop' the lock of the small Alfa Romeo and hide in the rear.

He guessed she would venture out at some point during the evening, perhaps for dinner or to visit friends, and so when the rain began, he reasoned she would more than likely take her car rather than walk the streets of Rome in the dark. If she didn't, and either stayed ensconced or took a taxi, his plan would be ruined and he would have to abort the surveillance until the next day.

He'd sat cramped in the rear foot-well of the Alfa for almost two hours, covered with his jacket, fighting the boredom and the risk of being spotted by a chance passerby. So when he was just about to give up hope and abort the operation for the evening, he was handed a large dose of luck. From his vantage point beneath his cover, he made out a slim figure standing beside the rain splattered driver's door, fumbling with the keys.

He flicked the safety of the Tokarev pistol and smiled to himself. The rest of the kidnapping had been relatively by rote; the surprise to the victim, the isolation, the threat of violence and the drive to the secure warehouse on the edge of the city where he would set in place the necessary measures to conclude this now troublesome contract.

The garage had originally been used by a mechanic who had recently retired and it had been sitting empty for the past month. So when the vendor was offered double the monthly rental price for a quick and unregulated lease, he'd snapped it up and no questions asked.

The Alfa pulled up in front of the double garage doors, Marquez held the gun on her and they both exited the vehicle in tandem. A quick unlocking of the heavy padlock, a flick of the light and they were inside. He led her by the arm towards the chair in the small office; her prison cell for the rest of the evening. It was only when she turned that he'd sensed something wasn't right. His mind whirled with confusion. Same look, same build, similar clothes, but no, no, not quite the same. She was too young, he thought.

"Take off the glasses and the scarf," he said, rummaging in his pocket for the surveillance photo he carried of Sophia Argento. The girl, for she was younger than the Contessa by a good twenty years, slowly removed them and tossed them onto the floor. A quick glance at the photograph and then the young woman in front of him confirmed they were not the same person. But from a distance and in the dark, yes, it had been enough to fool him. He raised the gun and pointed it directly at her head.

"Who the hell are you?" he said, the words coming out in a bitter fury. Damn his foolishness for being deceived by a slip of a girl.

Nicole took a breath, trying her best to remain calm. "Who I am is of no matter. Suffice to say that the Contessa is now under our protection."

Marquez thought about it for a moment, finding it an effort to clear his mind. The Russians, it had to be the Russians. It was obvious really, the politician was a KGB deep cover asset and they would protect her at all costs. But how did they know he was planning to take her? Probably the same way that they'd had the edge on them in Marseilles and Paris? "Russian. You don't look Russian," he said.

"What is a Russian meant to look like?" She'd decided to play along with the ruse. Gorilla had told her of Gioradze's belief that they were Russian operatives there to protect the KGB agents. She saw no reason to dissuade this killer of that notion.

"Where is the Contessa?" Marquez stepped forward and ground the barrel of the gun deeper into the back of her neck; she felt the small metal front sight pushing against her skin. *"Where?"*

Nicole flinched from the pain. "I don't know. Far enough away from you though!"

Damn! His plan to kill the Contessa outside the Russian Embassy was in ruins. "Are you with the small man, the blond man? I bet that you are. Have you been to Marseilles recently my dear... were you in Paris? Have you been tracking me?" Her silence infuriated him even more. "No matter, we'll have plenty of time to talk soon enough. Now where is he?"

Still, she met his gaze with a cool silence. He lashed out with his shoe, kicking her hard in the shin, causing her to scream. She stifled the scream, but there were tears forming in her eyes. "He's... he's... at the apartment he uses. I don't know where it is," she lied. "It's more secure that way. I swear!"

"More secure," repeated Marquez, considering her answer. It made sense they would have cut-out procedures in place. It was standard practice for all intelligence operatives. But still, something wasn't adding up. "How do you get in touch with him?"

Nicole ignored him and turned her gaze to the floor. Marquez, noting her resistance, slapped her sharply across the face and then jammed the pistol barrel into the side of her knee. *"Tell me,* tell me now or I'll kill you piece by piece! Have you ever seen a kneecap shot off; it's not very nice, very painful, as are both knees, elbows, wrists, ankles..." His finger moved slowly nearer to the trigger.

"It's... it's... a phone number," she said, the tears now rolling down her cheeks.

Marquez stood back, lowered the Tokarev and smiled. "Excellent, you see how easy that was? Now what is the number?"

She gave him the telephone number of their apartment. *It's only a number,* she told herself. At least he can't connect the address to that. "He'll come for me. You know that, don't you?"

Marquez turned to look at her, his face as hard as stone. "My dear, I am absolutely counting on it."

* * *

Gorilla and Sophia had been back in the safe-house for just over an hour when the phone rang. He heard the peal of the antiquated telephone and picked up the receiver quickly, heard the clunk as the phone system sparked into life, and was greeted by sobbing from the other end of the line.

"Jack... it's me... I've..."

"Where are you, we were expecting you over half an hour ago?" It was the scream that caused him to jerk the handset away from his ear. "Nicole? *Nicole! Where are you?*"

There was a brief crackling as the handset was moved from the screaming girl over to a heavy breathing, male voice, as if the person on the other end had suddenly exerted himself physically.

"Who is this?" Gorilla demanded.

"You know who it is. We've met before; Marseilles, I'm guessing and certainly Paris, where you shot me. Not fatal, but enough to cause me intense pain," answered Marquez.

"We all have off days, next time I'll make sure I aim higher. That's a promise."

"Of course, of course. You speak very good English for a Russian."

"And you speak very good English for a soon to be dead man. But enough of the pleasantries. Give me the girl back," growled Gorilla.

"Ah, if only it was that easy."

Gorilla snarled into the phone. "Don't make me come over there, you won't like it... If you've hurt her!"

"Oh, only a little motivational force, nothing too permanent, but that could change," replied Marquez.

Gorilla held down his rage. This was how parents who have had their children ripped away from them must feel, he suspected. That sense of helplessness, and impotence.

He wanted to smash things, rip out his own teeth, inflict pain upon this man, shoot, slash and burn him, do anything to stop him and to stop the rage that was about to engulf him. But of course, he did none of these things. Instead, he listened to the assassin on the other end of the phone.

"I propose a trade. The girl for the Contessa; she is very beautiful. It would be a shame to have to destroy that beauty for the sake of stubbornness, my friend, a shame indeed," said Marquez.

Oh great, thought Gorilla. *He's a 'talker'. Likes the sound of his own voice and likes to tell the world about how ruthless and cunning he is.* That fact alone made Gorilla want to shoot him in the head, as quickly as possible.

"Do I have an answer?" an impatient Marquez said down the line. "An exchange? Your agent for my target?"

You're crazy, thought Gorilla. Even if he wanted to, the chances of him handing over an SIS asset to be executed were nonexistent. *But when in Rome,* he thought, as he decided to fall headlong and eyes wide open into the trap that Marquez was setting. "Alright. Where and when?"

"Tonight. You have ninety minutes. Bring the Contessa with you and you can have the girl back, relatively unharmed. Then you go your way and I go mine. If you bring back-up, I'll see it and kill her," said Marquez.

"No. Don't worry, there'll be no back up. It will just be me."

"Good."

"And the where?" asked Gorilla.

Marquez laughed down the phone. "Ah, yes of course, forgive me. I have chosen a most suitable location. Somewhere quite fitting in fact. The Piazza del Colosseo."

Gorilla frowned. "But isn't that the—"

"Yes, it is. You have ninety minutes."

* * *

Marquez replaced the phone into its cradle and looked at the young woman handcuffed to the radiator. He had nearly lost everything, but if he played the game correctly, he could still have his reward and win.

His original plan had been to kill the Contessa outside the Russian Embassy, but obviously, that part of the operation would now have to be scrapped. However, with a little improvising, he could still complete the final hit of his contract and wreak revenge on the KGB assassin and his bitch who had been following him.

Yes, improvisation was the key here. He picked up the rucksack that contained his weapons and the piece of chain he'd planned to use to secure the Contessa to the steering wheel of her car. He looked over at the young woman once more. She was sitting on the floor with her knees drawn up and head down.

"Come, we have much work to do; a final piece of theatre, one last act to play out," he said.

* * *

"Is she alright? Talk to me! What has happened?"

Gorilla turned to Sophia, his brow furrowed in concentration, but also something more. Then she sensed it, could tell by his hands clasping and unclasping like an animal's claws. It was suppressed rage.

"No, she's not. Things have taken a serious turn for the worse," he said. Gorilla was sick of it all. Sick of hiding in the shadows, sick of chasing this killer from one end of Europe to the next, sick of always being on the back foot and sick of having missed this bastard twice already. What he wanted was a good old-fashioned out in the open fight that would settle it once and for all! And so it seemed, did Marquez.

First things first, he thought. Nicole had clearly given Marquez the telephone number to their base and he couldn't take the risk that she'd also told him the address. It could be a double bluff. Barter for a meeting to lull him into a false sense of security and then launch a surprise attack on their apartment. No, the apartment had been compromised, there was nothing left to do but evacuate and quickly. He turned to Sophia. "Nicole's been grabbed, taken by the man sent here to kill you. He wants a trade – your life for hers."

She looked aghast. *Has it come to this,* she thought. My life being bartered, one spy for another?

Gorilla saw the look of horror on her face and put a hand up to re-assure her. "Don't worry, nothing's going to happen to you, I promise. But this location is compromised, we have to move to a new location and we're going to have to do it right now."

She nodded, feeling her knees weaken, she slumped slowly onto the chair. "But what about Nicole?" she said. "She was taken by this maniac whilst trying to protect me, if anything were to happen to her.

"It won't. Trust me, I'm going to get her back and finish this once and for all." His first job was to let Masterman know the game had taken a twist. He picked up the phone and went through the whistles and clicks of the operator until he'd reached Masterman on his private line.

"I was about to go to a Regimental dinner, Jack, this better be good," said Masterman.

"It is. Listen up, I don't have much time. This operation's about to come to an end," he said. Gorilla talked swiftly. Told of the subterfuge to disguise Nicole as agent LYRA, the snatching by the killer Marquez, and the 'trade' that was to take place later that night.

"Okay. What do you need?" said Masterman, ever the leader of men. He knew when to give his operatives whatever they needed to get the job done. That was one of his strengths; the ability to cut through the bull.

"I need a new safe-house in Rome, immediately, for agent *LYRA*. Plus, there'll need to be armed security on it as well. I can't risk leaving her unprotected, in case Marquez squeezes the information from Nicole."

"Alright, you can't go to the Embassy, that would blow her cover; we need to keep her at arm's length as much as possible. Give me a few minutes, I'll see what we've got nearby," said Masterman.

"Okay, but as quick as you can, we don't have much time on this one. The clock's ticking. In truth, I think the request for me to hand over *LYRA* is just a ruse. It's partly me he wants. He wants to finish me off with a bullet in my head, probably kneeling and begging for my life. LYRA would just be a bonus."

"And you think you can get the girl back, Jack? Get her back and take him out as well? You up for that, are you?"

"I'll have to be, won't I?" murmured Gorilla. He gave Masterman five minutes to return the call, but the Colonel phoned back in two.

"There's a place not too far from you. *LYRA* can hide out for the next few hours. It's safe, secure and more importantly, the man running it is armed and more than capable. It's not ideal, but at short notice it's the best we've got." Masterman gave him the address. The *Sant' Anselmo all ' Aventino* church in Piazza dei Cavalieri di Malta in the center of the city.

Gorilla guessed it was no more than fifteen minutes' drive away. Hopefully, he should have more than enough time to make it to the rendezvous with Marquez. "A church! You've got to be kidding. Who are we meeting? Who runs the safe-house?"

Masterman told him. "You should be happy Jack; it's not often that people in our trade get to meet legends. Now get going."

* * *

The drive was uneventful. Gorilla had been correct, the Church of St Anselms of the Aventine was no more than a quarter of an hour's drive away from their apartment base, but just to be on the safe side, he took them on a circuitous counter-surveillance route around the city that added an extra twenty minutes onto the journey time.

He glanced at his watch. Just under an hour left until he had to be at the Coliseum. It was cutting it fine, but it was still manageable.

The car pulled up and Gorilla scanned the area before exiting. He wrapped a protective arm around Sophia and quickly hurried her to shelter out of the rain. They made their way around the side of the building as Masterman had instructed. "Ignore the main entrance to the church and go to the side of the building to the sacristy. He'll be expecting you. Give him my codename; that's the contact procedure," he had said.

Gorilla banged on the thick door with a fist. There was a pause and then from inside, came the grinding noise of metal bolts and chains being retracted. The heavy wooden door was pulled back to reveal a glow of candlelight burning bright. The shape of a large, heavily built man wearing a traditional cassock and collar greeted him. The man had the look of a heavyweight prize fighter and he glared down with somber eyes from beneath a greying head of hair and weather-beaten face. "Si," said the priest.

"I come from Sentinel," said Gorilla.

The man stepped back, showing them the interior of the sacristy. "Come quickly, inside, hurry. I am Father Mario Frazzano," he said as he hefted a Schmeisser MP40 sub-machine gun that he'd been concealing behind his back. "I understand that there is danger in Rome tonight. It pays for the wise man to take serious precautions."

* * *

Masterman had been right, a legend indeed. An old one, but a legend nonetheless!

Father Mario Frazzano, known as the *Diavolo Sacerdote*, the 'Devil Priest', was a living legend within SIS and for the Redaction team especially. Gorilla had once heard him speak as a guest lecturer on a service training course, on working in enemy-held territory. The man had been both humble and tough.

In the latter years of the war, the young priest had been the leader of a resistance cell on the island of Sicily and the link man between the various resistance groups and SIS back in London. For those few years leading up to the invasion, Mario Frazzano had, by day, been a humble priest, but by night had been the scourge of the German forces. Sabotage, assassination, and insurrection had all come under the remit of *Diavolo Sacerdote*. Legend had it that he had personally slaughtered seven senior SS officers with his own hands.

Since the end of the war, he had still occasionally helped the British with several of their operations; mainly offering introductions, providing safe-houses, emptying dead-drops. But no more killing. Those few years during the war had washed his hands with enough blood to last a lifetime. So no killing.

That is, unless he had to.

* * *

Gorilla had been left in the Sacristy while Sophia had been taken to the small house at the rear of the church.

Five minutes later the priest returned, still hefting the MP40. "She is resting, don't worry, she'll be fine. I have recruited one of my people to keep guard over her while we talk. If anyone chooses to disturb our guest tonight, they will be greeted by Franco's *Lupara*. Franco is an honorable man, a man of respect, who knows when to keep quiet."

Gorilla nodded. The priest seemed like a contradiction, a man of peace who was ready to kill. But then, Gorilla knew the man's history and knew better than to try to second guess him.

Father Frazzano poured them both a small glass of grappa and handed one to Gorilla. "I don't want to know who she is, it's better that I don't, but I would like to know what we are dealing with. If SENTINEL is involved, then I assume it is serious?"

Gorilla downed the grappa in one slug and placed the glass carefully on the table. He nodded. "It's serious enough. A professional killer has his sights set on her. She's the last one on his kill list and he has to complete his contract. It's just the way he is."

Frazzano nodded gravely. "I see. And there is no way of the police tracking him down?"

"No, Father. This is a below the radar operation. No one can know. He will carry on, unless I can kill him first." Gorilla looked at his watch. "I have to go. One of our people will be in touch to collect her when it is safe."

The priest stood up, holding the sub-machine gun in the crook of his arm as he opened the sacristy door for his guest. "Then go with God, my son."

Gorilla stood there staring at him for a few final seconds, then moved out into the night, into the rain. "No final words of prayer, Father? No absolution for my sins?" he asked, half mockingly.

"I don't think that it's prayers you need. You have the look of a man well-acquainted with death," said Frazzano, with a touch of sadness.

"How can you tell?" asked Gorilla. Was he marked, was there a stain that was visible, which showed he was a killer, a killer many times over.

But the priest simply closed the door, bolting it behind him, as if that was answer enough. Besides, Gorilla thought he knew what the priest had meant, knowing the *Diavolo's* history, it took one to know one.

* * *

"I've heard it said that when a man hunts another man to the death, he can never go back to hunting animals. Everything else seems rather flat and inconsequential. Almost as if the hunter had peaked with tracking and killing his fellow man. Mere beasts would be a bit of a letdown. What do you think of that?"

They were sat in C's new office on the top floor of Century House. The decorators had been in and given the place a spruce up before the Chief was finally allowed into his private domain. It was as if someone had uprooted his old office and thrown it across the river; everything was in its familiar place just as it had been at Broadway. The only difference was a new view; the spire of Big Ben and Parliament evident across the Thames.

"I have heard that too, sir," said Masterman.

"And what are your thoughts on it?"

Masterman pondered the question. "I think it is a fair summation."

In fact, he thought it was a load of balls. Masterman had hunted men in all manner of conflicts, some declared and some very much underground, it was never easy and at times distasteful, but in the final analysis it was a job that he'd been expected to carry out. It certainly didn't stop him from going pheasant or deer hunting in Scotland when the season was right. It was a lot of nonsense, but when the Chief of the Secret Intelligence Service was trying to make a point, he found it best to play along.

"So where are we, with Operation... oh damn, what's it called?" asked C.

"Mace, Sir."

C nodded, getting the details clear in his mind. "Yes, exactly Mace, one has so many operations to remember. What's the state of play thus far?"

The Chief had summoned him at the end of the working day for 'a quiet chat'. So a brisk drive from Pimlico to Lambeth and whisked upstairs past the senior officers' rooms to C's new river view office. Masterman still had his uniform on from tonight's now-cancelled Regimental dinner.

"It's Italy; the final stages are to be played out in Rome. Marquez tried to snatch *LYRA* but made a hash of it, not the least because my team had gotten there first and scuppered his plans. She is currently in a secure safe-house, under armed protection," said Masterman.

"I see, and everything is on track? Your people are ready to take this killer down?"

Masterman shifted uncomfortably in his chair. Nobody liked giving bad news to a superior officer, no matter how avuncular he might seem. "I've just spoken to my unit leader in Rome; it seems there's been a problem. One of my officers has been taken by Marquez, and he's expecting a trade, my officer in exchange for agent *LYRA*.

C reclined back in his chair and frowned. "We can assume the officer has talked, has he, to this Marquez?"

"It's a she, Sir. Nicole Quayle, a junior officer who had been seconded to Redaction for the duration of Mace."

C's head snapped up. "Good grief, Stephen! When one is handed an operational overview, one doesn't always read the fine details of personnel. A young woman of our service, you say?"

"According to my man in Rome, Marquez is under the impression that my team are, in fact, Russian agents there to wipe him out. From what I understand, it's a ruse that he's been encouraged to believe."

"Well, that's something. So the covers of Constellation's agents are still unblemished, it's nothing to do with us, it's the Russians protecting their investment in their spies. Is that a fair summation?"

"So far, sir," replied Masterman.

"And this man of yours, he's ready and primed to remove the last of these killers?"

Masterman nodded. "He is, as we speak, on his way to a rendezvous with Marquez. My officer has never let me down before. I fully expect him to finish what he started."

"That's excellent news, Stephen, I'm sure he will. After all, for the moment we have the upper hand in this game. Don't want us to lose that advantage, do we? Do you know, when I first proposed the creation of Redaction many years ago, I envisioned it to be a stealth-like creature, separate from the mainstream intelligence gathering of the rest of the Service, something that could be used when all other options were nullified," said C.

Masterman smiled. He remembered his first few weeks as the newly-appointed Head of Redaction, and how it had been drummed into him that Redaction was never to be seen, never to be heard, and never to be caught during an operation. They were the ghosts of SIS.

C continued, "I would hate to have to destroy my creation because it had become too loud and noisy, a distraction from the Service's usual operating style. Mace ends tonight, come hell or high water. I want all evidence and enemies expunged. Do I make myself clear?"

Masterman understood. Mace had been a difficult operation, far bigger and more widespread than anything the unit had been called on to handle before. The shootings and Redactions across Europe had given the senior command at SIS the vapors. "Of course. But what about the far-reaching consequences of Operation Mace? Mopping up the mess, so that the agents can survive?"

C waved it away. "Oh, I think we've done all we can for the moment. Let Porter and his case officers handle bringing Constellation back into the fold. Your man is armed and in place and the Americans are, as we speak, tracking down, if they haven't already, the culprits behind this rogue operation."

"So I'm led to believe," said Masterman.

C raised his hands in a reflective gesture. "Then for the moment, we can do nothing but sit back and see how the cards fall. It's the nature of intelligence work; you plan and plot and recruit and manipulate, but at the end of it all, we just have to sit in the hospital delivery ward and wait for the midwife to deliver our little progeny."

Masterman reflected on the amount of times he'd sat in the back of a jeep, or stood on a street corner or had been huddled inside a covert surveillance van, waiting for something to happen. The sense of frustration at having little or no control once the operation was in play never seemed to wane.

"In time, sooner rather than later, we'll give the Americans a friendly push to remind them how we helped them out during this debacle, use it as currency. Manipulate their embarrassment a little to make them more compliant. I rather fancy some more of that new-fangled satellite surveillance intelligence that the CIA has access to. Perhaps they'll feel like sharing it as and when we need it from now on," said C.

"And do you think they'll roll over that easily?"

"Oh, I know they will. It's what we do isn't it, take advantage of lesser beings. After all, our Service's job is to gain intelligence by any means, even if that does mean hamstringing our nearest and dearest colleagues. Well, don't let me keep you Stephen; I'm sure you'll want to keep a close eye on your operation. Do keep me informed about how it all goes and I very much look forward to meeting your officer when he returns victorious." C stood and ushered Masterman out of his office and returned to his desk.

A good man that, thought C. A credit to his father.

He pulled the next manila file across from his pending pile. It had the words OPERATION SHREDDER printed along the top. SHRED-DER, the next step along in SIS's greatest deception operation of the Cold War.

Chapter Four

Gorilla sat in the little Fiat, fuming, his knuckles white with tension on the steering wheel. He'd been locked in traffic for the past ten minutes and time was running out fast for him. He could see the Coliseum in the distance; he almost felt like he could touch it, that's how close it was.

The problem was that the traffic was backed all the way along the *Via de San Gregorio*, the result of a motor collision caused by the rain and the ensuing shunting of over a dozen vehicles had all but closed off most of the road. He had driven like the Devil from the church, throwing the small car around bends and speeding up on the long straight stretches. He had no idea of the roads he was driving down, or if he was even going the right way. Once or twice, he felt the rear end of the car sliding on the wet road surfaces. He revved the engine and held down the horn to keep pedestrians and other cars out of his way. So far, it had worked. *Probably by Italian driving standards, it was pretty tame,* he thought to himself.

All he could do was keep the spectacle of the Coliseum, rising like a mountain in the distance, in his sights. He knew that he would reach it soon... that was, until he finally made it onto the main arterial route that led directly to the Coliseum and everything stopped. Bastard bloody traffic! He had less than fifteen minutes to get to the rendezvous, less than that, in all truth, to help Nicole. He could sit here like a fool or do something!

"Bollocks to it," he growled. He lurched forward and began to feed the car through the lines of backed up traffic and after much horn blaring and obscene gesticulation from his fellow drivers, he managed to get the car over to the curbside on the right. One final surge of power and the car finally rested half on and half off the roadside. He kicked open the door, aware of the glowering looks of the other drivers, tightened his coat around him and set off into the rain.

Half a mile, he guessed, so he ran. He ran at full pelt. One arm holding onto the weight of the gun in the holster on his hip, covered by his coat. The restrictions of his suit and the heaviness of the overcoat all hampered his speed. The sweat was creasing the collar of his shirt and tie.

The snake of stalled traffic passed him by, his legs pumping fast. He barely noticed the cause of the delay as he sped by; a delivery truck had skidded and overturned, which had caused the pile up that was now blocking the traffic lanes. The drivers and passengers were now berating each other in angry Italian.

His breath rasped as he left the accident behind and the roads became miraculously clear, as if a stream had been brooked. The pavement began to climb gently until he was at the huge roundabout that was the *Via Celio Vibenna.* He crossed the road and spent a hair-raising few seconds dodging the traffic until, safely across, he finally made his way down the steps that led him onto the cobbled forecourt of the twelve story Coliseum. He wiped away the rain from his eyes and looked about for an access point. He ignored the main entrance, which was gated and locked. *No,* he thought, *not the tourist entrance that's too obvious, even at this time of night.*

He circled counter clockwise around the ancient building, looking for a not-so-obvious way in. Unsurprisingly, all the alcoves were secured with huge iron gates. He tested a few to gauge their resolve, but found that there would be no way of penetrating them without the help of an acetylene cutting kit. By the few people out on the street tonight, and those that were hurrying to escape from the rainstorm,

Gorilla was barely given a second glance. He would be classed as just another businessman on his way home and of no importance.

He checked his watch; it was less than five minutes before he had to confront Marquez and hand over a nonexistent agent. He doubted the killer would give him any more time and would probably execute Nicole on the spot. *Think, think, reason it out,* he told himself. Marquez must have found a way in, there must be a weak point that he took advantage of.

It was halfway through his second search when he found it. A small metal gate that looked locked, but wasn't. No security guard. Where was he? The gate had evidently been opened and the padlock had been replaced, but not locked shut. Why wouldn't he lock the padlock after him? *Because he wants you inside, you bloody idiot,* he chided himself. *He wants you inside to kill you; he's left you a clue so that you can enter unhindered.*

Gorilla checked around, but with no one in the vicinity, he swiftly pulled apart the rusty padlock from the bolt on the metal gate. He entered and reversed the process, ensuring that the padlock was merely held in place. To the casual observer, it would look like a secured gate. *Plus, it's better to have a quick escape point too,* he thought.

He turned and stepped into the shadow of the arch which formed the outer ring of the building, pulled the '39 from his hip holster and attached the silencer. A quick chamber check and a flicking off of the safety and he was ready. He moved slowly forward in the assassin's crouch, the pistol held one handed and out in front in the three quarter hip position, while his other hand hovered at his side in case of a surprise attack. He moved slowly forward, keeping to the shadows, and into the arena of death.

* * *

Gaining access to the Coliseum had actually been surprisingly easy, thought Marquez. In fact, it had been the easiest task of his whole time here in Rome. Simplicity itself.

He had kept the girl close; their arms linked and the gun in his pocket rammed into the side of her body. She had already been warned not to shout out or make a noise, and to play along. Play along or it would go very badly for her.

They had circled the Coliseum in the miserable rain storm, looking for a guard whom they could engage in conversation. On the first half rotation, they'd found him; an old man in an ill-fitting security guard uniform patrolling with his flashlight. Marquez had called out to the guard through the metal fence with the locked Judas gate built into it. He'd played the desperate tourist with mangled Italian phrases, making him sound pathetic and non-threatening. "*Si prega di sir.*" Please, sir.

The guard had waved back and was about to carry on his patrolling routine. "*Siamo Chiusi.*" We are closed.

"Please help us. My wife is pregnant. She is in pain. She is ill… she needs to rest out of the rain. We need to call a doctor," cried out Marquez, pushing the woman at his side forward and into the light.

The old guard shone the light over at them, as if to confirm what he was being told. He saw a tall, dark haired man with a young woman, her head resting on his shoulder. The couple seemed to be holding each other tight, almost protectively.

To her credit, the girl had played the part perfectly. With her rain-streaked face, wet hair and vulnerable look. But then again, what else could she do? *The game had to play out to its natural conclusion,* thought Marquez.

"I… I am not supposed to let anyone in after closing time. It is the rules," said the guard, but Marquez noted the uncertainty in his voice.

"Please my friend… just so that she can rest. We have been touring the city all day, we are tired and my wife feels unwell."

"Oh… I don't know," called the guard.

Marquez thought he'd lost the ruse there and then. Thought the guard would turn around, throw his hands in the air and utter that it was not his problem and go back to his patrolling, safe inside the protection of the Coliseum. So it came as something of a surprise when the girl spoke, despite his orders not to, and clinched the deal for them. She probably thought she would help save the guard's life. *How wrong she was,* thought Marquez.

"I can't feel my baby moving... please I need to rest! Please, grandfather," she said in halting Italian, her fragile voice perfectly pitched to squeeze the old man's heart.

After that it had all been so easy. The guard had let them through the gate and began to usher them along to the security office. "Come, I will have Santos in the office make you comfortable," he said, now playing the role of the couple's designated protector. The man ambled ahead of them, chattering away contentedly.

Nicole knew it was coming, was expecting it, but that didn't stop the fact that when Marquez swung around in front of the guard and shot him in the head with the silenced pistol, she jumped involuntarily. Six weeks ago she would have screamed, but not now. The most that a Redaction agent would give away would be a temporary widening of the eyes and a sharp intake of breath. She had become hardened to death recently.

The rest, for Marquez, had been commonplace. One more murder – Santos in the security office – and then they had exclusive use of the Coliseum for at least the next hour or so. A simple shot to the back of the unsuspecting guard's head. Marquez grabbed her and pushed her face first against the stone columns in the warren of passageways that led down to the Hyperion, the underground section. She felt the gun pressed to the back of her head.

He rummaged in his shoulder bag and removed a length of chain that had been adapted. He knew she wouldn't struggle, she'd been warned too many times before, and he suspected she thought that by complying, she would be leading him into a trap, a trap that the blond assassin would be hoping to spring upon him. Marquez smiled inwardly to himself. Let her think whatever she liked, he had been a killer and a survivor of numerous double crosses in his career, and he was adept at outwitting the foolish.

"Hold still while I put this on you. You try to struggle and I'll shoot you in the elbow," he said. A minute later, the chain and its contents were fastened around Nicole's waist. He kept the wire that attached itself to the belt taut and tense. He whispered in her ear, "Stay close to me and don't try to escape."

* * *

Gorilla had only travelled a few feet when he found the security guard who had been on duty by the gate. The guard was old and was lying splayed out on the walkway. His official blue uniform was covered in dust and his peaked cap was a few feet away from his head, which had recently acquired a deep crimson third eye in its center. Gorilla knew there was no need to check for a pulse, you don't come back from a large caliber bullet to the head.

He moved onwards, his senses were keen and his hearing was just as important as his sight. The internal lamps inside the amphitheater had been reduced by fifty percent. *Marquez, trying to stay concealed for as long as possible,* he thought. He moved along the circumference of the ground level, taking it slowly, stalking his ground carefully. This is how he would have had it in the first place, if it had been his choice. This was Gorilla's forte. Both of them armed with handguns, hunting each other to the death, man against man – what could be simpler?

Up ahead, he made out a small watchman's hut that stood beside the main visitor entrance. A small desk inside, a lamp illuminating the interior so that it gave away the shape of a pair of feet protruding from the doorway. *Another dead watchman,* thought Gorilla. Shot in the back of the head this time, judging by the position of the body. He wondered how many more dead security guards he would find on his journey. Marquez certainly wanted the place to himself.

He bypassed the little hut and moved around the arc of the Coliseum, taking time to move from one archway to another, conscious of a potential threat waiting for him around every stone pillar. He moved the '39 into a two-handed grip, more aware than ever that his target could ambush him, anywhere from touching distance to over twenty feet away. Not that the man would get a chance, the only place that Marquez was going was to the ground. Gorilla was that fast and accurate with a gun.

Was Marquez concealed high on the upper levels, looking down at him through a sniper scope and taking a bead on a spot on his temple? One shot from long distance and he would be out of the game and the girl lost for good. But Gorilla didn't think so. Knowing Marquez's mind now, he knew the killer would want to settle this conflict up close and personal. He would want to see Gorilla's eyes roll up into his head and his lifeblood spill out onto the Roman stone.

Twenty feet up ahead, there was an area brightly lit by a series of arc lights, they cast a yellowish haze down into the ruins, and for those few moments as he stood there, he thought the Coliseum looked magical, even beautiful, but from a tactical point of view it was a hunter's nightmare.

He would be visible right across the grounds, and no matter how fast he could run, the distance would be too great for him not to be spotted, and potentially fired upon.

Gorilla turned and fired – *Phut, Phut, Phut* – the suppressed '39 making hardly any sound amid the battering rainstorm. The lights blinked out in quick succession and then Gorilla was on the move, running as fast as he could, being careful not to slip. Over his head, he could feel the bullets from a silenced pistol smack into the column walls, sending shards of stone flying out. There were three shots that he was aware of, coming from above and to the left. By the time he'd reached the end column he'd counted another three silenced shots. He brought his own weapon up, checking the angles and the shadows. He was ready to fire, but still there was no visible target.

He knew Marquez had to be near, very near, certainly no more than twenty yards away, but in which direction he had no idea. He'd hunted the assassin in Marseilles and had been within a few seconds of eliminating him. The same had been true in Paris, when he'd wounded him before the man had escaped. This time, however, the tables had been turned, albeit temporarily, and Gorilla was the quarry.

Gorilla removed his dead magazine and slammed in the spare. Satisfied, he moved carefully up the stone steps to the next level. He hated negotiating stairs during room combat. They were a pain to go up and a pain to go down. The risk of taking a shot to the head on the way up or taking a shot to the legs on the way down was greatly increased. Neither option was perfect, but he knew from past experience that sometimes you just had to bite the bullet and step out into the unknown.

Taking the steps incrementally, the muzzle of the '39 leading the way, his finger resting on the trigger, he found himself on the second floor level, near the viewing platform. He glanced down at the spectacle of the Coliseum's floor. The rain and the lights gave it an otherworldly feel, almost as though he was viewing an alien planet from deep space. To imagine men and beasts fighting to the death down there for sport, gave him a sense of his own mortality.

"Where is the Contessa?" The voice, nothing more than a conversational whisper, echoed through the walkway.

"She's long gone," said Gorilla, who even now was moving position as Marquez's Tokarev fired at where he thought the voice had come from. "Give up the girl." Again Gorilla had moved as soon as he spoke, and he heard the silenced bullets take shards out of the stone where he'd stood only seconds before. He crouched down at the base of a column, scanning the area by the steps where he thought the shots had come from. He watched and waited. If he'd calculated correctly, the killer should be moving along to his left any second now.

Moments later, Gorilla was rewarded when he saw a pair of shadows edging along the curvature of the building. They stopped and he could see the rear of one trouser leg jutting from the cover of the stone column. Then it moved, hidden behind the stone column. Gone!

Gorilla began to track along the passageway between the blocks. There was more movement of feet, echoing here and there. The acoustics inside the amphitheater proved disorientating. What sounded like

it was coming from one direction, was in fact coming from the opposite way. Gorilla scanned around; temporarily frightened that he'd lost
his bearings on them. Suddenly he heard a noise only a few feet away,
a gasp. As though someone had been pulled suddenly and the shock
had caught them unawares. *Nicole.*

From his peripheral vision, he was aware of the side of a man's body
less than two columns away, about twenty feet. The right side rear of
the man was showing; a back, a leg and an elbow. They must have
passed, moving only a few meters from each other in the darkness,
until Marquez and Nicole were now at his rear.

Gorilla immediately twisted his upper body around in one smooth
motion and thrust out his weapon arm. The gun was pointed at Marquez's back, like a firebrand preacher berating a congregation with an
accusing finger, and as he was about to fire, he saw the man begin to
move as if he had sensed an attack from behind.

Gorilla's instincts, as fast as ever, instantly recalculated a new target. He moved the line of the gun by a fraction, found his new target
and fired. He heard the scream from Marquez, and then once more
heard the shuffling of feet as the two bodies moved with purpose.

Gorilla moved along, testing the corners, wary of a surprise attack.
He glanced down to where his prey had been standing. A blood trail.
Further along there was more, then more about the stone seating area
as if the man had rested momentarily before moving off to recover
what was left of his plan. *A wounded opponent was the best type to
have,* thought Gorilla. They were easier to track, easier to finally take
down and easier to ramp up the pressure on. "You've run out of time.
You can't win," he said. Not shouting despite the size of the building
they were inside, but speaking in a casual, matter of fact tone.

The reply from Marquez came back instantaneously, the voice full
of both pain and anger. "Fuck you – this is my game and I always win!"

Gorilla decided to try a different tack. The amphitheater was just
too big for them to continue stalking each other indefinitely. He had
already wounded Marquez, but the longer he left it, the greater the
risk to Nicole. He needed to resolve this quickly. Weapons had been

used and had failed; now something different was needed from the gunfighter's arsenal, namely deception.

"QJ/WIN," he called. Silence from the walkway. Then the shuffling of feet, as if one person was moving another. "QJ/WIN? Do you hear me? I have a message." Aside from the beating rain, there was silence. "The message is from Mr. Knight," continued Gorilla. In the distance Gorilla heard the shuffling of feet moving frantically, but no response. "Come on out and I'll explain," prompted Gorilla.

"You think me a fool. I wouldn't make it three feet before you shot me down," came the rebuke from Marquez.

No, you're anything but a fool, thought Gorilla. *Brutal, sadistic, ruthless, but not a fool.* "I'll put the gun away. Just come out with the girl."

The silence hung in the air once more, and then, as if making up his mind Marquez shouted, "I can see you from here. Put the weapon away and we'll come out!"

Gorilla held the gun up high to show that he'd understood and was willing to comply. Then he quickly removed the silencer from the Smith and Wesson before placing them both back in the holster at his hip. He began to move backwards; two steps, three steps, four steps, and five. He lowered his hands to chest height, not so far that he couldn't reach the '39 in case he should need it, but far enough so that it reassured Marquez. "Okay, the gun's away. Now bring her out."

At first, Gorilla thought he hadn't shouted loud enough. Then slowly, they emerged from beneath the arches twenty yards away, Marquez held her from behind, like one lover caressing another. He had one hand arched around her throat and the other held the silenced Tokarev to her temple. Marquez was using her body as a shield to protect himself, in case the other man decided to make a move.

Gorilla took in the scene. The shot had seemingly hit Marquez in his left leg, blood poured from the wound, giving the leg of his trousers a wet, silky sheen. He thought the man looked at the end of his tether. Worn out, stressed, desperate. He'd seen the same look in the eyes of agents back from a long haul behind enemy lines and he saw it now in the eyes of his quarry. Desperate indeed... but desperate men are liable to do desperate things if they're backed into a corner, and the last thing he needed was a bloodbath.

Gorilla wondered if there was a masochistic streak prevalent for some field agents, contractors and mercenaries. Even though they are aware of a trap, they can't seem to help themselves but walk right into it? Was it blind faith, overconfidence or the delusion that they could master and beat the odds? Either way, this killer had gone the length of the rope and now needed to be redacted.

He turned his gaze to Nicole. She seemed unharmed, her coat buttoned up to the top. Her hands were handcuffed together in front of her. A slim metal link chain was looped through the handcuffs and encircled her waist, pinching together the fabric of her coat. Marquez had also taped and gagged up her mouth, a sensible precaution in case she should cry out during the hunt through the Coliseum, thought Gorilla.

"What is the message?" asked Marquez.

Gorilla stood there with rivulets of rain running down his face. Now he had a lie to sell. He just hoped his acting skills were up to it. "Mr. Knight says the contract is complete. It's time to stop. Hand over the girl and you can go free."

Marquez looked doubtful. "You are CIA?"

Gorilla shook his head. "Let's just say, I'm an interested party."

"Then, if that is the case, we are on the same side?"

"I don't have sides QJ/WIN, I'm a one-man army. Just let the girl go. *Now!*"

Gorilla heard the other man chuckle, a soft bitter laugh. "Please don't try to control me, my friend."

"The thought never crossed my mind. But this operation is over," growled Gorilla.

But your tone says otherwise, my friend, thought Marquez. It was the age-old ploy, tell the enemy exactly what they want to hear, then when he is relaxed, you slip a stiletto between his shoulder blades. *Well, not this time my little monkey man!* Marquez moved himself further behind the frame of the girl, the gun still pressing into her head. "How can it be over? There can only be one winner."

Gorilla shrugged in response. "Then make it about us, Marquez. We can settle this between us. The girl isn't a part of this anymore. Let her go."

Gorilla counted the beats in his head. Two, three, four. Marquez was definitely weighing up his options; to believe or dismiss, cut or run, kill or spare. He knew time was not on the Catalan killer's side. He was bleeding and his options were now limited. Who to believe in this game of smoke and mirrors?

Gorilla decided to force the issue and ramp up the pressure. *"Marquez! If you don't let her go, you'll die! Walk way, now!"*

The rain drummed against the stone floor. They had entered a momentary no-man's land, when the outcome could go either way. Then the fire returned to Marquez's eyes and he shouted, "In that case – *have her!"*

Gorilla watched as Marquez pushed Nicole from behind, causing her to topple forward. The killer then turned and ran into the shadows of the covered walkway dragging his wounded leg behind him. Gorilla was stuck between running forward to catch Nicole from tottering forward on her heels or picking up the '39 and going after Marquez to finish him off.

His mind weighed up the tactical and operational considerations. He instantly opted for the '39 and going for the kill. Nicole was safe; she was here, coming towards him. What he needed to do was close down his quarry and redact him.

That was his mission, and he had never defaulted on a mission before. The decision to go for the '39 saved his life.

In a split second, Gorilla took two huge strides forward, bent down smoothly to one knee and drew the weapon from the holster on his hip. He was a fast draw, always had been, and even now his hand was coming up, the iron sight beginning to center on Marquez's back as he limped away. He turned his gaze to Nicole, who had just... well... she was standing still... not moving. Why wasn't she running towards him? *Come on girl, get moving over here, quickly,* he thought. He held out his hand to her, a smile of devilment on his face that he was trying to share with her.

But Nicole started to back up, started to move away from him, her eyes burning into him, pleading with him. There was fear in those eyes. His finger relaxed on the trigger, some unknown sense gave him pause. He stood and slowly began to walk towards her, as if in a daze. He thought at that moment, that standing there in the rain looking fragile and innocent, with the stylish coat, the elegant heels and her dark hair plastered to the side of her face, that she had never looked more beautiful.

He had only taken a handful of steps when the flash took him and he was blown backwards onto the hard cold floor of the Coliseum.

* * *

The MK 2 Fragmentation grenade that Marquez had tied to the back of Nicole's chain belt had a five-second delay fuse. When the time was right, he had simply pulled the restraining pin, causing the clip to fly off, which in turn released the acid burning fuse which raced towards the high explosive at the grenade's center.

Nicole Quayle had heard the click of the grenade's pin being pulled, and then felt a jolt as Marquez's strong hand pushed her forward and out towards Gorilla.

She knew it was coming, had known from the moment Marquez handcuffed her, and had shown her the grenade he was duct taping to the chain looped around her waist and ran through the handcuffs. She tried to warn Gorilla, but it was no use. Marquez had played a double bluff and Gorilla had simply not seen it; in truth, how could he? She just hoped Gorilla would survive and for her, death would be quick. He was a good man; she would have liked to have known him in a different life.

She stood still and turned her face towards the rain. *I'm coming, mamma,* she thought. *Don't worry, I'll be with you soon.*

James Quinn

* * *

The explosion had popped his ear drums and aside from an internal ringing, he could only hear the muffled sounds of the environment around him. The air was permeated with a reddish matter that combined with the rain, created a crimson mist. He knew what it was, didn't want to look at it or think about where it had come from.

He turned his head to look at the spot where Nicole had been standing. Through the dark and smoke-filled haze he could see the small crater the grenade had created. He looked and he saw the brutalized remains of Nicole.

And there, in the theatre of death, he knelt down on his hands and knees, the rain and blood from what was left of Nicole Quayle's shattered body running along the stone pathway and down onto his splayed fingers.

He lowered his forehead to the ground as if in prayer, and for the first time in many a year, Jack Duncan Grant wept.

Chapter Five

Bath, England – June 1965

The memorial service for Nicole Quayle, former member of the Foreign Office, took place at Haycombe Cemetery, near her family's home town of Bath. It was a clear crisp day, with a radiant sun, and everybody agreed that it was the kind of day Nicole herself would have enjoyed.

It was attended by her father, looking his most frail but sporting his wartime medals, and a compendium of aunts and uncles, cousins, and immediate friends from her school days. All gathered around the patriarch of the family like a shield wall. It was a memorial service. Not so much a funeral per say, after all, how could you have a burial when there was so little of the body remaining? But the vicar said the correct things and everyone agreed that the choice of hymns was well picked. Who couldn't fail to be stirred by 'Jerusalem'?

Of her colleagues from work, only a handful attended, and those who did were there in an official capacity. All had been briefed on how to answer the question of her death.

"Terrible business, I'm afraid, the office was distraught about the death of a much-valued member of our staff. A gas explosion at her apartment – of course, foreign standards of workmanship aren't up to scratch like they are back in England, are they? Italy? Oh, yes – very glamorous, very *La Dolce Vita*. It seems she was seconded for a brief period, to cover some overlap of Embassy personnel leaving for another posting. Very decent of her, what with it being at such short notice, just a tragic way for a young life to end..."

The majority of these questions were fielded by Nicole's former department head, in truth, an SIS officer who had actually never met her, but was brought in to 'stage manage' the affair and to, in his own rather unfortunate choice of words, "kill this bloody scandal as quickly as possible, before every intelligence network in Europe comes crashing down on our bloody heads!"

The other official mourners from the Foreign Office were a tall, broad man with an unmistakable military bearing about him, "Call me Stephen, and yes, I had the good fortune to have worked with Nicole for a few weeks recently. It was the least I could do, to come over and pay my respects."

In fact, Masterman was here more as a 'minder' for the other man who had accompanied him. A small, stocky man with short blond hair who sat glowering at the back of the church. He looked like a Golem – on his own, and isolated from the rest of the congregation.

* * *

"Such a beautiful service," said Masterman. "One of the few I've been to recently where it hasn't been raining."

Once again, they were walking, as was their habit, from the cemetery, across the church grounds and heading to Masterman's car. Masterman was setting the pace, keeping it slow, wanting the other man to get the pent-up rage out of his system.

Off to the side and heading along the main road to a waiting car, Masterman noticed Toby and his 'Burrowers'; the old copper and the young lady with the scarred face, linked arm-in-arm. They had sat apart from the rest of the SIS people in the church, like ghosts at a wake.

"I always think it's a blessing when the sun shines on such a somber occasion. It doesn't seem half as gloomy and depressing," said Masterman.

There was a snort of derision from Grant. Not quite a laugh, but not a growl either.

"I say something funny, Jack?"

Grant had his head down, watching as his feet pounded into the grass. "Oh no, Colonel, not at all. Gloomy, well, I'll tell her father and her family that it's alright because the sun's shining and every cloud has a silver lining and about half a dozen other clichés that I can think of. They'll be chuffed to bits."

Masterman knew what it was that was eating at the smaller man. Known it since he'd received the telephone call that night from Rome: Grant in a hotel lobby somewhere, exhausted, out of breath and telling him that the operation was a failure. The girl dead and Marquez was gone! Bloody hell!

Masterman risked a sideways glance at Grant as they walked; saw the fury smeared across his face. Grant had looked the same when he'd finally made it home after the aborted Rome operation. He had paced back and forth before Masterman's desk, swearing revenge and wanting a 'hunting license' to go after Marquez wherever he was. Masterman had calmed him down, temporarily, but still that mark of rage stayed with him over the passing weeks. So had the talk of revenge.

"Let's go this way," said Masterman. He knew how Grant worked and he thought it best to let his rage run its course. "We'll take the long way back to the car."

"You see, I ran, Colonel, I ran like a fucking coward. I let that girl down, an officer under my care, I let her walk into a trap and she paid the price for my bloody mindedness. Then I scarpered before the Carabinieri got there. Because that's what we do, isn't it? We run away because we're deniable. Deniable fucking cowards who run," said Grant, determined not to let the conversation trail off.

Masterman rested a gentle hand on Grant's shoulder. "You did what was expected – your job. You're not paid to get caught, you're paid to be able to disappear when you have to. Nicole knew the risks, just as you do. You shouldn't carry this guilt on your shoulders."

Grant stopped and turned. He already knew what he was going to say to Masterman, had been rehearsing it for over a week. "Then let me go after him! I found him once, I can find him again. He's too dangerous to let live! For us, the Americans and even the Russians!"

"Sorry Jack, that ship has sailed. Orders from the top. The Chief and the Americans have come to an understanding, so I'm told. Something of mutual benefit for both our services and something far above *our* security clearance," said Masterman.

"Look, this is important! One of our field agents has been murdered! I've killed people for less on your orders! Why is this so very different?" shouted Grant, his hands clenching and unclenching in his coat pockets.

"Because the last time I looked, you weren't the man in charge of the British Secret Service and you don't make those decisions, Jack."

"If we don't react to this, then every agent in our network will doubt our intentions in the future! Well, won't they?" It was Grant's last roll of the dice and the one he hoped would sway the Head of the Redaction Unit over to his cause.

But Masterman was a player of hardball and simply glowered down at his protégé. He'd had enough of this self-flagellation of Grant's over the past few weeks. It was time to give him the hard facts. "Are you serious, Jack? You think that this operation has global significance? Well, let me educate you; it doesn't. It has been just one shitty operation in a whole week of shitty operations, and no one outside of our dirty little game will care one jot about whether we saved the lives of a team of patriotic British agents or not. They're more interested in their mortgages, rock and roll, and which stripper is performing down the local boozer this week. MACE was nothing unusual; we do it all the time. We do our best, we get the job done and we move onto the next task. So don't go giving yourself heirs and graces and imagine that you're some kind of a diva."

"So why do we bother then, eh? If all they care about is trivia, why should we give a monkey's?" snarled Grant.

Masterman smiled. "Because if we don't, no one will. Look, take some time out. It's been a long one, this one. Both sides have taken hits. Get yourself away on a holiday. We can manage for a few months without you."

Grant shook his head sadly. "No, I'm done, Colonel. I didn't think you'd back me on this, but I had to try. I've already left my resignation letter on your desk. I did it this morning, before you picked me up. I'm out!"

Masterman looked shocked and spoke in his best Commanding Officer's voice. "What do you think this is, a bloody golf club that you can march out of anytime you feel like it? You're an officer of this Service; you have a job to do!"

"Not this time. You can lock me up, you could even kill me, but you can't make me kill anyone I don't want to."

Masterman's face flushed with anger. "What about the people in Scotland, in Loch Lomond? Have you thought about how your actions will affect them? If you're not a part of the Service, neither are they. I can't promise protection for them if you leave."

Grant smiled. He knew Masterman was better than that. "But you will though, won't you, Colonel? You will, because you're a good and decent man and you love them just as much as I do."

Masterman gave him a hard glare. Damn him, he was right! Of course he would look after the people up north. They had all been through so much together, had forged a bond and besides, Grant had watched his back, and he Grant's, many, many times. Some debts just couldn't be ignored for expediency's sake. "Jack, Jack..."

But Jack Grant was already walking away, past Masterman's car and out into the country lane.

Just let him go, thought Masterman. *He'll be back. He's just on a long, long leash.*

Book Eight:
Checkmate

Epilogue

The Congo - September 1965

Marquez staggered out of the bar, worse for the amount of drink he'd taken that night. Cognac; a cheap brand that rotted the guts. It was awful, but better than nothing in this godforsaken steaming hell pit. He checked his watch; almost midnight.

His bleary eyes searched around the deserted roadside for where he had left the jeep. He staggered one way and then the next, before his memory kicked in and he saw it across the pathway. He sucked in a lungful of air, in the hope that it might sober him up. *Doubtful,* he thought, as he lumbered towards his ride home.

He fell into his vehicle, rummaged around for the keys. He started the engine of the two-seater jeep, heard it cough and rumble, and then he pulled away from the ramshackle provincial bar. *Really, it was just a hut with an ice box,* he thought. The drive was a ten-minute journey and considering the amount of alcohol he'd put away that night, it would be a miracle if he didn't crash the jeep before making it back to his house.

He'd been down here, keeping a low profile, trying to blend in, for almost four months. The Congo, once a country he'd worked in and loved, he now hated with a vile passion. The heat, the people, the flies, the life! Circumstances, and lack of options, had made this the place he'd returned to and for that, he wished he had never taken the last contract, met Mr. Knight or ever worked for the Americans. Fuckers! Double-crossing fuckers!

Following the killing in Rome, he'd moved quickly; the money that he'd been promised for the full terms of the contract had been non-existent and so he had quickly spent his remaining financial resources on escaping the heat.

He'd heard through the grapevine that there was an open-ended hit contract out on him; who the paymaster was, he didn't know. The CIA or KGB, it mattered not. What did matter was that he had to move.

The first hint of a threat had been the burning down of his business and home in Luxembourg. He'd missed the arson attack by two days. That had been close. Recognizing that he needed to get out of Europe undetected, he'd visited his tame forger in Antwerp and paid over the odds for a new passport. The Belgian forger had been surprised to see him, but had nonetheless 'run up' a set of new papers for him.

He had fled Europe with a suitcase full of cash, which would help him buy his way into a semi-secure lifestyle in the Congo. He'd taken former General, now President Mobutu, at his word and asked for asylum and protection.

The President had, of course, not seen him personally, but had nonetheless stuck to his word and allowed Marquez to remain and begin a new life. And what a life it was. Hell would have been a better term. Long days, even longer nights, living in a ramshackle, prefabricated house on the outskirts of Uvira, miles from anywhere. Terrible food, even worse liquor, and aside from the occasional dalliance with one or two of the young boys from the nearby town, precious else left for him to do.

He had tried to muscle in on several smuggling operations, less for the money, but more to keep his mind occupied, but thus far, he'd been frozen out. The warning had come down from the top; the President runs *all* operations in the Congo: keep away unless you want to visit one of the torture cells and then get kicked out of Africa. So he sat and waited and drank and despaired. His lot in life set, eternally.

Ten minutes later, he saw the prison cell that was his house. The headlights illuminated it momentarily before he remembered to jam on the brakes and stop. He leaned forward in the driver's seat, felt it creak and groan, to remove the keys from the ignition, whilst with the other hand, he fumbled for the latch to open the door of the jeep.

The volley of shots when they came were silent, but powerful. From below him, it sounded as if someone was playing a rapid drum beat on a biscuit tin lid and then his chest, bizarrely, opened up and sprayed a glutinous mass of blood and tissue over the interior windscreen. He looked down to see the ragged remains of his shirt and the cascade of red where his sternum had once been. Then the pain was everywhere; front, back – all over. He screamed, but couldn't move, and eventually, even the scream subsided and his speech was gone, replaced by an unhealthy gurgling sound from his butchered chest.

The second volley was aimed higher. The same rapid drum beat as it ripped out his throat and jaw. Less pain this time, but certainly more blood as his body slouched sideways, finally coming to rest upon the steering wheel of the jeep.

The silence of the African night returned once more.

* * *

Gorilla quietly eased himself out of the cramped space of the Jeep's luggage compartment. He'd covered himself with an old blanket to hide his body shape. Resting in his hands was a silenced, Sterling sub machine gun that he'd bought on the black market. He stretched, feeling the knotted muscles and joints click and contract, his shirt and linen trousers saturated with sweat from his prolonged confinement in the rear of the Jeep.

He stepped over the side, and his boots crunched on the dusty plain of the African roadside as he walked around to the driver's window to inspect the result of his work.

Gorilla removed the ear protectors and goggles which had been so necessary when he'd fired the silenced Sterling from his hidden position behind the driver's seat. Even with a fully suppressed firearm, the shock waves and noise from the weapon would have been enough to blow out his eardrums and damage his eyes in such a confined space.

He had tracked this man across Europe, first as part of Operation MACE, and now on his own ticket of revenge, to Africa. It was good to have the hunt settled once and for all. He narrowed his eyes, as he almost forensically, ran them over the gloomy bloodbath inside. The shots had taken out a large portion of the man's chest and throat... not bad. It had been messy, but quick.

It had been a private operation on Gorilla's part, and although he had officially resigned from SIS three months ago, he knew that if Masterman were to find out he was in Africa and hunting Marquez, he would have quickly been arrested and dropped down a very dark hole somewhere. So he had, carefully, slowly, set about tracking down leads and pooling resources.

Determined to send a message to the Catalan that he was marked; Gorilla had visited the man's antiques shop with the apartment above, broken in and petrol-bombed it. He knew that Marquez hadn't returned for many months; Gorilla just wanted the man frightened and on the run.

The first breakthrough had come when he'd re-visited the forger in Antwerp, following a tip-off from a friend in the Belgium SIS Section. The forger had been frightened and apparently received a recent visit from the Catalan killer. Dumont needed to see the little gunman who had a penchant for shooting up wine goblets. Urgently!

Marquez the fugitive had needed a new passport to get him out of Europe! The rest had been a mirror image of MACE; tracking the 'flagged' passport had led him to Africa and the Congo. The rest had been patience, bribes and watching.

Gorilla dug into his trouser pocket and retrieved his habitual cut-throat razor, flicking it open one-handed, until the lethal blade shimmered in the African moonlight. He grabbed the head of the dead man in the Jeep, turned it to the right and placed the razor blade behind the nub of the man's ear. With one powerful cut the ear came away in his hands.

The ear would be his proof of a kill. The CIA had put out an open-ended hit contract on Marquez following the operation in Europe. The man had become too much of an embarrassment and could not be allowed to live.

Gorilla had no intention of collecting the $15,000 bounty on the killer's head. This was personal. It was payback for a brave and beautiful young woman who he'd loved, and yet had ultimately failed to protect. He would send the ear to an old man in England, a father, with a simple note attached: 'Payback for Nicole'.

What had QJ/WIN said, when they were battling to the death in Rome? *'This is my game and I always win.'*

Well, not this time you don't sunshine, thought Gorilla. He dropped the Sterling and began to walk away, calling back over his shoulder as an afterthought.

"You lose. Game over."

Dear reader,

We hope you enjoyed reading *A Game For Assassins.* Please take a moment to leave a review in Amazon, even if it's a short one. Your opinion is important to us.

The story continues in *Sentinel Five.*

Discover more books by James Quinn at https://www.nextchapter.pub/authors/james-quinn-british-espionage-thriller-author

Want to know when one of our books is free or discounted for Kindle? Join the newsletter at http://eepurl.com/bqqB3H

Best regards,

James Quinn and the Next Chapter Team

Dedication

This book is dedicated to John.

He is a soldier, a statesman, secret warrior, philanthropist and mentor to many. Some people that we meet in our lives leave a lasting impression and go on to inspire us with their words of kindness and encouragement. John is such a person, but no matter how many times he asks me to call him by his Christian name, something in my psyche instantly compels me to treat him with the respect of a senior officer and call him "Sir." It just seems the right thing to do.

Hopefully, we can climb the stairs to the Special Forces Club again soon for a dram or two.

As a way of saying thank you for all his help and guidance over the years *A Game for Assassins* is in his honor, I hope he approves, for without him there would be no Masterman.

Acknowledgements

I would like to thank the following people for all their contributions and advice;

Mike Smith of Advanced Armament Corp, USA for his expertise on all weapons suppressed and for his fascinating insight into the SDK 'Gestapo' Rifle that Marquez uses.

To my old friend, science fiction writer, Daniel Webster for all his help and encouragement over the years and for helping me find Gorilla's favorite tool of the trade, the S&W '39. *Phut – Phut – Phut*!

To John Nuttall, for sharing his knowledge of the Cornish Coast and for his advice on all things 'boat' related. Any errors are mine and should in no way be attributed to John's excellent advice.

To my 'Scottish Editor', Claire Piercy, for advising me on the correct way that those north of the border converse. I owe you a dram.

To the fantastic LE Fitzpatrick for saving the day at the last moment with her magical skills of proofreading and formatting to make this book the best that it can possibly be.

To Rachel Graves, for putting to work her contacts and for guiding me through the fascinating world of forensic pathology and science.

The staff at the British Embassy in Vienna for all their help with getting the details of the old Embassy correct.

To 'Ned Brockman' former agent of the old Federal Narcotics Bureau (and later its renamed manifestation, the Drug Enforcement Administration) for all his help in guiding me through the type of operations that the DEA excels at. I was lucky enough to meet up with 'Ned' for lunch in London and I think it's only fair that next time, I pay!

And last, but not least, to 'Lulu' for writing the last line of the book. I couldn't have done it without you. xxx

* * *

QJ/WIN and WI/ROGUE were real agents recruited to work for the CIA in the 1960's. Their identities have never truly been revealed, and I have taken liberties with the backgrounds and operations that they may have been involved in during this period of history.

The character of Jack 'Gorilla' Grant is one I hope the readers will take to. He is the very antithesis of James Bond. He is a working class spy.

He is based, if he is based on anybody, upon a number of people that I know or have known. Some worked, and continue to work, in the secret world and some don't. I stole a piece of each of them and melded them into both a physical and personality-based profile.

Of Grant's SIS work name, 'Gorilla', I was searching around for a co-dename for my spy/assassin. I toyed with many, all, I admit, sounding a bit too gung-ho, macho, Roman Godlike or predatory animal. I wanted something almost banal, but that also conveyed a workmanlike approach to the job that Jack Grant has to do. None seemed to reflect the almost casual disdain that Grant has for such frivolities better than 'Gorilla'; after all, he's a worker, but he's got better things to worry about than what people call him… and anyway, what's in a name?

J.Q
London, 2015

About the Author

James Quinn spent 15 years in the secret world of covert operations, undercover investigations and international security before turning his hand to writing.

He is trained in hand to hand combat, and in the use of a variety of weaponry, including small edged weapons, Japanese swords and hunting bows. He is also a crack pistol shot for CQB (Close Quarter Battle) and many of his experiences he has incorporated into his works of fiction.

When the mood takes him he likes to indulge in a good single malt whisky or expensive Kentucky bourbon.

He lives in the United Kingdom and travels extensively around the globe.

http://jamesquinn.webs.com/
If you enjoyed "A Game for Assassins"
watch out for the forthcoming Jack "Gorilla" Grant book

Sentinel Five

The Chief of the Secret Intelligence Service has been assassinated and the government brought to its knees.

A disavowed team is assembled to hunt down the terrorists and called back from obscurity is the 'Gorilla', a freelancer with a Smith & Wesson' 39 and a cut-throat razor, who is ready to even the score.

But in a game where power players, traitors, and terrorists work hand in hand, sometimes the most serious threats come from within.

The Sentinel Five team turn their gunsights to the East, to Asia, and enter a killing ground of death.

Printed in Great Britain
by Amazon

85877075R00315